Miss Prudence

by Mrs. Nathaniel Conklin

I.

AFTER SCHOOL.

"Our content is our best having."—*Shakespeare*.

Nobody had ever told Marjorie that she was, as somebody says we all are, three people,—the Marjorie she knew herself, the Marjorie other people knew, and the Marjorie God knew. It was a "bother" sometimes to be the Marjorie she knew herself, and she had never guessed there was another Marjorie for other people to know, and the Marjorie God knew and understood she did not learn much about for years and years. At eleven years old it was hard enough to know about herself—her naughty, absent-minded, story-book-loving self. Her mother said that she loved story-books entirely too much, that they made her absent-minded and forgetful, and her mother's words were proving themselves true this very afternoon. She was a real trouble to herself and there was no one near to "confess" to; she never could talk about herself unless enveloped in the friendly darkness, and then the confessor must draw her out, step by step, with perfect frankness and sympathy; even then, a sigh, or sob, or quickly drawn breath and half inarticulate expression revealed more than her spoken words.

She was one of the children that are left to themselves. Only Linnet knew the things she cared most about; even when Linnet laughed at her, she could feel the sympathetic twinkle in her eye and the sympathetic undertone smothered in her laugh.

It was sunset, and she was watching it from the schoolroom window, the clouds over the hill were brightening and brightening and a red glare shone over the fields of snow. It was sunset and the schoolroom clock pointed to a quarter of five. The schoolroom was chilly, for the fire had died out half an hour since. Hollis Rheid had shoved big sticks into the stove until it would hold no more and had opened the draft, whispering to her as he passed her seat that he would keep her warm at any rate. But now she was shivering, although she had wrapped herself in her coarse green and red shawl, and tapped her feet on the bare floor to keep them warm; she was hungry, too; the noon lunch had left her unsatisfied, for she had given her cake to Rie Blauvelt in return for a splendid Northern Spy, and had munched the apple and eaten her two sandwiches wishing all the time for more. Leaving the work on her slate unfinished, she had dived into the depths of her home-made satchel and discovered two crumbs of molasses cake. That was an hour ago. School had closed at three o'clock to-day because it was Friday and she had been nearly two hours writing nervously on her slate or standing at the blackboard making hurried figures. For the first time in her life Marjorie West had been "kept in." And that "Lucy" book hidden in her desk was the cause of it; she had taken it out for just one delicious moment, and the moment had extended itself into an hour and a half, and the spelling lesson was unlearned and the three hard examples in complex fractions unworked. She had not been ignorant of what the penalty would be. Mr. Holmes had announced it at the opening of school: "Each word in spelling that is missed, must be written one hundred times, and every example not brought in on the slate must be put on the blackboard after school."

She had smiled in self-confidence. Who ever knew Marjorie West to miss in spelling? And had not her father looked over her examples last night and pronounced them correct? But on her way to school the paper on which the examples were solved had dropped out of her Geography, and she had been wholly absorbed in the "Lucy" book during the time that she had expected to study the test words in spelling. And the overwhelming result was doing three examples on the board, after school, and writing seven hundred words. Oh, how her back ached and how her wrist hurt her and how her strained eyes smarted! Would she ever again forget *amateur, abyss, accelerate, bagatelle, bronchitis, boudoir* and *isosceles*?

Rie Blauvelt had written three words one hundred times, laughed at her, and gone home; Josie Grey had written *isosceles* one hundred times, and then taken up a slate to help Marjorie; before Marjorie was aware Josie had written *abyss* seventy-five times, then suspecting something by the demureness of Josie's eyes she had snatched her slate and erased the pretty writing.

"You're real mean," pouted Josie; "he said he would take our word for it, and you could have answered some way and got out of it."

Marjorie's reply was two flashing eyes.

"You needn't take my head off," laughed Josie; "now I'll go home and leave you, and you may stay all night for all I care."

"I will, before I will deceive anybody," resented Marjorie stoutly.

Without another word Josie donned sack and hood and went out, leaving the door ajar and the cold air to play about Marjorie's feet.

But five o'clock came and the work was done!

More than one or two tears fell slowly on the neat writing on Marjorie's slate; the schoolroom was cold and she was shivering and hungry. It would have been such a treat to read the last chapter in the "Lucy" book; she might have curled her feet underneath her and drawn her shawl closer; but it was so late, and what would they think at home? She was ashamed to go home. Her father would look at her from under his eyebrows, and her mother would exclaim, "Why, Marjorie!" She would rather that her father would look at her from under his eyebrows, than that her mother would say, "Why, *Marjorie!*" Her mother never scolded, and sometimes she almost wished she would. It would be a relief if somebody would scold her tonight; she would stick a pin into herself if it would do any good.

Her photograph would not be in the group next time. She looked across at the framed photograph on the wall; six girls in the group and herself the youngest—the reward for perfect recitations and perfect deportment for one year. Her father was so proud of it that he had ordered a copied picture for himself, and, with a black walnut frame, it was hanging in the sitting-room at home. The resentment against herself was tugging away at her heart and drawing miserable lines on her brow and lips—on her sweet brow and happy lips.

It was a bare, ugly country schoolroom, anyway, with the stained floor, the windows with two broken panes, and the unpainted desks with innumerable scars made by the boys' jack-knives, and Mr. Holmes was unreasonable, anyway, to give her such a hard punishment, and she didn't care if she had been kept in, anyway!

Miss Prudence

In that "anyway" she found vent for all her crossness. Sometimes she said, "I don't care," but when she said, "I don't care, *anyway*!" then everybody knew that Marjorie West was dreadful.

"I'm *through*," she thought triumphantly, "and I didn't cheat, and I wasn't mean, and nobody has helped me."

Yes, somebody had helped her. She was sorry that she forgot to think that God had helped her. Perhaps people always did get through! If they didn't help themselves along by doing wrong and—God helped them. The sunshine rippled over her face again and she counted the words on her slate for the second time to assure herself that there could be no possible mistake. Slowly she counted seven hundred, then with a sudden impulse seized her pencil and wrote each of the seven words five times more to be "*sure* they were all right."

Josie Grey called her "horridly conscientious," and even Rie Blauvelt wished that she would not think it wicked to "tell" in the class, and to whisper about something else when they had permission to whisper about the lessons.

By this time you have learned that my little Marjorie was strong and sweet. I wish you might have seen her that afternoon as she crouched over the wooden desk, snuggled down in the coarse, plaid shawl, her elbows resting on the hard desk, her chin dropped in her two plump hands, with her eyes fixed on the long, closely written columns of her large slate. She was not sitting in her own seat, her seat was the back seat on the girls' side, of course, but she was sitting midway on the boys' side, and her slate was placed on the side of the double desk wherein H.R. was cut in deep, ugly letters. She had fled to this seat as to a refuge, when she found herself alone, with something of the same feeling, that once two or three years ago when she was away from home and homesick she used to kneel to say her prayers in the corner of the chamber where her valise was; there was home about the valise and there was protection and safety and a sort of helpfulness about this desk where her friend Hollis Rheid had sat ever since she had come to school. This was her first winter at school, her mother had taught her at home, but in family council this winter it had been decided that Marjorie was "big" enough to go to school.

The half mile home seemed a long way to walk alone, and the huge Newfoundland at the farmhouse down the hill was not always chained; he had sprung out at them this morning and the girls had huddled together while Hollis and Frank Grey had driven him inside his own yard. Hollis had thrown her an intelligent glance as he filed out with the boys, and had telegraphed something back to her as he paused for one instant at the door. Not quite understanding the telegraphic signal, she was waiting for him, or for something. His lips had looked like: "Wait till I come." If the people at home were not anxious about her she would have been willing to wait until midnight; it would never occur to her that Hollis might forget her.

Her cheeks flushed as she waited, and her eyes filled with tears; it was a soft, warm, round face, with coaxing, kissable lips, a smooth, low brow and the gentlest of hazel eyes: not a pretty face, excepting in its lovely childishness and its hints of womanly graces; some of the girls said she was homely. Marjorie thought herself that she was very homely; but she had comforted herself with, "God made my face, and he likes it this way." Some one says that God made the other features, but permits us to make the mouth. Marjorie's sweetness certainly made her mouth. But then she was born sweet. Josie Grey declared that she would rather see a girl "get mad" than cry, as Marjorie did when the boys washed her face in the snow.

Mr. Holmes had written to a friend that Marjorie West, his favorite among the girls, was "almost too sweet." He said to himself that he feared she "lacked character." Marjorie's quiet, observant father would have smiled at that and said nothing. The teacher said that she did not know how to take her own part. Marjorie had been eleven years in this grasping world and had not learned that she had any "part" to take.

Since her pencil had ceased scribbling the room was so still that a tiny mouse had been nibbling at the toe of her shoe. Just then as she raised her head and pinned her shawl more securely the door opened and something happened. The something happened in Marjorie's face. Hollis Rheid thought the sunset had burst across it. She did not exclaim, "Oh, I am so glad!" but the gladness was all in her eyes. If Marjorie had been more given to exclamations her eyes would not have been so expressive. The closed lips were a gain to the eyes and her friends missed nothing. The boy had learned her eyes by heart. How stoutly he would have resisted if some one had told him that years hence Marjorie's face would be a sealed volume to him.

But she was making her eyes and mouth to-day and years hence she made them, too. Perhaps he had something to do with it then as he certainly had something to do with it now.

"I came back with my sled to take you home. I gave Sam my last ten cents to do the night work for me. It was my turn, but he was willing enough. Where's your hood, Mousie? Any books to take?"

"Yes, my Geography and Arithmetic," she answered, taking her fleecy white hood from the seat behind her.

"Now you look like a sunbeam in a cloud," he said poetically as she tied it over her brown head. "Oh, ho!" turning to the blackboard, "you do make handsome figures. Got them all right, did you?"

"I knew how to do them, it was only that—I forgot."

"I don't think you'll forget again in a hurry. And that's a nice looking slate, too," he added, stepping nearer. "Mother said it was too much of a strain on your nervous system to write all that."

"I guess I haven't much of a nervous system," returned Marjorie, seriously; "the girls wrote the words they missed fifty times last Friday and he warned us about the one hundred to-day. I suppose it will be one hundred and fifty next Friday. I don't believe I'll *ever* miss again," she said, her lips trembling at the mention of it.

"I think I'll have a word or two to say to the master if you do. I wonder how Linnet would have taken it."

"She wouldn't have missed."

"I'll ask Mr. Holmes to put you over on the boys side if you miss next week," he cried mischievously, "and make you sit with us all the afternoon."

"I'd rather write each word five hundred times," she cried vehemently.

"I believe you would," he said good humoredly. "Never mind, Mousie, I know you won't miss again."

"I'll do my examples to-night and father will help me if I can't do them. He used to teach in this very schoolhouse; he knows as much as Mr. Holmes."

"Then he must be a Solomon," laughed the boy.

The stamp of Hollis' boots and the sound of his laughter had frightened the mouse back into its hiding-place in the chimney; Marjorie would not have frightened the mouse all day long.

The books were pushed into her satchel, her desk arranged in perfect order, her rubbers and red mittens drawn on, and she stood ready, satchel in hand, for her ride on the sled down the slippery hill where the boys and girls had coasted at noon and then she would ride on over the snowy road half a mile to the old, brown farmhouse. Her eyes were subdued a little, but the sunshine lingered all over her face. She knew Hollis would come.

He smiled down at her with his superior fifteen-year-old smile, she was such a wee mousie and always needed taking care of. If he could have a sister, he would want her to be like Marjorie. He was very much like Marjorie himself, just as shy, just as sensitive, hardly more fitted to take his own part, and I think Marjorie was the braver of the two. He was slow-tempered and unforgiving; if a friend failed him once, he never took him into confidence again. He was proud where Marjorie was humble. He gave his services; she gave herself. He seldom quarrelled, but never was the first to yield. They were both mixtures of reserve and frankness; both speaking as often out of a shut heart as an open heart. But when Marjorie could open her heart, oh, how she opened it! As for Hollis, I think he had never opened his; demonstrative sympathy was equally the key to the hearts of both.

But here I am analyzing them before they had learned they had any self to analyze. But they existed, all the same.

Marjorie was a plain little body while Hollis was noticeably handsome with eloquent brown eyes and hair with its golden, boyish beauty just shading into brown; his sensitive, mobile lips were prettier than any girl's, and there was no voice in school like his in tone or culture. Mr. Holmes was an elocutionist and had taken great pains with Hollis Rheid's voice. There was a courteous gentleness in his manner all his own; if knighthood meant purity, goodness, truth and manliness, then Hollis Rheid was a knightly school-boy. The youngest of five rough boys, with a stern, narrow-minded father and a mother who loved her boys with all her heart and yet for herself had no aims beyond kitchen and dairy, he had not learned his refinement at home; I think he had not *learned* it anywhere. Marjorie's mother insisted that Hollis Rheid must have had a praying grandmother away back somewhere. The master had written to his friend, Miss Prudence Pomeroy, that Hollis Rheid was a born gentleman, and had added with more justice and penetration than he had shown in reading Marjorie, "he has too little application and is too mischievous to become a real student. But I am not looking for geniuses in a country school. Marjorie and Hollis are bright enough for every purpose in life excepting to become leaders."

"Are you going to church, to-night?" Hollis inquired as she seated herself carefully on the sled.

"In the church?" she asked, bracing her feet and tucking the ends of her shawl around them.

"Yes; an evangelist is going to preach."

"Evangelist!" repeated Marjorie in a voice with a thrill in it.

"Don't you know what that is?" asked Hollis, harnessing himself into the sled.

"Oh, yes, indeed," said she. "I know about him and Christian."

Hollis looked perplexed; this must be one of Marjorie's queer ways of expressing something, and the strange preacher certainly had something to do with Christians.

"If it were not for the fractions I suppose I might go. I wish I wasn't stupid about Arithmetic."

"It's no matter if girls are stupid," he said consolingly. "Are you sure you are on tight? I'm going to run pretty soon. You won't have to earn your living by making figures."

"Shall you?" she inquired with some anxiety.

"Of course, I shall. Haven't I been three times through the Arithmetic and once through the Algebra that I may support myself and somebody else, sometime?"

This seemed very grand to child Marjorie who found fractions a very Slough of Despond.

"I'm going to the city as soon as Uncle Jack finds a place for me. I expect a letter from him every night."

"Perhaps it will come to-night," said Marjorie, not very hopefully.

"I hope it will. And so this may be your last ride on Flyaway. Enjoy it all you can, Mousie."

Marjorie enjoyed everything all she could.

"Now, hurrah!" he shouted, starting on a quick run down the hill. "I'm going to turn you over into the brook."

Marjorie laughed her joyous little laugh. "I'm not afraid," she said in absolute content.

"You'd better be!" he retorted in his most savage tone.

The whole west was now in a glow and the glorious light stretched across fields of snow.

"Oh, how splendid," Marjorie exclaimed breathlessly as the rapid motion of the sled and the rush of cold air carried her breath away.

"Hold on tight," he cried mockingly, "we're coming to the brook."

Laughing aloud she held on "tight." Hollis was her true knight; she would not have been afraid to cross the Alps on that sled if he had asked her to!

She was in a talkative mood to-night, but her horse pranced on and would not listen. She wanted to tell him about *vibgyor*. The half mile was quickly travelled and he whirled the sled through the large gateway and around the house to the kitchen door. The long L at the back of the house seemed full of doors.

"There, Mousie, here you are!" he exclaimed. "And don't you miss your lesson to-morrow."

"To-morrow is Saturday! oh, I had forgotten. And I can go to see Evangelist to-night."

"You haven't said 'thank you' for your last ride on Flyaway."

"I will when I'm sure that it is," she returned with her eyes laughing.

He turned her over into a snowdrift and ran off whistling; springing up she brushed the snow off face and hands and with a very serious face entered the kitchen. The kitchen was long and low, bright with the sunset shining in at two windows and cheery with its carpeting of red, yellow and green mingled confusingly in the handsome oilcloth.

Unlike Hollis, Marjorie was the outgrowth of home influences; the kitchen oilcloth had something to do with her views of life, and her mother's broad face and good-humored eyes had a great deal more. Good-humor in the mother had developed sweet humor in the child.

Now I wonder if you understand Marjorie well enough to understand all she does and all she leaves undone during the coming fifteen or twenty years?

II.

EVANGELIST.

"The value of a thought cannot be told."—*Bailey*.

Her mother's broad, gingham back and the twist of iron gray hair low in her neck greeted her as she opened the door, then the odor of hot biscuits intruded itself, and then there came a shout from somebody kneeling on the oilcloth near the stove and pushing sticks of dry wood through its blazing open door.

"Oh, Marjie, what happened to you?"

"Something *didn't* happen. I didn't have my spelling or my examples. I read the "Lucy" book in school instead," she confessed dolefully.

"Why, *Marjie*!" was her mother's exclamation, but it brought the color to Marjorie's face and suffused her eyes.

"We are to have company for tea," announced the figure kneeling on the oilcloth as she banged the stove door. "A stranger; the evangelist Mr. Horton told us about Sunday."

"I know," said Marjorie. "I've read about him in *Pilgrim's Progress*; he showed Christian the way to the Wicket Gate."

Linnet jumped to her feet and shook a chip from her apron. "O, Goosie! Don't you know any better?"

Fourteen-year-old Linnet always knew better.

"Where is he?" questioned Marjorie.

"In the parlor. Go and entertain him. Mother and I must get him a good supper: cold chicken, canned raspberries, currant jelly, ham, hot biscuit, plain cake and fruit cake and—butter and—tea."

"I don't know how," hesitated Marjorie.

"Answer his questions, that's all," explained Linnet promptly. "I've told him all I know and now it's your turn."

"I don't like to answer questions," said Marjorie, still doubtfully.

"Oh, only your age and what you study and—if—you are a Christian."

"And he tells you how if you don't know how," said Marjorie, eagerly; "that's what he's for."

"Yes," replied her mother, approvingly, "run in and let him talk to you."

Very shyly glad of the opportunity, and yet dreading it inexpressibly, Marjorie hung her school clothing away and laid her satchel on the shelf in the hall closet, and then stood wavering in the closet, wondering if she dared go in to see Evangelist. He had spoken very kindly to Christian. She longed, oh, how she longed! to find the Wicket Gate, but would she dare ask any questions? Last Sabbath in church she had seen a sweet, beautiful face that she persuaded herself must be Mercy, and now to have Evangelist come to her very door!

What was there to know any better about? She did not care if Linnet had laughed. Linnet never cared to read *Pilgrim's Progress*.

It is on record that the first book a child reads intensely is the book that will influence all the life.

At ten Marjorie had read *Pilgrim's Progress* intensely. Timidly, with shining eyes, she stood one moment upon the red mat outside the parlor door, and then, with sudden courage, turned the knob and entered. At a glance she felt that there was no need of courage; Evangelist was seated comfortably in the horse-hair rocker with his feet to the fire resting on the camp stool; he did not look like Evangelist at all, she thought, disappointedly; he reminded her altogether more of a picture of Santa Claus: massive head and shoulders, white beard and moustache, ruddy cheeks, and, as the head turned quickly at her entrance, she beheld, beneath the shaggy, white brows, twinkling blue eyes.

"Ah," he exclaimed, in an abrupt voice, "you are the little girl they were expecting home from school."

"Yes, sir."

He extended a plump, white hand and, not at all shyly, Marjorie laid her hand in it.

"Isn't it late to come from school? Did you play on the way home?"

"No sir; I'm too big for that"

"Doesn't school dismiss earlier?"

"Yes, sir," flushing and dropping her eyes, "but I was kept in."

"Kept in," he repeated, smoothing the little hand. "I'm sure it was not for bad behavior and you look bright enough to learn your lessons."

"I didn't know my lessons," she faltered.

"Then you should have done as Stephen Grellet did," he returned, releasing her hand.

"How did he do?" she asked.

Nobody loved stories better than Marjorie.

Pushing her mother's spring rocker nearer the fire, she sat down, arranged the skirt of her dress, and, prepared herself, not to "entertain" him, but to listen.

"Did you never read about him?"

"I never even heard of him."

"Then I'll tell you something about him. His father was an intimate friend and counsellor of Louis XVI. Stephen was a French boy. Do you know who Louis XVI was?"

"No, sir."

"Do you know the French for Stephen?"

"No, sir."

"Then you don't study French. I'd study everything if I were you. My wife has read the Hebrew Bible through. She is a scholar as well as a good housewife. It needn't hinder, you see."

"No, sir," repeated Marjorie.

"When little Etienne—that's French for Stephen—was five or six years old he had a long Latin exercise to learn, and he was quite disheartened."

Marjorie's eyes opened wide in wonder. Six years old and a long Latin exercise. Even Hollis had not studied Latin.

"Sitting alone, all by himself, to study, he looked out of the window abroad upon nature in all her glorious beauty, and remembered that God made the gardens, the fields and the sky, and the thought came to him: 'Cannot the same God give me memory, also?' Then he knelt at the foot of his bed and poured out his soul in prayer. The prayer was wonderfully answered; on beginning to study again, he found himself master of his hard lesson, and, after that, he acquired learning with great readiness."

It was wonderful, Marjorie thought, and beautiful, but she could not say that; she asked instead: "Did he write about it himself?"

"Yes, he has written all about himself."

"When I was six I didn't know my small letters. Was he so bright because he was French?"

The gentleman laughed and remarked that the French were a pretty bright nation.

"Is that all you know about him?"

"Oh, no, indeed; there's a large book of his memoirs in my library. He visited many of the crowned heads of Europe."

There was another question forming on Marjorie's lips, but at that instant her mother opened the door. Now she would hear no more about Stephen Grellet and she could not ask about the Wicket Gate or Mercy or the children.

Rising in her pretty, respectful manner she gave her mother the spring rocker and pushed an ottoman behind the stove and seated herself where she might watch Evangelist's face as he talked.

How the talk drifted in this direction Marjorie did not understand; she knew it was something about finding the will of the Lord, but a story was coming and she listened with her listening eyes on his face.

"I had been thinking that God would certainly reveal his will if we inquired of him, feeling sure of that, for some time, and then I had this experience."

Marjorie's mother enjoyed "experiences" as well as Marjorie enjoyed stories. And she liked nothing better than to relate her own; after hearing an experience she usually began, "Now I will tell you mine."

Marjorie thought she knew every one of her mother's experiences. But it was Evangelist who was speaking.

The little girl in the brown and blue plaid dress with red stockings and buttoned boots, bent forward as she sat half concealed behind the stove and drank in every word with intent, wondering, unquestioning eyes.

Her mother listened, also, with eyes as intent and believing, and years afterward, recalled this true experience, when she was tempted to take Marjorie's happiness into her own hands, her own unwise, haste-making hands.

"My wife had been dead about two years," began Evangelist again, speaking in a retrospective tone. "I had two little children, the elder not eight years old, and my sister was my housekeeper. She did not like housekeeping nor taking care of children. Some women don't. She came to me one day with a very serious face. 'Brother,' said she, 'you need a wife, you must have a wife. I do not know how to take care of your children and you are almost never at home.' She left me before I could reply, almost before I could think what to reply. I was just home from helping a pastor in Wisconsin, it was thirty-six degrees below zero the day I left, and I had another engagement in Maine for the next week. I *was* very little at home, and my children did need a mother. I had not thought whether I needed a wife or not; I was too much taken up with the Lord's work to think about it. But that day I asked the Lord to find me a wife. After praying about it three days it came to me that a certain young lady was the one the Lord had chosen. Like Peter, I drew back and said, 'Not so, Lord.' My first wife was a continual spiritual help to me; she was the Lord's own messenger every day; but this lady, although a church member, was not particularly spiritually minded. Several years before she had been my pupil in Hebrew and Greek. I admired her intellectual gifts, but if a brother in the ministry had asked me if she would be a helpful wife to him, I should have hesitated about replying in the affirmative. And, yet here it was, the Lord had chosen her for me. I said, 'Not so, Lord,' until he assured me that her heart was in his hand and he could fit her to become my wife and a mother to my children. After waiting until I knew I was obeying the mind of my Master, I asked her to marry me. She accepted, as far as her own heart and will were concerned, but refused, because her father, a rich and worldly-minded man, was not willing for her to marry an itinerant preacher.

"I had not had a charge for three years then. I was so continually called to help other pastors that I had no time for a charge of my own. So it kept on for months and months; her father was not willing, and she would not marry me without his consent. My sister often said to me, 'I don't see how you can want to marry a woman that isn't willing to have you,' but I kept my own counsel. I knew the matter was in safe hands. I was not at all troubled; I kept about my Master's business and he kept about mine. Therefore, when she wrote to say that suddenly and unexpectedly her father had withdrawn all opposition, I was not in the least surprised. My sister declared I was plucky to hold on, but the Lord held on for me; I felt as if I had nothing to do with it. And a better wife and mother God never blessed one of his servants with. She could do something beside read the Bible in Hebrew; she could practice it in English. For forty years [missing text] my companion and counsellor and dearest friend. So you see"—he added in his bright, convincing voice, "we may know the will of the Lord about such things and everything else."

"I believe it," responded Marjorie's mother, emphatically.

"Now tell me about all the young people in your village. How many have you that are unconverted?"

Was Hollis one of them? Marjorie wondered with a beating heart. Would Evangelist talk to him? Would he kiss him, and give him a smile, and bid him God speed?

But—she began to doubt—perhaps there was another Evangelist and this was not the very one in *Pilgrim's Progress*; somehow, he did not seem just like that one. Might she dare ask him? How would she say it? Before she was aware her thought had become a spoken thought; in the interval of quiet while her mother was counting the young people in the village she was very much astonished to hear her own timid, bold, little voice inquire:

"Is there more than one Evangelist?"

"Why, yes, child," her mother answered absently and Evangelist began to tell her about some of the evangelists he was acquainted with.

"Wonderful men! Wonderful men!" he repeated.

Before another question could form itself on her eager lips her father entered and gave the stranger a cordial welcome.

"We have to thank scarlet fever at the Parsonage for the pleasure of your visit with us, I believe," he said.

"Yes, that seems to be the bright side of the trouble."

"Well, I hope you have brought a blessing with you."

"I hope I have! I prayed the Lord not to bring me here unless he came with me."

"I think the hush of the Spirit's presence has been in our church all winter," said Mrs. West. "I've had no rest day or night pleading for our young people."

The words filled Marjorie with a great awe; she slipped out to unburden herself to Linnet, but Linnet was setting the tea-table in a frolicsome mood and Marjorie's heart could not vent itself upon a frolicsome listener.

From the china closet in the hall Linnet had brought out the china, one of her mother's wedding presents and therefore seldom used, and the glass water pitcher and the small glass fruit saucers.

"Can't I help?" suggested Marjorie looking on with great interest.

"No," refused Linnet, decidedly, "you might break something as you did the night Mrs. Rheid and Hollis were here."

"My fingers were too cold, then."

"Perhaps they are too warm, now," laughed Linnet.

"Then I can tell you about the primary colors; I suppose I won't break *them*," returned Marjorie with her usual sweet-humor.

Linnet moved the spoon holder nearer the sugar bowl with the air of a house wife, Marjorie stood at the table leaning both elbows upon it.

"If you remember *vibgyor*, you'll remember the seven primary colors!" she said mysteriously.

"Is it like cutting your nails on Saturday without thinking of a fox's tail and so never have the toothache?" questioned Linnet.

"*No*; this is earnest. It isn't a joke; it's a lesson," returned Marjorie, severely. "Mr. Holmes said a professor told it to him when he was in college."

"You see it's a joke! I remember *vibgyor*, but now I don't know the seven primary colors. You are always getting taken in, Goosie! I hope you didn't ask Mr. Woodfern if he is the man in *Pilgrim's Progress*."

"I know he isn't," said Marjorie, seriously, "there are a good many of them, he said so. I guess *Pilgrim's Progress* happened a long time ago. I shan't look for Great-heart, any more," she added, with a sigh.

Linnet laughed and scrutinized the white handled knives to see if there were any blemishes on the blades; her mother kept them laid away in old flannel.

"Now, Linnet, you see it isn't a joke," began Marjorie, protestingly; "the word is made of all the first letters of the seven colors,—just see!" counting on her fingers, "violet, indigo, blue, green, yellow, orange, red! Did you see how it comes right?"

"I didn't see, but I will as soon as I get time. You were not taken in that time, I do believe. Did Mr. Woodfern ask you questions?"

"Not *that* kind! And I'm glad he didn't. Linnet, I haven't any 'experience' to talk about."

"You are not old enough," said Linnet, wisely.

"Are you?"

"Yes, I have a little bit."

"Shall you tell him about it?" asked Marjorie curiously.

"I don't know."

"I wish I had some; how do you get it?"

"It comes."

"From where?"

"Oh, I don't know."

"Then you can't tell me how to get it," pleaded Marjorie.

"No," said Linnet, shaking her sunshiny curls, "perhaps mother can."

"When did you have yours?" Marjorie persisted.

"One day when I was reading about the little girl in the Sandwich Islands. Her father was a missionary there, and she wrote in her journal how she felt and I felt so, too,"

"Did you put it in your journal?"

"Some of it."

"Did you show it to mother?"

"Yes."

"Was she glad?"

"Yes, she kissed me and said her prayers were answered."

Marjorie looked very grave. She wished she could be as old as Linnet and have "experience" to write in her journal and have her mother kiss her and say her prayers were answered.

"Do you have it all the time?" she questioned anxiously as Linnet hurried in from the kitchen with a small platter of sliced ham in her hand.

"Not every day; I do some days."

"I want it every day."

"You call them to tea when I tell you. And you may help me bring things in."

When Marjorie opened the parlor door to call them to tea she heard Mr. Woodfern inquire:

"Do all your children belong to the Lord?"

"The two in heaven certainly do, and I think Linnet is a Christian," her mother was saying.

"And Marjorie," he asked.

"You know there are such things; I think Marjorie's heart was changed in her cradle."

With the door half opened Marjorie stood and heard this lovely story about herself.

"It was before she was three years old; one evening I undressed her and laid her in the cradle, it was summer and she was not ready to go to sleep; she had been in a frolic with Linnet and was all in a gale of mischief. She arose up and said she wanted to get out; I said 'no,' very firmly, 'mamma wants you to stay.' But she persisted with all her might, and I had to punish her twice before she would consent to lie still; I was turning to leave her when I thought her sobs sounded more rebellious than subdued, I knelt down and took her in my arms to kiss her, but she drew back and would not kiss me. I saw there was no submission in her obedience and made up my mind not to leave her until she had given up her will to mine. If you can believe it, it was two full hours before she would kiss me, and then she couldn't kiss me enough. I think when she yielded to my will she gave up so wholly that she gave up her whole being to the strongest and most loving will she knew. And as soon as she knew God, she knew—or I knew—that she had submitted to him."

"Come to tea," called Marjorie, joyfully, a moment later.

This lovely story about herself was only one of the happenings that caused Marjorie to remember this day and evening: this day of small events stood out clearly against the background of her childhood.

That evening in the church she had been moved to do the hardest, happiest thing she had ever done in her hard and happy eleven years. At the close of his stirring appeal to all who felt themselves sinners in God's sight, Evangelist (he would always be Evangelist to Marjorie) requested any to rise who had this evening newly resolved to seek Christ until they found him. A little figure in a pew against the wall, arose quickly, after an undecided, prayerful moment, a little figure in a gray cloak and broad, gray velvet hat, but it was such a little figure, and the radiant face was hidden by such a broad hat, and the little figure dropped back into its seat so hurriedly, that, in looking over the church, neither the pastor nor the evangelist noticed it. Her heart gave one great jump when the pastor arose and remarked in a grieved and surprised tone: "I am sorry that there is not one among us, young or old, ready to seek our Saviour to-night."

The head under the gray hat drooped lower, the radiant face became for one instant sorrowful. As they were moving down the aisle an old lady, who had been seated next to Marjorie, whispered to her, "I'm sorry they didn't see you, dear."

"Never mind," said the bright voice, "God saw me."

Hollis saw her, also, and his heart smote him. This timid little girl had been braver than he. From the group of boys in the gallery he had looked down at her and wondered. But she was a girl, and girls did not mind doing such things as boys did; being good was a part of Marjorie's life, she wouldn't be Marjorie without it. There was a letter in his pocket from his uncle bidding him to come to the city without delay; he pushed through the crowd to find Marjorie, "it would be fun to see how sorry she would look," but her father had hurried her out and lifted her into the sleigh, and he saw the gray hat in the moonlight close to her father's shoulder.

As he was driving to the train the next afternoon, he jumped out and ran up to the door to say good-bye to her.

Marjorie opened the door, arrayed in a blue checked apron with fingers stained with peeling apples.

"Good-bye, I'm off," he shouted, resisting the impulse to catch her in his arms and kiss her.

"Good-bye, I'm so glad, and so sorry," she exclaimed with a shadowed face.

"I wish I had something to give you to remember me by," he said suddenly.

"I think you *have* given me lots of things."

"Come, Hol, don't stand there all day," expostulated his brother from the sleigh.

"Good-bye, then," said Hollis.

"Good-bye," said Marjorie. And then he was off and the bells were jingling down the road and she had not even cautioned him "Be a good boy." She wished she had had something to give him to remember *her* by; she had never done one thing to help him remember her and when he came back in years and years they would both be grown up and not know each other.

"Marjie, you are taking too thick peels," remonstrated her mother. For the next half hour she conscientiously refrained from thinking of any thing but the apples.

"Oh, Marjie," exclaimed Linnet, "peel one whole, be careful and don't break it, and throw it over your right shoulder and see what letter comes."

"Why?" asked Magorie, selecting a large, fair apple to peel.

"I'll tell you when it comes," answered Linnet, seriously.

With an intent face, and slow, careful fingers, Marjorie peeled the handsome apple without breaking the coils of the skin, then poised her hand and gave the shining, green rings a toss over her shoulder to the oilcloth.

"*S! S!* Oh! what a handsome *S!*" screamed Linnet.

"Well, what does it mean?" inquired Marjorie, interestedly.

"Oh, nothing, only you will marry a man whose name begins with *S*," said Linnet, seriously.

"I don't believe I will!" returned Marjorie, contentedly. "Do you believe I will, mother?"

Mrs. West was lifting a deliciously browned pumpkin pie from the oven, she set it carefully on the table beside Marjorie's yellow dish of quartered apples and then turned to the oven for its mate.

"Now cut one for me," urged Linnet gleefully.

"But I don't believe it," persisted Marjorie, picking among the apples in the basket at her feet; "you don't believe it yourself."

"I never *knew* it to come true," admitted Linnet, sagely, "but *S* is a common letter. There are more Smiths in the world than any one else. A woman went to an auction and bought a brass door plate with *Smith* on it because she had six daughters and was sure one of them would marry a Smith."

"And *did* one?" asked Maijorie, in her innocent voice. Linnet was sure her lungs were made of leather else she would have burst them every day laughing at foolish little Marjorie.

"The story ended there," said Linnet.

"Stories always leave off at interesting places," said Marjorie, guarding Linnet's future with slow-moving fingers. "I hope mine won't."

"It will if you die in the middle of it," returned Linnet

Linnet was washing the baking dishes at the sink.

"No, it wouldn't, it would go on and be more interesting," said Marjorie, in her decided way; "but I do want to finish it all."

"Be careful, don't break mine," continued Linnet, as Marjorie gave the apple rings a toss. "There! you have!" she cried disappointedly. "You've spoiled my fortune, Marjie."

"Linnet! Linnet!" rebuked her mother, shutting the oven door, "I thought you were only playing. I wouldn't have let you go on if I had thought you would have taken it in earnest."

"I don't really," returned Linnet, with a vexed laugh, "but I did want to see what letter it would be."

"It's *O*," said Marjorie, turning to look over her shoulder.

"Rather a crooked one," conceded Linnet, "but it will have to do."

"Suppose you try a dozen times and they all come different," suggested practical Marjorie.

"That proves it's all nonsense," answered her mother.

"And suppose you don't marry anybody," Marjorie continued, spoiling Linnet's romance, "some letter, or something *like* a letter has to come, and then what of it?"

"Oh, it's only fun," explained Linnet.

"I don't want to know about my *S*" confessed Marjorie. "I'd rather wait and find out. I want my life to be like a story-book and have surprises in the next chapter."

"It's sure to have that," said her mother. "We mustn't *try* to find out what is hidden. We mustn't meddle with our lives, either. Hurry providence, as somebody says in a book."

"And we can't ask anybody but God," said Marjorie, "because nobody else knows. He could make any letter come that he wanted to."

"He will not tell us anything that way," returned her mother.

"I don't want him to," said Marjorie.

"Mother, I was in fun and you are making *serious*," cried Linnet with a distressed face.

"Not making it dreadful, only serious," smiled her mother.

"I don't see why the letter has to be about your husband," argued Marjorie, "lots of things will happen to us first"

"But that is exciting," said Linnet, "and it is the most of things in story-books."

"I don't see why," continued Marjorie, unconvinced, turning an apple around in her fingers, "isn't the other part of the story worth anything?"

"Worth anything!" repeated Linnet, puzzled.

"Doesn't God care for the other part?" questioned the child. "I've got to have a good deal of the other part."

"So have all unmarried people," said her mother, smiling at the quaint gravity of Marjorie's eyes.

"Then I don't see why—" said Marjorie.

"Perhaps you will by and by," her mother replied, laughing, for Marjorie was looking as wise as an owl; "and now, please hurry with the apples, for they must bake before tea. Mr. Woodfern says he never ate baked apple sauce anywhere else."

Marjorie hoped he would not stay a whole week, as he proposed, if she had to cut the apples. And then, with a shock and revulsion at herself, she remembered that her father had read at worship that morning something about giving even a cup of cold water to a disciple for Christ's sake.

Linnet laughed again as she stooped to pick up the doubtful *O* and crooked *S* from the oilcloth.

But the letters had given Marjorie something to think about.

I had decided to hasten over the story of Marjorie's childhood and bring her into her joyous and promising girlhood, but the child's own words about the "other part" that she must have a "good deal" of have changed my mind. Surely God does care for the "other part," too.

And I wonder what it is in you (do you know?) that inclines you to hurry along and skip a little now and then, that you may discover whether Marjorie ever married Hollis? Why can't you wait and take her life as patiently as she did?

That same Saturday evening Marjorie's mother said to Marjorie's father, with a look of perplexity upon her face,

"Father, I don't know what to make of our Marjorie."

He was half dozing over the *Agriculturist*; he raised his head and asked sharply, "Why? What has she done now?"

Everybody knew that Marjorie was the apple of her father's eye.

"Nothing new! Only everything she does *is* new. She is two Marjories, and that's what I can't make out. She is silent and she is talkative; she is shy, very shy, and she is as bold as a little lion; sometimes she won't tell you anything, and sometimes she tells you everything; sometimes I think she doesn't love me, and again she loves me to death; sometimes I think she isn't as bright as other girls, and then again I'm sure she is a genius. Now Linnet is always the same; I always know what she will do and say; but there's no telling about Marjorie. I don't know what to make of her," she sighed.

"Then I wouldn't try, wife," said Marjorie's father, with his shrewd smile. "I'd let somebody that knows."

After a while, Marjorie's mother spoke again:

"I don't know that you help me any."

"I don't know that I can; girls are mysteries—you were a mystery once yourself. Marjorie can respond, but she will not respond, unless she has some one to respond *to*, or some *thing* to respond to. Towards myself I never find but one Marjorie!"

"That means that you always give her something to respond to!"

"Well, yes, something like it," he returned in one of Marjorie's contented tones.

"She'll have a good many heart aches before she's through, then," decided Mrs. West, with some sharpness.

"Probably," said Marjorie's father with the shadow of a smile on his thin lips.

III.
WHAT "DESULTORY" MEANS.

"A rose with all its sweetest leaves yet folded."

"Miss Prudence! O, Miss Prudence!"

It was summer time and Marjorie was almost fourteen years old. Her soul was looking out of troubled eyes to-day. Just now life was all one unanswered question.

"Marjorie! O, Marjorie!" mimicked Miss Prudence.

"I don't know what *desultory* means," said Marjorie.

"And you don't know where to find a dictionary?"

Miss Prudence

"Mustn't I ask you questions when I can find the answer myself?" asked Marjorie, straightforwardly.

"I think it's rather impertinent, don't you?"

"Yes," considered Marjorie, "rather."

Miss Prudence was a fair vision in Marjorie's eyes and Marjorie was a radiant vision in Miss Prudence's eyes. The radiant vision was not clothed in gorgeous apparel; the radiance was in the face and voice and in every motion; the apparel was simply a stiffly starched blue muslin, that had once belonged to Linnet and had been "let down" for Marjorie, and her head was crowned with a broad-brimmed straw hat, around the crown of which was tied a somewhat faded blue ribbon, also a relic of Linnet's summer days; her linen collar was fastened with an old-fashioned pin of her mother's; her boots were new and neatly fitting, her father had made them especially for herself.

Her sense of the fitness of things was sometimes outraged; one of the reasons why she longed to grow up was that she might have things of her own; things bought for her and made for her as they always were for Linnet. But Linnet was pretty and good and was going away to school!

The fair vision was clothed in white, a soft white, that fell in folds and had no kinship with starch. Marjorie had never seen this kind of white dress before; it was a part of Miss Prudence's loveliness. The face was oval and delicate, with little color in the lips and less in the cheeks, smooth black hair was brushed away from the thoughtful forehead and underneath the heavily pencilled black brows large, believing, gray eyes looked unquestioningly out upon the world. Unlike Marjorie, Miss Prudence's questions had been answered. She would have told Marjorie that it was because she had asked her questions of One who knew how to answer. She was swinging in her hammock on the back porch; this back porch looked over towards the sea, a grass plat touched the edge of the porch and then came the garden; it was a kitchen garden, and stretched down to the flat rocks, and beyond the flat rocks were the sand and the sea.

Marjorie had walked two miles and a half this hot afternoon to spend two or three hours with her friend, Miss Prudence. Miss Prudence was boarding at Marjorie's grandfather's; this was the second summer that she had been at this farmhouse by the sea. She was the lady of whom Marjorie had caught a glimpse so long ago in church, and called her Mercy. Throwing aside her hat, Marjorie dropped down on the floor of the porch, so near the gently swaying hammock that she might touch the soft, white drapery, and in a position to watch Miss Prudence's face.

"I don't see the use of learning somethings," Marjorie began; that is, if she could be said to begin anything with Miss Prudence, the beginning of all her questions had been so long ago. So long ago to Marjorie; long ago to Miss Prudence was before Marjorie was born.

There were no books or papers in the hammock. Miss Prudence had settled herself comfortably, so comfortably that she was not conscious of inhabiting her body when Marjorie had unlatched the gate.

"Which one of the things, for instance?"

In the interested voice there was not one trace of the delicious reverie she had been lost in.

"Punctuation," said Marjorie, promptly; "and Mr. Holmes says we must be thorough in it. I can't see the use of anything beside periods, and, of course, a comma once in a while."

A gleam of fun flashed into the gray eyes. Miss Prudence was a born pedagogue.

"I'll show you something I learned when I was a little girl; and, after this, if you don't confess that punctuation has its work in the world, I have nothing more to say about it."

Marjorie had been fanning herself with her broad brim, she let it fall in her eagerness and her eyes were two convincing arguments against the truth of her own theory, for they were two emphasized exclamation points; sometimes when she was very eager she doubled herself up and made an interrogation point of herself.

"Up in my room on the table you will find paper and pencil; please bring them to me."

Marjorie flew away and Miss Prudence gave herself up to her interrupted reverie. To-day was one of Miss Prudence's hard-working days; that is, it was followed by the effect of a hard-working day; the days in which she felt too weak to do anything beside pray she counted the successful days of her life. She said they were the only days in her life in which she accomplished anything.

Marjorie was at home in every part of her grandfather's queer old house; Miss Prudence's room was her especial delight. It was a low-studded chamber, with three windows looking out to the sea, the wide fireplace was open, filled with boughs of fragrant hemlock; the smooth yellow floor with its coolness and sweet cleanliness invited you to enter; there were round braided mats spread before the bureau and rude washstand, and more pretentious ones in size and beauty were laid in front of the red, high-posted bedstead and over the brick hearth. There were, beside, in the apartment, two tables, an easy-chair with arms, its cushions covered with red calico, a camp stool, three rush-bottomed chairs, a Saratoga trunk, intruding itself with ugly modernness, also, hanging upon hooks, several articles of clothing, conspicuously among them a gray flannel bathing suit. The windows were draperied in dotted swiss, fastened back with green cord; her grandmother would never have been guilty of those curtains. Marjorie was sure they had intimate connection with the Saratoga trunk. Sunshine, the salt-breath of the sea and the odor of pine woods as well!

There were rollicking voices outside the window, Marjorie looked out and spied her five little cousins playing in the sand. Three of them held in their hands, half-eaten, the inevitable doughnut; morning, noon, and night those children were to be found with doughnuts in their hands.

She laughed and turned again to the contemplation of the room; on the high mantel was a yellow pitcher, that her grandmother knew was a hundred years old, and in the centre of the mantel were arranged a sugar bowl and a vinegar cruet that Miss Prudence had coaxed away from the old lady; her city friends would rave over them, she said. The old lady had laughed, remarking that "city folks" had ways of their own.

"I've given away a whole set of dishes to folks that come in the yachts," she said. "I should think you would rather have new dishes."

Miss Prudence never dusted her old possessions; she told Marjorie that she had not the heart to disturb the dust of ages.

Marjorie was tempted to linger and linger; in winter this room was closed and seemed always bare and cold when she peeped into it; there was no temptation to stay one moment; and now she had to tear herself away. It must be Miss Prudence's spirit that brooded over it and gave it sweetness and sunshine. This was the way Marjorie put the thought to herself. The child was very poetical when she lived alone with herself. Miss Prudence's wicker work-basket with its dainty lining of rose-tinted silk, its shining scissors and gold thimble, with its spools and sea-green silk needlebook was a whole poem to the child; she thought the possession of one could make any kind of sewing, even darning stockings, very delightful work. "Stitch, stitch, stitch," would not seem dreadful, at all.

How mysterious and charming it was to board by the seashore with somebody's grandfather! And then, in winter, to go back to some bewildering sort of a fairyland! To some kind of a world where people did not talk all the time about "getting along" and "saving" and "doing without" and "making both ends meet." How Marjorie's soul rebelled against the constant repetition of those expressions! How she thought she would never *let* her little girls know what one of them meant! If she and her little girls had to be saving and do without, how brave they would be about it, and laugh over it, and never ding it into anybody's ears! And she would never constantly be asking what things cost! Miss Prudence never asked such questions. But she would like to know if that gold pen cost so very much, and that glass inkstand shaped like a pyramid, and all that cream note-paper with maple tassels and autumn leaves and butterflies and ever so many cunning things painted in its left corners. And there was a pile of foolscap on the table, and some long, yellow envelopes, and some old books and some new books and an ivory paper-cutter; all something apart from the commonplace world she inhabited. Not apart from the world her thoughts and desires revelled in; not her hopes, for she had not gotten so far as to hope to live in a magical world like Miss Prudence. And yet when Miss Prudence did not wear white she was robed in deep mourning; there was sorrow in Miss Prudence's magical world.

It was some few moments before the roving eyes could settle themselves upon the paper and pencil she had been sent for; she would have liked to choose a sheet of the thick cream-paper with the autumn leaves painted on it, but that was not for study, and Miss Prudence certainly intended study, although there was fun in her eyes. She selected carefully a sheet of foolscap and from among the pen oils a nicely sharpened Faber number three. With the breath of the room about her, and the beauty and restfulness of it making a glory in her eyes, she ran down to the broad, airy hall.

Glancing into the sitting-room as she passed its partly opened door she discovered her grandfather asleep in his arm-chair and her grandmother sitting near him busy in slicing apples to be strung and hung up in the kitchen to dry! With a shiver of foreboding the child passed the door on tiptoe; suppose her grandmother *should* call her in to string those apples! The other children never strung them to suit her and she "admired" Marjorie's way of doing them. Marjorie said once that she hated apple blossoms because they turned into dried apples. But that was when she had stuck the darning needle into her thumb.

I'm afraid you will think now that Marjorie is not as sweet as she used to be.

She presented the paper, congratulating herself upon her escape, and Miss Prudence lifted herself in the hammock and took the pencil, holding it in her fingers while she meditated. What a little girl she was when her whiteheaded old teacher had bidden her write this sentence on the blackboard. She wrote it carefully, Marjorie's attentive eyes following each movement of the pencil.

"The persons inside the coach were Mr Miller a clergyman his son a lawyer Mr Angelo a foreigner his lady and a little child" In the entire sentence there was not one punctuation mark.

"Read it, please."

Marjorie began to read, then stopped and laughed.

"I can't."

"You wouldn't enjoy a book very much written in that style, would you?"

"I couldn't enjoy it at all. I wouldn't read it"

"Well, if you can't read it, explain it to me. How many persons are in the coach?"

"That's easy enough! There's Mr. Miller, that's one; there's the clergyman, that's two!"

"Perhaps that is only one; Mr. Miller may be a clergyman."

"So he may. But how can I tell?" asked Marjorie, perplexed. "Well, then, his son makes two."

"Whose son?"

"Why, Mr. Miller's!"

"Perhaps he was the clergyman's son," returned Miss Prudence seriously.

"Well, then," declared Marjorie, "I guess there were eight people! Mr. Miller, the clergyman, the son, the lawyer, Mr. Angelo, a foreigner, a lady, and a child!"

"Placing a comma after each there are eight persons," said Miss Prudence making the commas.

"Yes," assented Marjorie, watching her.

Beneath it Miss Prudence wrote the sentence again, punctuating thus:

"The persons inside the conch were Mr. Miller, a clergyman; his son, a lawyer; Mr. Angelo, a foreigner, his lady; and a little child."

"Now how many persons are there inside this coach?"

"Three gentlemen, a lady and child," laughed Marjorie—"five instead of eight. Those little marks have caused three people to vanish."

"And to change occupations."

"Yes, for Mr. Miller is a clergyman, his son a lawyer, and Mr. Angelo has become a foreigner."

The pencil was moving again and the amused, attentive eyes were steadfastly following.

"The persons inside the coach were Mr. Miller; a clergyman, his son; a lawyer, Mr. Angelo; a foreigner, his lady, and a little child."

Miss Prudence

Marjorie uttered an exclamation; it was so funny!

"Now, Mr. Miller's son is a clergyman instead of himself, Mr. Angelo is a lawyer, and nobody knows whether he is a foreigner or not, and we don't know the foreigner's name, and he has a wife and child."

Miss Prudence smiled over the young eagerness, and rewrote the sentence once again causing Mr. Angelo to cease to be a lawyer and giving the foreigner a wife but no little child.

"O, Miss Prudence, you've made the little thing an orphan all alone in a stage-coach all through the change of a comma to be a semi-colon!" exclaimed Marjorie in comical earnestness. "I think punctuation means ever so much; it isn't dry one bit," she added, enthusiastically.

"You couldn't enjoy Mrs. Browning very well without it," smiled Miss Prudence.

"I never would know what the 'Cry of the Children' meant, or anything about Cowper's grave, would I? And if I punctuated it myself, I might not get all *she* meant. I might make a meaning of my own, and that would be sad."

"I think you do," said Miss Prudence; "when I read it to you and the children, there were tears in your eyes, but the others said all they liked was my voice."

"Yes," said Marjorie, "but if somebody had stumbled over every line I shouldn't have felt it so. I know the good there is in studying elocution. When Mr. Woodfern was here and read 'O, Absalom, my son! My son, Absalom!' everybody had tears in their eyes, and I had never seen tears about it before. And now I know the good of punctuation. I guess punctuation helps elocution, too."

"I shouldn't wonder," replied Miss Prudence, smiling at Marjorie's air of having discovered something. "Now, I'll give you something to do while I close my eyes and think awhile."

"Am I interrupting you?" inquired Marjorie in consternation. "I didn't know how I could any more than I can interrupt—"

"God" was in her thought, but she did not give it utterance.

"I shall not allow you," returned Miss Prudence, quietly. "You will work awhile, and I will think and when I open my eyes you may talk to me about anything you please. You are a great rest to me, child."

"Thank you," said the child, simply.

"You may take the paper and change the number of people, or relationship, or professions again. I know it may be done."

"I don't see how."

"Then it will give you really something to do."

Seating herself again on the yellow floor of the porch, within range of Miss Prudence's vision, but not near enough to disturb her, Marjorie bit the unsharpened end of her pencil and looked long at the puzzling sentences on the foolscap. With the attitude of attentiveness she was not always attentive; Mr. Holmes told her that she lacked concentration and that she could not succeed without it. Marjorie was very anxious to "succeed." She scribbled awhile, making a comma and a dash, a parenthesis, an interrogation point, an asterisk and a line of asterisks! But the sense was not changed; there was nobody new in the stage-coach and nobody did anything new. Then she rewrote it again, giving the little child to the foreigner and lady; she wanted the child to have a father and mother, even if the father were a foreigner and did not speak English; she called the foreigner Mr. Angelo, and imagined him to be a brother of the celebrated Michael Angelo; making a dive into the shallow depths of her knowledge of Italian nomenclature she selected a name for the child, a little girl, of course—Corrinne would do, or it might be a boy and named for his uncle Michael. In what age of the world had Michael Angelo lived? At the same time with Petrarch and Galileo, and Tasso and—did she know about any other Italians? Oh, yes. Silvio Pellico,—wasn't he in prison and didn't he write about it? And was not the leaning tower of Pisa in Italy? Was that one of the Seven Wonders of the World? And weren't there Seven Wise Men of Greece? And wasn't there a story about the Seven Sleepers? But weren't they in Asia? And weren't the churches in Revelation in Asia? And wasn't the one at Laodicea lukewarm? And did people mix bread with lukewarm water in summer as well as winter? And wasn't it queer—why how had she got there? But it *was* queer for the oriental king to refuse to believe and say it wasn't so—that water couldn't become hard enough for people to walk on it! And it was funny for the East Indian servant to be alarmed because the butter was "spoiled," just because when they were up in the mountains it became hard and was not like oil as it was down in Calcutta! And that was where Henry Martyn went, and he dressed all in white, and his face was so lovely and pure, like an angel's; and angels *were* like young men, for at the resurrection didn't it say they were young men! Or was it some other time? And how do you spell *resurrection*? Was that the word that had one *s* and two *r's* in it? And how would you write two *r's*? Would punctuation teach you that? Was *B* a word and could you spell it?

"Well, Marjorie?"

"Oh, dear me!" exclaimed Marjorie. "I've been away off! I always do go away off! I don't remember what the last thing I thought of was. I never shall be concentrated," she sighed. "I believe I could go right on and think of fifty other things. One thing always reminds me of some thing else."

"And some day," rebuked Miss Prudence, "when you must concentrate your thoughts you will find that you have spoiled yourself."

"I have found it out now," acknowledged Marjorie humbly.

"I have to be very severe with myself."

"I ought to be," Marjorie confessed with a rueful face, "for it spoils my prayers so often. I wouldn't dare tell you all the things I find myself thinking of. Why, last night—you know at the missionary meeting they asked us to pray for China and so I thought I'd begin last night, and I had hardly begun when it flashed into my mind—suppose somebody should make me Empress of China, and give me supreme power, of course. And I began to make plans as to how I should make them all Christians. I thought I wouldn't *force* them or destroy their temples, but I'd have all my officers real Christians; Americans, of course; and I thought I *would* compel them to send the children to Christian schools. I'd have such grand schools. I had you as principal for the grandest one. And I'd have the Bible and all our best books, and all our best Sunday School books translated into Chinese and I *would* make the Sabbath a holy day all over the land. I didn't know what I would do about that room in every large house called the Hall of Ancestors. You know they worship their grandparents and great-great-grandparents there. I think I should have to let them read the old books. Isn't it queer that one of the proverbs should be like the Bible? 'God hates the proud and is kind to the humble.' Do you know all about Buddha?"

"Is that as far as you got in your prayer?" asked Miss Prudence, gravely.

"About as far. And then I was so contrite that I began to pray for myself as hard as I could, and forgot all about China."

"Do you wander off in reading the Bible, too?"

"Oh, no; I can keep my attention on that. I read Genesis and Exodus last Sunday. It is the loveliest story-book I know. I've begun to read it through. Uncle James said once, that when he was a sea-captain, he brought a passenger from Germany and he used to sit up all night and read the Bible. He told me last Sunday because he thought I read so long. I told him I didn't wonder. Miss Prudence," fixing her innocent, questioning eyes upon Miss Prudence's face, "why did a lady tell mother once that she didn't want her little girl to read the Bible through until she was grown up? It was Mrs. Grey,—and she told mother she ought not to let me begin and read right through."

"What did your mother say?"

"She said she was glad I wanted to do it."

"I think Mrs. Grey meant that you might learn about some of the sin there is in the world. But if you live in the world, you will be kept from the evil, because Christ prayed that his disciples might be thus kept; but you must know the sin exists. And I would rather my little girl would learn about the sins that God hates direct from his lips than from any other source. As soon as you learn what sin is, you will learn to hate it, and that is not sure if you learn it in any other way. I read the Bible through when I was about your age, and I think there are some forms of sin I never should have hated so intensely if I had not learned about them in the way God thinks best to teach us his abhorrence of them. I never read any book in which a sin was fully delineated that I did not feel some of the excitement of the sin—some extenuation, perhaps, some glossing over, some excuse for the sinner,—but in the record God gives I always intensely hate the sin and feel how abominable it is in his sight. The first book I ever cried over was the Bible and it was somebody's sin that brought the tears. I would like to talk to Mrs. Grey!" cried Miss Prudence, her eyes kindling with indignation. "To think that God does not know what is good for his children."

"I wish you would," said Marjorie with enthusiasm, "for I don't know how to say it. Mother knows a lady who will not read Esther on Sunday because God isn't in it"

"The name of God, you mean," said Miss Prudence smiling. "I think Esther and Mordecai and all the Jews thought God was in it."

"I will try not to build castles," promised Marjorie often a silent half minute. "I've done it so much to please Linnet. After we go to bed at night she says, 'Shut your eyes, Marjie, and tell me what you see,' Then I shut my eyes and see things for us both. I see ourselves grown up and having a splendid home and a real splendid husband, and we each have three children. She has two boys and one girl, and I have two girls and one boy. And we educate them and dress them so nice, and they do lovely things. We travel all around the world with them, and I tell Linnet all we see in Europe and Asia. Our husbands stay home and send us money. They have to stay home and earn it, you know," Marjorie explained with a shrewd little smile. "Would you give that all up?" she asked disappointedly.

"Yes, I am sure I would. You are making a disappointment for yourself; your life may not be at all like that. You may never marry, in the first place, and you may marry a man who cannot send you to Europe, and I think you are rather selfish to spend his money and not stay home and be a good wife to him," said Miss Prudence, smiling.

"Oh. I write him splendid long letters!" said Marjorie quickly. "They are so splendid that he thinks of making a book of them."

"I'm afraid they wouldn't take," returned Miss Prudence seriously, "books of travel are too common nowadays."

"Is it wrong to build castles for any other reason than for making disappointments?" Marjorie asked anxiously.

"Yes, you dwell only on pleasant things and thus you do not prepare yourself, or rather un-prepare yourself for bearing trial. And why should a little girl live in a woman's world?"

"Oh, because it's so nice!" cried Marjorie.

"And are you willing to lose your precious childhood and girlhood?"

"Why no," acknowledged the child, looking startled.

"I think you lose a part of it when you love best to look forward to womanhood; I should think every day would be full enough for you to live in."

"To-day is full enough; but some days nothing happens at all."

"Now is your study time; now is the time for you to be a perfect little daughter and sister, a perfect friend, a perfect helper in every way that a child may help. And when womanhood comes you will be ready to enjoy it and to do its work. It would be very sad to look back upon a lost or blighted or unsatisfying childhood."

"Yes," assented Marjorie, gravely.

"Perhaps you and Linnet have been reading story-books that were not written for children."

"We read all the books in the school library."

"Does your mother look over them?"

"No, not always."

"They may harm you only in this way that I see. You are thinking of things before the time. It would be a pity to spoil May by bringing September into it."

"All the girls like the grown-up stories best" excused Marjorie.

"Perhaps they have not read books written purely for children. Think of the histories and travels and biographies and poems piled up for you to read!"

"I wish I had them. I read all I could get."

"I am sure you do. O, Marjorie, I don't want you to lose one of your precious days. I lost so many of mine by growing up too soon. There are years and years to be a woman, but there are so few years to be a child and a girl."

Marjorie scribbled awhile thinking of nothing to say. Had she been "spoiling" Linnet, too? But Linnet was two years older, almost old enough to think about growing up.

"Marjorie, look at me!"

Marjorie raised her eyes and fixed them upon the glowing eyes that were reading her own. Miss Prudence's lips were white and tremulous.

"I have had some very hard things in my life and I fully believe I brought many of them upon myself. I spoiled my childhood and early girlhood by light reading and castle-building; I preferred to live among scenes of my own imagining, than in my own common life, and oh, the things I left up done! The precious girlhood I lost and the hard womanhood I made for myself."

The child's eyes were as full of tears as the woman's.

"Please tell me what to do," Marjorie entreated. "I don't want to lose anything. I suppose it is as good to be a girl as a woman."

"Get all the sweetness out of every day; *live* in to-day, don't plan or hope about womanhood; God has all that in his safe hands. Read the kind of books I have spoken of and when you read grown-up stories let some one older and wiser choose them for you. By and by your taste will be so formed and cultivated that you will choose only the best for yourself. I hope the Bible will spoil some other books for you."

"I *devour* everything I can borrow or find anywhere."

"You don't eat everything you can borrow or find anywhere. If you choose for your body, how much more ought you to choose for your mind."

"I do get discontented sometimes and want things to happen as they do in books; something happens in every chapter in a book," acknowledged Marjorie.

"There's nothing said about the dull, uneventful days that come between; if the author should write only about the dull days no one would read the book."

"It wouldn't be like life, either," said Marjorie, quickly, "for something does happen, sometimes nothing has happened yet to me, though. But I suppose something will, some day."

"Then if I should write about your thirteen years the charm would have to be all in the telling."

"Like Hector in the Garden," said Marjorie, brightly. "How I do love that. And he was only nine years old."

"But how far we've gotten away from punctuation!"

Next to prayer children were Miss Prudence's most perfect rest. They were so utterly unconscious of what she was going through. It seemed to Miss Prudence as if she were always going through and never getting through.

"Are you fully satisfied that punctuation has its work in the world?"

"Yes, ever so fully. I should never get along in the Bible without it."

"That reminds me; run upstairs and bring me my Bible and I'll show you something.

"And, then, after that will you show me the good of remembering *dates*. They are so hard to remember. And I can't see the good. Do you suppose you *could* make it as interesting as punctuation?"

"I might try. The idea of a little girl who finds punctuation so interesting having to resort to castle-building to make life worth living," laughed Miss Prudence.

"Mother said to-day that she was afraid I was growing deaf, for she spoke three times before I answered; I was away off somewhere imagining I had a hundred dollars to spend, so she went down cellar for the butter herself."

Marjorie walked away with a self-rebuked air; she did dread to pass that open sitting-room door; Uncle James had come in in his shirt sleeves, wiping his bald head with his handkerchief and was telling her grandfather that the hay was poor this year; Aunt Miranda was brushing Nettie's hair and scolding her for having such greasy fingers; and her grandmother had a pile, *such* a pile of sliced apple all ready to be strung. Her head was turning, yes, she would see her and then she could not know about dates or have a lesson in reading poetry! Tiptoeing more softly still and holding the skirt of her starched muslin in both hands to keep it from rustling, she at last passed the ordeal and breathed freely as she gained Miss Prudence's chamber. The spirit of handling things seemed to possess her this afternoon, for, after finding the Bible, she went to the mantel and took into her hands every article placed upon it; the bird's nest with the three tiny eggs, the bunch of feathers that she had gathered for Miss Prudence with their many shades of brown, the old pieces of crockery, handling these latter very carefully until she seized the yellow pitcher; Miss Prudence had paid her grandmother quite a sum for the pitcher, having purchased it for a friend; Marjorie turned it around and around in her hands, then, suddenly, being startled by a heavy, slow step on the stairs which she recognized as her grandmother's, and having in fear those apples to be strung, in attempting to lift it to the high mantel, it fell short of the mantel edge and dropped with a crash to the hearth.

For an instant Marjorie was paralyzed with horror; then she stifled a shriek and stood still gazing down through quick tears upon the yellow fragments. Fortunately her grandmother, being very deaf, had passed the door and heard no sound. What would have happened to her if her grandmother had looked in!

How disappointed Miss Prudence would be! It belonged to her friend and how could she remedy the loss?

Stooping, with eyes so blinded with tears that she could scarcely see the pieces she took into her hand, she picked up each bit, and then on the spur of the moment hid them among the thick branches of hemlock. Now what was she to do next? Could she earn money to buy another hundred-years-old yellow pitcher? And if she could earn the money, where could she find the pitcher? She would not confess to Miss Prudence until she found some way of doing something for her. Oh, dear! This was not the kind of thing that she had been wishing would happen! And how could she go down with such a face to hear the rest about punctuation?

"Marjorie! Marjorie!" shouted Uncle James from below, "here's Cap'n Rheid at the gate, and if you want to catch a ride you'd better go a ways with him."

The opportunity to run away was better than the ride; hastening down to the hammock she laid the Bible in Miss Prudence's lap.

"I have to go, you see," she exclaimed, hurriedly, averting her face.

"Then our desultory conversation must be finished another time."

"If that's what it means, it means delightful!" said Marjorie. "Thank you, and good-bye."

The blue muslin vanished between the rows of currant bushes. She was hardly a radiant vision as she flew down to the gate; in those few minutes what could have happened to the child?

IV.

A RIDE, A WALK, A TALK, AND A TUMBLE.

"Children always turn toward the light"

"Well, Mousie!"

The old voice and the old pet name; no one thought of calling her
"Mousie" but Hollis Rheid.

Her mother said she was noisier than she used to be; perhaps he would not call her Mousie now if he could hear her sing about the house and run up and down stairs and shout when she played games at school. That time when she was so quiet and afraid of everybody seemed ages ago; ages ago before Hollis went to New York. He had returned home once since, but she had been at her grandfather's and had not seen him. Springing to the ground, he caught her in his arms, this tall, strange boy, who had changed so much, and yet who had not changed at all, and lifted her into the back of the open wagon.

"Will you squeeze in between us—there's but one seat you see, and father's a big man, or shall I make a place for you in the bottom among the bags?"

"I'd rather sit with the bags," said Marjorie, her timidity coming back. She had always been afraid of Hollis' father; his eyes were the color of steel, and his voice was not encouraging. He thought he was born to command. People said old Captain Rheid acted as if he were always on shipboard. His wife said once in the bitterness of her spirit that he always marched the quarter-deck and kept his boys in the forecastle.

"You don't weigh more than that bag of flour yourself, not as much, and that weighs one hundred pounds."

"I weigh ninety pounds," said Marjorie.

"And how old are you?"

"Almost fourteen," she answered proudly.

"Four years younger than I am! Now, are you comfortable? Are you afraid of spoiling your dress? I didn't think of that?"

"Oh, no; I wish I was," laughed Marjorie, glancing shyly at him from under her broad brim.

It was her own bright face, yet, he decided, with an older look in it, her eyelashes were suspiciously moist and her cheeks were reddened with something more than being lifted into the wagon.

Marjorie settled herself among the bags, feeling somewhat strange and thinking she would much rather have walked; Hollis sprang in beside his father, not inclined to make conversation with him, and restrained, by his presence, from turning around to talk to Marjorie.

Oh, how people misunderstand each other! How Captain Rheid misunderstood his boys and how his boys misunderstood him! The boys said that Hollis was the Joseph among them, his father's favorite; but Hollis and his father had never opened their hearts to each other. Captain Rheid often declared that there was no knowing what his boys would do if they were not kept in; perhaps they had him to thank that they were not all in state-prison. There was a whisper among the country folks that the old man himself had been in prison in some foreign country, but no one had ever proved it; in his many "yarns" at the village store, he had not even hinted at such a strait. If Marjorie had not stood quite so much in fear of him she would have enjoyed his adventures; as it was she did enjoy with a feverish enjoyment the story of thirteen days in an open boat on the ocean. His boys were fully aware that he had run away from home when he was fourteen, and had not returned for fourteen years, but they were not in the least inclined to follow his example. Hollis' brothers had all left home with the excuse that they could "better" themselves elsewhere; two were second mates on board large ships, Will and Harold, Sam was learning a trade in the nearest town, he was next to Hollis in age, and the eldest, Herbert, had married and was farming on shares within ten miles of his father's farm. But Captain Rheid held up his head, declaring that his boys were good boys, and had always obeyed him; if they had left him to farm his hundred and fifty acres alone, it was only because their tastes differed from his. In her lonely old age, how his wife sighed for a daughter!—a daughter that would stay at home and share her labors, and talk to her, and read to her on stormy Sundays, and see that her collar was on straight, and that her caps were made nice. Some mothers had daughters, but she had never had much pleasure in her life!

"Like to come over to your grandfather's, eh?" remarked Captain Rheid, looking around at the broad-brimmed hat among the full bags.

"Yes, sir," said Marjorie, denting one of the full bags with her forefinger and wondering what he would do to her if she should make a hole in the bag, and let the contents out.

She rarely got beyond monosyllables with Hollis' father.

"Your uncle James isn't going to stay much longer, he tells me,"

"No, sir," said Marjorie, obediently.

"Wife and children going back to Boston, too?"

"Yes, sir."

Her forefinger was still making dents.

"Just come to board awhile, I suppose?"

"I thought they *visited*" said Marjorie.

"Visited? Humph! *Visit* his poor old father with a wife and five children!"

Marjorie wanted to say that her grandfather wasn't poor.

"Your grandfather's place don't bring in much, I reckon."

"I don't know," Marjorie answered.

"How many acres? Not more'n fifty, and some of that *made* land. I remember when some of your grandfather's land was water! I don't see what your uncle James had to settle down to business in Boston for—*that's* what comes of marrying a city girl! Why didn't he stay home and take care of his old father?"

Marjorie had nothing to say. Hollis flushed uncomfortably.

"And your mother had to get married, too. I'm glad I haven't a daughter to run away and get married?"

"She didn't run away," Marjorie found voice to answer indignantly.

"O, no, the Connecticut schoolmaster had to come and make a home for her."

Marjorie wondered what right he had to be so disagreeable to her, and why should he find fault with her mother and her uncle, and what right had he to say that her grandfather was poor and that some of his land had once been water?

"Hollis shan't grow up and marry a city girl if I can help it," he growled, half good-naturedly.

Hollis laughed; he thought he was already grown up, and he did admire "city girls" with their pretty finished manners and little ready speeches.

Marjorie wished Hollis would begin to talk about something pleasant; there were two miles further to ride, and would Captain Rheid talk all the way?

If she could only have an errand somewhere and make an excuse to get out! But the Captain's next words relieved her perplexity; "I can't take you all the way, Sis, I have to branch off another road to see a man about helping me with the hay. I would have let Hollis go to mill, but I couldn't trust him with these horses."

Hollis fidgeted on his seat; he had asked his father when they set out to let him take the lines, but he had replied ungraciously that as long as he had hands he preferred to hold the reins.

Hollis had laughed and retorted: "I believe that, father."

"Shall I get out now?" asked Marjorie, eagerly. "I like to walk. I expected to walk home."

"No; wait till we come to the turn."

The horses were walking slowly up the hill; Marjorie made dents in the bag of flour, in the bag of indian meal, and in the bag of wheat bran, and studied Hollis' back. The new navy-blue suit was handsome and stylish, and the back of his brown head with its thick waves of brownish hair was handsome also—handsome and familiar; but the navy-blue suit was not familiar, and the eyes that just then turned and looked at her were not familiar either. Marjorie could get on delightfully with *souls*, but bodies were something that came between her soul and their soul; the flesh, like a veil, hid herself and hid the other soul that she wanted to be at home with. She could have written to the Hollis she remembered many things that she could not utter to the Hollis that she saw today. Marjorie could not define this shrinking, of course.

"Hollis has to go back in a day or two," Captain Rheid announced; "he spent part of his vacation in the country with Uncle Jack before he came home. Boys nowadays don't think of their fathers and mothers."

Hollis wondered if *he* thought of his mother and father when he ran away from them those fourteen years: he wished that his father had never revealed that episode in his early life. He did not miss it that he did not love his father, but he would have given more than a little if he might respect him. He knew Marjorie would not believe that he did not think about his mother.

"I wonder if your father will work at his trade next winter," continued Captain Rheid.

"I don't know," said Marjorie, hoping the "turn" was not far off.

"I'd advise him to—summers, too, for that matter. These little places don't pay. Wants to sell, he tells me."

"Yes, sir."

"Real estate's too low; 'tisn't a good time to sell. But it's a good time to buy; and I'll buy your place and give it to Hollis if he'll settle down and work it."

"It would take more than *that* farm to keep me here," said Hollis, quickly; "but, thank you all the same, father; Herbert would jump at the chance."

"Herbert shan't have it; I don't like his wife; she isn't respectful to Herbert's father. He wants to exchange it for city property, so he can go into business, he tells me."

"Oh, does he?" exclaimed Marjorie. "I didn't know that."

"Girls are rattlebrains and chatterboxes; they can't be told everything," he replied shortly.

"I wonder what makes you tell me, then," said Marjorie, demurely, in the fun of the repartee forgetting for the first time the bits of yellow ware secreted among the hemlock boughs.

Throwing back his head Captain Rheid laughed heartily, he touched the horses with the whip, laughing still.

"I wouldn't mind having a little girl like you," he said, reining in the horses at the turn of the road; "come over and see marm some day."

"Thank you," Marjorie said, rising.

Giving the reins to Hollis, Captain Rheid climbed out of the wagon that he might lift the child out himself.

"Jump," he commanded, placing her hands on his shoulders.

Marjorie jumped with another "thank you."

"I haven't kissed a little girl for twenty years—not since my little girl died—but I guess I'll kiss you."

Marjorie would not withdraw her lips for the sake of the little girl that died twenty years ago.

"Good-bye, Mousie, if I don't see you again," said Hollis.

"Good-bye," said Marjorie.

She stood still till the horses' heads were turned and the chains had rattled off in the distance, then, very slowly, she walked on in the dusty road, forgetting how soft and green the grass was at the wayside.

"She's a proper nice little thing," observed Hollis' father; "her father wouldn't sell her for gold. I'll exchange my place for his if he'll throw her in to boot. Marm is dreadful lonesome."

"Why don't she adopt a little girl?" asked Hollis.

"I declare! That *is* an idea! Hollis, you've hit the nail on the head this time. But I'd want her willing and loving, with no ugly ways. And good blood, too. I'd want to know what her father had been before her."

"Are your boys like *you*, father?" asked Hollis.

"God forbid!" answered the old man huskily. "Hollis, I want you to be a better man than your father. I pray every night that my boys may be Christians; but my time is past, I'm afraid. Hollis, do you pray and read your Bible, regular?"

Hollis gave an embarrassed cough. "No, sir," he returned.

"Then I'd see to it that I did it. That little girl joined the Church last Sunday and I declare it almost took my breath away. I got the Bible down last Sunday night and read a chapter in the New Testament. If you haven't got a Bible, I'll give you money to buy one."

"Oh, I have one," said Hollis uneasily.

"Git up, there!" shouted Captain Rheid to his horses, and spoke not another word all the way home.

After taking a few slow steps Marjorie quickened her pace, remembering that Linnet did not like to milk alone; Marjorie did not like to milk at all; at thirteen there were not many things that she liked to do very much, except to read and think.

"I'm afraid she's indolent," sighed her mother; "there's Linnet now, she's as spry as a cricket"

But Linnet was not conscious of very many things to think about and Marjorie every day discovered some new thought to revel in. At this moment, if it had not been for that unfortunate pitcher, she would have been reviewing her conversation with Miss Prudence. It *was* wonderful about punctuation; how many times a day life was "wonderful" to the growing child!

Along this road the farmhouses were scattered at long distances, there was one in sight with the gable end to the road, but the next one was fully quarter of a mile away; she noted the fact, not that she was afraid or lonely, but it gave her something to think of; she was too thoroughly acquainted with the road to be afraid of anything by night or by day; she had walked to her grandfather's more times than she could remember ever since she was seven years old. She tried to guess how far the next house was, how many feet, yards or rods; she tried to guess how many quarts of blueberries had grown in the field beyond; she even wondered if anybody could count the blades of grass all along the way if they should try! But the remembrance of the broken pitcher persisted in bringing itself uppermost, pushing through the blades of grass and the quarts of blueberries; she might as well begin to plan how she was to earn another pitcher! Or, her birthday was coming—in a month she would be fourteen; her father would certainly give her a silver dollar because he was glad that he had had her fourteen years. A quick, panting breath behind her, and the sound of hurrying feet, caused her to turn her head; she fully expected to meet the gaze of some big dog, but instead a man was close upon her, dusty, travel-stained, his straw hat pushed back from a perspiring face and a hand stretched out to detain her.

On one arm he carried a long, uncovered basket in which were arranged rows and piles of small bottles; a glance at the basket reassured her, every one knew Crazy Dale, the peddler of essences, cough-drops and quack medicines.

"It's lonesome walking alone; I've been running to overtake you; I tried to be in time to catch a ride; but no matter, I will walk with you, if you will kindly permit."

She looked up into his pleasant countenance; he might have been handsome years ago.

"Well," she assented, walking on.

"You don't know where I could get a girl to work for me," he asked in a cracked voice.

"No sir."

"And you don't want a bottle of my celebrated mixture to teach you how to discern between the true and the false! Rub your head with it every morning, and you'll never believe a lie."

"I don't now," replied Marjorie, taking very quick steps.

"How do you know you don't?" he asked keeping step with her. "Tell me how to tell the difference between a lie and the truth!"

"Rub your head with your mixture," she said, laughing.

But he was not disconcerted, he returned in a simple tone.

"Oh, *that's* my receipt, I want yours. Yours may be better than mine."

"I think it is."

"Tell me, then, quick."

"Don't you want to go into that house and sell something?" she asked, pointing to the house ahead of them.

"When I get there; and you must wait for me, outside, or I won't go in."

"Don't you know the way yourself?" she evaded.

"I've travelled it ever since the year 1, I ought to know it," he replied, contemptuously. "But you've got to wait for me."

"Oh, dear," sighed Marjorie, frightened at his insistence; then a quick thought came to her: "Perhaps they will keep you all night."

"They won't, they always refuse. They don't believe I'm an angel unawares. That's in the Bible."

"I'd ask them, if I were you," said Marjorie, in a coaxing, tremulous voice; "they're nice, kind people."

"Well, then, I will," he said, hurrying on.

She lingered, breathing more freely; he would certainly overtake her again before she could reach the next house and if she did not agree with everything he proposed he might become angry with her. Oh, dear! how queerly this day was ending! She did not really want anything to happen; the quiet days were the happiest, after all. He strode on before her, turning once in a while, to learn if she were following.

"That's right; walk slow," he shouted in a conciliatory voice.

By the wayside, near the fence opposite the gate he was to enter, there grew a dense clump of blackberry vines; as the gate swung behind him, she ran towards the fence, and, while he stood with his back towards her in the path talking excitedly to a little boy who had come to meet him, she squeezed herself in between the vines and the fence, bending her head and gathering the skirt of her dress in both hands.

He became angry as he talked, vociferating and gesticulating; every instant she the more congratulated herself upon her escape; some of the girls were afraid of him, but she had always been too sorry for him to be much afraid; still, she would prefer to hide and keep hidden half the night rather than be compelled to walk a long, lonely mile with him. Her father or mother had always been within the sound of her voice when he had talked with her; she had never before had to be a protection to herself. Peering through the leaves, she watched him, as he turned again towards the gate, with her heart beating altogether too rapidly for comfort: he opened the gate, strode out to the road and stood looking back.

He stood a long, long time, uttering no exclamation, then hurried on, leaving a half-frightened and very thankful little girl trembling among the leaves of the blackberry vines. But, would he keep looking back? And how could she ever pass the next house? Might he not stop there and be somewhere on the watch for her? If some one would pass by, or some carriage would only drive along! The houses were closer together a mile further on, but how dared she pass that mile? He would not hurt her, he would only look at her out of his wild eyes and talk to her. Answering Captain Rheid's questions was better than this! Staying at her grandfather's and confessing about the pitcher was better than this!

Suddenly—or had she heard it before, a whistle burst out upon the air, a sweet and clear succession of notes, the air of a familiar song: "Be it ever so humble, there's no place like home."

Some one was at hand, she sprang through the vines, the briers catching the old blue muslin, extricating herself in time to run almost against the navy-blue figure that she had not yet become familiar with.

The whistle stopped short—"Well, Mousie! Here you are!"

"O, Hollis," with a sobbing breath, "I'm so glad!"

"So am I. I jumped off and ran after you. Why, did I frighten you? Your eyes are as big as moons."

"No," she laughed, "I wasn't frightened."

"You look terribly like it."

"Perhaps some things are *like*—" she began, almost dancing along by his side, so relieved that she could have poured out a song for joy.

"What do you do nowadays?" he asked presently. "You are more of a *live* mouse than you used to be! I can't call you Mousie any more, only for the sake of old times."

"I like it," said Marjorie.

"But what do you do nowadays?"

"I read all the time—when I can, and I work, different kinds of work. Tell me about the little city girls."

"I only know my cousins and one or two others, their friends."

"What do they look like?"

"Like girls! Don't you know how girls look?"

"Not city girls."

"They are pretty, most of them, and they dress older than you and have a *manner;* they always know how to reply and they are not awkward and too shy; they know how to address people, and introduce people, and sometimes to entertain them, they seem to know what to talk about, and they are bright and wide-awake. They play and sing and study the languages and mathematics. The girls I know are all little ladies."

Marjorie was silent; her cheeks were burning and her eyes downcast. She never could be like that; she never could be a "little lady," if a little lady meant all those unattainable things.

"Do they talk differently from us—from country girls?" she asked after a long pause.

"Yes, I think they do. Mira Crane—I'll tell you how the country girls talk—says 'we am,' and 'fust rate,' and she speaks rudely and abruptly and doesn't look directly at a person when she speaks, she says 'good morning' and 'yes' and 'no' without 'sir' or 'ma'am' or the person's name, and answers 'I'm very well' without adding 'thank you.'"

"Yes," said Marjorie, taking mental note of each expression.

"And Josie Grey—you see I've been studying the difference in the girls since I came home—"

Had he been studying *her*?

"Is there so much difference?" she asked a little proudly.

"Yes. The difference struck me. It is not city or country that makes the difference, it is the *homes* and the *schools* and every educating influence. Josie Grey has all sorts of exclamations like some old grandmother, and she says 'I tell you,' and 'I declare,' and she hunches all up when she sits or puts her feet out into the middle of the room."

"Yes," said Marjorie, again, intently.

"And Nettie Trevor colors and stammers and talks as if she were afraid of you. My little ladies see so many people that they become accustomed to forgetting themselves and thinking of others. They see people to admire and imitate, too."

"So do I," said Marjorie, spiritedly. "I see Miss Prudence and I see Mrs. Proudfit, our new minister's wife, and I see—several other people."

"I suppose I notice these things more than some boys would. When I left home gentleness was a new language to me; I had never heard it spoken excepting away from home. I was surprised at first that a master could command with gentleness and that those under authority could obey with gentleness."

Marjorie listened with awe; this was not like Hollis; her old Hollis was gone, a new, wise Hollis had come instead. She sighed a little for the old Hollis who was not quite so wise.

"I soon found how much I lacked. I set myself to reading and studying. From the first of October all through the winter I attend evening school and I have subscribed to the Mercantile Library and have my choice among thousands of books. Uncle Jack says I shall be a literary business man."

A "literary business man" sounded very grand to Marjorie. Would she stay home and be ignorant and never be or do anything? At that instant a resolve was born in her heart; the resolve to become a scholar and a lady. But she did not speak, if possible she became more quiet. Hollis should not be ashamed of being her friend.

"Mousie! Why don't you talk to me?" he asked, at last.

"Which of your cousins do you like best?"

"Helen," he said unhesitatingly.

"How old is she?" she asked with a sinking at her heart.

"Seventeen. *She's* a lady, so gentle and bright, she never rustles or makes a noise, she never says anything to hurt any one's feelings: and how she plays and sings. She never once laughed at me, she helps me in everything; she wanted me to go to evening school and she told me about the Mercantile Library. She's a Christian, too. She teaches in a mission school and goes around among poor people with Aunt Helen. She paints and draws and can walk six miles a day. I go everywhere with her, to lectures and concerts and to church and Sunday school."

How Marjorie's eyes brightened! She had found her ideal; she would give herself no rest until she had become like Helen Rheid. But Helen Rheid had everything to push her on, every one to help her. For the first time in her life Marjorie was disheartened. But, with a reassuring conviction, flashed the thought—there were years before *she* would be seventeen.

"Wouldn't you like to see her, Mousie?"

"Indeed, I would," said Marjorie, enthusiastically.

"I brought her photograph to mother—how she looked at me when 'marm' slipped out one day. The boys always used to say 'Marm,'" he said laughing.

Marjorie remembered that she had been taught to say "grandmarm," but as she grew older she had softened it to "grandma."

"I'll bring you her photograph when I come to-morrow to say good-bye. Now, tell me what you've been looking sad about."

Is it possible that she was forgetting?

"Oh, perhaps you can help me!"

"Help you! Of course I will."

"How did you know I was troubled?" she asked seriously, looking up into his eyes.

"Have I eyes?" he answered as seriously. "Father happened to think that mother had an errand for him to do on this road, so I jumped off and ran after you."

"No, you ran after your mother's errand," she answered, jealously.

"Well, then, I found you, my precise little maiden, and now you must tell me what you were crying about."

"Not spilt milk, but only a broken milk pitcher! *Do* you think you can find me a yellow pitcher, with yellow figures—a man, or a lion, or something, a hundred or two hundred years old?"

"In New York? I'm rather doubtful. Oh, I know—mother has some old ware, it belonged to her grandmother, perhaps I can beg a piece of it for you. Will it do if it isn't a pitcher?"

Miss Prudence

"I'd rather have a pitcher, a yellow pitcher. The one I broke belongs to a friend of Miss Prudence."

"Prudence! Is she a Puritan maiden?" he asked.

Marjorie felt very ignorant, she colored and was silent. She supposed Helen Rheid would know what a Puritan maiden was.

"I won't tease you," he said penitently. "I'll find you something to make the loss good, perhaps I'll find something she'll like a great deal better."

"Mr. Onderdonk has a plate that came from Holland, it's over two hundred years old he told Miss Prudence; oh, if you *could* get that!" cried Marjorie, clasping her hands in her eagerness.

"Mr. Onderdonk? Oh, the shoemaker, near the schoolhouse. Well, Mousie, you shall have some old thing if I have to go back a century to get it. Helen will be interested to know all about it; I've told her about you."

"There's nothing to tell about me," returned Marjorie.

"Then I must have imagined it; you used to be such a cunning little thing."

"*Used to be!*" repeated sensitive Marjorie, to herself. She was sure Hollis was disappointed in her. And she thought he was so tall and wise and handsome and grand! She could never be disappointed in him.

How surprised she would have been had she known that Helen's eyes had filled with tears when Hollis told her how his little friend had risen all alone in that full church! Helen thought she could never be like Marjorie.

"I wish you had a picture of how you used to look for me to show Helen."

Not how she looked to-day! Her lips quivered and she kept her eyes on her dusty shoes.

"I suppose you want the pitcher immediately."

Two years ago Hollis would have said "right away."

After that Marjorie never forgot to say "immediately."

"Yes, I would," she said, slowly. "I've hidden the pieces away and nobody knows it is broken."

"That isn't like you," Hollis returned, disappointedly.

"Oh, I didn't do it to deceive; I couldn't. I didn't want her to be sorry about it until I could see what I could do to replace it"

"That sounds better."

Marjorie felt very much as if he had been finding fault with her.

"Will you have to pay for it?"

"Not if mother gives it to me, but perhaps I shall exact some return from you."

She met his grave eyes fully before she spoke. "Well, I'll give you all I can earn. I have only seventy-three cents; father gives me one tenth of the eggs for hunting them and feeding the chickens, and I take them to the store. That's the only way I can earn money," she said in her sweet half-abashed voice.

A picture of Helen taking eggs to "the store" flashed upon Hollis' vision; he smiled and looked down upon his little companion with benignant eyes.

"I could give you all I have and send you the rest. Couldn't I?" she asked.

"Yes, that would do. But you must let me set my own price," he returned in a business like tone.

"Oh I will. I'd do anything to get Miss Prudence a pitcher," she said eagerly.

The faded muslin brushed against him; and how odd and old-fashioned her hat was! He would not have cared to go on a picnic with Marjorie in this attire; suppose he had taken her into the crowd of girls among which his cousin Helen was so noticeable last week, how they would have looked at her! They would think he had found her at some mission school. Was her father so poor, or was this old dress and broad hat her mother's taste? Anyway, there was a guileless and bright face underneath the flapping hat and her voice was as sweet as Helen's even it there was such an old-fashioned tone about it. One word seemed to sum up her dress and herself—old-fashioned. She talked like some little old grandmother. She was more than quaint—she was antiquated. That is, she was antiquated beside Helen. But she did not seem out of place here in the country; he was thinking of her on a city pavement, in a city parlor, or among a group of fluttering, prettily dressed city girls, with their modulated voices, animated gestures and laughing, bright replies. There was light and fire about them and Marjorie was such a demure little mouse.

"Don't fret about it any more," he said, kindly, with his grown-up air, patting her shoulder with a light, caressing touch. "I will take it into my hands and you need not think of it again."

"Oh, thank you! thank you!" she cried, her eyes brimming over.

It was the old Hollis, after all; he could do anything and everything she wanted.

Forgetting her shyness, after that home-like touch upon her shoulder, she chatted all the way home. And he did not once think that she was a quiet little mouse.

He did not like "quiet" people; perhaps because his own spirit was so quiet that it required some effort for him to be noisy. Hollis admired most characteristics unlike his own; he did not know, but he *felt* that Marjorie was very much like himself. She was more like him than he was like her. They were two people who would be very apt to be drawn together under all circumstances, but without special and peculiar training could never satisfy each other. This was true of them even now, and, if possible with the enlarged vision of experience, became truer as they grew older. If they kept together they might grow together; but, the question is, whether of themselves they would ever have been drawn very close together. They were close enough together now, as Marjorie chatted and Hollis listened; he had many questions to ask about the boys and girls of the village and Marjorie had many stories to relate.

"So George Harris and Nell True are really married!" he said. "So young, too!"

"Yes, mother did not like it. She said they were too young. He always liked her best at school, you know. And when she joined the Church she was so anxious for him to join, too, and she wrote him a note about it and he answered it and they kept on writing and then they were married."

"Did he join the Church?" asked Hollis,

"He hasn't yet."

"It is easier for girls to be good than for boys," rejoined Hollis in an argumentative tone,

"Is it? I don't see how."

"Of course you don't. We are in the world where the temptations are; what temptations do *you* have?"

"I have enough. But I don't want to go out in the world where more temptations are. Don't you know—" She colored and stopped,

"Know what?"

"About Christ praying that his disciples might be kept from the evil that was in the world, not that they might be taken out of the world. They have *got* to be in the world."

"Yes."

"And," she added sagely, "anybody can be good where no temptations are."

"Is that why girls are good?"

"I don't think girls are good."

"The girls I know are."

"You know city girls," she said archly. "We country girls have the world in our own hearts."

There was nothing of "the world" in the sweet face that he looked down into, nothing of the world in the frank, true voice. He had been wronging her; how much there was in her, this wise, old, sweet little Marjorie!

"Have you forgotten your errand?" she asked, after a moment.

"No, it is at Mr. Howard's, the house beyond yours."

"I'm glad you had the errand."

"So am I. I should have gone home and not known anything about you."

"And I should have stayed tangled in the black berry vines ever so long," she laughed.

"You haven't told me why you were there."

"Because I was silly," she said emphatically.

"Do silly people always hide in blackberry vines?" he questioned, laughing.

"Silly people like me," she said.

At that moment they stopped in front of the gate of Marjorie's home; through the lilac-bushes—the old fence was overgrown with lilacs—Hollis discerned some bright thing glimmering on the piazza. The bright thing possessed a quick step and a laugh, for it floated towards them and when it appeared at the gate Hollis found that it was only Linnet.

There was nothing of the mouse about Linnet.

"Why, Marjie, mother said you might stay till dark."

Linnet was seventeen, but she was not too grown up for "mother said" to be often on her lips.

"I didn't want to," said Marjorie. "Good-bye, Hollis. I'm going to hunt eggs."

"I'd go with you, it's rare fun to hunt eggs, only I haven't seen Linnet—yet."

"And you must see Linnet—yet," laughed Linnet, "Hollis, what a big boy you've grown to be!" she exclaimed regarding him critically; the new suit, the black onyx watch-chain, the blonde moustache, the full height, and last of all the friendly brown eyes with the merry light in them.

"What a big girl you've grown to be, Linnet," he retorted surveying her critically and admiringly.

There was fun and fire and changing lights, sauciness and defiance, with a pretty little air of deference, about Linnet. She was not unlike his city girl friends; even her dress was more modern and tasteful than Marjorie's.

"Marjorie is so little and doesn't care," she often pleaded with their mother when there was not money enough for both. And Marjorie looked on and held her peace.

Self-sacrifice was an instinct with Marjorie.

"I am older and must have the first chance," Linnet said.

So Marjorie held back and let Linnet have the chances.

Linnet was to have the "first chance" at going to school in September. Marjorie stayed one moment looking at the two as they talked, proud of Linnet and thinking that Hollis must think she, at least, was something like his cousin Helen, and then she hurried away hoping to return with her basket of eggs before Hollis was gone. Hollis was almost like some one in a story-book to her. I doubt if she ever saw any one as other people saw them; she always saw so much. She needed only an initial; it was easy enough to fill out the word. She hurried across the yard, opened the large barn-yard gate, skipped across the barn-yard, and with a little leap was in the barn floor. Last night she had forgotten to look in the mow; she would find a double quantity hidden away there to-night. She wondered if old Queen Bess were still persisting in sitting on nothing in the mow's far dark corner; tossing away her hindering hat and catching up an old basket, she ran lightly up the ladder to the mow. She never remembered that she ran up the ladder.

An hour later—Linnet knew that it was an hour later—Marjorie found herself moving slowly towards the kitchen door. She wanted to see her mother. Lifting the latch she staggered in.

She was greeted with a scream from Linnet and with a terrified exclamation from her mother.

"Marjorie, what *is* the matter?" cried her mother catching her in her arms.

"Nothing," said Marjorie, wondering.

"Nothing! You are purple as a ghost!" exclaimed Linnet, "and there's a lump on your forehead as big as an egg."

"Is there?" asked Marjorie, in a trembling voice.

"Did you fall? Where did you fall?" asked her mother shaking her gently.
"Can't you speak, child?"

"I—didn't—fall," muttered Marjorie, slowly.

"Yes, you did," said Linnet. "You went after eggs."

"Eggs," repeated Marjorie in a bewildered voice.

"Linnet, help me quick to get her on to the sitting-room lounge! Then get pillows and a comforter, and then run for your father to go for the doctor."

"There's nothing the matter," persisted the child, smiling weakly. "I can walk, mother. Nothing hurts me."

"Doesn't your head ache?" asked Linnet, guiding her steps as her head rested against her mother's breast.

"No."

"Don't you ache *anywhere*?" questioned her mother, as they led her to the lounge.

"No, ma'am. Why should I? I didn't fall."

Linnet brought the pillow and comforter, and then ran out through the back yard calling, "Father! Father!"

Down the road Hollis heard the agonized cry, and turning hastened back to the house.

"Oh, go for the doctor quick!" cried Linnet, catching him by the arm; "something dreadful has happened to Marjorie, and she doesn't know what it is."

"Is there a horse in the stable?"

"Oh, no, I forgot. And mother forgot Father has gone to town."

"I'll get a horse then—somewhere on the road—don't be so frightened.
Dr. Peck will be here in twenty minutes after I find him."

Linnet flew back to satisfy her mother that the doctor had been sent for, and found Marjorie reiterating to her mother's repeated inquiries:

"I don't ache anywhere; I'm not hurt at all."

"Where were you, child."

"I wasn't—anywhere," she was about to say, then smiled, for she knew she must have been somewhere.

"What happened after you said good-bye to Hollis?" questioned Linnet, falling on her knees beside her little sister, and almost taking her into her arms.

"Nothing."

"Oh, dear, you're crazy!" sobbed Linnet.

Marjorie smiled faintly and lifted her hand to stroke Linnet's cheeks.

"I won't hurt *you*," she comforted tenderly.

"I know what I'll do!" exclaimed Mrs. West suddenly and emphatically, "I can put hot water on that bump; I've heard that's good."

Marjorie closed her eyes and lay still; she was tired of talking about something that had not happened at all. She remembered afterward that the doctor came and opened a vein in her arm, and that he kept the blood flowing until she answered "Yes, sir," to his question, "Does your head hurt you *now*?" She remembered all their faces—how Linnet cried and sobbed, how Hollis whispered, "I'll get a pitcher, Mousie, if I have to go to China for it," and how her father knelt by the lounge when he came home and learned that it had happened and was all over, how he knelt and thanked God for giving her back to them all out of her great danger. That night her mother sat by her bedside all night long, and she remembered saying to her:

"If I had been killed, I should have waked up in Heaven without knowing that I had died. It would have been like going to Heaven without dying."

V.

TWO PROMISES.

"He who promiseth runs in debt."

Hollis held a mysterious looking package in his hand when he came in the next day; it was neatly done up in light tissue paper and tied with yellow cord. It looked round and flat, not one bit like a pitcher, unless some pitchers a hundred years ago *were* flat.

Marjorie lay in delicious repose upon the parlor sofa, with the green blinds half closed, the drowsiness and fragrance of clover in the air soothed her, rather, quieted her, for she was not given to nervousness; a feeling of safety enwrapped her, she was *here* and not very much hurt, and she was loved and petted to her heart's content. And that is saying a great deal for Marjorie, for *her* heart's content was a very large content. Linnet came in softly once in a while to look at her with anxious eyes and to ask, "How do you feel now?" Her mother wandered in and out as if she could rest in nothing but in looking at her, and her father had given her one of his glad kisses before he went away to the mowing field. Several village people having heard of the accident through Hollis and the doctor had stopped at the door to inquire with a sympathetic modulation of voice if she were any better. But the safe feeling was the most blessed of all. Towards noon she lay still with her white kitten cuddled up in her arms, wondering who would come next; Hollis had not come, nor Miss Prudence, nor the new minister, nor grandma, nor Josie Grey; she was wishing they would all come to-day when she heard a quick step on the piazza and a voice calling out to somebody.

"I won't stay five minutes, father."

The next instant the handsome, cheery face was looking in at the parlor door and the boisterous "vacation" voice was greeting her with,

"Well, Miss Mousie! How about the tumble down now?"

But her eyes saw nothing excepting the mysterious, flat, round parcel in his hand.

"Oh, Hollis, I'm so glad!" she exclaimed, raising herself upon one elbow.

The stiff blue muslin was rather crumpled by this time, and in place of the linen collar and old-fashioned pin her mother had tied a narrow scarf of white lace about her throat; her hair was brushed back and braided in two heavy braids and her forehead was bandaged in white.

"Well, Marjorie, you *are* a picture, I must say," he cried, bounding in.
"Why don't you jump up and take another climb?"

"I want to. I want to see the swallow's nest again; I meant to have fed the swallows last night"

"Where are they?"

"Oh, up in the eaves. Linnet and I have climbed up and fed them."

As he dropped on his knees on the carpet beside the sofa she fell back on her pillow.

"Father is waiting for me to go to town with him and I can't stay. You will soon be climbing up to see the swallows again and hunting eggs and everything as usual."

"Oh, yes, indeed," said Marjorie, hopefully.

Watching her face he laid the parcel in her hand. "Don't open it till I'm gone. I had something of a time to get it. The old fellow was as obstinate as a mule when he saw that my heart was set on it. Mother hadn't a thing old enough—I ransacked everywhere—if I'd had time to go to grandmother's I might have done better. She's ninety-three, you know, and has some of her grandmother's things. This thing isn't a beauty to look at, but it's old, and that's the chief consideration. Extreme old age will compensate for its ugliness; which is an extenuation that I haven't for mine. I'm going to-morrow."

"Oh, I want to see it," she exclaimed, not regarding his last remark.

"That's all you care," he said, disappointedly. "I thought you would be sorry that I'm going."

"You know I am," she returned penitently, picking at the yellow cord.

"Perhaps when I am two hundred years old you'll be as anxious to look at me as you are to look at that!"

"Oh, Hollis, I do thank you so."

"But you must promise me two things or you can't have it!"

"I'll promise twenty."

"Two will do until next time. First, will you go and see my mother as soon as you get well, and go often?"

"That's too easy; I want to do something *hard* for you," she answered earnestly.

"Perhaps you will some day, who knows? There are hard enough things to do for people, I'm finding out. But, have you promised?"

"Yes, I have promised."

"And I know you keep your promises. I'm sure you won't forget. Poor mother isn't happy; she's troubled."

"About you?"

"No, about herself, because she isn't a Christian."

"That's enough to trouble anybody," said Marjorie, wisely.

"Now, one more promise in payment. Will you write to me every two weeks?"

"Oh, I couldn't," pleaded Marjorie.

"Now you've found something too hard to do for me," he said, reproachfully.

"Oh, I'll do it, of course; but I'm afraid."

"You'll soon get over that. You see mother doesn't write often, and father never does, and I'm often anxious about them, and if you write and tell me about them twice a month I shall be happier. You see you are doing something for me."

"Yes, thank you. I'll do the best I can. But I can't write like your cousin Helen," she added, jealously.

"No matter. You'll do; and you will be growing older and constantly improving and I shall begin to travel for the house by and by and my letters will be as entertaining as a book of travels."

"Will you write to me? I didn't think of that."

"Goosie!" he laughed, giving her Linnet's pet name. "Certainly I will write as often as you do, and you mustn't stop writing until your last letter has not been answered for a month."

"I'll remember," said Marjorie, seriously. "But I wish I could do something else. Did you have to pay money for it?"

Marjorie was accustomed to "bartering" and that is the reason that she used the expression "pay money."

"Well, yes, something," he replied, pressing his lips together.

He was angry with the shoemaker about that bargain yet.

"How much? I want to pay you."

"Ladies never ask a gentleman such a question when they make them a present," he said, laughing as he arose. "Imagine Helen asking me how much I paid for the set of books I gave her on her birthday."

The tears sprang to Marjorie's eyes. Had she done a dreadful thing that Helen would not think of doing?

Long afterward she learned that he gave for the plate the ten dollars that his father gave him for a "vacation present."

"Good-bye, Goosie, keep both promises and don't run up a ladder again until you learn how to run down."

But she could not speak yet for the choking in her throat.

"You have paid me twice over with those promises," he said. "I am glad you broke the old yellow pitcher."

So was she even while her heart was aching. Her fingers held the parcel tightly; what a hearts-ease it was! It had brought her peace of mind that was worth more hard promises than she could think of making.

"He said his father's great-grandfather had eaten out of that plate over in Holland and he had but one more left to bequeath to his little grandson."

"I'm glad the great-grandfather didn't break it," said Marjorie.

Hollis would not disturb her serenity by remarking that the shoemaker *might* have added a century to the age of his possession; it looked two hundred years old, anyway.

"Good-bye, again, if you don't get killed next time you fall you may live to see me again. I'll wear a linen coat and smell of cheese and smoke a pipe too long for me to light myself by that time—when I come home from Germany."

"Oh, don't," she exclaimed, in a startled voice.

"Which? The coat or the cheese or the pipe."

"I don't care about the cheese or the coat—"

"You needn't be afraid about the pipe; I promised mother to-day that I would never smoke or drink or play cards."

"That's good," said Marjorie, contentedly.

"And so she feels safe about me; safer than I feel about myself, I reckon. But it *is* good-bye this time. I'll tell Helen what a little mouse and goose you are!"

"Hollis! *Hollis!*" shouted a gruff voice, impatiently.

"Aye, aye, sir," Hollis returned. "But I must say good-bye to your mother and Linnet."

Instead of giving him a last look she was giving her first look to her treasure. The first look was doubtful. It was not half as pretty as the pitcher. It was not very large and there were innumerable tiny cracks interlacing each other, there were little raised figures on the broad rim and a figure in the centre, the colors were buff and blue. But it was a treasure, twofold more a treasure than the yellow pitcher, for it was twice as old and had come from Holland. The yellow pitcher had only come from England. Miss Prudence would be satisfied that she had not hidden the pitcher to escape detection, and perhaps her friend might like this ancient plate a great deal better and be glad of what had befallen the pitcher. But suppose Miss Prudence did believe all this time that she had hidden the broken pieces and meant, never to tell! At that, she could not forbear squeezing her face into the pillow and dropping a few very sorrowful tears. Still she was glad, even with a little contradictory faint-heartedness, for Hollis would write to her and she would never lose him again. And she could *do* something *for* him, something hard.

Her mother, stepping in again, before the tears were dried upon her cheek, listened to the somewhat incoherent story of the naughty thing she had done and the splendid thing Hollis had done, and of how she had paid him with two promises.

Mrs. West examined the plate critically. "It's old, there's no sham about it. I've seen a few old things and I know. I shouldn't wonder if he gave five dollars for it"

"Five dollars!" repeated Marjorie in affright "Oh, I hope not."

"Well, perhaps not, but it is worth it and more, too, to Miss Prudence's friend."

"And I'll keep my promises," said Marjorie's steadfast voice.

"H'm," ejaculated her mother. "I rather think Hollis has the best of it."

"That depends upon me," said wise little Marjorie.

VI.
MARJORIE ASLEEP AND AWAKE.

"She was made for happy thoughts."—*Mary Howlet.*

I wonder if there is anything, any little thing I should have said, that tries a woman more than the changes in her own face, a woman that has just attained two score and—an unmarried woman. Prudence Pomeroy was discovering these changes in her own face and, it may be undignified, it may be unchristian even, but she was tried. It was upon the morning of her fortieth birthday, that, with considerable shrinking, she set out upon a voyage of discovery upon the unknown sea of her own countenance. It was unknown, for she had not cared to look upon herself for some years, but she bolted her chamber door and set herself about it with grim determination this birthday morning. It was a weakness, it may be, but we all have hours of weakness within our bolted chamber doors.

She had a hard early morning all by herself; but the battle with herself did not commence until she shoved that bolt, pushed back the white curtains, and stationed herself in the full glare of the sun light with her hand-glass held before her resolute face. It was something to go through; it was something to go through to read the record of a score of birthdays past: but she had done that before the breakfast bell rang, locked the old leathern bound volume in her trunk and arranged herself for breakfast, and then had run down with her usual tripping step and kept them all amused with her stories during breakfast time. But that was before the door was bolted. She gazed long at the reflection of the face that Time had been at work upon for forty years; there were the tiniest creases in her forehead, they were something like the cracks in the plate two hundred years old that Marjorie had sent to her last night, there were unmistakable lines under her eyes, the pale tint of her cheek did not erase them nor the soft plumpness render them invisible, they stared at her with the story of relentless years; at the corners of her lips the artistic fingers of Time had chiselled lines, delicate, it is true, but clearly defined—a line that did not dent the cheeks of early maidenhood, a line that had found no place near her own lips ten years ago; and above her eyes—she had not discerned that, at first—there was a lack of fullness, you could not name it hollowness; that was new, at least new to her, others with keener eyes may have noticed it months ago, and there was a yellowness—she might as well give it boldly its right name—at the temple, decrease of fairness, she might call it, but that it was a positive shade of that yellowness she had noticed in others no older than herself; and, then, to return to her cheeks, or rather her chin, there was a laxity about the muscles at the sides of her mouth that gave her chin an elderly outline! No, it was not only the absence of youth, it was the presence of age—her full forty years. And her hair! It was certainly not as abundant as it used to be, it had wearied her, once, to brush out its thick glossy length; it was becoming unmistakably thinner; she was certainly slightly bald about the temples, and white hairs were straggling in one after another, not attempting to conceal themselves. A year ago she had selected them from the mass of black and cut them short, but now they were appearing too fast for the scissors. It was a sad face, almost a gloomy one, that she was gazing into: for the knowledge that her forty years had done their work in her face as surely, and perhaps not as sweetly as in her life had come to her with a shock. She was certainly growing older and the signs of it were in her face, nothing could hide it, even her increasing seriousness made it more apparent; not only growing older, but growing old, the girls would say. Twenty years ago, when she first began to write that birthday record, she had laughed at forty and called it "old" herself. As she laid the hand-glass aside with a half-checked sigh, her eyes fell upon her hand and wrist; it was certainly losing its shapeliness; the fingers were as tapering as ever and the palm as pink, but—there was a something that reminded her of that plate of old china. She might be like a bit of old china, but she was not ready to be laid upon the shelf, not even to be paid a price for and be admired! She was in the full rush of her working days. Awhile ago her friends had all addressed her as "Prudence," but now, she was not aware when it began or how, she was "Miss Prudence" to every one who was not within the nearest circle of intimacy. Not "Prudie" or "Prue" any more. She had not been "Prudie" since her father and mother died, and not "Prue" since she had lost that friend twenty years ago.

In ten short years she would be fifty years old, and fifty was half a century: old enough to be somebody's grandmother. Was she not the bosom friend of somebody's grandmother to-day? Laura Harrowgate, her friend and schoolmate, not one year her senior, was the grandmother of three-months-old Laura. Was it possible that she herself did not belong to "the present generation," but to a generation passed away? She had no daughter to give place to, as Laura had, no husband to laugh at her wrinkles and gray hairs, as Laura had, and to say, "We're growing old together." If it were only "together" there would be no sadness in it. But would she want it to be such a "together" as certain of her friends shared?

Laura Harrowgate was a grandmother, but still she would gush over that plate from Holland two centuries old, buy a bracket for it and exhibit it to her friends. A hand-glass did not make *her* dolorous. A few years since she would have rebelled against what the hand-glass revealed; but, to-day, she could not rebel against God's will; assuredly it *was* his will for histories to be written in faces. Would she live a woman's life and adorn herself with a baby's face? Had not her face been moulded by her life? Had she stopped thinking and working ten years ago she might, to-day, have looked at the face she looked at ten years ago. No, she demurred, not a baby's face, but—then she laughed aloud at herself—was not her fate the common fate of all? Who, among her friends, at forty years of age, was ever taken, or mistaken, for twenty-five or thirty? And if *she* were, what then? Would her work be worth more to the world? Would the angels encamp about her more faithfully or more lovingly? And, then, was there not a face "marred"? Did he live his life upon the earth with no sign of it in his face? Was it not a part of his human nature to grow older? Could she be human and not grow old? If she lived she must grow old; to grow old or to die, that was the question, and then she laughed again, this time more merrily. Had she made the changes herself by fretting and worrying; had she taken life too hard? Yes; she had taken life hard. Another glance into the glass revealed another fact: her neck was not as full and round and white as it once was: there was a suggestion of old china about that, too. She would discard linen collars and wear softening white ruffles; it would not be deceitful to hide Time's naughty little tracery. She smiled this time; she *was* coming to a hard place in her life. She had believed—oh, how much in vain!—that she had come to all the hard places and waded through them, but here there was looming up another, fully as hard, perhaps harder, because it was not so tangible and, therefore, harder to face and fight. The acknowledging that she had come to this hard place was something. She remembered the remark of an old lady, who was friendless and poor: "The hardest time of my life was between forty and forty-five; I had to accept several bitter facts that after became easier to bear." Prudence Pomeroy looked at herself, then looked up to God and accepted, submissively, even cheerfully, his fact that she had begun to grow old, and then, she dressed herself for a walk and with her sun-umbrella and a volume of poems started out for her tramp along the road and through the fields to find her little friend Marjorie. The china plate and pathetic note last night had moved her strangely. Marjorie was in the beginning of things. What was her life worth if not to help such as Marjorie live a worthier life than her own two score years had been?

A face flushed with the long walk looked in at the window upon Marjorie asleep. The child was sitting near the open window in a wooden rocker with padded arms and back and covered with calico with a green ground sprinkled over with butterflies and yellow daisies; her head was thrown back against the knitted tidy of white cotton, and her hands were resting in her lap; the blue muslin was rather more crumpled than when she had seen it last, and instead of the linen collar the lace was knotted about her throat. The bandage had been removed from her forehead, the swelling had abated but the discolored spot was plainly visible; her lips were slightly parted, her cheeks were rosy; if this were the "beginning of things" it was a very sweet and peaceful beginning.

Entering the parlor with a soft tread Miss Prudence divested herself of hat, gloves, duster and umbrella, and, taking a large palm leaf fan from the table, seated herself near the sleeper, gently waving the fan to and fro as a fly lighted on Marjorie's hands or face. On the window seat were placed a goblet half filled with lemonade, a small Bible, a book that had the outward appearance of being a Sunday-school library book, and a copy in blue and gold of the poems of Mrs. Hemans. Miss Prudence remembered her own time of loving Mrs. Hemans and had given this copy to Marjorie; later, she had laid her aside for Longfellow, as Marjorie would do by and by, and, in his turn, she had given up Longfellow for Tennyson and Mrs. Browning, as, perhaps, Marjorie would never do. She had brought Jean Ingelow with her this morning to try "Brothers and a Sermon" and the "Songs of Seven" with Marjorie. Marjorie was a natural elocutionist; Miss Prudence was afraid of spoiling her by unwise criticism. The child must thoroughly appreciate a poem, forget herself, and then her rendering would be more than Miss Prudence with all her training could perfectly imitate.

"Don't teach her too much; she'll want to be an actress," remonstrated Marjorie's father after listening to Marjorie's reading one day.

Miss Prudence laughed and Marjorie looked perplexed.

"Marjorie is to comfort with her reading as some do by singing," she replied. "Wait till you are old and she reads the Bible to you!"

"She reads to me now," he said. "She read 'The Children of the Lord's Supper' to me last night."

Miss Prudence moved the fan backward and forward and studied the sleeping, innocent face. I had almost written "sweet" again; I can scarcely think of her face, as it was then, without writing sweet. It would be long, Miss Prudence mused, before lines and creases intruded here and there in that smooth forehead, and in the tinted cheeks that dimpled at the least provocation; but life would bring them in time, and they would add beauty if there were no bitterness nor hardness in them. If the Holy Spirit dwelt in the temple of the body were not the lines upon the face his handwriting? She knew more than one old face that was growing more attractive with each year of life.

The door was pushed open and Mrs. West's broad shoulders and motherly face appeared. Miss Prudence smiled and laid her finger on her lips and, smiling, too, the mother moved away. Linnet, in her kitchen apron, and with the marks of the morning's baking on her fingers, next looked in, nodded and ran away. After awhile, the sleeping eyelids quivered and lifted themselves; a quick flush, a joyous exclamation and Marjorie sprang into her friend's arms.

"I *felt* as if I were not alone! How long have you been here? Oh, why *didn't* you speak to me or touch me?"

"I wanted to have the pleasure all on my side. I never saw you asleep before."

"I hope I didn't keep my mouth open and snore."

"Oh, no, your lips were gently apart and you breathed regularly as they would say in books!"

Marjorie laughed, released Miss Prudence from the tight clasp and went back to her chair.

"You received my note and the plate," she said anxiously.

"Both in perfect preservation. There was not one extra crack in the plate, it was several hours older than when it left your hands, but that only increases its value."

"And did you think I was dreadful not to confess before?" asked Marjorie, tremulously.

"I thought you were dreadful to run away from me instead of *to* me."

"I was so sorry; I wanted to get something else before you knew about it. Did you miss it?"

"I missed something in the room, I could not decide what it was."

"Will the plate do, do you think? Is it handsome enough?"

"It is old enough, that is all the question. Do you know all about Holland when that plate first came into existence?"

"No; I only know there *was* a Holland."

"That plate will be a good point to begin with. You and I will study up Holland some day. I wonder what you know about it now."

"Is that why your friend wants the plate, because she knows about Holland two hundred years ago?"

"No; I'm afraid not. I don't believe she knows more than you do about it. But she will delight in the plate. Which reminds me, your uncle has promised to put the unfortunate pitcher together for me. And in its mended condition it will appear more ancient than ever. I cannot say that George Washington broke it with his little hatchet; but I can have a legend about you connected with it, and tell it to your grandchildren when I show it to them fifty years hence. Unto them I will discover—not a swan's nest among the reeds, as Mrs. Browning has it, but an old yellow pitcher that their lovely grandmother was in trouble about fifty years ago."

"It will be a hundred and fifty years old then," returned Marjorie, seriously, "and I think," she added rebukingly, "that *you* were building castles then."

"I had you and the pitcher for the foundation," said Miss Prudence, in a tone of mock humility.

"Don't you think—" Marjorie's face had a world of suggestion in it—"that 'The Swan's Nest' is bad influence for girls? Little Ellie sits alone and builds castles about her lover, even his horse is 'shod in silver, housed in azure' and a thousand serfs do call him master, and he says 'O, Love, I love but thee.'"

"But all she looks forward to is showing him the swan's nest among the reeds! And when she goes home, around a mile, as she did daily, lo, the wild swan had deserted and a rat had gnawed the reeds. That was the end of her fine castle!"

"'If she found the lover, ever,
Sooth, I know not, but I know
She could never show him, never,
That swan's nest among the reeds,'"

quoted Marjorie. "So it did all come to nothing."

"As air-castles almost always do. But we'll hope she found something better."

"Do people?" questioned Marjorie.

"Hasn't God things laid up for us better than we can ask or think or build castles about?"

"I *hope* so," said Marjorie; "but Hollis Rheid's mother told mother yesterday that her life was one long disappointment."

"What did your mother say?"

"She said 'Oh, Mrs. Rheid, it won't be if you get to Heaven, at last.'"

"I think not."

"But she doesn't expect to go to Heaven, she says. Mother says she's almost in 'despair' and she pities her so!"

"Poor woman! I don't see how she can live through despair. The old proverb 'If it were not for hope, the heart would break,' is most certainly true."

"Why didn't you come before?" asked Marjorie, caressing the hand that still played with the fan.

"Perhaps you never lived on a farm and cannot understand. I could not come in the ox-cart because the oxen were in the field, and every day since I heard of your accident your uncle has had to drive your aunt to Portland on some business. And I did not feel strong enough to walk until this morning."

"How good you are to walk!"

"As good as you are to walk to see me."

"Oh, but I am young and strong, and I wanted to see you so, and ask you questions so."

"I believe the latter," said Miss Prudence smiling.

"Well, I'm happy now," Marjorie sighed, with the burden of her trouble still upon her. "Suppose I had been killed when I fell and had not told you about the pitcher nor made amends for it."

"I don't believe any of us could be taken away without one moment to make ready and not leave many things undone—many tangled threads and rough edges to be taken care of. We are very happy if we have no sin to confess, no wrong to make right."

"I think Hollis would have taken care of the plate for me," said Marjorie, simply; "but I wanted to tell you myself. Mother wants to go home as suddenly as that would have been for me, she says. I shouldn't wonder if she prays about it—she prays about everything. Do people have *that* kind of a prayer answered?"

"I have known more than one instance—and I read about a gentleman who had desired to be taken suddenly and he was killed by lightning while sitting on his own piazza."

"Oh!" said Marjorie.

"That was all he could have wished. And the mother of my pastor at home, who was over ninety, was found dead on her knees at her bedside, and she had always wished to be summoned suddenly."

"When she was speaking to him, too," murmured Marjorie. "I like old people, don't you? Hollis' grandmother is at his house and Mrs. Rheid wants me to go to see her; she is ninety-three and blind, and she loves to tell stories about herself, and I am to stay all day and listen to her and take up her stitches when she drops them in her knitting work and read the Bible to her. She won't listen to anything but the Bible; she says she's too old to hear other books read."

"What a treat you will have!"

"Isn't it lovely? I never had *that* day in my air-castles, either. Nor you coming to stay all day with me, nor writing to Hollis. I had a letter from him last night, the funniest letter! I laughed all the time I was reading it. He begins: 'Poor little Mousie,' and ends, 'ours, till next time.' I'll show it to you. He doesn't say much about Helen. I shall tell him if I write about his mother he must write about Helen. I'm sorry to tell him what his mother said yesterday about herself but I promised and I must be faithful."

"I hope you will have happy news to write soon."

"I don't know; she says the minister doesn't do her any good, nor reading the Bible nor praying. Now what can help her?"

"God," was the solemn reply. "She has had to learn that the minister and Bible reading and prayer are not God. When she is sure that God will do all the helping and saving, she will be helped and saved. Perhaps she has gone to the minister and the Bible instead of to God, and she may have thought her prayers could save her instead of God."

"She said she was in despair because they did not help her and she did not know where to turn next," said Marjorie, who had listened with sympathetic eyes and aching heart.

"Don't worry about her, dear, God is teaching her to turn to himself."

"I told her about the plate, but she did not seem to care much. What different things people *do* care about!" exclaimed Marjorie, her eyes alight with the newness of her thought.

"Mrs. Harrowgate will never be perfectly satisfied until she has a memorial of Pompeii. I've promised when I explore underground I'll find her a treasure. Your Holland plate is something for her small collection; she has but eighty-seven pieces of china, while a friend of hers has gathered together two hundred."

"What do *you* care for most, Miss Prudence?

"In the way of collections? I haven't shown you my penny buried in the lava of Mt. Vesuvius; I told my friend that savored of Pompeii, the only difference is one is above ground and the other underneath, but I couldn't persuade her to believe it."

"I don't mean collecting coins or things; I mean what do you care for *most*?"

"If you haven't discovered, I cannot care very much for what I care for most."

Marjorie laughed at this way of putting it, then she answered gravely: "I do know. I think you care most—" she paused, choosing her phrase carefully—"to help people make something out of themselves."

"Thank you. That's fine. I never put it so excellently to myself."

"I haven't found out what I care most for."

"I think I know. You care most to make something out of yourself."

"Do I? Isn't that selfish? But I don't know how to help any one else, not even Linnet."

"Making the best of ourselves is the foundation for making something out of others."

"But I didn't say *that*" persisted Marjorie. "You help people to do it for themselves."

"I wonder if that is my work in the world," rejoined Miss Prudence, musingly. "I could not choose anything to fit me better—I had no thought that I have ever succeeded; I never put it to myself in that way."

"Perhaps I'll begin some day. Helen Rheid helps Hollis. He isn't the same boy; he studies and buys books and notices things to be admired in people, and when he is full of fun he isn't rough. I don't believe I ever helped anybody."

"You have some work to do upon yourself first. And I am sure you have helped educate your mother and father."

Marjorie pulled to pieces the green leaf that had floated in upon her lap and as she kept her eyes on the leaf she pondered.

Her companion was "talking over her head" purposely to-day; she had a plan for Marjorie and as she admitted to herself she was "trying the child to see what she was made of."

She congratulated herself upon success thus far.

"That children do educate their mothers is the only satisfactory reason I have found when I have questioned why God does give children to *some* mothers."

"Then what becomes of the children?" asked Marjorie, alarmed.

"The Giver does not forget them; he can be a mother himself, you know."

Marjorie did not know; she had always had her mother. Had she lost something, therefore, in not thus finding out God? Perhaps, in after life she would find his tenderness by losing—or not having—some one else. It was not too bad, for it would be a great pity if there were not such interruptions, but at this instant Linnet's housewifely face was pushed in at the door, and her voice announced: "Dinner in three minutes and a half! Chicken-pie for the first course and some new and delicious thing for dessert."

"Oh, splendid!" cried Marjorie, hopping up. "And we'll finish everything after dinner, Miss Prudence."

"As the lady said to the famous traveller at a dinner party: 'We have five minutes before dinner, please tell me all about your travels,'" said Miss Prudence, rising and laughing.

"You remember you haven't told me what you sent me for the Bible to show me that unhappy—no, happy time—I broke the picture," reminded Marjorie, leading the way to the dining-room.

VII.

UNDER THE APPLE-TREE.

"Never the little seed stops in its growing."—*Mrs. Osgood.*

Linnet moved hither and thither, after the dinner dishes were done, all through the house, up stairs and down, to see that everything was in perfect order before she might dress and enjoy the afternoon. Linnet was pre-eminently a housekeeper, to her mother's great delight, for her younger daughter was not developing according to her mind in housewifely arts.

"That will come in time," encouraged Marjorie's father when her mother spoke faultfindingly of some delinquency in the kitchen.

"I should like to know *what* time!" was the sharp reply.

It was queer about Marjorie's mother, she was as sharp as she was good-humored.

"Linnet has no decided tastes about anything but housekeeping and fancy-work, and Marjorie has some other things to be growing in," said her father.

"I wish she would grow to some purpose then," was the energetic reply.

"As the farmer said about his seed before it was time for it to sprout," laughed the children's father.

This father and mother could not talk confidentially together five minutes without bringing the "children" in.

Their own future was every day; but the children had not begun to live in theirs yet; their golden future, which was to be all the more golden because of their parents' experiences.

This mother was so very old-fashioned that she believed that there was no career open to a girl beside marriage; the dreadful alternative was solitary old-maidenhood. She was a good mother, in many respects a wise mother; but she would not have slept that night had she believed that either of her daughters would attain to thirty years unmarried. This may have been owing to a defect of education, or it may have been that she was so happily married to a husband six years her junior—whom she could manage. And she was nearly thirty when she was married herself and had really begun to believe that she should never be married at all. She believed marriage to be so honorable in all, that the absence of it, as in Miss Prudence's case, was nearly dishonorable. She was almost a Jewish mother in her reverence for marriage and joyfulness for the blessing of children. This may have been the result of her absorbed study of the Old Testament Scriptures. Marjorie had wondered why her mother in addressing the Lord had cried, "O, Lord God of Israel," and instead of any other name nearer New Testament Christians, she would speak of him as "The Holy One of Israel." Sometimes I have thought that Marjorie's mother began her religious life as a Jew, and that instead of being a Gentile Christian she was in reality a converted Jew, something like what Elizabeth would have been if she had been more like Marjorie's mother and Graham West's wife. This type of womanhood is rare in this nineteenth century; for aught I know, she is not a representative woman, at all; she is the only one I ever knew, and perhaps you never saw any one like her. She has no heresies, she can prove every assertion from the Bible, her principles are as firm as adamant and her heart as tender as a mother's. Still, marriage and motherhood have been her education; if the Connecticut, school-teacher had not realized her worth, she might have become what she dreaded her own daughters becoming—an old maid with uncheerful views of life. In planning their future she looked into her own heart instead of into theirs.

The children were lovely blossomings of the seed in the hearts of both parents; of seeds, that in them had not borne abundant fruitage.

"How did two such cranky old things ever have such happy children!" she exclaimed one day to her husband.

"Perhaps they will become what we stopped short of being," he replied.

Graham West was something of a philosopher; rather too much of a philosopher for his wife's peace of mind. To her sorrow she had learned that he had no "business tact," he could not even scrape a comfortable living off his scrubby little farm.

But I began with Linnet and fell to discoursing about her mother; it was Linnet, as she appeared in her grayish brown dress with a knot of crimson at her throat, running down the stairway, that suggested her mother's thought to me.

"Linnet is almost growing up," she had said to herself as she removed her cap for her customary afternoon nap. This afternoon nap refreshed her countenance and kept her from looking six years older than her husband. Mrs. West was not a worldly woman, but she did not like to look six years older than her husband.

Linnet searched through parlor and hall, then out on the piazza, then looked through the front yard, and, finally, having explored the garden, found Marjorie and her friend in camp-chairs on the soft green turf under the low hanging boughs of an apple-tree behind the house. There were two or three books in Marjorie's lap, and Miss Prudence was turning the leaves of Marjorie's Bible. She was answering one of Marjorie's questions Linnet supposed and wondered if Marjorie would be satisfied with the answer; she was not always satisfied, as the elder sister knew to her grievance. For instance: Marjorie had said to her yesterday, with that serious look in her eyes: "Linnet, father says when Christ was on earth people didn't have wheat ground into fine flour as we do;—now when it is so much nicer, why do you suppose he didn't tell them about grinding it fine?"

"Perhaps he didn't think of it," she replied, giving the first thought that occurred to her.

"That isn't the reason," returned Marjorie, "for he could think of everything he wanted to."

"Then—for the same reason why didn't he tell them about chloroform and printing and telegraphing and a thousand other inventions?" questioned Linnet in her turn.

"That's what I want to know," said Marjorie.

Linnet settled herself on the turf and drew her work from her pocket; she was making a collar of tatting for her mother's birthday and working at it at every spare moment. It was the clover leaf pattern, that she had learned but a few weeks ago; the thread was very fine and she was doing it exquisitely. She had shown it to Hollis because he was in the lace business, and he had said it was a fine specimen of "real lace." To make real lace was one of Linnet's ambitions. The lace around Marjorie's neck was a piece that their mother had made towards her own wedding outfit. Marjorie's mother sighed and feared that Marjorie would never care to make lace for her wedding outfit.

Linnet frowned over her clover leaf and Marjorie watched Miss Prudence as she turned the leaves. Marjorie did not care for the clover leaf, only as she was interested in everything that Linnet's fingers touched, but Linnet did care for the answer to Marjorie's question. She thought perhaps it was about the wheat.

The Bible leaves were still, after a second Miss Prudence read:

"'For many walk, of whom I have told you often, and now tell you even weeping, that they are the enemies of the cross of Christ.'"

That was not the answer, Linnet thought.

"What does that mean to you, Marjorie?" asked Miss Prudence.

"Why—it can't mean anything different from what it says. Paul was so sorry about the people he was writing about that he wept as he told them—he was so sorry they were enemies of the cross of Christ."

"Yes, he told them even weeping. But I knew an old gentleman who read the Bible unceasingly—I saw one New Testament that he had read through fifteen times—and he told me once that some people were so grieved because they were the enemies of the cross of Christ that they were enemies even weeping. I asked 'Why did they continue enemies, then?' and he said most ingenuously that he supposed they could not help it. Then I remembered this passage, and found it, and read it to him as I read it to you just now. He was simply astounded. He put on his spectacles and read it for himself. And then he said nothing. He had simply put the comma in the wrong place. He had read it in this way: 'For many walk, of whom I have told you often and now tell you, even weeping that they are the enemies of the cross of Christ.'"

"Oh," cried Marjorie, drawing an astonished long breath, "what a difference it does make."

"Now I know, it's punctuation you're talking about," exclaimed Linnet. "Marjorie told me all about the people in the stage-coach. O, Miss Prudence, I don't love to study; I want to go away to school, of course, but I can't see the *use* of so many studies. Marjorie *loves* to study and I don't; perhaps I would if I could see some use beside 'being like other people.' Being like other people doesn't seem to me to be a *real* enough reason."

Linnet had forgotten her clover leaf, she was looking at Miss Prudence with eyes as grave and earnest as Marjorie's ever were. She did not love to study and it was one of the wrong doings that she had confessed in her prayers many a time.

"Well, don't you see the reason now for studying punctuation?"

"Yes, I do," she answered heartily. "But we don't like dates, either of us."

"Did you ever hear about Pompeii, the city buried long ago underground?"

Linnet thought that had nothing to do with her question.

"Oh, yes," said Marjorie, "we have read about it. 'The Last Days of Pompeii' is in the school library. I read it, but Linnet didn't care for it."

"Do you know *when* it was buried?"

"No," said Linnet, brightening.

"Have you any idea?"

"A thousand years ago?" guessed Marjorie.

"Then you do not know how long after the Crucifixion?"

"No," they replied together.

"You know when the Crucifixion was, of course?"

"Why—yes," admitted Linnet, hesitatingly.

"Christ was thirty-three years old," said Marjorie, "so it must have been in the year 33, or the beginning of 34."

"Of course I know *Anno Domini*," said Linnet; "but I don't always know what happened before and after."

"Suppose we were walking in one of the excavated streets of Pompeii and I should say, 'O, girls! Look at that wall!' and you should see a rude cross carved on it, what would you think?"

"I should think they knew about Christ," answered Linnet.

The clover leaf tatting had fallen into her lap and the shuttle was on the grass.

"Yes, and is that all?"

"Why, yes," she acknowledged.

"Pompeii wasn't so far, so very far from Jerusalem and—they could hear," said Marjorie.

"And you two would pass on to a grand house with a wonderful mosaic floor and think no more about the cross."

"I suppose we would," said Linnet "Wouldn't you?"

"But I should think about the cross. I should think that the city was destroyed in 79 and be rejoiced that the inhabitants had heard of the Cross and knew its story before swift destruction overtook them. It was destroyed about forty-five years after the Crucifixion."

"I *like* to know that," said Marjorie. "Perhaps some of the people in it had seen St. Paul and heard him tell about the Cross."

"I see some use in that date," said Linnet, picking up her shuttle.

"Suppose I should tell you that once on a time a laborer would have to work fifteen years to earn enough to buy a Bible and then the Bible must be in Latin, wouldn't you like to know when it was."

"I don't know when the Bible was printed in English," confessed Marjorie.

"If you did know and knew several other things that happened about that time you would be greatly interested. Suppose I should tell you about something that happened in England, you would care very much more if you knew about something that was linked with it in France, and in Germany. If I say 1517 I do not arouse your enthusiasm; you don't know what was happening in Germany then; and 1492 doesn't remind you of anything—"

"Yes, it does," laughed Marjorie, "and so does 1620."

"Down the bay on an island stand the ruins of a church, and an old lady told me it was built in 1604. I did not contradict her, but I laughed all to myself."

"I know enough to laugh at that," said Linnet.

"But I have seen in America the spot where Jamestown stood and that dates almost as far back. Suppose I tell you that Martin Luther read *Pilgrims Progress* with great delight, do you know whether I am making fun or not? If I say that Queen Elizabeth wrote a letter to Cleopatra, do you know whether I mean it or not? And if I say that Richard the Third was baptized by St. Augustine, can you contradict it? And Hannah More wrote a sympathetic letter to Joan of Arc, and Marie Antoinette danced with Charlemagne, and George Washington was congratulated on becoming President by Mary Queen of Scots."

The girls could laugh at this for they had an idea that the Queen of Scots died some time before the first president of the United States was born; but over the other names and incidents they looked at each other gravely.

"Life is a kind of conglomeration without dates," said Linnet.

"I wonder if you know how long ago the flood was!" suggested Miss Prudence, "or if Mahomet lived before the flood or after," she added, seriously.

Marjorie smiled, but Linnet was serious.

"You confuse me so," said Linnet. "I believe I don't know when anything *was*. I don't know how long since Adam was made. Do you, Marjorie?"

"No," in the tone of one dreadfully ashamed.

"And now I'll tell you a lovely thought out of the Bible that came through dates. I did not discover it myself, of course."

"I don't see why 'of course,'" Marjorie said in a resentful tone. "You *do* discover things."

"I discover little girls once in a while," returned Miss Prudence with a rare softening of lips and eyes.

If it had not been for a few such discoveries the lines about Miss Prudence's lips might have been hard lines.

"Of course you both remember the story of faithful old Abraham, how he longed and longed for a son and hoped against hope, and, after waiting so long, Isaac was born at last. He had the sure promise of God that in his seed all the nations of the earth should be blessed. Do you know how many nations Abraham knew about? Did he know about France and England and America, the Empire of Russia and populous China?"

Linnet looked puzzled; Marjorie was very grave.

"Did he know that the North American Indians would be blessed in him? Did he know they would learn that the Great Spirit had a Son, Jesus Christ? And that Jesus Christ was descended from him?"

"I—don't—know," said Marjorie, doubtfully. "I get all mixed up."

"It was because all the world would be blessed that he was so anxious to have a son. And, then, after Isaac was born and married for years and years the promise did not seem to come true, for he had no child. Must the faithful, hopeful old father die with his hope deferred? We read that Abraham died in a good old age, an old man, full of years, and Isaac and Ishmael buried him, and farther on in the same chapter we find that the twin boys are born, Jacob and Esau. But their old grandfather was dead. He knew now how true God is to his promises, because he was in Heaven, but we can't help wishing he had seen those two strong boys from one of whom the Saviour of the whole world was to descend. But if we look at Abraham's age when he died, and comparing it with Isaac's when the twins were born, we find that the old man, truly, had to wait twenty years before they were born, but that he really lived to see them seventeen or eighteen years of age. He lived to tell them with his own lips about that wonderful promise of God."

"Oh, I'm so glad!" cried Marjorie, enthusiastically.

"He had another long time to wait, too," said Linnet.

"Yes, he had hard times all along," almost sighed Miss Prudence.

Forty years old did not mean to her that her hard times were all over.

"But he had such a good time with the boys," said Marjorie, who never could see the dark side of anything. "Just to think of *dates* telling us such a beautiful thing."

"That's all you hate, dates and punctuation," Linnet declared; "but I can't see the use of ever so many other things."

"If God thought it worth while to make the earth and people it and furnish it and govern it with laws, don't you think it worth your poor little while to learn what he has done?" queried Miss Prudence, gently.

"Oh!" exclaimed Linnet, "is *that* it?"

"Just it," said Miss Prudence, smiling, "and some day I will go over with you each study by itself and show you how it will educate you and help you the better to do something he asks you to do."

"Oh, how splendid!" cried Linnet. "Before I go to school, so the books won't seem hard and dry?"

"Yes, any day that you will come to me. Marjorie may come too, even though she loves to study."

"I wonder if you can find any good in Natural Philosophy," muttered Linnet, "and in doing the examples in it. And in remembering the signs of the Zodiac! Mr. Holmes makes us learn everything; he won't let us skip."

"He is a fine teacher, and you might have had, if you had been so minded, a good preparation for your city school."

"I haven't," said Linnet. "If it were not for seeing the girls and learning how to be like city girls, I would rather stay home."

"Perhaps that knowledge would not improve you. What then?"

"Why, Miss Prudence!" exclaimed Marjorie, "don't you think we country girls are away behind the age?"

"In the matter of dates! But you need not be. With such a teacher as you have you ought to do as well as any city girl of your age. And there's always a course of reading by yourself."

"It isn't always," laughed Linnet, "it is only for the studiously disposed."

"I was a country girl, and when I went to the city to school I did not fail in my examination."

"Oh, *you*!" cried Linnet.

"I see no reason why you, in your happy, refined, Christian home, with all the sweet influences of your healthful, hardy lives, should not be as perfectly the lady as any girl I know."

Marjorie clapped her hands. Oh, if Hollis might only hear this! And Miss Prudence *knew*.

"I thought I had to go to a city school, else I couldn't be refined and lady-like," said Linnet.

"That does not follow. All city girls are not refined and lady-like; they may have a style that you haven't, but that style is not always to their advantage. It is true that I do not find many young ladies in your little village that I wish you to take as models, but the fault is in them, as well as in some of their surroundings. You have music, you have books, you have perfection of beauty in shore and sea, you have the Holy Spirit, the Educator of mankind."

The girls were awed and silent.

"I have been shocked at the rudeness of city girls, and I have been charmed with the tact and courtesy of more than one country maiden. Nowadays education and the truest culture may be had everywhere."

"Even in Middlefield," laughed Marjorie her heart brimming over with the thought that, after all, she might be as truly a lady as Helen Rheid.

Miss Prudence

If Linnet had been as excited as Marjorie was, at that moment, she would have given a bound into the grass and danced all around. But Marjorie only sat still trembling with a flush in eyes and cheeks.

"I think I'll keep a list of the books I read," decided Marjorie after a quiet moment.

"That's a good plan. I'll show you a list I made in my girlhood, some day. But you mustn't read as many as an Englishman read,—Thomas Henry Buckle,—his library comprised twenty-two thousand."

"He didn't read them *all*," cried Linnet.

"He read parts of all, and some attentively, I dare say. He was a rapid reader and had the rare faculty of being able to seize on what he needed to use. He often read three volumes a day. But I don't advise you to copy him. I want you to read, mark, learn, and inwardly digest. He could absorb, but, we'll take it for granted that you must plod on steadily, step by step. He read through Johnson's Dictionary to enlarge his vocabulary."

"Vocabulary!" repeated Linnet.

"His stock of words," exclaimed Marjorie. "Miss Prudence!" with a new energy in her voice, "I'm going to read Webster through."

"Well," smiled Miss Prudence.

"Don't you believe I *can*?"

"Oh, yes."

"Then I will. I'll be like Buckle in one thing. I'll plan to read so many pages a day. We've got a splendid one; mother got it by getting subscriptions to some paper. Mother will do *anything* to help us on, Miss Prudence."

"I have learned that. I have a plan to propose to her by and by."

"Oh, can't you tell us?" entreated Linnet, forgetting her work.

"Not yet."

"Does it concern *us*?" asked Marjorie.

"Yes, both of you."

Two hours since it had "concerned" only Marjorie, but in this hour under the apple-tree Miss Prudence had been moved to include Linnet, also. Linnet was not Marjorie, she had mentally reasoned, but she was Linnet and had her own niche in the world. Was she not also one of her little sisters that were in the world and not of it?

"When may we know?" questioned Linnet

"That depends. Before I leave your grandfather's, I hope."

"I know it is something good and wonderful, because you thought of it," said Marjorie. "Perhaps it is as good as one of our day-dreams coming true."

"It may be something very like one of them, but the time may not be yet. It will not do you any harm to know there's something pleasant ahead, if it can be arranged."

"I do like to know things that are going to happen to us," Linnet confessed. "I used to wish I could dream and have the dreams come true."

"Like the wicked ancients who used to wrap themselves in skins of beasts and stay among the graves and monuments to sleep and dream—and in the temples of the idols, thinking the departed or the idols would foretell to them in dreams. Isaiah reproves the Jews for doing this. And Sir Walter Scott, in his notes to 'The Lady of the Lake,' tells us something about a similar superstition among the Scotch."

"I like to know about superstitions," said Linnet, "but I'd be afraid to do that."

"Miss Prudence, I haven't read 'The Lady of the Lake'!" exclaimed Marjorie.

"No, imitator of Buckle, you haven't. But I'll send it to you when I go home."

"What did Buckle *do* with all his learning?" inquired Marjorie.

"I haven't told you about half of his learning. He wrote a work of great learning, that startled the world somewhat, called 'The History of Civilization,' in which he attempted to prove that the differences between nations and peoples were almost solely to be attributed to physical causes that food had more to do with the character of a nation than faith."

"Didn't the Israelites live on the same food that the Philistines did?" asked Marjorie, "and didn't—"

"Are you getting ready to refute him? The Jews could not eat pork, you remember."

"And because they didn't eat pork they believed in one true God!" exclaimed Marjorie, indignantly. "I don't like his book, Miss Prudence."

"Neither do I. And we need not read it, even if he did study twenty-two thousand books and Johnson's Dictionary to help him write it."

"Why didn't he study Webster?" asked Linnet.

"Can't you think and tell me?"

"No."

"Can you not, Marjorie?"

"Because he was English, I suppose, and Johnson wrote the English Dictionary and Webster the American."

"An Irish lady told me the other day that Webster was no authority. I wish I could tell you all about Johnson; I love him, admire him, and pity him."

Marjorie laughed and squeezed Miss Prudence's hand. "Don't you wish you could tell us about every *body* and every *thing*, Miss Prudence?"

"And then help you use the knowledge. I am glad of your question, Marjorie, 'What did Mr. Buckle *do* with his knowledge?' If I should learn a new thing this week and not use it next week I should feel guilty."

"I don't know how to use knowledge," said Linnet.

"You are putting your knowledge of tatting to very good service."

"Miss Prudence, will you use your things on me?" inquired Marjorie, soberly.

"That is just what I am hoping to do."

"Hillo! Hillo! Hillo!" sounded a voice behind the woodshed. After a moment a tall figure emerged around a corner, arrayed in coarse working clothes, with a saw over his shoulders.

"Hillo! gals, I can't find your father. Tell him I left my saw here for him to file."

"I will," Linnet called back.

"That's African John," explained Linnet as the figure disappeared around the corner of the woodshed. "I wish I had asked him to stay and tell you some of his adventures."

"*African* John. He is not an African;" said Miss Prudence.

"No, oh no; he's Captain Rheid's cousin. People call him that because he was three years in Africa. He was left on the coast. It happened this way. He was only a sailor and he went ashore with another sailor and they got lost in a jungle or something like it and when they came back to the shore they saw the sails of their ship in the distance and knew it had gone off and left them. The man with him fell down dead on the sand and he had to stay three years before a ship came. He's an old man now and that happened years and years ago. Captain Rheid can't tell anything more frightful than that. Mother had a brother lost at sea, they supposed so, for he never came back; if I ever have anybody go and not come back I'll never, never, *never* give him up."

"Never, never, never give him up," echoed Miss Prudence in her heart.

"They thought Will Rheid was lost once, but he came back! Linnet didn't give him up, and his father and mother almost did."

"I'd never give him up," said Linnet again, emphatically.

"Will Rheid," teased Marjorie, "or anybody?"

"Anybody," replied Linnet, but she twitched at her work and broke her thread.

"Now, girls, I'm going in to talk to your mother awhile, and then perhaps Linnet will walk part of the way home with me," said Miss Prudence.

"To talk about *that*," cried Marjorie.

"I'll tell you by and by."

VIII.

BISCUITS AND OTHER THINGS.

"I am rather made for giving than taking."—*Mrs. Browning.*

Mrs. West had been awakened from her nap with an uncomfortable feeling that something disagreeable had happened or was about to happen; she felt "impressed" she would have told you. Pushing the light quilt away from her face she arose with a decided vigor, determined to "work it off" if it were merely physical; she brushed her iron gray hair with steady strokes and already began to feel as if her presentiment were groundless; she bathed her cheeks in cool water, she dressed herself carefully in her worn black and white barège, put on her afternoon cap, a bit of black lace with bows of narrow black ribbon, fastened the linen collar Linnet had worked with button-hole stitch with the round gold and black enamelled pin that contained locks of the light hair of her two lost babes, and then felt herself ready for the afternoon, even ready for the minister and his stylish wife, if they should chance to call. But she was not ready without her afternoon work; she would feel fidgety unless she had something to keep her fingers moving; the afternoon work happened to be a long white wool stocking for Linnet's winter wear. Linnet must have new ones, she decided; she would have no time to darn old ones, and Marjorie might make the old ones do another winter; it was high time for Marjorie to learn to mend.

The four shining knitting needles were clicking in the doorway of the broad little entry that opened out to the green front yard when Miss Prudence found her way around to the front of the house. The ample figure and contented face made a picture worth looking at, and Miss Prudence looked at it a moment before she announced her presence by speaking.

"Mrs. West, I want to come to see you a little while—may I?"

Miss Prudence had a pretty, appealing way of speaking, oftentimes, that caused people to feel as if she were not quite grown up. There was something akin to childlikeness in her voice and words and manner, to-day. She had never felt so humble in her life, as to-day when her whole life loomed up before her—one great disappointment.

"I was just thinking that I would go and find you after I had turned the heel; I haven't had a talk with you yet."

"I want it," returned the younger lady, seating herself on the upper step and leaning back against the door post. "I've been wanting to be *mothered* all day. I have felt as if the sunshine were taking me into its arms, and as if the soft warm grass were my mother's lap."

"Dear child, you have had trouble in your life, haven't you?" replied the motherly voice.

Miss Prudence was not impulsive, at least she believed that she had outgrown yielding to a sudden rush of feeling, but at these words she burst into weeping, and drawing nearer dropped her head in the broad lap.

"There, there, deary! Cry, if it makes you feel any better," hushed the voice that had rocked babies to sleep.

Miss Prudence

After several moments of self-contained sobbing Miss Prudence raised her head. "I've never told any one, but I feel as if I wanted to tell you. It is so long that it makes me feel old to speak of it. It is twenty years ago since it happened. I had a friend that I love as girls love the man they have chosen to marry; father admired him, and said he was glad to leave me with such a protector. Mother had been dead about a year and father was dying with consumption; they had no one to leave me with excepting this friend; he was older than I, years older, but I admired him all the more for that. Father had perfect trust in him. I think the trouble hastened father's death. He had a position of trust—a great deal of money passed through his hands. Like every girl I liked diamonds and he satisfied me with them; father used to look grave and say: 'Prudie, your mother didn't care for such things.' But I cared for mine. I had more jewels than any of my friends; and he used to promise that I should have everything I asked for. But I did not want anything if I might have him. My wedding dress was made—our wedding tour was all planned: we were to come home to his beautiful house and father was to be with us. Father and I were so contented over our plans; he seemed just like himself that last evening that we laughed and talked. But he—my friend was troubled and left early; when he went away he caught me in his arms and held me. 'God bless you, bless you' he said, and then he said, 'May he forgive me!' I could not sleep that night, the words sounded in my ears. In the morning I unburdened myself to father, I always told him everything, and he was as frightened as I. Before two days we knew all. He had taken—money—that was not his own, thousands of dollars, and he was tried and sentenced. I sent them all my diamonds and everything that would bring money, but that was only a little of the whole. They sent him—to state-prison, to hard labor, for a term of five years. Father died soon after and I had not any one nearer than an aunt or cousin. I thought my heart broke with the shame and dishonor. I have lived in many places since. I have money enough to do as I like—because I do not like to do very much, perhaps. But I can't forget. I can't forget the shame. And I trusted him so! I believed in him. He had buried a young wife years ago, and was old and wise and good! When I see diamonds they burn into me like live coals. I would have given up my property and worked for my living, but father made me bind myself with a solemn promise that I would not do it. But I have sought out many that he wronged, and given them all my interest but the sum I compelled myself to live on. I have educated two or three orphans, and I help every month several widows and one or two helpless people who suffered through him. Father would be glad of that, if he knew how comfortably I can live on a limited income. I have made my will, remembering a number of people, and if they die before I do, I shall keep trace of their children. I do all I can; I would, rather give all my money up, but it is my father's money until I die."

Mrs. West removed a knitting needle from between her lips and knit it into the heel she had "turned."

"Where is he—now?" she asked.

"I never saw him after that night—he never wrote to me; I went to him in prison but he refused to see me. I have heard of him many times through his brother; he fled to Europe as soon as he was released, and has never returned home—to my knowledge. I think his brother has not heard from him for some years. When I said I had not a friend, I did not mention this brother; he was young when it happened, too young to have any pity for his brother; he was very kind to me, they all were. This brother was a half-brother—there were two mothers—and much younger."

"What was his name?"

Mrs. West did not mean to be inquisitive, but she did want to know and not simply for the sake of knowing.

"Excuse me—but I must keep the secret for his brother's sake. He's the only one left."

"I may not know the name of the bank then?"

"If you knew that you would know all. But *I* know that your husband lost his small patrimony in it—twenty-five hundred dollars—"

"H'm," escaped Mrs. West's closely pressed lips.

"And that is one strong reason why I want to educate your two daughters."

The knitting dropped from the unsteady fingers.

"And I've fretted and fretted about that money, and asked the Lord how my girls ever were to be educated."

"You know now," said Miss Prudence. "I had to tell you, for I feared that you would not listen to my plan. You may guess how I felt when your sister-in-law, Mrs. Easton, told me that she was to take Linnet for a year or two and let her go to school. At first I could not see my way clear, my money is all spent for a year to come—I only thought of taking Marjorie home with me—but, I have arranged it so that I can spare a little; I have been often applied to to take music pupils, and if I do that I can take one of the girls home with me and send her to school; next year I will take all the expense upon myself, wardrobe and all. There is a cheap way of living in large cities as well as an expensive one. If Linnet goes to Boston with her aunt, she will be kept busy out of school hours. Mrs. Easton is very kindhearted but she considers no one where her children are concerned. If I wore diamonds that Linnet's money purchased, aren't you willing she shall eat bread and butter my money purchases?"

"But you gave the diamonds up?"

"I wore them, though."

"That diamond plea has done duty a good many times, I guess," said Mrs. West, smiling down upon the head in her lap.

"No, it hasn't. His brother has done many things for me; people are ready enough to take money from his brother, and the widows are my friends. It has not been difficult. It would have been without him."

"The nights I've laid awake and made plans. My little boys died in babyhood. I imagine their father and I would have mortgaged the farm, and I would have taken in washing, and he would have gone back to his trade to send those boys through college. But the girls don't need a college education. The boys might have been ministers—one of them, at least. But I would like the girls to have a piano, they both play so well on the melodeon! I would like them to be—well, like you, Miss Prudence, and not like their rough, hardworking old mother. I've shed tears enough about their education, and told the Lord about it times enough. If the Boston plan didn't suit, we had another, Graham and I—he always listens and depends upon my judgment. I'm afraid, sometimes, I depend upon my own judgment more than upon the Lord's wisdom. But this plan was—" the knitting needle was being pushed vigorously through her back hair now, "to exchange the farm for a house and lot in town—Middlefield is quite a town, you know—and he was to go back to his trade, and I was to take boarders, and the girls were to take turns in schooling and accomplishments. I am not over young myself, and he isn't over strong, but we had decided on that. I shed some tears over it, and he looked pale and couldn't sleep, for we've counted on this place as the home of our old age which isn't so far off as it was when he put that twenty-five hundred dollars into that bank. But I do breathe freer if I think we may have this place to live and die on, small as it is and the poor living it gives us. Father's place isn't much to speak of, and James will come in for his share of that, so we haven't much to count on anywhere. I don't know, though," the knitting needle was doing duty in the stocking again, "about taking *your* money. You were not his wife, you hadn't spent it or connived at his knavery."

"I felt myself to be his wife—I am happier in making all the reparation in my power. All I could do for one old lady was to place her in The Old Ladies' Home. I know very few of the instances; I would not harrow my soul with hearing of those I could not help. I have done very little, but that little has been my exceeding comfort."

"I guess so," said Mrs. West, in a husky voice. "I'll tell father what you say, we'll talk it over and see. I know you love my girls—especially Marjorie."

"I love them both," was the quick reply.

"Linnet is older, she ought to have the first chance."

Miss Prudence thought, but did not say, "As Laban said about Leah," she only said, "I do not object to that. We do Marjorie no injustice. This is Linnet's schooltime. There does seem to be a justice in giving the first chance to the firstborn, although God chose Jacob instead of the elder Esau, and Joseph instead of his older brethren, and there was little David anointed when his brothers were refused."

Miss Prudence's tone was most serious, but her eyes were full of fun. She was turning the partial mother's weapons against herself.

"But David and Jacob and Joseph were different from the others," returned the mother, gravely, "and in this case, the elder is as good as the younger."

It almost slipped off Miss Prudence's tongue, "But she will not take the education Marjorie will," but she wisely checked herself and replied that both the girls were as precious as precious could be.

"And now don't you go home to-night, stay all night and I'll talk to father," planned Mrs. West, briskly; "as Marjorie would say, Giant Despair will get Diffidence his wife to bed and they will talk the matter over. She doesn't read *Pilgrim's Progress* as much as she used to, but she calls you Mercy yet. And you are a mercy to us."

With the tears rolling down her cheeks the mother stooped over and kissed the lover of her girls.

"Mr. Holmes is coming to see Marjorie to-night, he hasn't called since her accident, and to talk to father, he likes to argue with him, and it will be pleasanter to have you here. And Will Rheid is home from a voyage, and he'll be running in. It must be lonesome for you over there on the Point. It used to be for me when I was a girl."

"But I'm not a girl," smiled Miss Prudence.

"You'll pass for one any day. And you can play and make it lively. I am not urging you with disinterested motives."

"I can see through you; and I *am* anxious to know how Mr. West will receive my proposal."

"He will see through my eyes in the end, but he always likes to argue a while first. I want you to taste Linnet's cream biscuit, too. She made them on purpose for you. There's father, now, coming with African John, and there *is* Will Rheid coming across lots. Well, I'm glad Linnet did make the biscuits."

Miss Prudence arose with a happy face, she did not go back to the girls at once, there was a nook to be quiet in at the foot of the kitchen garden, and she felt as if she must be alone awhile. Mrs. West, with her heart in a tremor that it had not known since Marjorie was born, tucked away her knitting behind the school-books on the dining-room table, tied on her blue checked apron, and went out to the kitchen to kindle the fire for tea, singing in her mellow voice, "Thus far the Lord hath led me on," suddenly stopping short as she crammed the stove with shavings to exclaim, "His name *was* Holmes! And that's the school-master's name. And that's why he's in such a fume when the boys cheat at marbles. Well, did I *ever*!"

Linnet ran in to exchange her afternoon dress for a short, dark calico, and to put on her old shoes before she went into the barnyard to milk Bess and Brindle and Beauty. Will Rheid found her in time to persuade her to let him milk Brindle, for he was really afraid he would get his hand out, and it would never do to let his wife do all the milking when his father bequeathed him a fifth of his acres and two of his hardest-to-be-milked cows. Linnet laughed, gave him one of her pails, and found an other milking stool for him.

Marjorie wandered around disconsolate until she discovered Miss Prudence in the garden.

She was perplexed over a new difficulty which vented itself in the question propounded between tasting currants.

"Ought I—do you think I ought—talk to people—about—like the minister—about—"

"No, child!" and Miss Prudence laughed merrily. "You ought to talk to people like Marjorie West! Like a child and not like a minister."

IX.

JOHN HOLMES.

"Courage to endure and to obey."—*Tennyson.*

It was vacation-time and yet John Holmes was at work. No one knew him to take a vacation, he had attempted to do it more than once and at the end of his stipulated time had found himself at work harder than ever. The last lazy, luxurious vacation that he remembered was his last college vacation. What a boyish, good-for-nothing, aimless fellow he was in those days! How his brother used to snap him up and ask if he had nothing better to do than to dawdle around into Maple Street and swing Prudence under the maples in that old garden, or to write rhymes with her and correct her German exercises! How he used to tease her about having by and by to color her hair white and put on spectacles, or else she would have to call her husband "papa." And she would dart after him and box his ears and laugh her happy laugh and look as proud as a queen over every teasing word. He had told her that she grew prettier every hour as her day of fate drew nearer, and then had audaciously kissed her as he bade her good-by, for, in one week would she not be his sister, the only sister he had ever had? He stood at the gate watching her as she tripped up to her father's arm-chair on the piazza, and saw her bend her head down to his, and then he had gone off whistling and thinking that his brother certainly had a share of all of earth's good things position, a good name, money, and now this sweet woman for a wife. Well, the world was all before *him* where to choose, and he would have money and a position some day and the very happiest home in the land.

The next time he saw Prudence she looked like one just risen out of a grave: pallid, with purple, speechless lips, and eyes whose anguish rent his soul. Her father had been suddenly prostrated with hemorrhage and he stayed through the night with her, and afterward he made arrangements for the funeral, and his mother and himself stood at the grave with her. And then there was a prison, and after that a delirious fever for himself, when for days he had not known his mother's face or Prudence's voice.

The other boys had gone back to college, but his spirit was crushed, he could not hold up his head among men. He had lost his "ambition," people said. Since that time he had taught in country schools and written articles for the papers and magazines; he had done one thing beside, he had purchased books and studied them. In the desk in his chamber there were laid away to-day four returned manuscripts, he was only waiting for leisure to exchange their addressee and send them forth into the world again to seek their fortunes. A rejection daunted him no more than a poor recitation in the schoolroom; where would be the zest in life if one had not the chance of trying again?

John Holmes was a hermit, but he was a hermit who loved boys; girls were too much like delicate bits of china, he was afraid of handling for fear of breaking. Girls grown up were not quite so much like bits of china, but he had no friend save one among womankind, his sister that was to have been, Prudence Pomeroy. He had not addressed her with the name his brother had given her since that last day in the garden; she was gravely Prudence to him, in her plain attire, her smooth hair and little unworldly ways, almost a veritable Puritan maiden.

As to her marrying—again (he always thought "again"), he had no more thought of it than she had. He had given to her every letter he had received from his brother, but they always avoided speaking his name; indeed Prudence, in her young reverence for his age and wisdom, had seldom named his Christian name to others or to himself, he was "Mr. Holmes" to her.

John Holmes was her junior by three years, yet he had constituted himself friend, brother, guardian, and sometimes, he told her, she treated him as though he were her father, beside.

"It's good to have all in one," she once replied, "for I can have you all with me at one time."

After being a year at Middlefield he had written to her about the secluded homestead and fine salt bathing at the "Point," urging her to spend her summer there. Marjorie had seen her face at church one day in early spring as she had stopped over the Sabbath at the small hotel in the town on her way on a journey farther north.

This afternoon, while Prudence had been under the apple-tree and in the front entry, he had bent over the desk in his chamber, writing. This chamber was a low, wide room, carpeted with matting, with neither shades nor curtains at the many-paned windows, containing only furniture that served a purpose—a washstand, with a small, gilt-framed glass hanging over it, one rush-bottomed chair beside the chair at the desk, that boasted arms and a leather cushion, a bureau, with two large brass rings to open each drawer, and a narrow cot covered with a white counterpane that his hostess had woven as a part of her wedding outfit before he was born, and books! There were books everywhere—in the long pine chest, on the high mantel, in the bookcase, under the bed, on the bureau, and on the carpet wherever it was not absolutely necessary for him to tread.

Prudence and Marjorie had climbed the narrow stairway once this summer to take a peep at his books, and Prudence had inquired if he intended to take them all out West when he accepted the presidency of the college that was waiting for him out there.

"I should have to come back to my den, I couldn't write anywhere else."

"And when somebody asks me if you are dead, as some king asked about the author of Butler's 'Analogy' once, I'll reply, as somebody replied: 'Not dead, but buried.'"

"That is what I want to be," he had replied. "Don't you want a copy of my little pocket dictionary? It just fits the vest pocket, you see. You don't know how proud I was when I saw a young man on the train take one from his pocket one day!"

He opened his desk and handed her a copy; Marjorie looked at it and at him in open-eyed wonder. And dared she recite to a teacher who had made a book?

"When is your Speller coming out?"

"In the fall. I'm busy on my Reader now."

Prudence stepped to his desk and examined the sheets of upright penmanship; it could be read as easily as print.

"And the Arithmetic?"

"Oh, I haven't tackled that yet. That is for winter evenings, when my fire burns on the hearth and the wind blows and nobody in the world cares for me."

"Then it won't be *this* winter," said Marjorie, lifting her eyes from the binding of the dictionary.

"Why not?" he questioned.

"Because somebody cares for you," she answered gravely.

He laughed and shoved his manuscript into the desk. He was thinking of her as he raised his head from the desk this afternoon and found the sun gone down; he thought of her and remembered that he had promised to call to see her to-night. Was it to take tea? He dreaded tea-parties, when everybody talked and nobody said anything. A dim remembrance of being summoned to supper a while ago flashed through his mind; but it hardly mattered—Mrs. Devoe would take her cup of tea alone and leave his fruit and bread and milk standing on the tea-table; it was better so, she would not pester him with questions while he was eating, ask him why he did not take more exercise, and if his room were not suffocating this hot day, and if he did not think a cup of good, strong tea would not be better for him than that bowl of milk!

Mrs. Devoe, a widow of sixty-five, and her cat, Dolly, aged nineteen, kept house and boarded the school-master. Her house was two miles nearer the shore than the school-building, but he preferred the walk in all weathers and he liked the view of the water. Mrs. Devoe had never kept a boarder before, her small income being amply sufficient for her small wants, but she liked the master, he split her wood and his own, locked the house up at night, made no trouble, paid his board, two dollars per week, regularly in advance, never went out at night, often read to her in the evening after her own eyes had given out, and would have been perfect if he had allowed her to pile away his books and sweep his chamber every Friday.

"But no man is perfect," she had sighed to Mrs. Rheid, "even my poor husband would keep dinner waiting."

After a long, absent-minded look over the meadows towards the sea, where the waves were darkening in the twilight, he arose in haste, threw off his wrapper, a gray merino affair, trimmed with quilted crimson silk, that Prudence had given him on a birthday three years ago, and went to the wash-stand to bathe his face and brush back that mass of black hair. He did not study his features as Prudence had studied hers that morning; he knew so little about his own face that he could scarcely distinguish a good portrait of himself from a poor one; but Prudence knew it by heart. It was a thin, delicate face, marred with much thought, the features not large, and finely cut, with deep set eyes as black as midnight, and, when they were neither grave nor stern, as soft as a dove's eyes; cheeks and chin were closely shaven; his hair, a heavy black mass, was pushed back from a brow already lined with thought or care, and worn somewhat long behind the ears; there was no hardness in any line of the face, because there was no hardness in the heart, there was sin and sorrow in the world, but he believed that God is good.

The slight figure was not above medium height; he had a stoop in the shoulders that added to his general appearance of delicacy; he was scholarly from the crown of his black head to the very tip of his worn, velvet slipper; his slender hands, with their perfectly kept nails, and even the stain of ink on the forefinger of his right hand, had an air of scholarship about them. His black summer suit was a perfect fit, his boots were shining, the knot of his narrow black neck tie was a little towards one side, but that was the only evidence that he was careless about his personal appearance.

"I want my boys to be neat," he had said once apologetically to Mrs. Devoe, when requesting her to give away his old school suit preparatory to buying another.

All he needed to be perfect was congenial social life, Prudence believed, but that, alas, seemed never to enter his conception. He knew it never had since that long ago day when he had congratulated his brother upon his perfect share of this world's happiness. And, queerly enough, Prudence stood too greatly in awe of him to suggest that his life was too one-sided and solitary.

"Some people wonder if you were ever married," Mrs. Devoe said to him that afternoon when he went down to his late supper. Mrs. Devoe never stood in awe of anybody.

"Yes, I was married twenty years ago—to my work," he replied, gravely; "there isn't any John Holmes, there is only my work."

"There is something that is John Holmes to me," said the widow in her quick voice, "and there's a John Holmes to the boys and girls, and I guess the Lord thinks something of you beside your 'work,' as you call it."

Meditatively he walked along the grassy wayside towards the brown farmhouse:

"Perhaps there *is* a John Holmes that I forget about," he said to himself.

X.

LINNET.

"Use me to serve and honor thee,
And let the rest be as thou wilt"—*E.L.E.*

Marjorie's laugh was refreshing to the schoolmaster after his hard day's work. She was standing behind her father, leaning over his shoulder, and looking at them both as they talked; some word had reminded Mr. Holmes of the subject of his writing that day and he had given them something of what he had been reading and writing on Egyptian slavery. Mr. Holmes was always "writing up" something, and one of Mr. West's usual questions was: "What have you to tell us about now?"

The subject was intensely interesting to Marjorie, she had but lately read "Uncle Tom's Cabin" and her tears and indignation were ready to burst forth at any suggestion of injustice or cruelty. But the thing that she was laughing at was a quotation from one of the older versions of the Bible, Roger's Version Mr. Holmes told them when he quoted the passage: "And the Lord was with Joseph and he was a luckie felowe." She lifted her head from her father's shoulder and ran out into the little front yard to find her mother and the others that she might tell them about Joseph and ask Miss Prudence what "Roger's Version" meant. But her mother was busy in the milkroom and Linnet was coming towards the house walking slowly with her eyes on the ground. Will Rheid was walking as slowly toward his home as Linnet was toward hers.

Miss Prudence made a picture all by herself in her plain black dress, with no color or ornament save the red rose in her black crape scarf, as she sat upright in the rush-bottomed, straight-backed chair in the entry before the wide-open door. Her eyes were towards the two who had parted so reluctantly on the bridge over the brook. Marjorie danced away to find her mother, suddenly remembering to ask if she might share the spare chamber with Miss Prudence, that is—if Linnet did not want to very much.

Marjorie never wanted to do anything that Linnet wanted to very much.

Opening the gate Linnet came in slowly, with her eyes still on the ground, shut the gate, and stood looking off into space; then becoming aware of the still figure on the piazza hurried toward it.

Linnet's eyes were stirred with a deeper emotion than had ever moved her before; Miss Prudence did not remember her own face twenty years ago, but she remembered her own heart.

Will Rheid was a good young fellow, honest and true; Miss Prudence stifled her sigh and said, "Well, dear" as the young girl came and stood beside her chair.

"I was wishing—I was saying to Will, just now, that I wished there was a list of things in the Bible to pray about, and then we might be sure that we were asking right."

"And what did he say?"

"He said he'd ask anyhow, and if it came, it was all right, and if it didn't, he supposed that was all right, too."

"That was faith, certainly."

"Oh, he has faith," returned Linnet, earnestly. "Don't you know—oh, you don't remember—when the Evangelist—that always reminds me of Marjorie"—Linnet was a somewhat fragmentary talker like her mother—"but when Mr. Woodfern was here four of the Rheid boys joined the Church, all but Hollis, he was in New York, he went about that time. Mr. Woodfern was so interested in them all; I shall never forget how he used to pray at family worship: 'Lord, go through that Rheid family.' He prayed it every day, I really believe. And they all joined the Church at the first communion time, and every one of them spoke and prayed in the prayer meetings. They used to speak just as they did about anything, and people enjoyed it so; it was so genuine and hearty. I remember at a prayer meeting here that winter Will arose to speak 'I was talking to a man in town today and he said there was nothing *in* religion. But, oh, my! I told him there was nothing *out* of it.' I told him about that to-night and he said he hadn't found anything outside of it yet."

"He's a fine young fellow," said Miss Prudence. "Mr. Holmes says he has the 'right stuff' in him, and he means a great deal by that."

A pleasant thought curved Linnet's lips.

"But, Miss Prudence," sitting down on the step of the piazza, "I do wish for a list of things. I want to know if I may pray that mother may never look grave and anxious as she did at the supper table, and father may not always have a cough in winter time, and Will may never have another long voyage and frighten us all, and that Marjorie may have a chance to go to school, too, and—why, *ever* so many things!"

A laugh from the disputants in the parlor brought the quick color to Miss Prudence's cheeks. No mere earthly thing quickened her pulses like John Holmes' laugh. And I do not think that was a mere earthly thing; there was so much grace in it.

"Doesn't St. Paul's 'everything' include your '*ever* so many things?'" questioned Miss Prudence, as the laugh died away.

"I don't know," hesitatingly. "I thought it meant about people becoming Christians, and faith and patience and such good things."

"Perhaps your requests are good things, too. But I have thought of something that will do for a list of things; it is included in this promise: 'Whatsoever things ye desire when ye pray, believe that ye receive them and ye shall have them.' Desire *when* ye pray! That's the point."

"Does the time when we desire make any difference?" asked Linnet, interestedly.

There were some kind of questions that Linnet liked to ask.

"Does it not make all the difference? Suppose we think of something we want while we are ease-loving, forgetful of duty, selfish, unforgiving, neither loving God or our neighbor, when we feel far from him, instead of near him, can we believe that we shall have such a heart's desire as that would be? Would your desire be according to his will, his unselfish, loving, forgiving will?"

"No, oh, no," said Linnet, earnestly. "But I do think about father and mother and Marjorie going to school and—when I am praying."

"Then ask for everything you desire while you are praying; don't be afraid."

"*Is* mother troubled about something?"

"Not troubled, really; only perplexed a little over something we have been planning about; and she is very glad, too."

"I don't like to have her troubled, because her heart hurts her when she worries. Marjorie don't know that, but she told me. That's one reason—my strongest reason—for being sorry about going to Boston."

"But your father is with her and he will watch over her."

"But she depends on *me*," pleaded Linnet.

"Marjorie is growing up," said Miss Prudence, hopefully.

"Marjorie! It doesn't seem to me that she will ever grow up; she is such a little puss, always absent-minded, with a book in her hand. And she can't mend or sew or even make cake or clear up a room neatly. We spoil her, mother and I, as much as she spoils her kitten, Pusheen. Did you know that *pusheen* is Irish for puss? Mr. Holmes told us. I do believe he knows everything."

"He comes nearer universal knowledge than the rest of us," said Miss Prudence, smiling at the girl's eagerness.

"But he's a book himself, a small volume, in fine print, printed in a language that none of us can read," said Linnet.

"To most people he is," granted Miss Prudence; "but when he was seven I was ten, I was a backward child and he used to read to me, so he is not a dead language to me."

Linnet pulled at the fringe of her white shawl; Will Rheid had brought that shawl from Ireland a year ago.

"Miss Prudence, *do* we have right desires, desires for things God likes, while we are praying?"

"If we feel his presence, if we feel as near to him as Mary sitting at the feet of Christ, if we thank him for his unbounded goodness, and ask his forgiveness for our sins with a grateful, purified, and forgiving heart, how can we desire anything selfish—for our own good only and not to honor him, anything unholy, anything that it would hurt him to grant; if our heart is ever one with his heart, our will ever one with his will, is it not when we are nearest to him, nearest in obeying, or nearest in praying? Isn't there some new impulse toward the things he loves to give us every time we go near to him?"

Linnet assented with a slight movement of her head. She understood many things that she could not translate into words.

"Yesterday I saw in the paper the death of an old friend." They had been silent for several minutes; Miss Prudence spoke in a musing voice. "She was a friend in the sense that I had tried to befriend her. She was unfortunate in her home surroundings, she was something of an invalid and very deaf beside. She had lost money and was partly dependent upon relatives. A few of us, Mr. Holmes was one of them, paid her board. She was not what you girls call 'real bright,' but she was bright enough to have a heartache every day. Reading her name among the deaths made me glad of a kindness I grudged her once."

"I don't believe you grudged it," interrupted Marjorie, who had come in time to lean over the tall back of the chair and rest her hand on Miss Prudence's shoulder while she listened to what promised to be a "story."

"I did, notwithstanding. One busy morning I opened one of her long, complaining, badly-written letters; I could scarcely decipher it; she was so near-sighted, too, poor child, and would not put on glasses. Her letters were something of a trial to me. I read, almost to my consternation, 'I have been praying for a letter from you for three weeks.' Slipping the unsightly sheet back into the envelope, hastily, rather too hastily, I'm afraid, I said to myself: 'Well, I don't see how you will get it.' I was busy every hour in those days, I did not have to rest as often as I do now, and how could I spare the hour her prayer was demanding? I could find the time in a week or ten days, but she had prayed for it yesterday and would expect it to-day, would pray for it to-day and expect it to-morrow. 'Why could she not pray about it without telling me?' I argued as I dipped my pen in the ink, not to write to her but to answer a letter that must be answered that morning. I argued about it to myself as I turned from one thing to another, working in nervous haste; for I did more in those days than God required me to do, I served myself instead of serving him. I was about to take up a book to look over a poem that I was to read at our literary circle when words from somewhere arrested me: 'Do you like to have the answer to a prayer of yours put off and off in this way?' and I answered aloud, 'No, I *don't*.' 'Then answer this as you like to have God answer you.' And I sighed, you will hardly believe it, but I *did* sigh. The enticing poem went down and two sheets of paper came up and I wrote the letter for which the poor thing a hundred miles away had been praying three weeks. I tried to make it cordial, spirited and sympathetic, for that was the kind she was praying for. And it went to the mail four hours after I had received her letter."

"I'm so glad," said sympathetic Linnet. "How glad she must have been!"

"Not as glad as I was when I saw her death in the paper yesterday."

"You do write to so many people," said Marjorie.

"I counted my list yesterday as I wrote on it the fifty-third name."

"Oh, dear," exclaimed Linnet, who "hated" to write letters. "What do you do it for?"

"Perhaps because they need letters, perhaps because I need to write them. My friends have a way of sending me the names of any friendless child, or girl, or woman, who would be cheered by a letter, and I haven't the heart to refuse, especially as some of them pray for letters and give thanks for them. Instead of giving my time to 'society' I give it to letter writing. And the letters I have in return! Nothing in story books equals the pathos and romance of some of them."

"I like that kind of good works," said Marjorie, "because I'm too bashful to talk to people and I can *write* anything."

How little the child knew that some day she would write anything and everything because she was "too bashful to talk." How little any of us know what we are being made ready to do. And how we would stop to moan and weep in very self-pity if we did know, and thus hinder the work of preparation from going on.

Linnet played with the fringe of her shawl and looked as if something hard to speak were hovering over her lips.

"Did mother tell you about Will?" she asked, abruptly, interrupting one of Miss Prudence's stories to Marjorie of which she had not heeded one word.

"About Will!" repeated Marjorie. "What has happened to him?"

Linnet looked up with arch, demure eyes. "He told mother and me while we were getting supper; he likes to come out in the kitchen. The first mate died and he was made first mate on the trip home, and the captain wrote a letter to his father about him, and his father is as proud as he can be and says he'll give him the command of the bark that is being built in Portland, and he mustn't go away again until that is done. Captain Rheid is the largest owner, he and African John, so they have the right to appoint the master. Will thinks it grand to be captain at twenty-four."

"But doesn't Harold feel badly not to have a ship, too?" asked Marjorie, who was always thinking of the one left out.

"But he's younger and his chance will come next. He doesn't feel sure enough of himself either. Will has studied navigation more than he has. Will went to school to an old sea-captain to study it, but Harold didn't, he said it would get knocked into him, somehow. He's mate on a ship he likes and has higher wages than Will will get, at first, but Will likes the honor. It's so wonderful for his father to trust him that he can scarcely believe it; he says his father must think he is some one else's son. But that letter from the old shipmaster that Captain Rheid used to know has been the means of it."

"Is the bark named yet?" asked Marjorie. "Captain Rheid told father he was going to let Mrs. Rheid name it."

"Yes," said Linnet, dropping her eyes to hide the smile in them, "she is named LINNET."

"Oh, how nice! How splendid," exclaimed Marjorie, "Won't it look grand in the *Argus*—'Bark LINNET, William Rheid, Master, ten days from Portland'?"

"Ten days to where?" laughed Linnet.

"Oh, to anywhere. Siberia or the West Indies. I *wish* he'd ask us to go aboard, Linnet. *Don't* you think he might?"

"We might go and see her launched! Perhaps we all have an invitation; suppose you run and ask mother," replied Linnet, with the demure smile about her lips.

Marjorie flew away, Linnet arose slowly, gathering her shawl about her, and passed through the entry up to her own chamber.

Miss Prudence did not mean to sigh, she did not mean to be so ungrateful, there was work enough in her life, why should she long for a holiday time? Girls must all have their story and the story must run on into womanhood as hers had, there was no end till it was all lived through.

"When thou passest *through* the waters I will be with thee."

Miss Prudence dropped her head in her hands; she was going through yet.

Will Rheid was a manly young fellow, just six feet one, with a fine, frank face, a big, explosive voice, and a half-bashful, half-bold manner that savored of land and sea. He was as fresh and frolicsome as a sea breeze itself, as shrewd as his father, and as simple as Linnet.

But—Miss Prudence came back from her dreaming over the past,—would Linnet go home with her and go to school? Perhaps John Holmes would take Marjorie under his special tutelage for awhile, until she might come to her, and—how queer it was for her to be planning about other people's homes—why might he not take up his abode with the Wests, pay good board, and not that meagre two dollars a week, take Linnet's seat at the table, become a pleasant companion for Mr. West through the winter, and, above all, fit Marjorie for college? And did not he need the social life? He was left too much to his own devices at old Mrs. Devoe's. Marjorie, her father with his ready talk, her mother, with a face that held remembrance of all the happy events of her life, would certainly be a pleasant exchange for Mrs. Devoe, and Dolly, her aged cat. She would go home to her own snuggery, with Linnet to share it, with a relieved mind if John Holmes might be taken into a family. And it was Linnet, after all, who was to make the changes and she had only been thinking of Marjorie.

When Linnet came to her to kiss her good night, Miss Prudence looked down into her smiling eyes and quoted:

"'Keep happy, sweetheart, and grow wise.'"

The low murmur of voices reached Miss Prudence in her chamber long after midnight, she smiled as she thought of Giant Despair and his wife Diffidence. And then she prayed for the wanderer over the seas, that he might go to his Father, as the prodigal did, and that, if it were not wrong or selfish to wish it, she might hear from him once more before she died.

And then the voices were quiet and the whole house was still.

XI.

GRANDMOTHER.

"Even trouble may be made a little sweet"—*Mrs. Platt.*

"Here she is, grandmarm!" called out the Captain. "Run right in, Midget."

His wife was *marm* and his mother *grandmarm*.

Marjorie ran in at the kitchen door and greeted the two occupants of the roomy kitchen. Captain Rheid had planned his house and was determined he said that the "women folks" should have room enough to move around in and be comfortable; he believed in having the "galley" as good a place to live in as the "cabin."

It was a handsome kitchen, with several windows, a fine stove, a well-arranged sink, a large cupboard, a long white pine table, three broad shelves displaying rows of shining tinware, a high mantel with three brass candlesticks at one end, and a small stone jar of fall flowers at the other, the yellow floor of narrow boards was glowing with its Saturday afternoon mopping, and the general air of freshness and cleanliness was as refreshing as the breath of the sea, or the odor of the fields.

Marm and grandmarm liked it better.

"Deary me!" ejaculated grandma, "it's an age since you were here."

"A whole week," declared Marjorie, standing on tiptoe to hang up her sack and hat on a hook near the shelves.

"Nobody much comes in and it seems longer," complained the old lady.

"I think she's very good to come once a week," said Hollis' sad-faced mother.

"Oh, I like to come," said Marjorie, pushing one of the wooden-bottomed chairs to grandmother's side.

"It seems to me, things have happened to your house all of a sudden," said Mrs. Rheid, as she gave a final rub to the pump handle and hung up one of the tin washbasins over the sink.

"So it seems to us," replied Marjorie; "mother and I hardly feel at home yet. It seems so queer at the table with Linnet gone and two strangers—well, Mr. Holmes isn't a stranger, but he's a stranger at breakfast time."

"Don't you know how it all came about?" inquired grandmother, who "admired" to get down to the roots of things.

"No, I guess—I think," she hastily corrected, "that nobody does. We all did it together. Linnet wanted to go with Miss Prudence and we all wanted her to go; Mr. Holmes wanted to come and we all wanted him to come; and then Mr. Holmes knew about Morris Kemlo, and father wanted a boy to do the chores for winter and Morris wanted to come, because he's been in a drug store and wasn't real strong, and his mother thought farm work and sea air together would be good for him."

"And you don't go to school?" said Mrs. Rheid, bringing her work, several yards of crash to cut up into kitchen towels and to hem. Her chair was also a hard kitchen chair; Hollis' mother had never "humored" herself, she often said, there was not a rocking chair in her house until all her boys were big boys; she had thumped them all to sleep in a straight-backed, high, wooden chair. But with this her thumping had ceased; she was known to be as lax in her government as the father was strict in his.

She was a little woman, with large, soft black eyes, with a dumb look of endurance about the lips and a drawl in her subdued voice. She had not made herself, her loving, rough boys, and her stern, faultfinding husband, had moulded not only her features, but her character. She was afraid of God because she was afraid of her husband, but she loved God because she knew he must love her, else her boys would not love her.

"Is Linnet homesick?" she questioned as her sharp shears cut through the crash.

"Yes, but not very much. She likes new places. She likes the school, and the girls, so far, and she likes Miss Prudence's piano. Hollis has been to see her, and Helen Rheid has called to see her, and invited her and Miss Prudence to come to tea some time. Miss Prudence wrote me about Helen, and she's *lovely*, Mrs. Rheid."

"So Hollis said. Have you brought her picture back?"

"Yes'm."

Marjorie slowly drew a large envelope from her pocket, and taking the imperial from it gazed at it long. There was a strange fascination to her in the round face, with its dark eyes and mass of dark hair piled high on the head. It was a vignette and the head seemed to be rising from folds of black lace, the only ornament was a tiny gold chain on which was placed a small gold cross.

To Marjorie this picture was the embodiment of every good and beautiful thing. It was somebody that she might be like when she had read all the master's books, and learned all pretty, gentle ways. She never saw Helen Rheid, notwithstanding Helen Rheid's life was one of the moulds in which some of her influences were formed. Helen Rheid was as much to her as Mrs. Browning was to Miss Prudence. After another long look she slipped the picture back into the envelope and laid it on the table behind her.

"You are going with Miss Prudence when Linnet is through, I suppose?" asked Mrs. Rheid.

"So mother says. It seems a long time to wait, but I am studying at home. Mother cannot spare me to go to school, now, and Mr. Holmes says he would rather hear me recite than not. So I am learning to sew and do housework as well."

"You need that as much as schooling," returned Mrs. Rheid, decidedly. "I wish one of my boys could have gone to college, there's money enough to spare, but their father said he had got his learning knocking around the world and they could get theirs the same way."

"Hollis studies—he's studying French now."

"Did you bring a letter from him?" inquired his mother, eagerly.

"Yes," said Marjorie, disappointedly, "but I wanted to keep it until the last thing. I wanted you to have the best last."

"If I ever do get the best it will be last!" said the subdued, sad voice.

"Then you shall have this first," returned the bright, childish voice.

But her watchful eyes had detected a stitch dropped in grandmother's work and that must be attended to first. The old lady gave up her work willingly and laid her head back to rest while Marjorie knit once around. And then the short letter was twice read aloud and every sentence discussed.

"If I ever wrote to him I suppose he'd write to me oftener," said his mother, "but I can't get my hands into shape for fine sewing or for writing. I'd rather do a week's washing than write a letter."

Marjorie laughed and said she could write letters all day.

"I think Miss Prudence is very kind to you girls," said Mrs. Rheid. "Is she a relation?"

"Not a *real* one," admitted Marjorie, reluctantly.

"There must be some reason for her taking to you and for your mother letting you go. Your mother has the real New England grit and she's proud enough. Depend upon it, there's a reason."

"Miss Prudence likes us, that's the reason, and we like her."

"But that doesn't repay *money*."

"She thinks it does. And so do we."

"How much board does the master pay?" inquired grandmother.

"I don't know; I didn't ask. He has brought all his books and the spare chamber is full. He let me help him pile them up. But he says I must not read one without asking him."

"I don't see what you want to read them for," said the old lady sharply.
"Can't your mother find enough for you to do. In my day—"

"But your day was a long time ago," interrupted her daughter-in-law.

"Yes, yes, most a hundred, and girls want everything they can get now.
Perhaps the master hears your lessons to pay his board."

"Perhaps," assented Marjorie.

"They say bees pay their board and work for you beside," said Mrs. Rheid. "I guess he's like a bee. I expect the Widow Devoe can't help wishing he had stayed to her house."

"He proposed to come himself," said Marjorie, with a proud flash of her eyes, "and he proposed to teach me himself."

"Oh, yes, to be sure, but she and the cat will miss him all the same."

"It's all sudden."

"[missing text] happen sudden, nowadays. I keep my eyes shut and things keep whirling around."

Grandmother was seated in an armchair with her feet resting on a home-made foot stool, clad in a dark calico, with a little piece of gray shawl pinned closely around her neck, every lock of hair was concealed beneath a black, borderless silk cap, with narrow black silk strings tied under her trembling chin, her lips were sunken and seamed, her eyelids partly dropped over her sightless eyes, her withered, bony fingers were laboriously pushing the needles in and out through a soft gray wool sock, every few moments Marjorie took the work from her to pick up a dropped stitch or two and to knit once around. The old eyes never once suspected that the work grew faster than her own fingers moved. Once she remarked plaintively: "Seems to me it takes you a long time to pick up one stitch."

"There were three this time," returned Marjorie, seriously.

"What does the master learn you about?" asked Mrs. Rheid.

"Oh, the school studies! And I read the dictionary by myself."

"I thought you had some new words."

"I want some good words," said Marjorie.

"Now don't you go and get talking like a book," said grandmother, sharply, "if you do you can't come and talk to me."

"But you can talk to me," returned Marjorie, smiling, "and that is what I want. Hollis wrote me that I mustn't say 'guess' and I do forget so often."

"Hollis is getting ideas," said Hollis' mother; "well, let him, I want him to learn all he can."

Marjorie was wondering where her own letter to Hollis would come in; she had stowed away in the storehouse of her memory messages enough from mother and grandmother to fill one sheet, both given with many explanations, and before she went home Captain Rheid would come in and add his word to Hollis. And if she should write two sheets this time would her mother think it foolish? It was one of Mrs. West's old-fashioned ways to ask Marjorie to let her read every letter that she wrote.

With her reserve Marjorie could open her heart more fully to Miss Prudence than she could to one nearer her; it was easier to tell Miss Prudence that she loved her than to tell her mother that she loved her, and there were some things that she could say to Mr. Holmes that she could not say to her father. It may be a strange kind of reserve, but it is like many of us. Therefore, under this surveillance, Marjorie's letters were not what her heart prompted them to be.

If, in her own young days, her mother had ever felt thus she had forgotten it.

But for this Marjorie's letters would have been one unalloyed pleasure. One day it occurred to her to send her letter to the mail before her mother was aware that she had written, but she instantly checked the suggestion as high treason.

Josie Grey declared that Marjorie was "simple" about some things. A taint of deceit would have caused her as deep remorse as her heart was capable of suffering.

"Grandma, please tell me something that happened when you were little," coaxed Marjorie, as she placed the knitting back in the old fingers. How pink and plump the young fingers looked as they touched the old hands.

"You haven't told me about the new boy yet," said the old lady. "How old is he? Where did he come from? and what does he look like?"

"*We* want another boy," said Mrs. Rheid, "but boys don't like to stay here. Father says I spoil them."

"Our 'boy,'—Morris Kemlo,—don't you think it's a pretty name? It's real funny, but he and I are twins, we were born on the same day, we were both fourteen this summer. He is taller than I am, of course, with light hair, blue eyes, and a perfect gentleman, mother says. He is behind in his studies, but Mr. Holmes says he'll soon catch up, especially if he studies with me evenings. We are to have an Academy at our house. His mother is poor, and has other children, his father lost money in a bank, years ago, and died afterward. It was real dreadful about it—he sold his farm and deposited all his money in this bank, he thought it was so sure! And he was going into business with the money, very soon. But it was lost and he died just after Morris was born. That is, it was before Morris was born that he lost the money, but Morris talks about it as if he knew all about it. Mr. Holmes and Miss Prudence know his mother, and Miss Prudence knew father wanted a boy this winter. He is crazy to go to sea, and says he wants to go in the *Linnet*. And that's all I know about him, grandma."

"Is he a *good* boy?" asked Mrs. Rheid.

"Oh, yes," said Marjorie, "he brings his Bible downstairs and reads every night. I like everything but doing his mending, and mother says I must learn to do that. Now, grandma, please go on."

"Well, Marjorie, now I've heard all the news, and Hollis' letter, if you'll stay with grandmarm I'll run over and see Cynthy! I want to see if her pickles are as green as mine, and I don't like to leave grandmarm alone. You must be sure to stay to supper."

"Thank you; I like to stay with grandma."

"But I want hasty pudding to-night, and you won't be home in time to make it, Hepsie," pleaded the old lady in a tone of real distress.

"Oh, yes, I will, Marjorie will have the kettle boiling and she'll stir it while I get supper."

Mrs. Rheid stooped to pick up the threads that had fallen on her clean floor, rolled up her work, took her gingham sun-bonnet from its hook, and stepped out into the sunshine almost as lightly as Marjorie would have done.

"Cynthy" was African John's wife, a woman of deep Christian experience, and Mrs. Rheid's burdened heart was longing to pour itself out to her.

Household matters, the present and future of their children, the news of the homes around them, and Christian experience, were the sole topics that these simply country women touched upon.

"Well, deary, what shall I tell you about? I must keep on knitting, for Hollis must have these stockings at Christmas, so he can tell folks in New York that his old grandmarm most a hundred knit them for him all herself. Nobody helped her, she did it all herself. She did it with her own old fingers and her own blind eyes. I'll drop too many stitches while I talk, so I'll let you hold it for me. It seems as if it never will get done," she sighed, dropping it from her fingers.

"Oh, yes," said Marjorie, cheerily, "it's like your life, you know; that has been long, but it's 'most done.'"

"Yes, I'm most through," sighed the old lady with a long, resigned breath, "and there's nobody to pick up the stitches I've dropped all along."

"Won't God?" suggested Marjorie, timidly.

"I don't know, I don't know about things. I've never been good enough to join the Church. I've been afraid."

"Do you have to be *good* enough?" asked the little church member in affright. "I thought God was so good he let us join the Church just as he lets us go into Heaven—and he makes us good and we try all we can, too."

"That's an easy way to do, to let him make you good. But when the minister talks to me I tell him I'm afraid."

"I wouldn't be afraid," said Marjorie; "because you want to do as Christ commands, don't you? And he says we must remember him by taking the bread and wine for his sake, to remember that he died for us, don't you know?"

"I never did it, not once, and I'm most a hundred!"

"Aren't you sorry, don't you want to?" pleaded Marjorie, laying her warm fingers on the hard old hand.

"I'm afraid," whispered the trembling voice. "I never was good enough."

"Oh, dear," sighed Marjorie, her eyes brimming over, "I don't know how to tell you about it. But won't you listen to the minister, he talks so plainly, and he'll tell you not to be afraid."

"They don't go to communion, my son nor his wife; they don't ask me to."

"But they want you to; I know they want you to—before you die," persuaded Marjorie. "You are so old now."

"Yes, I'm old. And you shall read to me out of the Testament before you go. Hepsie reads to me, but she gets to crying before she's half through; she can't find 'peace,' she says."

"I wish she could," said Marjorie, almost despairingly.

"Now I'll tell you a story," began the old voice in a livelier tone. "I have to talk about more than fifty years ago—I forget about other things, but I remember when I was young. I'm glad things happened then, for I can remember them."

"Didn't things happen afterward?" asked Marjorie, laughing.

"Not that I remember."

This afternoon was a pleasant change to Marjorie from housework and study, and she remembered more than once that she was doing something to help pay Hollis for the Holland plate.

"Where shall I begin?" began the dreamy, cracked voice, "as far back as I can remember?"

"As far back as you can," said Marjorie, eagerly. "I like old stories best."

"Maybe I'll get things mixed up with my mother and grandmother and not know which is me."

"Rip Van Winkle thought his son was himself," laughed Marjorie, "but you will think you are your grandmother."

"I think over the old times so, sitting here in the dark. Hepsie is no hand to talk much, and Dennis, he's out most of the time, but bedtime comes soon and I can go to sleep. I like to have Dennis come in, he never snaps up his old mother as he does Hepsie and other folks. I don't like to be in the dark and have it so still, a dog yapping is better than no noise, at all. I say, 'Now I lay me' ever so many times a day to keep me company."

"You ought to live at our house, we have noisy times; mother and I sing, and father is always humming about his work. Mr. Holmes is quiet, but Morris is so happy he sings and shouts all day."

"It used to be noisy enough once, too noisy, when the boys were all making a racket together, and Will made noise enough this time he was home. He used to read to me and sing songs. I don't wonder Hepsie is still and mournful, like. It's a changed home to her with the boys away. My father's house had noise enough in it; he had six wives."

"Not all at once," cried Marjorie alarmed, confounding a hundred years ago with the partriarchal age.

But the old story-teller never heeded interruptions.

"And my marm was the last wife but one. My father was a hundred years and one day when he died. I've outlived all the children, I guess, for I never hear from none of them—I most forget who's dead. Some of them was married before I was born. I was the youngest, and I never remember my own mother, but I had a good mother, all the same."

"You had four step-mothers before you were born," said Marjorie seriously, "and one own mother and then another step-mother. Girls don't have so many step-mothers nowadays."

"And our house was one story—a long house, with the eaves most touching the ground and big chimneys at both ends. It was full of folks."

"I should *think* so," interposed Marjorie.

"And Sunday nights we used to sing 'God of my childhood and my youth.'
Can you sing that? I wish you'd sing it to me. I forget what comes next."

"I never heard of it before; I wish you *could* remember it all, it's so pretty."

"Amzi used to sit next to me and sing—he was my twin brother—as loud and clear as a bell. And when he died they put this on his tombstone:

"'Come see ye place where I do lie
As you are now so once was I:
As I be now so you will be,
Prepare for death and follow me.'"

"Oh," shivered Marjorie, "I don't like it. I like a Bible verse better."

"Isn't that in the Bible?" she asked, angrily.

"I don't believe it is."

"'Prepare to meet thy God' is."

"Yes," said Marjorie, "that was the text last Sunday."

"And on father's tombstone mother put this verse:

'O, my dear wife, do think of me
Although we've from each other parted,
O, do prepare to follow me
Where we shall love forever.'

"I wish I could remember some more."

"I wish you could," said Marjorie. "Didn't you have all the things we have? You didn't have sewing machines."

"Sewing machines!" returned the old lady, indignantly, "we had our fingers and pins and needles. But sometimes we couldn't have pins and had to pin things together with thorns. How would you like that?"

"I'd rather be born now," said Marjorie. "I wouldn't want to have so many step-mothers as you had, and I'd rather be named Marjorie than *Experience*."

"Experience is a good name, and I'd have earned it by this time if my mother hadn't given it to me," and the sunken lips puckered themselves into a smile. "I could tell you some *dreadful* things, too, but Hepsie won't like it if I do. I'll tell you one, though. I don't like to think about the dreadful things myself. I used to tell them to my boys and they'd coax me to tell them again, about being murdered and such things. A girl I knew found out after she was married that her husband had killed a peddler, to steal his money to marry her with, and people found it out and he was hanged and she was left a widow!"

"Oh, dear, *dear*," exclaimed Marjorie, "have dreadful things been always happening? Did she die with a broken heart?"

"No, indeed, she was married afterward and had a good husband. She got through, as people do usually, and then something good happened."

"I'll remember that," said Marjorie, her hazel eyes full of light; "but it was dreadful."

"And there were robbers in those days."

"Were there giants, too?"

"I never saw a giant, but I saw robbers once. The women folks were alone, not even a boy with us, and six robbers came for something to eat and they ransacked the house from garret to cellar; they didn't hurt us at all, but we *were* scared, no mistake. And after they were gone we found out that the baby was gone, Susannah's little black baby, it had died the day before and mother laid it on a table in the parlor and covered it with a sheet and they had caught it up and ran away with it."

"Oh, *dear*," ejaculated Marjorie.

"Father got men out and they hunted, but they never found the robbers or the baby. If Susannah didn't cry nobody ever did! She had six other children but this baby was so cunning! We used to feed it and play with it and had cried our eyes sore the day it died. But we never found it."

"It wasn't so bad as if it had been alive," comforted Marjorie, "they couldn't hurt it. And it was in Heaven before they ran away with the body. But I don't wonder the poor mother was half frantic."

"Poor Susannah, she used to talk about it as long as she lived."

"Was she a slave?"

"Of course, but we were good to her and took care of her till she died. My father gave her to me when I was married. That was years and years and *years* before we came to this state. I was fifteen when I was married—"

"*Fifteen*," Marjorie almost shouted. That was queerer than having so many step-mothers.

"And my husband had four children, and Lucilla was just my age, the oldest, she was in my class at school. But we got on together and kept house together till she married and went away. Yes, I've had things happen to me. People called it our golden wedding when we'd been married fifty years, and then he died, the next year, and I've lived with my children since. I've had my ups and downs as you'll have if you live to be most a hundred."

"You've had some *ups* as well as downs," said Marjorie.

"Yes, I've had some good times, but not many, not many."

Marjorie answered indignantly: "I think you have good times now, you have a good home and everybody is kind to you."

"Yes, but I can't see and Hepsie don't talk much."

"This afternoon as I was coming along I saw an old hunch-backed woman raking sticks together to make a bonfire in a field, don't you think she had a hard time?"

"Perhaps she liked to; I don't believe anybody made her, and she could *see* the bonfire."

Marjorie's eyes were pitiful; it must be hard to be blind.

"Shall I read to you now?" she asked hurriedly.

"How is the fire? Isn't it most time to put the kettle on? I shan't sleep a wink if I don't have hasty pudding to-night and I don't like it *raw*, either."

"It shan't be raw," laughed Marjorie, springing up. "I'll see to the fire and fill the kettle and then I'll read to you."

The old lady fumbled at her work till Marjorie came back to her with the family Bible in her hands.

She laid the Bible on the table and moved her chair to the table.

"Where shall I read?"

"About Jacob and all his children and all his troubles, I never get tired of that. He said few and evil had been his days and he was more than most a hundred."

"Well," said Marjorie, lingering over the word and slowly turning back to Genesis. She had opened to John, she wanted to read to the grumbling old heart that was "afraid" some of the comforting words of Jesus: "Let not your heart be troubled, neither let it be afraid."

"Begin about Jacob and read right on."

With a voice that could not entirely conceal her disappointment, she "began about Jacob and read right on" until Mrs. Rheid's light step touched the plank at the kitchen door. There was a quiet joyfulness in her face, but she did not say one word; she bent over to kiss Marjorie as she passed her, hung up her gingham sun-bonnet, and as the tea kettle was singing, poured the boiling water into an iron pot, scattered a handful of salt in it and went to the cupboard for the Indian meal.

"I'll stir," said Marjorie, looking around at the old lady and discovering her head dropped towards one side and the knitting aslant in her fingers.

"The pudding stick is on the shelf next to the tin porringer," explained
Mrs. Rheid.

Marjorie moved to the stove and stood a moment holding the wooden pudding stick in her hand.

"You may tell Hollis," said Hollis' mother, slowly dropping the meal into the boiling water, "that I have found peace, at last."

Majorie's eyes gave a quick leap.

"Peace in *believing*—there is no peace anywhere else," she added.

XII.

A BUDGET OF LETTERS.

"The flowers have with the swallows fled,
 And silent is the cricket;
The red leaf rustles overhead,
 The brown leaves fill the thicket

 "With frost and storm comes slowly on
The year's long wintry night time."—*J. T. Trowbridge*

"*New York, Nov.* 21, 18—.

"MY DARLING MARJORIE:

"You know I hate to write letters, and I do not believe I should have begun this this evening if Miss Prudence had not made me. She looks at me with her eyes and then I am *made*. I am to be two weeks writing this, so it is a journal. To think I have been at school two years and am beginning a third year. And to think I am really nineteen years old. And you are sixteen, aren't you? Almost as old as I was when I first came. But your turn is coming, poor dear! Miss Prudence says I may go home and be married next summer, if I can't find anything better to do, and Will says I can't. And I shouldn't wonder if we go to Europe on our wedding tour. That sounds grand, doesn't it? But it only means that Captain Will Rheid will take his wife with him if the owners' do not object too strongly, and if they do, the captain says he will let the *Linnet* find another master; but I don't believe he will, or that anybody will object. That little cabin is just large enough for two of us to turn around in, or we would take you. Just wait till Will has command of a big East Indiaman and you shall go all around the world with us. We are in our snuggery this evening, as usual. I think you must know it as well as I do by this time. The lovely white bed in the alcove, the three windows with lace curtains dropping to the floor, the grate with its soft, bright fire, the round table under the chandelier, with Miss Prudence writing letters and I always writing, studying, or mending. Sometimes we do not speak for an hour. Now my study hours are over and I've eaten three Graham wafers to sustain my sinking spirits while I try to fill this sheet. Somehow I can think of enough to say—how I would talk to you if you were in that little rocker over in the corner. But I think you would move it nearer, and you would want to do some of the talking yourself. I haven't distinguished myself in anything, I have not taken one prize, my composition has never once been marked T. B. R, *to be read*; to be read aloud, that is; and I have never done anything but to try to be perfect in every recitation and to be ladylike in deportment. I am always asked to sing, but any bird can sing. I was discouraged last night and had a crying time down here on the rug before the grate. Miss Prudence had gone to hear Wendell Phillips, with one of the boarders, so I had a good long time to cry my cry out all by myself. But it was not all out when she came, I was still floating around in my own briny drops, so, of course, she would know the cause of the small rain storm I was drenched in, and I had to stammer out that—I—hadn't—improved—my time and—I knew she was ashamed of me—and sorry she—had tried to—make anything out of me. And then she laughed. You never heard her laugh like that—nor any one else. I began to laugh as hard as I had been crying. And, after that, we talked till midnight. She said lovely things. I wish I knew how to write them, but if you want to hear them just have a crying time and she will say them all to you. Only you can never get discouraged. She began by asking somewhat severely: 'Whose life do you want to live?' And I was frightened and said, 'My own, of course,' that I wouldn't be anybody else for anything, not even Helen Rheid, or you. And she said that my training had been the best thing for my own life, that I had fulfilled all her expectations (not gone beyond them), and she knew just what I could do and could not do when she brought me here. She had educated me to be a good wife to Will, and an influence for good in my little sphere in my down-east home; she knew I would not be anything wonderful, but she had tried to help me make the most of myself and she was satisfied that I had done it. I had education enough to know that I am an ignorant thing (she didn't say *thing*, however), and I had common sense and a loving heart. I was not to go out into the world as a bread-winner or 'on a mission,' but I was to stay home and make a home for a good man, and to make it such a sweet, lovely home that it was to be like a little heaven. (And then I had to put my head down and cry again.) So it ended, and I felt better and got up early to write it all to Will.—There's a knock at the door and a message for Miss Prudence.

"Later. The message was that Helen Rheid is very sick and wants her to come to sit up with her to-night. Hollis brought the word but would not come upstairs. And now I must read my chapter in the Bible and prepare to retire. Poor Helen! She was here last week one evening with Hollis, as beautiful as a picture and so full of life. She was full of plans. She and Miss Prudence are always doing something together.

Miss Prudence

"23d. Miss Prudence has not come home yet and I'm as lonesome as can be. Coming home from school to-day I stopped to inquire about Helen and saw nobody but the servant who opened the door; there were three doctors upstairs then, she said, so I came away without hearing any more; that tells the whole story. I wish Hollis would come and tell me. I've learned my lessons and read my chapters in history and biography, and now I am tired and stupid and want to see you all. I do not like it here, in this stiff house, without Miss Prudence. Most of the boarders are gentlemen or young married ladies full of talk among themselves. Miss Prudence says she is going back to her Maple Street home when she takes you, and you and she and her old Deborah are to live alone together. She is tired of boarding and so I am, heartily tired. I am tired of school, to-night, and everything. Your letter did not come to-day, and Will's was a short, hurried one, and I'm homesick and good-for-nothing.

"27th. I've been studying hard to keep up in geometry and astronomy and have not felt a bit like writing. Will has sailed for Liverpool and I shall not see him till next spring or later, for he may cross the Mediterranean, and then back to England, and nobody knows where else, before he comes home. It all depends upon "freights." As if freight were everything. Hollis called an hour ago and stayed awhile. Helen is no better. She scarcely speaks, but lies patient and still. He looked in at her this morning, but she did not lift her eyes. Oh, she is so young to die! And she has so much to *do*. She has not even begun to do yet. She has so much of herself to do with, she is not an ignoramus like me. Her life has been one strong, pure influence Hollis said to-night. He is sure she will get well. He says her father and mother pray for her night and day. And his Aunt Helen said such a beautiful thing yesterday. She was talking to Hollis, for she knows he loves her so much. She said something like this: (the tears were in his eyes when he told me) 'I was thinking last night, as I stood looking at her, about that blood on the lintel—the blood of the lamb that was to keep the first-born safe among the children of Israel. She is our first-born and the blood of Jesus Christ is in all our thoughts while we plead for her life—for his sake—for the sake of his blood.' Hollis broke down and had to go away without another word. Her life has done him good. I wish she could talk to him before she goes away, because he is not a Christian. But he is so good and thoughtful that he will *think* now more than he ever did before. Miss Prudence stays all the time. Helen notices when she is not there and Mrs. Rheid says she can rest while Miss Prudence is in the room.

"I am such a poor stick myself, and Helen could do so much in the world; and here I am, as strong and well as can be, and she is almost dying. But I do not want to take her place. I have so much to live for—so many, I ought to say. I thought of writing a long journal letter, but I have not the heart to think of anything but Helen.

"Hollis is to start next week on his first trip as a 'commercial traveller,' and he is in agony at the thought of going and not knowing whether Helen will live or die. I'll finish this in the morning, because I know you are anxious to hear from us.

"In the morning. I am all ready for school, with everything on but my gloves. I don't half know my geometry and I shall have to copy my composition in school. It is as stupid as it can be; it is about the reign of Queen Anne. There isn't any heart in it, because all I care about is the present—and the future. I'll send it to you as soon as it is returned corrected. You will laugh at the mistakes and think, if you are too modest to say so, that you can do better. I pity you if you can't. I shall stop on the way to inquire about Helen, and I am afraid to, too.

"School, Noon Recess. I met Hollis on the walk as I stood in front of Helen's—there was no need to ask. Black and white ribbon was streaming from the bell handle. I have permission to go home. I have cried all the morning. I hope I shall find Miss Prudence there. She must be so tired and worn out. Hollis looked like a ghost and his voice shook so he could scarcely speak.

"With ever so much love to all,

"YOUR SISTER LINNET.

"P. S. Hollis said he would not write this week and wants you to tell his mother all about it."

* * * * *

The next letter is dated in the early part of the following month.

"*In my Den, Dec.* 10, 18—,

"MY FRIEND PRUDENCE:

"My heart was with you, as you well know, all those days and nights in that sick chamber that proved to be the entrance to Heaven. She smiled and spoke, lay quiet for awhile with her eyes closed, and awoke in the presence of the Lord. May you and I depart as easily, as fearlessly. I cannot grieve as you do; how much she is saved! To-night I have been thinking over your life, and a woman's lot seems hard. To love so much, to suffer so much. You see I am desponding; I am often desponding. You must write to me and cheer me up. I am disappointed in myself. Oh how different this monotonous life from the life I planned! I dig and delve and my joy comes in my work. If it did not, where would it come in, pray? I am a joyless fellow at best. There! I will not write another word until I can give you a word of cheer. Why don't you toss me overboard? Your life is full of cheer and hard work; but I cannot be like you. Marjorie and Morris were busy at the dining-room table when I left them, with their heads together over my old Euclid. We are giving them a lift up into the sunshine and that is something. What do you want to send Marjorie to school for? What can school do for her when I give her up to you? Give yourself to her and keep her out of school. The child is not always happy. Last communion Sunday she sat next to me; she was crying softly all the time. You could have said something, but, manlike, I held my peace. I wonder whether I don't know what to say, or don't know how to say it. I seem to know what to say to you, but, truly Prudence, I don't know how to say it. I have been wanting to tell you something, fourteen, yes, fourteen years, and have not dared and do not dare to night. Sometimes I am sure I have a right, a precious right, a sacred right, and then something bids me forbear, and I forbear. I am forbearing now as I sit up here in my chamber alone, crowded in among my books and the wind is wild upon the water. I am gloomy to-night and discouraged. My book, the book I have lost myself in so long, has been refused the fourth time. Had it not been for your hand upon my arm awhile ago it would be now shrivelled and curling among the ashes on my hearth.

"Who was it that stood on London Bridge and did not throw his manuscript over? Listen! Do you hear that grand child of yours asking who it was that sat by his hearth and did not toss his manuscript into the fire? Didn't somebody in the Bible toss a roll into the fire on the hearth? I want you to come to talk to me. I want some one not wise or learned, except learned and wise in such fashion as you are, to sit here beside me, and look into the fire with me, and listen to the wind with me, and talk to me or be silent with me. If my book had been accepted, and all the world were wagging their tongues about it, I should want that unwise, unlearned somebody. That friend of mine over the water, sitting in his lonely bungalow tonight studying Hindoostanee wants somebody, too. Why did you not go with him, Prudence? Shall you never go with any one; shall you and I, so near to each other, with so much to keep us together, go always uncomforted. But you *are* comforted. You loved Helen, you love Linnet and Marjorie and a host of others; you do not need me to bid you be brave. You are a brave woman. I am not a brave man. I am not brave to-night, with that four-times-rejected manuscript within reach of my hand. Shall I publish it myself? I want some one to think well enough of it to take the risk.

"Prudence, I have asked God for something, but he gives me an answer that I cannot understand. Write to me and tell me how that is.

"Yours to-day and to-morrow."

"J. H."

* * * * *

"*New York, Dec.* 20, 18—.

"MY DEAR JOHN:

"I have time but for one word to-night, and even that cannot be at length. Linnet and I are just in from a lecture on Miss Mitford! There were tears running down over my heart all the time that I was listening. You call me brave; she was brave. Think of her pillowed up in bed writing her last book, none to be kind to her except those to whom she paid money. Linnet was delighted and intends to 'write a composition' about her. Just let me keep my hand on your arm (will you?) when evil impulses are about. You do not quite know how to interpret the circumstances that seem to be in answer to your prayer? It is as if you spoke to God in English and the answer comes in Sanscrit. I think I have received such answers myself. And if we were brutes, with no capacity of increasing our understanding, I should think it very queer. Sometimes it is hard work to pray until we get an answer and then it is harder still to find out its meaning. I imagine that Linnet and Marjorie, even Will Rheid, would not understand that; but you and I are not led along in the easiest way. It must be because the answer is worth the hard work: his Word and Spirit can interpret all his involved and mystical answers. Think with a clear head, not with any pre-formed judgment, with a heart emptied of all but a willingness to read his meaning aright, be that meaning to shatter your hopes or to give bountifully your desire—with a sincere and abiding determination to take it, come what may, and you will understand as plainly as you are understanding me. Try it and see. I have tried and I know. There may be a wound for you somewhere, but oh, the joy of the touch of his healing hand. And after that comes obedience. Do you remember one a long time ago who had half an answer, only a glimmer of light on a dark way? He took the answer and went on as far as he understood, not daring to disobey, but he went on—something like you, too—in 'bitterness,' in the heat of his spirit, he says; he went on as far as he could and stayed there. That was obedience. He stayed there 'astonished' seven days. Perhaps you are in his frame of mind. Nothing happened until the end of the seven days, then he had another word. So I would advise you to stay astonished and wait for the end of your seven days. In our bitterness and the heat of our spirit we are apt to think that God is rather slow about our business. Ezekiel could have been busy all that seven days instead of doing nothing at all, but it was the time for him to do nothing and the time for God to be busy within him. You have inquired of the Lord, that was your busy time, now keep still and let God answer as slowly as he will, this is his busy time. Now Linnet and I must eat a cracker and then say good-night to all the world, yourself, dear John, included.

"Yours,

"PRUDENCE"

* * * * *

"*Washington, Dec.* 21, 18—.

"DEAR MARJORIE:

"Aunt Helen sent me your letter; it came an hour ago. I am full of business that I like. I have no time for sight-seeing. I wish I had! Washington is the place for Young America to come to. But Young America has to come on business this time. Perhaps I will come here on my wedding trip, when there is no business to interfere. I am not ashamed to say that if I had been a girl I would have cried over your letter. Helen was *something* to everybody; she used to laugh and then look grave when she read your letters about her and the good she was to you. There will never be another Helen. There is one who has a heartache about her and no one knows it except himself and me. She refused him a few days before she was taken ill. He stood a long time and looked at her in her coffin, as if he forgot that any one was looking at him. I told him it was of no use to ask her, but he persisted. She had told me several times that he was disagreeable to her. Her mother wonders who will take her place to us all, and we all say no one ever can. I thank God that she lived so long for my sake. You and she are like sisters to me. You do me good, too. I should miss your letters very much, for I hear from home so seldom. You are my good little friend, and I am grateful to you. Give my best love to every one at home and tell mother I like my business. Mother's photograph and yours and Helen's are in my breast pocket. If I should die to-night would I be as safe as Helen is?

"Your true friend,

"HOLLIS RHEID."

* * * * *

"*The Homestead, Jan.* 4, 18—.

"DEAR FRIEND HOLLIS:

"Thank you for your letter from Washington. I took it over to your mother and read it to her and your father, all excepting about the young man who stood and looked at Helen in her coffin. I thought, perhaps, that was in confidence. Your father said: 'Tell Hollis when he is tired of tramping around to come home and settle down near the old folks,' and your mother followed me to the door and whispered: 'Tell him I cannot feel that he is safe until I know that he has repented and been forgiven.' And now, being through all this part, my conscience is eased and I can tell you everything else I want to.

Miss Prudence

"Look in and see us in a snow-storm. Mother is reading for the one hundred and twenty-second and a half time somebody's complete works on the New Testament, and father and Mr. Holmes are talking about—let me see if I know—ah, yes, Mr. Holmes is saying, 'Diversity of origin,' so you know all about it.

"Sometimes I listen instead of studying. I would listen to this if your letter were not due for the mail to-morrow. Father sits and smiles, and Mr. Holmes walks up and down with his arms behind him as he used to do during recitation in school. Perhaps he does it now, only you and I are not there to see. I wish you were here to listen to him; father speaks now and then, but the dialogue soon develops into a monologue and the master entertains and instructs us all. If you do not receive this letter on time know that it is because I am learning about the Jew; how he is everywhere proving the truth of prophecy by becoming a resident of every country. And yet while he is a Jew he has faces of all colors. In the plains of the Ganges, he is black; in Syria, lighter and yet dusky; in Poland his complexion is ruddy and his hair as light as yours. There was a little Jewess boarding around here last summer as olive as I imagine Rebekah and Sarah, and another as fair and rosy as a Dane. But have you enough of this? Don't you care for what Livingstone says or Humboldt? Don't you want to know the four proofs in support of unity of origin? I do, and if I write them I shall remember them; 1. Bodily Structure. 2. Language. 3. Tradition. 4. Mental Endowment. Now he is telling about the bodily structure and I do want to listen.—And I *have* listened and the minute hand of the clock has been travelling on and my pen has been still. But don't you want to know the ten conclusions that have been established—I know you do. And if I forget, I'll nudge Morris and ask him. Oh, I see (by looking over his shoulder) he has copied them all in one of his exercise books.

"You may skip them if you want to, but I know you want to see if your experience in your extensive travels correspond with the master's authority. Now observe and see if the people in Washington—all have the same number of teeth, and of additional bones in their body. As that may take some time, and seriously interfere with your 'business' and theirs, perhaps you had better not try it. And, secondly, they all shed their teeth in the same way (that will take time also, so, perhaps, you may better defer it until your wedding trip, when you have nothing else to do); and, thirdly, they all have the upright position, they walk and look upward; and, fourthly, their head is set in every variety in the same way; fifthly, they all have two hands; sixthly, they all have smooth bodies with hair on the head; seventhly, every muscle and every nerve in every variety are the same; eighthly, they all speak and laugh; ninthly, they eat different kind of food, and live in all climates; and, *lastly*, they are more helpless and grow more slowly than other animals. Now don't you like to know that? And now he has begun to talk about language and I *must* listen, even if this letter is never finished, because language is one of my hobbies. The longer the study of language is pursued the more strongly the Bible is confirmed, he is saying. You ought to see Morris listen. His face is all soul when he is learning a new thing. I believe he has the most expressive face in the whole world. He has decided to be a sailor missionary. He says he will take the Gospel to every port in the whole world. Will takes Bibles and tracts always. Morris reads every word of *The Sailors Magazine* and finds delightful things in it. I have almost caught his enthusiasm. But if I were a man I would be professor of languages somewhere and teach that every word has a soul, and a history because it has a soul. Wouldn't you like to know how many languages there are? It is *wonderful*. Somebody says—Adelung (I don't know who he is)—three thousand and sixty-four distinct languages, Balbi (Mr. Holmes always remembers names) eight hundred languages and five thousand dialects, and Max Müller says there are nine hundred known languages. Mr. Holmes can write a letter in five languages and I reverence him, but what is that where there are, according to Max Müller, eight hundred and ninety-five that he does not know a word of? Mr. Holmes stands still and puts his hands in front of him (where they were meant to be), and says he will tell us about Tradition to-morrow night, as he must go up to his den and write letters. But he does say Pandora's box is the story of the temptation and the fall. You know she opened her box out of curiosity, and diseases and wars leaped out to curse mankind. That is a Greek story. The Greek myths all seem to mean something. Father says: 'Thank you for a pleasant evening,' as Mr. Holmes takes his lamp to leave us, and *he* says: 'You forget what I have to thank you all for.'

"My heart *bursts* with gratitude to him, sometimes; I have his books and I have him; he is always ready so gently and wisely to teach and explain and never thinks my questions silly, and Morris says he has been and is his continual inspiration. And we are only two out of the many whom he stimulates. He says we are his recreation. Dull scholars are his hard work. Morris is never dull, but I can't do anything with geometry; he outstripped me long ago. He teaches me and I do the best I can. He has written on his slate, 'Will you play crambo?' Crambo was known in the time of Addison, so you must know that it is a very distinguished game. Just as I am about to say 'I will as soon as this page is finished,' father yawns and looks up at the clock. Mother remarks: 'It is time for worship, one of the children will read, father.' So while father goes to the door to look out to see what kind of a night it is and predict to-morrow and while mother closes her book with a lingering, loving sigh, and Morris pushes his books away and opens the Bible, I'll finish my last page. And, lo, it is finished and you are glad that stupidity and dullness do sometime come to an abrupt end.

"FRIEND MARJORIE."

* * * * *

"*In the Schoolroom, Jan.* 23, 18—.

"MY BLESSED MOTHER:

"Your last note is in my breast pocket with all the other best things from you. What would boys do without a breast pocket, I wonder. There is a feeling of study in the very air, the algebra class are 'up' and doing finely. The boy in my seat is writing a note to a girl just across from us, and the next thing he will put it in a book and ask, with an unconcerned face, 'Mr. Holmes, may I hand my arithmetic to somebody?' And Mr. Holmes, having been a fifteen-year-old boy himself, will wink at any previous knowledge of such connivings, and say 'Yes,' as innocently! It isn't against the rules to do it, for Mr. Holmes, never, for a moment, supposes such a rule a necessity. But I never do it. Because Marjorie doesn't come to school. And a pencil is slow for all I want to say to her. She is my talisman. I am a big, awkward fellow, and she is a zephyr that is content to blow about me out of sheer good will to all human kind. But, in school, I write notes to another girl, to my mother. And I write them when I have nothing to say but that I am well and strong and happy, content with the present, hopeful for the future, looking forward to the day when you will see me captain of as fine a ship as ever sailed the seas. And won't I bring you good things from every country in the world, just because you are such a blessed mother to

"Your unworthy boy,

"M.K."

* * * * *

"New York, Jan. 30, 18—.

"MY MARJORIE:

"Your long letter has been read and re-read, and then read aloud to Linnet. She laughed over it, and brushed her eyes over it; and then it was laid away in my archives for future reference. It is a perfect afternoon, the sun is shining, and the pavements are as dry as in May. Linnet endeavored to coax me out, as it is her holiday afternoon, and Broadway will be alive with handsome dresses and handsome faces, and there are some new paintings to be seen. But I was proof against her coaxing as this unwritten letter pressed on my heart, so she has contented herself with Helen's younger sister, Nannie, and they will have a good time together and bring their good time home to me, for Nannie is to come home to dinner with her. Linnet looked like a veritable linnet in her brown suit with the crimson plume in her brown hat; I believe the girl affects grays and brown with a dash of crimson, because they remind her of a linnet, and she *is* like a linnet in her low, sweet voice, not strong, but clear. She will be a lovely, symmetrical woman when she comes out of the fire purified. How do I know she will ever be put in any furnace? Because all God's children must suffer at some times, and then they know they are his children. And she loves Will so vehemently, so idolatrously, that I fear the sorrow may be sent through him; not in any withdrawing of his love, he is too thoroughly true for that, not in any great wickedness he may commit, he is too humble and too reliant upon the keeping power of God to be allowed to fall into that, but—she may not have him always, and then, I fear, her heart would really break.

"She reminds me of my own young vehemence and trust. But the taking away will be the least sorrow of all. Why! How sorrowfully I am writing to-day: no, how truly I am writing of life to-day: of the life you and she are entering—are already entered upon. But God is good, God is good, hold to that, whatever happens. Some day, when you are quite an old woman and I am really an old woman, I will tell you about my young days.

"Your letter was full of questions; do not expect me to answer them all at once. First, about reading the Bible. You poor dear child! Do you think God keeps a book up in Heaven to put down every time you fail to read the Bible through in a year? Because you have read it three times in course, so many chapters a weekday, and so many a Sunday, do you think you must keep on so or God will keep it laid up against you?

"Well, be a law keeper if you must, but keep the whole law, and keep it perfectly, in spirit and in letter, or you will fail! And if you fail in one single instance, in spirit or in letter, you fail in all, and must bear the curse. You must continue in *all things* written in the law to do them. Are you ready to try that? Christ could do it, and he did do it, but can you? And, if not, what? You must choose between keeping the law and trusting in Christ who has kept it for you. You cannot serve two masters: the Law and Christ. Now, I know I cannot keep the law and so I have given up; all I can do is to trust in Christ to save me, in Christ who is able to obey all God's law for me, and so I trust him and love him, and obey him with the strength he gives me. If we love him, we will keep his commandments, he says. 'I can do all things through Christ strengthening me'—even keep his commandments, which are not grievous. If you must be a law keeper in your own strength, give up Christ and cling to the law to save you, or else give up keeping the law for your salvation and cling to Christ. Keep his commandments because you love him, and not keep the old law to save your soul by your own obedience. Read the Bible because you love it, every word. Read till you are full of some message he gives you, and then shut it up; don't keep on, because you must read so many chapters a day.

"My plan is—and I tell you because it has been blessed to me—to ask him to feed me with his truth, feed me *full*, and then I open the Book and read. One day I was filled full with one clause: '*Because they fainted*.' I closed it, I could read no more. At another time I read a whole Epistle before I had all I was hungry for. One evening I read a part of Romans and was so excited that I could not sleep for some time that night. Don't you like that better than reading on and on because you have set yourself to do it, and ending with a feeling of relief because it is *done*, at last? These human hearts are naughty things and need more grace continually. Just try my way—not my way but God's way for me,—and see how full you will be fed with your daily reading.

"I just bethought myself of a page in an old journal; I'll copy it for you. It has notes of my daily reading. I wish I had kept the references, but all I have is the thought I gathered. I'll give it to you just as I have it.

"'April 24, 18—. Preparation is needed to receive the truth.

"'25. Ezekiel saw the glory before he heard the Voice.

"'26. He permits long waiting.

"'27. It is blessed to hear his voice, even if it be to declare punishment.

"'28. The word of God comes through the lips of men.

"'29. God works with us when we work with him.

"'30. God's work, and not man's word, is the power,

"'May 1. Man fails us, *then* we trust in God.

"'2. Death is wages, Life is a gift.

"'3. Paul must witness at Jerusalem before going to Rome.

"'4. When God wills, it is not *to be*, it *is*.

"'5. To man is given great power, but it is not his own power.

"'6. Even his great love Christ *commends* to us.

"'7. To seek and find God all beside must be put away.

"'11. The day of the Lord is darkness to those who do not seek him.

"'12. For all there were so many yet was not the net broken.

"'13. Even after Aaron's sin the Lord made him High Priest.

"'14. Therefore I take pleasure in infirmities—for Christ's sake.

"'15. It is *spirit* and not letter that God looks at.

"'16. His choices rule all things.

"'17. That which is not forbidden may be inquired about.

"'18. Captivity is turned upon repentance and obedience.

"'19. Rejoicing comes after understanding his words.

"'20. A way of escape is made for sin.

"'21. Faith waits as long as God asks it to wait.

"'22. He strengthens our hearts through waiting to wait longer.

"'23. Anything not contrary to the revealed will of God we may ask in prayer.'

"These lessons I took to my heart each day. Another might have drawn other lessons from the same words, but these were what I needed then. The page is written in pencil, and some words were almost erased. But I am glad I kept them all this time; I did not know I was keeping them for you, little girl. I have so fully consecrated myself to God that sometimes I think he does not let any of me be lost; even my sins and mistakes I have used to warn others, and through them I have been led to thank him most fervently that he has not left me to greater mistakes, greater sins. Some day your heart will almost break with thankfulness.

"And now, childie, about your praying. You say you are *tired out* when your prayer is finished. I should think you would be, poor child, if you desire each petition with all your intense nature. Often one petition uses all my strength and I can plead no more—in words. You seem to think that every time you kneel you must pray about every thing that can be prayed about, the church, the world, all your friends, all your wants, and everything that everybody wants.

"What do you think of my short prayers? This morning all I could ejaculate was: 'Lord, this is thy day, every minute of it.' I have had some blessed minutes. When the sinner prayed, 'Lord, be merciful to me a sinner,' he did not add, 'and bless my father and mother, brothers and sisters, and all the sick and sinful and sorrowing, and send missionaries to all parts of the world, and hasten thy kingdom in every heart.' And when Peter was sinking he cried: 'Lord, save me, I perish,' and did not add, 'strengthen my faith for this time and all time, and remember those who are in the ship looking on, and wondering what will be the end of this; teach them to profit by my example, and to learn the lesson thou art intending to teach by this failure of mine.' And when the ship was almost overwhelmed and the frightened disciples came to him—but why should I go on? Child, *pour* out your heart to him, and when, through physical weariness, mental exhaustion, or spiritual intensity of feeling, the heart refuses to be longer poured out, *stop*, don't pump and pump and *pump* at an exhausted well for water that has been all used up. We are not heard for much speaking or long praying. Study the prayer he gave us to pray, study his own prayer. He continued all night in prayer but he was not hard upon his weak disciples, who through weariness and sorrow fell asleep while he had strength to keep on praying. Your master is not a hard master. We pray when we do not utter one word. Let the Spirit pray in you and don't try to do it all yourself. Don't make crosses for yourself. Before you begin to pray think of the loving, lovely Saviour and pitiful Father you are praying to and ask the Spirit to help you pray, and then pray and be joyful. Pray the first petition that comes out of your heart, and then the second and the third, and thank him for everything.

"But here come the girls laughing upstairs and I must listen to the story of their afternoon. Linnet will tell you about the pictures.

"More than ever your sympathizing friend,

"*P. P.*"

* * * * *

"*Feb.* 2, 18—.

"DEAR HOLLIS:

"Your mother asked me to write to you while I am here, in your home, so that it may seem like a letter from her. It is evening and I am writing at the kitchen table with the light of one candle. How did I come to be here at night? I came over this afternoon to see poor grandma and found your mother alone with her; grandma had been in bed three days and the doctor said she was dying of old age. She did not appear to suffer, she lay very still, recognizing us, but not speaking even when we spoke to her.

"How I did want to say something to help her, for I was afraid she might be troubled, she was always so 'afraid' when she thought about joining the Church. But as I stood alone, looking down at her, I did not dare speak. I did not like to awaken her if she were comfortably asleep. Then I thought how wicked I was to withhold a word when she might hear it and be comforted and her fear taken away, so I stooped over and said close to her ear, 'Grandma,' and all she answered was, in her old way, 'Most a hundred;' and then I said, '"The blood of Jesus Christ cleanseth from all sin, even the sins of most a hundred years;"' and she understood, for she moaned, 'I've been very wicked;' and all I could do was to say again, '"The blood of Jesus Christ cleanseth from all sin."' She made no reply and we think she did not speak again, for your mother's cousin, Cynthy, was with her at the last and says she bent over her and found that she did not breathe, and all the time she was with her she did not once speak.

"The house is so still, they all move around so softly and speak in whispers. Your mother thinks you may be in Philadelphia or Baltimore when this reaches New York, and that you will not hear in time to come to the funeral. I hope you can come; she does *so* want to see you. She says once a year is so seldom to see her youngest boy. I believe I haven't seen you since the day you brought me the plate so long, so long ago. I've been away both times since when you were home. I have kept my promise, I think; I do not think I have missed one letter day in writing to you. I have come to see your mother as often as I could. Grandma will not be buried till the fifth; they have decided upon that day hoping you can get here by that time. Morris was to come for me if I did not get home before dark and there's the sound of sleigh bells now. Here comes your mother with her message. She says: 'Tell Hollis to come if he *any way* can; I shall look for him.' So I know you will.

"That *is* Morris, he is stamping the snow off his feet at the door. Why do you write such short letters to me? Are mine too long? O, Hollis, I want you to be a Christian; I pray for you every day.

"Your friend,

"MARJORIE"

* * * * *

"Feb 15, 18—.

"MY DARLING LINNET:

"Now I am settled down for a long letter to you, up here in the master's chamber, where no one will dare interrupt me. I am sitting on the rug before the fire with my old atlas on my lap; his desk with piles of foolscap is so near that when my own sheet gives out, and my thoughts and incidents are still unexhausted, all I have to do is to raise the cover of his desk, take a fresh sheet and begin again. I want this to be the kind of a three-volumed letter that you like; I have inspiration enough—for I am surrounded by books containing the wisdom of all the past. No story books, and I know you want a story letter. This room is as cozy as the inside of an egg shell, with only the fire, the clock, the books and myself. There is nothing but snow, snow, snow, out the window, and promise of more in the threatening sky. I am all alone to-day, too, and I may be alone to-night. I rather like the adventure of staying alone; perhaps something will happen that never happened to any one before, and I may live to tell the tale to my grandchildren. It is early in the morning, that is, early to be writing a letter, but I shall not have much dinner to get for myself and I want to write letters all day. *That* is an adventure that never happened to me before. How do you think it happens that I am alone? Of course Morris and the master have taken their dinners and gone to school; mother has been in Portland four days, and father is to go for her to-day and bring her home to-morrow; Morris is to go skating to-night and to stay in Middlefield with some of the boys; and I told Mr. Holmes that he might go to the lecture on Turkey and stay in Middlefield, too, if he would give my note to Josie Grey and ask her to come down after school and stay with me. He said he would come home unless she promised to come to stay with me, so I don't suppose I shall have my adventurous night alone, after all.

"I don't believe father has gone yet, I heard his step down-stairs, I'll run down to say good-bye again and see if he wants anything, and go down cellar and get me some apples to munch on to keep me from being lonesome. Father will take the horses and they will not need to be fed, and I told Morris I could feed the two cows and the hens myself, so he need not come home just for that. But father is calling me.

"Afternoon. Is it years and *years* since I began this letter? My hair has not turned white and I am not an old woman; the ink and paper look fresh, too, fresher than the old bit of yellow paper that mother keeps so preciously, that has written on it the invitation to her mother's wedding that somebody returned to her. How slowly I am coming to it! But I want to keep you in suspense. I am up in the master's chamber again, sitting on the hearth before a snapping fire, and I haven't written one word since I wrote you that father was calling me.

"He did call me, and I ran down and found that he wanted an extra shawl for mother; for it might be colder to-morrow, or it might be a snow-storm. I stood at the window and saw him pass and listened to the jingling of his bells until they were out of hearing, and then I lighted a bit of a candle (ah, me, that it was not longer) and went down cellar for my apples. I opened one barrel and then another until I found the ones I wanted, the tender green ones that you used to like; I filled my basket and, just then hearing the back door open and a step in the entry over my head, I turned quickly and pushed my candlestick over, and, of course, that wee bit of light sputtered out. I was frightened, for fear a spark might have fallen among the straw somewhere, and spent some time feeling around to find the candlestick and to wait to see if a spark *had* lighted the straw; and then, before I could cry out, I heard the footsteps pass the door and give it a pull and turn the key! Father always does that, but this was not father. I believe it was Captain Rheid, father left a message for him and expected him to call, and I suppose, out of habit, as he passed the door he shut it and locked it. I could not shout in time, he was so quick about it, and then he went out and shut the outside door hard.

"I think I turned to stone for awhile, or fainted away, but when I came to myself there I stood, with the candlestick in my hand, all in the dark. I could not think what to do. I could not find the outside doors, they are trap doors, you know, and have to be pushed up, and in winter the steps are taken down, and I don't know where they are put. I had the candle, it is true, but I had no match. I don't know what I did do. My first thought was to prowl around and find the steps and push up one of the doors, and I prowled and prowled and prowled till I was worn out. The windows—small windows, too,—are filled up with straw or something in winter, so that it was as dark as a dungeon; it *was* a dungeon and I was a prisoner.

"If I hadn't wanted the apples, or if the light hadn't gone out, or if Captain Rheid hadn't come, or if he hadn't locked the door! Would I have to stay till Josie came? And if I pounded and screamed wouldn't she be frightened and run away?

"After prowling around and hitting myself and knocking myself I stood still again and wondered what to do! I wanted to scream and cry, but that wouldn't have done any good and I should have felt more alone than ever afterward. Nobody could come there to hurt me, that was certain, and I could stamp the rats away, and there were apples and potatoes and turnips to eat? But suppose it had to last all night! I was too frightened to waste any tears, and too weak to stand up, by this time, so I found a seat on the stairs and huddled myself together to keep warm, and prayed as hard as I ever did in my life.

"I thought about Peter in prison; I thought about everything I could think of. I could hear the clock strike and that would help me bear it, I should know when night came and when morning came. The cows would suffer, too, unless father had thrown down hay enough for them; and the fires would go out, and what would father and mother think when they came home to-morrow? Would I frighten them by screaming and pounding? Would I add to my cold, and have quinsy sore throat again? Would I faint away and never 'come to'? When I wrote 'adventure' upstairs by the master's fire I did not mean a dreadful thing like this! Staying alone all night was nothing compared to this. I had never been through anything compared to this. I tried to comfort myself by thinking that I might be lost or locked up in a worse place; it was not so damp or cold as it might have been, and there was really nothing to be afraid of. I had nothing to do and I was in the dark. I began to think of all the stories I knew about people who had been imprisoned and what they had done. I couldn't write a Pilgrim's Progress, I couldn't even make a few rhymes, it was too lonesome; I couldn't sing, my voice stopped in my throat. I thought about somebody who was in a dark, solitary prison, and he had one pin that he used to throw about and lose and then crawl around and find it in the dark and then lose it again and crawl around again and find it. I had prowled around enough for the steps; that amusement had lost its attraction for me. And then the clock struck. I counted eleven, but had I missed one stroke? Or counted too many? It was not nine when I lighted that candle. Well, that gave me something to reason about, and something new to look forward to. How many things could I do in an hour? How many could I count? How many Bible verses could I repeat? Suppose I began with A and repeated all I could think of, and then went on to B. 'Ask, and ye shall receive.' How I did ask God to let me out in some way, to bring somebody to help me? To *send* somebody. Would not Captain Rheid come back again? Would not Morris change his mind and come home to dinner? or at night? And would Mr. Holmes certainly go to hear that lecture? Wasn't there anybody to come? I thought about you and how sorry you would be, and, I must confess it, I did think that I would have something to write to you and Hollis about. (Please let him see this letter; I don't want to write all this over again.)

"So I shivered and huddled myself up in a heap and tried to comfort myself and amuse myself as best I could. I said all the Bible verses I could think, and then I went back to my apples and brought the basket with me to the stairs. I would not eat one potato or turnip until the apples had given out. You think I can laugh now; so could you, after you had got out. But the clock didn't strike, and nobody came, and I was sure it must be nearly morning I was so faint with hunger and so dizzy from want of sleep. And then it occurred to me to stumble up the stairs and try to burst the door open! That lock was loose, it turned very easily! In an instant I was up the stairs and trying the door. And, lo, and behold, it opened easily, it was not locked at all! I had only imagined I heard the click of the lock. And I was free, and the sun was shining, and I was neither hungry nor dizzy.

"I don't know whether I laughed or cried or mingled both in a state of ecstasy. But I was too much shaken to go on with my letter, I had to find a story book and a piece of apple pie to quiet my nerves. The fires were not out and the clock had only struck ten. But when you ask me how long I stayed in that cellar I shall tell you one hundred years! Now, isn't that adventure enough for the first volume?

"Vol. II. Evening. I waited and waited downstairs for somebody to come, but nobody came except Josie Grey's brother, to say that her mother was taken ill suddenly and Josie could not come. I suppose Mr. Holmes expected her to come and so he has gone to Middlefield, and Morris thought so, too; and so I am left out in the cold, or rather in by the fire. Mr. Holmes' chamber is the snuggest room in the house, so full of books that you can't be lonely in it, and then the fire on the hearth is company. It began to snow before sun down and now the wind howls and the snow seems to rush about as if it were in a fury. You ask what I have read this winter. Books that you will not like: Thomson's 'Seasons,' Cowper's 'Task,' Pollok's 'Course of Time,' Milton's 'Paradise Regained,' Strickland's 'Queens of England,' 'Nelson on Infidelity,' 'Lady Huntington and her Friends,' 'Lady of the Lake,' several of the 'Bridgewater Treatises,' Paley's 'Natural Theology,' 'Trench on Miracles,' several dozens of the best story books I could find to make sandwiches with the others, somebody's 'Travels in Iceland,' and somebody's 'Winter in Russia,' and 'Rasselas,' and 'Boswell's Johnson,' and I cannot remember others at this moment. Morris says I do not think anything dry, but go right through everything. Because I have the master to help me, and I did give 'Paradise Lost' up in despair. Mother says I shall never make three quilts for you if I read so much, but I do get on with the patch work and she already has one quilt joined, and Mrs. Rheid is coming to help her quilt it next week. There is a pile of blocks on the master's desk now and I intend to sit here in his arm chair and sew until I am sleepy. I wonder if you will do as much for me when my Prince comes. Mine is to be as handsome as Hollis, as good as Morris, as learned as the master, and as devoted as your splendid Will. And if I cannot find all these in one I will—make patch work for other brides and live alone with Miss Prudence. And I'll begin now to make the patch work. Oh, dear, I wish you and Miss Prudence were here. Hark! there's somebody pounding on the outside kitchen door! Shall I go down or let them pound? I don't believe it is Robin Hood or any of his merry men, do you? I'll screw my courage up and go.

"Vol. III. Next Day. I won't keep you in suspense, you dear, sympathetic Linnet. I went down with some inward quaking but much outward boldness as the pounding increased, and did not even ask 'Who's there?' before I opened the door. But I *was* relieved to find Morris, covered with snow, looking like a storm king. He said he had heard through Frank Grey that Josie couldn't come and he would not let me stay alone in a storm. I was so glad, if I had been you I should have danced around him, but as it was I and not you I only said how glad I was, and made him a cup of steaming coffee and gave him a piece of mince pie for being so good. To-day it snows harder than ever, so that we do not expect father and mother; and Mr. Holmes has not come out in the storm, because Morris saw him and told him that he was on the way home. Not a sleigh has passed, we have not seen a single human being to-day. I could not have got out to the stable, and I don't know what the cows and hens would have done without Morris. He has thrown down more hay for the cows, and put corn where the hens may find it for to-morrow, in case he cannot get out to them. The storm has not lessened in any degree; I never knew anything like it, but I am not the 'oldest inhabitant.' Wouldn't I have been dreary here alone?

"This does seem to be a kind of adventure, but nothing happens. Father is not strong enough to face any kind of a storm, and I am sure they will not attempt to start. Morris says we are playing at housekeeping and he helps me do everything, and when I sit down to sew on your patch work he reads to me. I let him read this letter to you, forgetting what I had said about my Prince, but he only laughed and said he was glad that he was *good* enough for me, even if he were not handsome enough, or learned enough, or devoted enough, and said he would become devoted forthwith, but he could not ever expect to attain to the rest. He teases me and says that I meant that the others were not good enough. He has had a letter from Will promising to take him before the mast next voyage and he is hilarious over it. His mother tries to be satisfied, but she is afraid of the water. When so many that we know have lost father or brother or husband on the sea it does seem strange that we can so fearlessly send another out. Mrs. Rheid told me about a sea captain that she met when she was on a voyage with Captain Rheid. He had been given up for lost when he was young and when he came back he found his wife married to another man, but she gave up the second husband and went back to the first. She was dead when Mrs. Rheid met him; she said he was a very sad man. His ship was wrecked on some coast, I've forgotten where, and he was made to work in a mine until he was rescued. I think I would have remained dead to her if she had forgotten me like that. But isn't this a long letter? Morris has made me promise to write regularly to him; I told him he had never given me a Holland plate two hundred years old, but he says he will go to Holland and buy me one and that is better.

"I am glad Hollis wrote such a long letter to his mother if he could not come home. I wish he would write to her oftener; I do not think she is quite satisfied to have him write to me instead. I will write to him to-morrow, but I haven't anything to say, I have told you everything. O, Linnet, how happy I shall be when your school days are over. Miss Prudence shall have the next letter; I have something to ask her, as usual.

"The end of my story in three volumes isn't very startling. But this snow-storm is. If we hadn't everything under cover we would have to do without some things.

"Yours,

"MARJORIE"

XIII.

A WEDDING DAY.

"A world-without-end bargain."—*Shakespeare.*

A young girl stood in the doorway, shading her eyes with her hand as she gazed down the dusty road; she was not tall or slight, but a plump, well-proportioned little creature, with frank, steadfast eyes, a low, smooth forehead with brown hair rippling away from it, a thoughtful mouth that matched well with the eyes; an energetic maiden, despite the air of study that somehow surrounded her; you were sure her voice would be sweet, and as sure that it would be sprightly, and you were equally sure that a wealth of strength was hidden behind the sweetness. She was only eighteen, eighteen to-day, but during the last two years she had rapidly developed into womanhood. The master told Miss Prudence this morning that she was trustworthy and guileless, and as sweet and bright as she was good; still, he believed, as of old, that she did not quite know how to take her own part; but, as a woman, with a man to fight for her, what need had she of fighting? He would not have been at all surprised had he known that she had chosen, that morning, a motto, not only for her new year, but, as she told Morris, for her lifetime: "The Lord shall fight for you, and ye shall hold your peace." And he had said: "May I fight for you, too, Marjorie?" But she had only laughed and answered: "We don't live in the time of the Crusades."

Although it was Linnet's wedding day Marjorie, the bridesmaid, was attired in a gingham, a pretty pink and white French gingham; but there were white roses at her throat and one nestled in her hair. The roses were the gift of the groomsman, Hollis, and she had fastened them in under the protest of Morris' eyes. Will and Linnet had both desired Hollis to "stand up" with Marjorie; the bridesmaid had been very shy about it, at first; Hollis was almost a stranger, she had seen him but once since she was fourteen, and their letters were becoming more and more distant. He was not as shy as Marjorie, but he was not easy and at home with her, and never once dared to address the maiden who had so suddenly sprung into a lovely woman with the old names, Mousie, or Goosie. Indeed, he had nearly forgotten them, he could more readily have said: "Miss Marjorie."

He had grown very tall; he was the handsomest among the brothers, with an air of refinement and courtesy that somewhat perplexed them and set him apart from them. Marjorie still prayed for him every day, that is, for the Hollis she knew, but this Hollis came to her to-day a stranger; her school-boy friend was a dream, the friend she had written to so long was only her ideal, and this tall man, with the golden-red moustache, dark, soft eyes and deep voice, was a fascinating stranger from the outside world. She could never write to him again; she would never have the courage.

And his heart quickened in its beating as he stood beside the white-robed figure and looked down into the familiar, strange face, and he wondered how his last letter could have been so jaunty and off-hand. How could he ever write "Dear Marjorie" again, with this face in his memory? She was as much a lady as Helen had been, he would be proud to take her among his friends and say: "This is my old school friend."

But he was busy bringing chairs across the field at this moment and Marjorie stood alone in the doorway looking down the dusty road. This doorway was a fitting frame for such a rustic picture as a girl in a gingham dress, and the small house itself a fitting background.

The house was a story and a half, with a low, projecting roof, a small entry in the centre, and square, low-studded rooms on both sides, a kitchen and woodshed stretched out from the back and a small barn stood in the rear; the house was dazzling in the sun, with its fresh coat of white paint, and the green blinds gave a cooling effect to the whole; the door yard was simply a carpet of green with lilac bushes in one corner and a tall pine standing near the gate; the fence rivalled the house in its glossy whiteness, and even the barn in the rear had a new coat of brown to boast of. Every room inside the small house was in perfect order, every room was furnished with comfort and good taste, but plainly as it became the house of the captain of the barque *Linnet* to be. It was all ready for housekeeping, but, instead of taking instant possession, at the last moment Linnet had decided to go with her husband to Genoa.

"It is nonsense," Captain Rheid growled, "when the house is all ready."
But Will's mother pleaded for him and gained an ungracious consent.

"You never run around after me so," he said.

"Go to sea to-day and see what I will do," she answered, and he kissed her for the first time in so many years that she blushed like a girl and hurried away to see if the tea-kettle were boiling.

Linnet's mother was disappointed, for she wanted to see Linnet begin her pretty housekeeping; but Marjorie declared that it was as it should be and quite according to the Old Testament law of the husband cheering up his wife.

But Marjorie did not stay very long to make a picture of herself, she ran back to see if Morris had counted right in setting the plates on the long dining table that was covered with a heavy cloth of grandma's own making. There was a silk quilt of grandma's making on the bed in the "spare room" beside. As soon as the ceremony was performed she had run away with "the boys" to prepare the surprise for Linnet, a lunch in her own house. The turkeys and tongue and ham had been cooked at Mrs. Rheid's, and Linnet had seen only the cake and biscuits prepared at home, the fruit had come with Hollis from New York at Miss Prudence's order, and the flowers had arrived this morning by train from Portland. Cake and sandwiches, lemonade and coffee, would do very well, Linnet said, who had no thought of feasting, and the dining room at home was the only banqueting hall she had permitted herself to dream of.

Marjorie counted the chairs as Hollis brought them across the field from home, and then her eyes filled as he drew from his pocket, to show her, the deed of the house and ten acres of land, the wedding present from his father to the bride.

"Oh, he's too good," she cried. "Linnet will break down, I know she will."

"I asked him if he would be as good to my wife," answered Hollis, "and he said he would, if I would please him as well as Will had done."

"There's only one Linnet," said Marjorie.

"But bride's have sisters," said Morris. "Marjorie, where shall I put all this jelly? And I haven't missed one plate with a bouquet, have I? Now count everybody up again and see if we are all right."

"Marjorie and I," began Hollis, audaciously, pushing a chair into its place.

"Two," counted Morris, but his blue eyes flashed and his lip trembled.

"And Will and Linnet, four," began Marjorie, in needless haste, and father and mother, six, and Will's father and mother, eight, and the minister and his wife, ten, and Herbert and his wife, twelve, and Mr. Holmes and Miss Prudence, fourteen, and Sam and Harold, sixteen, and Morris, seventeen. That is all. Oh, and grandfather and grandmother, nineteen."

"Seventeen plates! You and I are to be waiters, Marjorie," said Morris.

"I'll be a waiter, too," said Hollis. "That will be best fun of all. I'm glad you didn't hire anybody, Marjorie."

"I wouldn't; I wanted to be primitive and do it all ourselves; I knew Morris would be grand help, but I was not so sure of you."

"Are you sure of me, now?" he laughed, like the old Hollis who used to go to school.

After that Marjorie would not have been surprised if he had called her "Mousie."

"Morris, what do you want to be a sailor for?" inquired Hollis, arranging the white rose in his button-hole anew.

"To sail," answered Morris seriously. "What do you want to be a salesman for?"

"To sell," said Hollis, as seriously, "Marjorie, what do you want to be yourself for?"

"To help you to be yourself," she answered promptly, and flew to the front door where there was a sound of shouting and laughter. They were all there, every one of the little home-made company; and the waiters ushered them into the kitchen, where the feast was spread, with great ceremony.

If Linnet had not been somebody's wife she would have danced around and clapped her hands with delight; as it was she nearly forgot her dignity, and exclaimed with surprise and pleasure sufficient to satisfy those who were in the secret of the feast.

Linnet was in her gray travelling suit, but the dash of crimson this time was in both cheeks; there was a haziness in her eyes that subdued the brightness of her face and touched them all. The bridegroom was handsome and proud, his own merry self, not a trifle abashed before them all on his wedding day, everything that he said seemed to be thought worth laughing at, and there was not a shadow on any face, except the flitting of a shadow ever and anon across Morris Kemlo's blue eyes.

The feast was ended, prayer offered by the pastor and the new home dedicated to him who is the Father in every home where his children dwell, and then kisses and congratulations and thanks mingled with the tears that the mothers must need shed out of their joy and natural regret. The mothers were both exultantly proud and sure that *her* child would not be the one to make the other unhappy. The carriages rolled away, Will and Linnet to take the train to Portland, for if the wind were fair the *Linnet* would sail the next day for New York and thence to Genoa. Linnet had promised to bring Marjorie some of the plastering of the chamber in which Christopher Columbus was born, and if they went down to Naples she would surely climb Mt. Vesuvius and bring her a branch of mulberry.

The mothers remained to wash the dishes and pack things away, to lock up the house, and brush the last flake of dust from any of Linnet's new possessions; Captain Rheid called to Hollis and asked him to walk over the farm with him and see where everything was planted. Hollis was to remain over night, but Morris was to take a late train to join the *Linnet's* crew, it being his first voyage as second mate.

The mothers took off their kitchen aprons, washed their hands at Linnet's new sink, and gave Morris the key of the front door to hang up in an out-of-the-way corner of the wood shed.

"It may better be here," said Mrs. Rheid, "and then any of us can get in at any time to see how things are without troubling anybody to find the key. The captain will see that every door and window is safe and as we have the silver I don't believe anybody will think of troubling the house."

"Oh, dear no," replied Mrs. West. "I always leave my clothes out on the line and we never think of locking a door at night."

"Our kitchen windows look over this way and I shall always be looking over. Now come home with me and see that quilt I haven't got finished yet for them. I told your husband to come to our house for you, for you would surely be there. I suppose Marjorie and Morris will walk back; we wouldn't have minded it, either, on our eighteenth birthday."

"Come, Marjorie, come see where I hang the key," said Morris.

Marjorie followed him down the kitchen steps, across the shed to a corner at the farther end; he found a nail and slipped it on and then asked her to reach it.

Even standing on tip toe her upstretched hand could not touch it.

"See how I put the key of my heart out of your reach," he said, seriously.

"And see how I stretch after it," she returned, demurely.

"I will come with you and reach it for you."

"How can you when you are demolishing plaster in Christopher Columbus' house or falling into the crater of Mt. Vesuvius? I may want to come here that very day."

"True; I will put it lower for you. Shall I put it under this stone so that you will have to stoop for it?"

"Mrs. Rheid said hang it over the window, that has been its place for generations. They lived here when they were first married, before they built their own house; the house doesn't look like it, does it? It is all made over new. I am glad he gave it to Will."

"He can build a house for Hollis," said he, watching her as he spoke.

"Let me see you put the key there," she returned, unconcernedly.

He hung the key on the nail over the small window and inquired if it were done to her satisfaction.

"Yes," she said. "I wonder how Linnet feels about going away from us all so far."

"She is with her husband," answered Morris. "Aren't you woman enough to understand that?"

"Possibly I am as much of a woman as you are."

"You are years ahead of me; a girl at eighteen is a woman; but a boy at eighteen is a boy. Will you tell me something out here among the wood? This wood pile that the old captain sawed and split ten years ago shall be our witness. Why do you suppose he gets up in winter before daylight and splits wood—when he has a pile that was piled up twenty years ago?"

"That is a question worthy the time and place and the wood pile shall be our witness."

"Oh, that isn't the question," he returned with some embarrassment, stooping to pick up a chip and toss it from him as he lifted himself. "Marjorie, *do* you like Hollis better than you like me?"

"You are only a boy, you know," she answered, roguishly.

"I know it; but do you like me better than Hollis?"

His eyes were on the chips at his feet, Marjorie's serious eyes were upon him.

"It doesn't matter; suppose I don't know; as the question never occurred to me before I shall have to consider."

"Marjorie, you are cruel," he exclaimed raising his eyes with a flash in them; he was "only a boy" but his lips were as white as a man's would have been.

"I am sorry; I didn't know you were in such earnest," she said, penitently. "I like Hollis, of course, I cannot remember when I did not like him, but I am not acquainted with him."

"Are you acquainted with me?" he asked in a tone that held a shade of relief.

"Oh, you!" she laughed lightly, "I know what you think before you can speak your thought."

"Then you know what I am thinking now."

"Not all of it," she returned, but she colored, notwithstanding, and stepped backward toward the kitchen.

"Marjorie," he caught her hand and held it, "I am going away and I want to tell you something. I am going far away this time, and I must tell you. Do you remember the day I came? You were such a little thing, you stood at the kitchen sink washing dishes, with your sleeves rolled back and a big apron up to your neck, and you stopped in your work and looked at me and your eyes were so soft and sorry. And I have loved you better than anybody every day since. Every day I have thought: 'I will study like Marjorie. I will be good like Marjorie. I will help everybody like Marjorie.'"

She looked up into his eyes, her own filled with tears.

"I am so glad I have helped you so."

"And will you help me further by saying that you like me better than Hollis."

"Oh, I do, you know I do," she cried, impulsively. "I am not acquainted with him, and I know every thought you think."

"Now I am satisfied," he cried, exultantly, taking both her hands in his and kissing her lips. "I am not afraid to go away now."

"Marjorie,"—the kitchen door was opened suddenly,—"I'm going to take your mother home with me. Is the key in the right place."

"Everything is all right, Mrs. Rheid," replied Morris. "You bolt that door and we will go out this way."

The door was closed as suddenly and the boy and girl stood silent, looking at each other.

"Your Morris Kemlo is a fine young man," observed Mrs. Rheid as she pushed the bolt into its place.

"He is a heartease to his mother," replied Mrs. West, who was sometimes poetical.

"Does Marjorie like him pretty well?"

"Why, yes, we all do. He is like our own flesh and blood. But why did you ask?"

"Oh, nothing. I just thought of it."

"I thought you meant something, but you couldn't when you know how Hollis has been writing to her these four years."

"Oh!" ejaculated Hollis' mother.

She did not make plans for her children as the other mother did.

The two old ladies crossed the field toward the substantial white farmhouse that overlooked the little cottage, and the children, whose birthday it was, walked hand in hand through the yard to the footpath along the road.

"Must you keep on writing to Hollis?" he asked.

"I suppose so. Why not? It is my turn to write now."

"That's all nonsense."

"What is? Writing in one's turn?"

"I don't see why you need write at all."

"Don't you remember I promised before you came?"

"But I've come now," he replied in a tone intended to be very convincing.

"His mother would miss it, if I didn't write; she thinks she can't write letters. And I like his letters," she added frankly.

"I suppose you do. I suppose you like them better than mine," with an assertion hardly a question in his voice.

"They are so different. His life is so different from yours. But he is shy, as shy as a girl, and does not tell me all the things you do. Your letters are more interesting, but *he* is more interesting—as a study. You are a lesson that I have learned, but I have scarcely begun to learn him."

"That is very cold blooded when you are talking about human beings."

"My brain was talking then."

"Suppose you let your heart speak."

"My heart hasn't anything to say; it is not developed yet."

"I don't believe it," he answered angrily.

"Then you must find it out for yourself. Morris, I don't want to be *in love* with anybody, if that's what you mean. I love you dearly, but I am not in love with you or with anybody."

"You don't know the difference," he said quickly.

"How do you know the difference? Did you learn it before I was born?"

"I love my mother, but I am in love with you; that's the difference."

"Then I don't know the difference—and I do. I love my dear father and Mr. Holmes and you,—not all alike, but I need you all at different times—"

"And Hollis," he persisted.

"I do not know him," she insisted. "I have nothing to say about that. Morris, I want to go with Miss Prudence and study; I don't want to be a housekeeper and have a husband, like Linnet! I have so much to learn; I am eager for everything. You see you *are* older than I am."

"Yes," he said, disappointedly, "you are only a little girl yet. Or you are growing up to be a Woman's Rights Woman, and to think a 'career' is better than a home and a man who is no better than other men to love you and protect you and provide for you."

"You know that is not true," she answered quietly; "but I have been looking forward so long to going to school."

"And living with Miss Prudence and becoming like her!"

"Don't you want me to be like her?"

"No," he burst out. "I want you to be like Linnet, and to think that little house and house-keeping, and a good husband, good enough for you. What is the good of studying if it doesn't make you more a perfect woman? What is the good of anything a girl does if it doesn't help her to be a woman?"

"Miss Prudence is a perfect woman."

Marjorie's tone was quiet and reasonable, but there was a fire in her eyes that shone only when she was angry.

"She would be more perfect if she stayed at home in Maple Street and made a home for somebody than she is now, going hither and thither finding people to be kind to and to help. She is too restless and she is not satisfied. Look at Linnet; she is happier to-day with her husband that reads only the newspapers, the nautical books, and his Bible, than Miss Prudence with all her lectures and concerts and buying books and knowing literary people! She couldn't make a Miss Prudence out of Linnet, but she will make a Miss Prudence twice over out of you."

"Linnet is happy because she loves Will, and she doesn't care for books and people, as we do; but we haven't any Will, poor Miss Prudence and poor Marjorie, we have to substitute people and books."

"You might have, both of you!" he went on, excitedly; "but you want something better, both of you,—*higher*, I suppose you think! There's Mr. Holmes eating his heart out with being only a friend to Miss Prudence, and you want me to go poking along and spoiling my life as he does, because you like books and study better!"

Marjorie laughed; the fire in Morris' blue eyes was something to see, and the tears in his voice would have overcome her had she not laughed instead. And he was going far away, too.

"Morris, I didn't know you were quite such a volcano. I don't believe Mr. Holmes stays here and *pokes* because of Miss Prudence. I know he is melancholy, sometimes, but he writes so much and thinks so much he can't be light-hearted like young things like us. And who does as much good as Miss Prudence? Isn't she another mother to Linnet and me? And if she doesn't find somebody to love as Linnet does Will, I don't see how she can help it."

"It isn't in her heart or she would have found somebody; it is what is in peoples' hearts that makes the difference! But when they keep the brain at work and forget they have any heart, as you two do—"

"It isn't Miss Prudence's brain that does her beautiful work. You ought to read some of the letters that she lets me read, and then you would see how much heart she has!"

"And you want to be just like her," he sighed, but the sigh was almost a groan.

Certainly, in some experiences he had outstripped Marjorie.

"Yes, I want to be like her," she answered deliberately.

"And study and go around and do good and never be married?" he questioned.

"I don't see the need of deciding that question to-day."

"I suppose not. You will when Hollis Rheid asks you to."

"Morris, you are not like yourself to-day, you are quarrelling with me, and we never quarrelled before."

"Because you are so unreasonable; you will not answer me anything."

"I have answered you truly; I have no other answer to give."

"Will you think and answer me when I come home?"

"I have answered you now."

"Perhaps you will have another answer then."

"Well, if I have I will give it to you. Are you satisfied?"

"No," he said; but he turned her face up to his and looked down into her innocent earnest eyes.

"You are a goosie, as Linnet says; you will never grow up, little Marjorie."

"Then, if I am only eight, you must not talk to me as if I were eighty."

"Or eighteen," he said. "How far on the voyage of life do you suppose Linnet and Captain Will are."

"Not far enough on to quarrel, I hope."

"They will never be far enough for that, Will is too generous and Linnet will never find anything to differ about; do you know, Marjorie, that girl has no idea how Will loves her?"

Marjorie stopped and faced him with the utmost gravity.

"Do you know, Morris, that man has no idea how Linnet loves him?"

And then the two burst into a laugh that restored them both to the perfect understanding of themselves and each other and all the world. And after an early supper he shook hands with them all—excepting "Mother West," whom he kissed, and Marjorie, whom he asked to walk as far as "Linnet's" with him on his way to the train—and before ten o'clock was on board the *Linnet*, and congratulating again the bridegroom, who was still radiant, and the bride, who was not looking in the least bit homesick.

"Will," said Linnet with the weight of tone of one giving announcement to a mighty truth, "I wouldn't be any one beside myself for *anything*."

"And I wouldn't have you any one beside yourself for *anything*," he laughed, in the big, explosive voice that charmed Linnet every time afresh.

XIV.

A TALK AND ANOTHER TALK.

"Life's great results are something slow."—Howells.

Morris had said good-bye with a look that brought sorrow enough in Marjorie's eyes to satisfy him—almost, and had walked rapidly on, not once turning to discover if Marjorie were standing still or moving toward home; Mr. Holmes and Miss Prudence had promised to start out to meet her, so that her walk homeward in the starlight would not be lonely.

But they were not in sight yet to Marjorie's vision, and she stood leaning over the gate looking at the windows with their white shades dropped and already feeling that the little, new home was solitary. She did not turn until a footstep paused behind her; she was so lost in dreams of Linnet and Morris that she had not noticed the brisk, hurried tread. The white rose had fallen from her hair and the one at her throat had lost several petals; in her hand was a bunch of daisies that Morris had picked along the way and laughingly asked her to try the childish trick of finding out if he loved her, and she had said she was afraid the daisies were too wise and would not ask them.

"Haven't you been home all this time?" asked Hollis, startling her out of her dream.

"Oh, yes, and come back again."

"Do you find the cottage so charming?"

"I find it charming, but I could have waited another day to come and see it. I came to walk part of the way with Morris."

She colored, because when she was embarrassed she colored at everything, and could not think of another word to say.

Among those who understood him, rather, among those he understood, Hollis was a ready talker; but, seemingly, he too could not think of another word to say.

Marjorie picked her daisies to pieces and they went on in the narrow foot path, as she and Morris had done in the afternoon; Hollis walking on the grass and giving her the path as her other companion had done. She could think of everything to say to Morris, and Morris could think of everything to say to her; but Morris was only a boy, and this tall stranger was a gentleman, a gentleman whom she had never seen before.

"If it were good sleighing I might take you on my sled," he remarked, when all the daisies were pulled to pieces.

"Is Flyaway in existence still?" she asked brightly, relieved that she might speak at last.

"'Stowed away,' as father says, in the barn, somewhere. Mr. Holmes is not as strict as he used to be, is he?"

"No, he never was after that. I think he needed to give a lesson to himself."

"He looks haggard and old."

"I suppose he is old; I don't know how old he is, over forty."

"That *is* antiquated. You will be forty yourself, if you live long enough."

"Twenty-two years," she answered seriously; "that is time enough to do a good many things in."

"I intend to do a good many things," he answered with a proud humility in his voice that struck Marjorie.

"What—for example?"

"Travel, for one thing, make money, for another."

"What do you want money for?" she questioned.

"What does any man want it for? I want it to give me influence, and I want a luxurious old age."

"That doesn't strike me as being the highest motives."

"Probably not, but perhaps the highest motives, as you call them, do not rule my life."

And she had been praying for him so long.

"Your mother seems to be a happy woman," was her reply, coming out of a thought that she did not speak.

"She is," he said, emphatically. "I wish poor old father were as happy."

"Do you find many happy people?" she asked.

"I find you and my mother," he returned smiling.

"And yourself?"

"Not always. I am happy enough today. Not as jubilant as old Will, though. Will has a prize."

"To be sure he has," said Marjorie.

"What are you going to do next?"

"Go to that pleasant home in Maple Street with Miss Prudence and go to school." She was jubilant, too, today, or she would have been if Morris had not gone away with such a look in his eyes.

"You ought to be graduated by this time, you are old enough. Helen was not as old as you."

"But I haven't been at school at all, yet," she hastened to say. "And Helen was so bright."

"Aren't you bright?" he asked, laughing.

"Mr. Holmes doesn't tell me that I am."

"What will your mother do?"

"Oh, dear," she sighed, "that is what I ask myself every day. But she insists that I shall go, Linnet has had her 'chance' she says, and now it is my turn. Miss Prudence is always finding somebody that needs a home, and she has found a girl to help mother, a girl about my age, that hasn't any friends, so it isn't the work that will trouble me; it is leaving mother without any daughter at all."

"She is willing to let Linnet go, she ought to be as willing to let you."

"Oh, she is, and father is, too. I know I don't deserve such good times, but I do want to go. I love Miss Prudence as much as I do mother, I believe, and I am only forty miles from home. Mr. Holmes is about leaving, too. How father will miss *him*! And Morris gone! Mother sighs over the changes and then says changes must needs come if boys and girls will grow up."

"Where is Mr. Holmes going?"

"To California. The doctor says he must go somewhere to cure his cough. And he says he will rest and write another book. Have you read his book?"

"No, it is too dry for me."

"We don't think it is dry; Morris and I know it by heart."

"That is because you know the author."

"Perhaps it is. The book is everything but a story book. Miss Prudence has a copy in Turkey morocco. Do you see many people that write books?"

"No," he said, smiling at her simplicity. "New York isn't full of them."

"Miss Prudence sees them," replied Marjorie with dignity.

"She is a bird of their feather. I do not fly, I walk on the ground—with my eyes on it, perhaps."

"Like the man with the muck rake," said Marjorie, quoting from her old love, *Pilgrims Progress*, "don't you know there was a crown held above his head, and his eyes were on the ground and he could not see it."

"No, I do not know it, but I perceive that you are talking an allegory at me."

"Not at you, *to* you," she corrected.

"You write very short letters to me, nowadays."

"Your letters are not suggestive enough," she said, archly.

"Like my conversation. As poor a talker as I am, I am a better talker than writer. And you—you write a dozen times better than you talk."

"I'm sorry I'm so unentertaining to-night. When Linnet writes she says: "'I wish I could *talk* to you,' and when I talk I think: 'I wish I could write it all to you.'"

"As some one said of some one who could write better than he talked, 'He has plenty of bank notes, but he carries no small change, in his pocket.'"

"It is so apt to be too small," she answered, somewhat severely.

"I see you are above talking the nonsense that some girls talk. What do you do to get rested from your thoughts?"

How Marjorie laughed!

"Hollis, do talk to me instead of writing. And I'll write to you instead of talking."

"That is, you wish me near to you and yourself far away from me. That is the only way that we can satisfy each other. Isn't that Miss Prudence coming?"

"And the master. They did not know I would have an escort home. But do come all the way, father will like to hear you talk about the places you have visited."

"I travel, I don't visit places. I expect to go to London and Paris by and by. Our buyer has been getting married and that doesn't please the firm; he wanted to take his wife with him, but they vetoed that. They say a married man will not attend strictly to business; see what a premium is paid to bachelorhood. I shall understand laces well enough soon: I can pick a piece of imitation out of a hundred real pieces now. Did Linnet like the handkerchief and scarf?"

"You should have seen her! Hasn't she spoken of them?"

"No, she was too full of other things."

"Marriage isn't all in getting ready, to Linnet," said Marjorie, seriously, "I found her crying one day because she was so happy and didn't deserve to be."

"Will is a good fellow," said Hollis. "I wish I were half as good. But I am so contradictory, so unsatisfied and so unsatisfying. I understand myself better than I want to, and yet I do not understand myself at all."

"That is because you are *growing*," said Marjorie, with her wise air. "I haven't settled down into a real Marjorie yet. I shouldn't know my own picture unless I painted it myself."

"We are two rather dangerous people, aren't we?" laughed Hollis. "We will steer clear of each other, as Will would say, until we can come to an understanding."

"Unless we can help each other," Marjorie answered. "But I don't believe you need to be pulled apart, but only to be let alone to grow—that is, if the germ is perfect."

"A perfect germ!" he repeated. Hollis liked to talk about himself to any one who would help him to self-analysis.

But the slowly moving figures were approaching, the black figure with bent shoulders and a slouched hat, the tall slight figure at his side in light gray with a shawl of white wool across her shoulders and drawn up over her hair, the fleecy whiteness softening the lines of a face that were already softened.

"O, Prudence, how far ahead we are of those two," exclaimed the school-master, "and they are wiser than we, perhaps, because they do not know so much."

"They do not know so much of each other, surely," she replied with a low laugh. That very day Mr. Holmes had quoted to her, giving it a personal application: "What she suffered she shook off in the sunshine."

He had been arguing within himself all day whether or not to destroy that letter in his pocket or to show it to her. Would it give her something else to shake off in the sunshine?

Hollis was wondering if this Marjorie, with her sweet, bright face, her graceful step and air of ladyhood, with modest and quick replies, not at all intruding herself, but giving herself, unconsciously, could be the same half-bashful little girl that he had walked with on a country road four years before; the little girl who fell so far behind his ideal, the little girl so different from city girls; and now, who among his small circle of girlhood at home could surpass her? And she was dressed so plainly, and there were marks of toil upon her fingers, and even freckles hidden beneath the fresh bloom of her cheek! She would hunt eggs tomorrow and milk the cows, she might not only weed in the garden, but when the potatoes were dug she might pick them up, and even assist her father in assorting them. Had he not said that Marjorie was his "boy" as well as her mother's girl? Had she not taken the place of Morris in all things that a girl could, and had she not taken his place with the master and gone on with Virgil where Morris left off?

"Marjorie, I don't see the *need* of your going to school?" he was saying when they joined the others.

"Hollis, you are right," repeated the master, emphatically, "that is only a whim, but she will graduate the first year, so it doesn't matter."

"You see he is proud of his work," said Marjorie, "he will not give any school the credit of me."

"I will give you into Miss Prudence's keeping for a term of years, to round you off, to make you more of a woman and less of a student—like herself."

Marjorie's eyes kindled, "I wish Morris might hear that! He has been scolding me,—but that would satisfy him."

After several moments of light talk, if the master ever could be said to encourage light talk, he touched Miss Prudence, detaining her with him, and Marjorie and Hollis walked on together.

Marjorie and Hollis were not silent, nor altogether grave, for now and then her laugh would ripple forth and he would join, with a ringing, boyish laugh that made her forget that he had grown up since that day he brought her the plate.

But the two behind them were altogether grave; Miss Prudence was speaking, for Mr. Holmes had asked her what kind of a day she had had.

"To-morrow is to be one of our anniversaries, you know," she replied; "twenty-four years ago—to-morrow—was to have been to me what to-day is to Linnet. I wonder if I *were* as light hearted as Linnet."

"You were as blithe a maiden as ever trod on air," he returned smiling sadly. "Don't I remember how you used to chase me around that old garden. When we go back let us try another chase, shall we?"

"We will let Marjorie run and imagine it is I."

"Prudence, if I regain my strength out there, I am coming home to tell you something, may I?"

"I want you to regain your strength, but I am trembling when I think of anything to be told. Is it anything—about—"

"Jerome? Yes, it is about him and about my self. It is about our last interview when we spoke of you. Do you still believe that he is living?"

"Yes, we are living, why should he not be alive?"

"Do yon know how old he would be?"

"He was just twenty years older than I."

"Then he must be sixty-four. That is not young, Prudence, and he had grown old when I said goodbye to him on the steamer—no, it was not a steamer, he avoided the publicity, he went in a merchant ship, there was not even one passenger beside himself. He had a fine constitution and he knew how to take care of himself; it was the—worry that made him look old. He was very warm-hearted and lovable."

"Yes," escaped Miss Prudence's lips.

"But he was weak and lead astray—it seems strange that your silver wedding day might be almost at hand, and that tall boy and girl in front of you my brother's children to call me Uncle John."

"John," she sobbed, catching her breath.

"Poor child! Now I've brought the tears. I was determined to get that dead look out of your eyes that was beginning to come to-night. It shall go away to-night and you shall not awake with it in the morning. Do you know what you want? Do you want to tell me what you pray about on your wedding day?"

"Yes, and you can pray with me to-morrow. I always ask repentance and remission of sins for him and for myself that I may see him once more and make him believe that I have forgiven him."

"Did you ever wish that you had been his wife and might have shared his exile?"

"Not at first; I was too indignant; I did not forgive him, at first; but since I have wished it; I know he has needed me."

"But he threw you off."

"No, he would not let me share his disgrace."

"He did not love you well enough to keep the disgrace from you, it seems," said John Holmes, bitterly.

"No, I could not keep him from sin. The love of a woman is not the love of God. I failed as many a woman has failed. But I did not desert him; I went—but he would not see me."

"He was sorry afterward, he tried to write to you, but he always broke down and could not go on; you were so young and he had been a shame to you."

"You never told me this before."

"Because I hated him, I hated my brother, for disgracing you and disgracing my mother and myself; I have grown forgiving since, since God has forgiven me. He said that last day that you must not forget him."

"He knew I would not forget," said Miss Prudence, proudly.

"Did you ever hate him?"

"Yes, I think I did. I believed he hastened poor father's death; I knew he had spoiled all my life; yes, I hated him until my heart was softened by many sorrows—John, I loved that man who went away—so far, without me, but I held myself bound, I thought your brother would come back and claim [missing text] was while Jerome was in—before he went to Europe— and I said the shame and horror was too great, I could not become anybody's happy wife with that man who was so nearly my husband in such a place."

"Have you regretted that decision since?" he questioned in a dry hard tone.

"Yes."

How quiet her voice was! "I was sorry—when I read of his sudden death two years ago—and I almost hated your brother again for keeping so much from me—it is so hard not to hate with a bitter hatred when we have been so wronged. How I have prayed for a forgiving heart," she sighed.

"Have you had any comfort to-day?"

"Yes, I found it in my reading this morning. Linnet was up and singing early and I was sitting at my window over her head and I learned a lesson of how God waits before he comforts in these words that were given new to me. 'And the napkin that was about his head, not lying with the linen clothes, but wrapped together in a place by itself.'"

"I cannot see any comfort in that."

There was a broken sound in the master's voice that Miss Prudence had never heard before, a hopelessness that was something deeper than his old melancholy. Had any confession that she had made touched him anew? Was he troubled at that acknowledged hardness towards his brother? Or was it sorrow afresh at the mention of her disappointments? Or was it sympathy for the friend who had given her up and gone away without her?

Would Miss Prudence have been burdened as she never had been burdened before could she have known that he had lost a long-cherished hope for himself? that he had lived his lonely life year after year waiting until he should no longer be bound by the promise made to his brother at their parting? The promise was this; that he should not ask Prudence, "Prue" his brother had said, to marry him until he himself should be dead; in pity for the brother who had educated him and had in every way been so generous, and who now pleaded brokenly for this last mercy, he had given the promise, rather it had been wrung out of him, and for a little time he had not repented. And then when he forgot his brother and remembered himself, his heart died within him and there was nothing but hard work left to live for; this only for a time, he found God afterward and worked hard for him.

He had written to his brother and begged release, but no word of release had come, and he was growing old and his health had failed under the stress of work and the agony of his self-control, "the constant anguish of patience."

But the letter in his pocket was of no avail now, Prudence had loved him only as a brother all these long years of his suspense and hope and waiting; that friend whose sudden death had moved her so had been in her thoughts, and he was only her dear friend and—Jerome's brother.

It is no wonder that the bent shoulders drooped lower and that the slouched hat was drawn over a face that fain would have hidden itself. Prudence, his sister Prudence, was speaking to him and he had not heard a word. How that young fellow in front was rattling on and laughing as though hearts never ached or broke with aching, and now he was daring Marjorie to a race, and the fleet-footed girl was in full chase, and the two who had run their race nearly a quarter of a century before walked on slowly and seriously with more to think about and bear than they could find words for.

"I found comfort in that. Shall I tell you?" she asked.

"Yes," he said, "if you can make me understand."

"I think you will understand, but I shall not make you; I shall speak slowly, for I want to tell you all I thought. The Lord was dead; he had been crucified and laid away within the sepulchre three days since, and they who had so loved him and so trusted in his promises were broken-hearted because of his death. Our Christ has never been dead to us, John; think what it must have been to them to know him *dead*. 'Let not your heart be troubled' he said; but their hearts were troubled, and he knew it; he knew how John's heart was rent, and how he was sorrowing with the mother he had taken into his own home; he knew how Peter had wept his bitter tears, how Martha and Mary and Lazarus were grieving for him, how all were watching, waiting, hoping and yet hardly daring to hope,—oh, how little our griefs seem to us beside such grief as theirs! And the third day since he had been taken from them. Did they expect again to hear his footfall or his voice? He could see, all this time, the hands outstretched in prayer, he could hear their cries, he could feel the beating of every heart, and yet how slowly he was going forth to meet them. How could he stay his feet? Were not Peter and John running towards him? Was not Mary on her way to him? And yet he did not hasten; something must first be done, such little things; the linen clothes must be laid aside and the napkin that had been about his head must be wrapped together in a place by itself. Such a little thing to think of, such a little thing to do, before he could go forth to meet them! Was it necessary that the napkin should be wrapped together in a place by itself? As necessary as that their terrible suspense should be ended? As necessary as that Peter and John and Martha and Mary and his mother should be comforted one little instant sooner? Could you or I wait to fold a napkin and lay it away if we might fly to a friend who was wearying for us? Suppose God says: 'Fold that napkin and lay it away,' do we do it cheerfully and submissively, choosing to do it rather than to hasten to our friend? If a leper had stood in the way, beseeching him, if the dead son of a widow were being carried out, we could understand the instant's delay, if only a little child were waiting to speak to the Lord, but to keep so many waiting just to lay the linen clothes aside, and, most of all, to wrap together that napkin and lay it by itself. Only the knowing that the doing this was doing the will of God reconciles me to the waiting that one instant longer, that his mother need not have waited but for that. So, John, perhaps you and I are waiting to do some little thing, some little thing that we do not know the meaning of, before God's will can be perfect concerning us. It may be as near to us as was the napkin about the head of the Lord. I was forgetting that, after he died for us, there was any of the Father's will left for him to do. And I suppose he folded that napkin as willingly as he gave himself up to the cross. John, that does help me—I am so impatient at interruptions to what I call my 'work,' and I am so impatient for the Lord to work for me."

"Yes," he answered slowly, "it is hard to realize that we *must* stop to do every little thing. But I do not stop, I pass the small things by. Prudence, I am burning up with impatience to-night."

"Are you? I am very quiet."

"If you knew something about Jerome that I do not know, and it would disturb me to know it, would you tell me?"

"If I should judge you by myself I should tell you. How can one person know how a truth may affect another? Tell me what you know; I am ready."

But she trembled exceedingly and staggered as she walked.

"Take my arm," he said, quietly.

She obeyed and leaned against him as they moved on slowly; it was too dark for them to see each other's faces clearly, a storm was gathering, the outlines of the house they were approaching, were scarcely distinguishable.

"We are almost home," she said.

"Yes, there! Our light is flashing out. Marjorie is lighting the parlor lamp. I have in my pocket a letter from Jerome; I have had it a week; you seemed so quiet and happy I had not the heart to disturb you. It was sent to the old address, I told him some one there would always find me. He has not written because he thought we did not care to hear. He has the name of an honest man there, he says."

"Is that all?" she questioned, her heart beating with a rapid pulsation.
How long she had waited for this.

"He is not in Europe now, he is in California. His wife is dead and he has a little girl ten years old. He refers to a letter written twelve years ago—a letter that I never received; but it would have made no difference if I had received it. I wrote to him once begging him to release me from a promise that I made rashly out of great pity for him, it was cruel and selfish in him to force me to it, but I was not sure of myself then, and it was all that I could do for him. But, as I said, he released me when he chose to do it, and it does not matter. Perhaps it is better that I had the promise to bind me; you are happier for it, I think, and I have not been selfish in any demand upon you."

"John, I don't know what you mean," she said, perplexed.

"I don't mean anything that I can tell you."

"I hope he did not deceive her—his wife, that he told her all about himself."

"She died nine years ago, he writes, and now he is very ill himself and wishes to leave his little daughter in safe hands; her mother was an orphan, it seems, and the child has no relatives that he cares to leave her with; her mother was an English girl, he was married in England. He wishes me to come to him and take charge of the child."

"That is why you so suddenly chose California instead of Minnesota for your winter?"

"Yes."

"Have you written to him?"

"Yes."

"Is he very ill?"

"Yes; he may never receive my letter."

"I would like to write to him," said Miss Prudence.

"Would you like to see the letter?"

"No; I would rather not. You have told me all?" with a slight quiver in the firm voice.

"All excepting his message to you."

After a moment she asked: "What is it?"

"He wants you to take the guardianship of his child with me. I have not told you all—he thinks we are married."

The brave voice trembled in spite of his stern self-control.

"Oh!" exclaimed Prudence, and then: "Why should he think that?" in a low, hesitating voice.

"Because he knew me so well. Having only each other, it was natural, was it not?"

"Perhaps so. Then that is all he says."

"Isn't that enough?"

"No, I want to know if he has repented, if he is another man. I am glad I may write to him; I want to tell him many things. We will take care of the little girl, John."

"If I am West and you are East—"

"Do you want to keep her with you?"

"What could I do with her? She will be a white elephant to me. I am not her father; I do not think I understand girls—or boys, or men. I hardly understand you, Prudence."

"Then I am afraid you never will. Isn't it queer how I always have a little girl provided for me? Marjorie is growing up and now I have this child, your niece, John, to be my little girl for a long time. I wonder what her name is."

"He did tell me that! I may have passed over something else; you might better see the letter."

"No; handwriting is like a voice, or a perfume to me—I could not bear it to-night. John, I feel as if it would *kill* me. It is so long ago—I thought I was stronger—O, John," she leaned her head upon his arm and sobbed convulsively like a little child.

He laid his hand upon her head as if she were indeed the little child, and for a long time no words were spoken.

"Prudence, there is something else, there is the photograph of the little girl—her mother named her Jeroma."

"I will take that," she said, lifting her head, "and I will write to her to-night."

That night before she slept she wrote a long letter to the child with the brown eyes and sunny curls, describing the home in Maple Street, and promising to take her into her heart and keep her there always, to adopt her for her very own little daughter for her own sake and for her father's sake, whom she knew long ago, ending it thus:

"You cannot come to me too soon, for I am waiting for you with a hungry heart. I knew there was something good coming to me, and I know you will be my blessing.

"Your Loving Aunt Prue."

XV.

JEROMA.

"Whom hast them pitied? And whom forgiven I"—*Wills*.

The child had risen early that she might have a good time looking at the sea lions; the huge creatures covered the rocks two hundred yards away from her, crawling and squirming, or lying still as if as dead as the rock itself, their pointed heads and shining bodies giving her a delightful shiver of affright, their howling and groaning causing her to run every now and then back to her father's chair on the veranda, and then she would dance back again and stand and watch them—the horrible, misshapen monsters—as they quarrelled, or suckled their young, or furious and wild as they tumbled about and rolled off the craggy cliffs into the sea. She left her chamber early every morning to watch them and never grew weary of the familiar, strange Bight. Not that this sight had been so long familiar, for her father was ever seeking new places along the coast to rest in, or grow strong in. Nurse had told her that morning that there was not any place for her papa to get well in.

He had breakfasted, as usual, upon the veranda, and, the last time that she had brought her gaze from the fascinating monsters to look back at him, he was leaning against the cushions of his rolling chair, with his eyes fixed upon the sea. He often sat for hours and hours looking out upon the sea.

Jeroma had played upon the beach every day last winter, growing ruddy and strong, but the air had revived him only for a little time, he soon sank back into weakness and apathy. He had dismissed her with a kiss awhile ago, and had seemed to suffer instead of respond to her caresses.

"Papa gets tired of loving me," she had said to Nurse last night with a quivering of the lip.

"Papa is very sick," Nurse had answered guardedly, "and he had letters to-day that were too much for him."

"Then he shouldn't have letters," said the child, decidedly. "I'll tell him so to-morrow."

As she danced about, her white dress and sunny curls gleaming in and out among the heliotrope and scarlet geranium that one of the flower-loving boarders was cultivating, her father called her name; it was a queer name, and she did not like it. She liked her second name, Prudence, better. But Nurse had said, when she complained to her, that the girls would call her "Prudy" for short, and "Jerrie" was certainly a prettier name than that.

"Jerrie," her father called.

The sound was so weak and broken by a cough that she did not turn her head or answer until he had called more than twice. But she flew to him when she was sure that he had called her, and kissed his flabby cheek and smoothed back the thin locks of white hair. His black eyes were burning like two fires beneath his white brows, his lips were ashy, and his breath hot and hurried. Two letters were trembling in his hand, two open letters, and one of them was in several fluttering sheets; this handwriting was a lady's, Jeroma recognized that, although she could not read even her own name in script.

"O, papa, those are the letters that made you sick! I'll throw them away to the lions," she cried, trying to snatch them. But he kept them in his fingers and tried to speak.

"I'll be rested in a moment, eat those strawberries—and then I have—something to talk to you about."

She surveyed the table critically, bread and fruit and milk; there was nothing beside.

"I've had my breakfast! O, papa, I've forgotten your flowers! Mrs. Heath said you might have them every morning."

"Run and get them then, and never wait for me to call you—it tires me too much."

"Poor papa! And I can howl almost as loud as the lions themselves."

"Don't howl at me then, for I might want to roll off into the sea," he said, smiling as she danced away.

The child seemed never to walk, she was always frisking about, one hardly knew if her feet touched the ground.

"Poor child! happy child," he groaned, rather than murmured, as she disappeared around the corner of the veranda. She was a chubby, roundfaced child, with great brown eyes and curls like yellow floss; from her childishness and ignorance of what children at ten years of age are usually taught, she was supposed by strangers to be no more than eight years of age; she was an imperious little lady, impetuous, untrained, self-reliant, and, from much intercourse with strangers, not at all shy, looking out upon the world with confiding eyes, and knowing nothing to be afraid of or ashamed of. Nurse had been her only teacher; she could barely read a chapter in the New Testament, and when her father gave her ten cents and then five more she could not tell him how many cents she held in her hand.

"No matter, I don't want you to count money," he said.

Before he recovered his breath and self-possession she was at his side with the flowers she had hastily plucked—scarlet geranium, heliotrope, sweet alyssum, the gorgeous yellow and orange poppy, and the lovely blue and white lupine. He received them with a listless smile and laid them upon his knee; as he bade her again to eat the strawberries she brought them to his side, now and then coaxing a "particularly splendid" one into his mouth, pressing them between his lips with her stained fingers.

"Papa, your eyes shine to-day! You are almost well. Nurse doesn't know."

"What does Nurse say?"

"That you will die soon; and then where shall I go?"

"Would you like to know where you will go?"

"I don't want to go anywhere; I want to stay here with you."

"But that is impossible, Jerrie."

"Why! Who says so?" she questioned, fixing her wondering eyes on his.

"God," he answered solemnly.

"Does he know all about it?"

"Yes."

"Has it *got* to be so, then?" she asked, awed.

"Yes."

"Well, what is the rest, then?"

"Sit down and I'll tell you."

"I'd rather stand, please. I never like to sit down."

"Stand still then, dear, and lean on the arm of my chair and not on me; you take my breath away,"

"Poor papa! Am I so big? As big as a sea lion?"

Not heeding her—more than half the time he heard her voice without heeding her words—he turned the sheets in his fingers, lifted them as if to read them and then dropped his hand.

"Jerrie, what have I told you about Uncle John who lives near the other ocean?"

Jerrie thought a moment: "That he is good and will love me dearly, and be ever so kind to me and teach me things?"

"And Prue, Aunt Prue; what do you know about her?"

"I know I have some of her name, not all, for her name is Pomeroy; and she is as beautiful as a queen and as good; and she will love me more than Uncle John will, and teach me how to be a lovely lady, too."

"Yes, that is all true; one of these letters is from her, written to you—"

"Oh, to me! to *me*."

"I will read it to you presently."

"I know which is hers, the thin paper and the writing that runs along."

"And the other is from Uncle John."

"To me?" she queried.

"No, this is mine, but I will read it to you. First I want to tell you about Aunt Prue's home."

"Is it like this? near the sea? and can I play on the beach and see the lions?"

"It is near the sea, but it is not like this; her home is in a city by the sea. The house is a large house. It was painted dark brown, years ago, with red about the window frames, and the yard in front was full of flowers that Aunt Prue had the care of, and the yard at the back was deep and wide with maples in it and a swing that she used to love to swing in; she was almost like a little girl then herself."

"She isn't like a little girl now, is she?"

"No, she is grown up like that lady on the beach with the children; but she describes herself to you and promises to send her picture!"

"Oh, good!" exclaimed the child, dancing around the chair, and coming back to stand quietly at her father's side.

"What is the house like inside? Like this house?"

"No, not at all. There is a wide, old-fashioned hall, with a dark carpet in it and a table and several chairs, and engravings on the walls, and a broad staircase that leads to large, pleasant rooms above; and there is a small room on the top of the house where you can go up and see vessels entering the harbor. Down-stairs the long parlor is the room that I know best; that had a dark carpet and dark paper on the walls and many windows, windows in front and back and two on the side, there were portraits over the mantel of her father and mother, and other pictures around everywhere, and a piano that she loved to play for her father on, and books in book cases, and, in winter, plants; it was not like any one else's parlor, for her father liked to sit there and she brought in everything that would please him. Her father was old like me, and sick, and she was a dear daughter like you."

"Did he die?" she asked.

"Yes, he died. He died sooner than he would have died because some one he thought a great deal of did something very wicked and almost killed his daughter with grief. How would I feel if some one should make you so unhappy and I could not defend you and had to die and leave you alone."

"Would you want to kill him—the man that hurt me?"

But his eyes were on the water and not on her face; his countenance became ashy, he gasped and hurried his handkerchief to his lips. Jeroma was not afraid of the bright spots that he sought to conceal by crumpling the handkerchief in his hand, she had known a long time that when her father was excited those red spots came on his handkerchief. She knew, too, that the physician had said that when he began to cough he would die, but she had never heard him cough very much, and could not believe that he must ever die.

"Papa, what became of the man that hurt Aunt Prue and made her father die?"

"He lived and was the unhappiest wretch in existence. But Aunt Prue tried to forgive him, and she used to pray for him as she always had done before. Jerrie, when you go to Aunt Prue I want you to take her name, your own name, Prudence, and I will begin to-day to call you 'Prue,' so that you may get used to it."

"Oh, will you?" she cried in her happy voice. "I don't like to be 'Jerrie,' like the boy that takes care of the horses. When Mr. Pierce calls so loud 'Jerry!' I'm always afraid he means me; but Nurse says that Jerry has a *y* in it and mine is *ie*, but it sounds like my name all the time. But Prue is soft like Pussy and I like it. What made you ever call me Jerrie, papa?"

"Because your mamma named you after my name, Jerome. We used to call you Roma, but that was long for a baby, so we began to call you Jerrie."

"I like it, papa, because it is your name, and I could tell the girls at Aunt Prue's that it is my father's name, and then I would be proud and not ashamed."

"No, dear, always write it Prudence Holmes—forget that you had any other name. It is so uncommon that people would ask how you came by it and then they would know immediately who your father was."

"But I like to tell them who my father was. Do people know you in Aunt Prue's city?"

"Yes, they knew me once and they are not likely to forget. Promise me, Jerrie—Prue, that you will give up your first name."

"I don't like to, now I must, but I will, papa, and I'll tell Aunt Prue you liked her name best, shall I?"

"Yes, tell her all I've been telling you—always tell her everything—never do anything that you cannot tell her—and be sure to tell her if any one speaks to you about your father, and she will talk to you about it."

"Yes, papa," promised the child in an uncomprehending tone.

"Does Nurse teach you a Bible verse every night as I asked her to do?"

"Oh, yes, and I like some of them. The one last night was about a name! Perhaps it meant Prue was a good name."

"What is it?" he asked.

"'A good name—a good name—'" she repeated, with her eyes on the floor of the veranda, "and then something about riches, great riches, but I do forget so. Shall I run and ask her, papa?"

"No, I learned it when I was a boy: 'A good name is rather to be chosen than great riches.' Is that it?"

"Yes, that's it: 'A good name is rather to be chosen than great riches.' I shan't forget next time; I'll think about your name, Jerome, papa; that is a good name, but I don't see how it is better than *great* riches, do you?"

The handkerchief was nervously at his lips again, and the child waited for him to speak.

"Jerrie, I have no money to leave you, it will all be gone by the time you and Nurse are safe at Aunt Prue's. Everything you have will come from her; you must always thank her very much for doing so much for you, and thank Uncle John and be very obedient to him."

"Will he make me do what I don't want to?" she asked, her lips pouting and her eyes moistening.

"Not unless it is best, and now you must promise me never to disobey him or Aunt Prue. Promise, Jerrie."

But Jerrie did not like to promise. She moved her feet uneasily, she scratched on the arm of his chair with a pin that she had picked up on the floor of the veranda; she would not lift her eyes nor speak. She did not love to be obedient; she loved to be queen in her own little realm of Self.

"Papa is dying—he will soon go away, and his little daughter will not promise the last thing he asks of her?"

Instantly, in a flood of penitent tears, her arms were flung about his neck and she was promising over and over, "I will, I will," and sobbing on his shoulder.

He suffered the embrace for a few moments and then pushed her gently aside.

"Papa is tired now, dear. I want to teach you a Bible verse, that you must never, never forget: 'The way of the transgressor is hard.' Say it after me."

The child brushed her tears away and stood upright.

"The way of the transgressor is hard," she repeated in a sobbing voice.

"Repeat it three times."

She repeated it three times slowly.

"Tell Uncle John and Aunt Prue that that was the last thing I taught you, will you?"

"Yes, papa," catching her breath with a little sob.

"And now run away and come back in a hour and I will read the letters to you. Ask Nurse to tell you when it is an hour."

The child skipped away, and before many minutes he heard her laughing with the children on the beach. With the letters in his hand, and the crumpled handkerchief with the moist red spots tucked away behind him in the chair, he leaned back and closed his eyes. His breath came easily after a little time and he dozed and dreamed. He was a boy again and it was a moonlight night, snow was on the ground, and he was walking home from town besides his oxen; he had sold the load of wood that he had started with before daylight; he had eaten his two lunches of bread and salt beef and doughnuts, and now, cold and tired and sleepy, he was walking back home at the side of his oxen. The stars were shining, the ground was as hard as stone beneath his tread, the oxen labored on slowly, it seemed as if he would never get home. His mother would have a hot supper for him, and the boys would ask what the news was, and what he had seen, and his little sister would ask if he had bought that piece of ginger bread for her. He stirred and the papers rustled in his fingers and there was a harsh sound somewhere as of a bolt grating, and his cell was small and the bed so narrow, so narrow and so hard, and he was suffocating and could not get out.

"Papa! papa! It's an hour," whispered a voice in his ear. The eyelids quivered, the eyes looked straight at her but did not see her.

"Ah Sing! Ah Sing! Get me to bed!" he groaned.

Frightened at the expression of his face the child ran to call Nurse and her father's man, Ah Sing. Nurse kept her out of her father's chamber all that day, but she begged for her letter and Nurse gave it to her. She carried it in her hand that day and the next, at night keeping it under her pillow.

Before many days the strange uncle came and he led her in to her father and let her kiss his hand, and afterward he read Aunt Prue's soiled letter to her and told her that she and Nurse were going to Aunt Prue's home next week.

"Won't you go, too?" she asked, clinging to him as no one had ever clung to him before.

"No, I must stay here all winter—I shall come to you some time."

She sobbed herself to sleep in his arms, with the letter held fast in her hand; he laid her on her bed, pressing his lips to her warm, wet face, and then went down and out on the beach, pacing up and down until the dawn was in the sky.

XVI.

MAPLE STREET.

"Work for some good, be it ever so slowly."—*Mrs. Osgood.*

The long room with its dark carpet and dark walls was in twilight, in twilight and in firelight, for without the rain was falling steadily, and in the old house fires were needed early in the season. In the time of which little Jeroma had heard, there had been a fire on the hearth in the front parlor, but to-night, when that old time was among the legends, the fire glowed in a large grate; in the back parlor the heat came up through the register. Miss Prudence had a way of designating the long apartment as two rooms, for there was an arch in the centre, and there were two mantels and two fireplaces. Prue's father would have said to-night that the old room was unchanged—nothing had been taken out and nothing new brought in since that last night that he had seen the old man pacing up and down, and the old man's daughter whirling around on the piano stool, as full of hope and trust and enthusiasm as ever a girl could be.

But to-night there was a solitary figure before the fire, with no memories and no traditions to disturb her dreaming, with no memories of other people's past that is, for there was a sad memory or a foreboding in the very droop of her shoulders and in her listless hands. The small, plump figure was arrayed in school attire of dark brown, with linen collar and cuffs, buttoned boots resting on the fender, and a black silk apron with pockets; there were books and a slate upon the rug, and a slate pencil and lead pencil in one of the apron pockets; a sheet of note paper had slipped from her lap down to the rug, on the sheet of paper was a half-finished letter beginning: "Dear Morris." There was nothing in the letter worth jotting down, she wondered why she had ever begun it. She was nestling down now with her head on the soft arm of the chair, her eyes were closed, but she was not asleep, for the moisture beneath the tremulous eyelids had formed itself into two large drops and was slowly rolling, unheeded, down her cheeks.

The rain was beating noisily upon the window panes, and the wind was rising higher and higher; as it lulled for a moment there was the sound of a footfall on the carpet somewhere and the door was pushed open from the lighted hall.

"Don't you want to be lighted up yet, Miss Marjorie?"

"No, Deborah, thank you! I'll light the lamps myself."

"Young things like to sit in the dark, I guess," muttered old Deborah, closing the door softly; adding to herself: "Miss Prudence used to, once on a time, and this girl is coming to it."

After that for a little time there was no sound, save the sound of the rain, and, now and then, the soft sigh that escaped Marjorie's lips.

How strange it was, she reasoned with herself, for her to care at all! What if Hollis did not want to answer that last letter of hers, written more than two months ago, just after Linnet's wedding day? That had been a long letter; perhaps too long. But she had been so lonesome, missing everybody. Linnet, and Morris, and Mr. Holmes, and Miss Prudence had gone to her grandfather's for the sea bathing, and the girl had come to help her mother, and she had walked over to his mother's and talked about everything to her and then written that long letter to him, that long letter that had been unanswered so long. When his letter was due she had expected it, as usual, and had walked to the post-office, the two miles and a half, for the sake of the letter and having something to do. She could not believe it when the postmaster handed her only her father's weekly paper, she stood a moment, and then asked, "Is that all?" And the next week came, and the next, and the next, and no letter from him; and then she had ceased, with a dull sense of loss and disappointment, to expect any answer at all. Her mother inquired briskly every day if her letter had come and urged her to write a note asking if he had received it, for he might be waiting for it all this time, but shyness and pride forbade that, and afterward his mother called and spoke of something that he must have read in that letter. She felt how she must have colored, and was glad that her father called her, at that moment, to help him shell corn for the chickens.

When she returned to the house, brightened up and laughing, her mother told her that Mrs. Rheid had said that Hollis had begun to write to her regularly and she was so proud of it. "She says it is because you are going away and he wants her to hear directly from him; I guess, too, it's because he's being exercised in his mind and thinks he ought to have written oftener before; she says her hand is out of practice and the Cap'n hates to write letters and only writes business letters when it's a force put. I guess she will miss you, Marjorie."

Marjorie thought to herself that she would.

But Marjorie's mother did not repeat all the conversation; she did not say that she had followed her visitor to the gate and after glancing around to be sure that Marjorie was not near had lowered her voice and said:

"But I do think it is a shame, Mis' Rheid, for your Hollis to treat my Marjorie so! After writing to her four years to give her the slip like this! And the girl takes on about it, I can see it by her looks, although she's too proud to say a word."

"I'm sure I'm sorry," said Mrs. Rheid. "Hollis wouldn't do a mean thing."

"I don't know what you call this, then," Marjorie's mother had replied spiritedly as she turned towards the house.

Mrs. Rheid pondered night and day before she wrote to Hollis what Marjorie's mother had said; but he never answered that part of the letter, and his mother never knew whether she had done harm or good. Poor little Marjorie could have told her, with an indignation that she would have been frightened at; but Marjorie never knew. I'm afraid she would not have felt like kissing her mother good-night if she had known it.

Her father looked grave and anxious that night when her mother told him, as in duty bound she was to tell him everything, how she was arranging things for Marjorie's comfort.

"That was wrong, Sarah, that was wrong," he said.

"How wrong? I don't see how it was wrong?" she had answered sharply.

"Then I cannot explain to you, Marjorie isn't hurt any; I don't believe she cares half as much as you do?"

"You don't know; you don't see her all the time."

"She misses Linnet and Morris, and perhaps she grieves about going away. You remind me of some one in the Bible—a judge. He had thirty sons and thirty daughters and he got them all married! It's well for your peace of mind that you have but two."

"It's no laughing matter," she rejoined.

"No, it is not," he sighed, for he understood Marjorie.

How the tears would have burned dry on Marjorie's indignant cheeks had she surmised one tithe of her mother's remonstrance and defence; it is true she missed his letters, and she missed writing her long letters to him, but she did not miss him as she would have missed Morris had some misunderstanding come between them. She was full of her home and her studies, and she felt herself too young to think grown-up thoughts and have grown-up experiences; she felt herself to be so much younger than Linnet. But her pride was touched, simple-hearted as she was she wanted Hollis to care a little for her letters. She had tried to please him and to be thoughtful about his mother and grandmother; and this was not a pleasant ending. Her mother had watched her, she was well aware, and she was glad to come away with Miss Prudence to escape her mother's keen eyes. Her father had kissed her tenderly more than once, as though he were seeking to comfort her for something. It was *such* a relief—and she drew a long breath as she thought of it—to be away from both, and to be with Miss Prudence, who never saw anything, or thought anything, or asked any questions. A few tears dropped slowly as she cuddled in the chair with her head on its arm, she hardly knew why; because she was alone, perhaps, and Linnet was so far off, and it rained, and Miss Prudence and her little girl might not come home to-night, and, it might be, because Miss Prudence had another little girl to love.

Miss Prudence had gone to New York, a week ago, to meet the child and to visit the Rheids. The nurse had relatives in the city and preferred to remain with them, but Prue would be ready to come home with Miss Prudence, and it was possible that they might come to-night.

The house had been so lonely with old Deborah it was no wonder that she began to cry! And, it was foolish to remember that Holland plate in Mrs. Harrowgate's parlor that she had seen to-day when she had stopped after school on an errand for Miss Prudence. What a difference it had made to her that it was that plate on the bracket and not that yellow pitcher. The yellow pitcher was in fragments now up in the garret; she must show it to Prue some rainy day and tell her about what a naughty little girl she had been that day.

That resolution helped to shake off her depression, she roused herself, went to the window and looked out into darkness, and then sauntered as far as the piano and seated herself to play the march that Hollis liked; Napoleon crossing the Alps. But scarcely had she touched the keys before she heard voices out in the rain and feet upon the piazza.

Deborah's old ears had caught an earlier sound, and before Marjorie could rush out the street door was opened and the travellers were in the hall.

Exclamations and warm embraces, and then Marjorie drew the little one into the parlor and before the fire. The child stood with her grave eyes searching out the room, and when the light from the bronze lamp on the centre table flashed out upon everything she walked up and down the length of the apartment, stopping now and then to look curiously at something.

Marjorie smiled and thought to herself that she was a strange little creature.

"It's just as papa said," she remarked, coming to the rug, her survey being ended. The childishness and sweet gravity of her tone were striking.

Marjorie removed the white hood that she had travelled from California in, and, brushing back the curls that shone in the light like threads of gold, kissed her forehead and cheeks and rosy lips.

"I am your Cousin Marjorie, and you are my little cousin."

"I like you, Cousin Marjorie," the child said.

"Of course you do, and I love you. Are you Prue, or Jeroma?"

"I'm Prue," she replied with dignity. "Don't you *ever* call me Jeroma again, ever; papa said so."

Marjorie laughed and kissed her again.

"I never, never will," she promised.

"Aunt Prue says 'Prue' every time."

Marjorie unbuttoned the gray cloak and drew off the gray gloves; Prue threw off the cloak and then lifted her foot for the rubber to be pulled off.

"I had no rubbers; Aunt Prue bought these in New York."

"Aunt Prue is very kind," said Marjorie, as the second little foot was lifted.

"Does she buy you things, too?" asked Prue.

"Yes, ever and ever so many things."

"Does she buy *everybody* things?" questioned Prue, curiously.

"Yes," laughed Marjorie; "she's everybody's aunt."

"No, I don't buy everybody things. I buy things for you and Marjorie because you are both my little girls."

Turning suddenly Marjorie put both arms about Miss Prudence's neck: "I've missed you, dreadfully, Miss Prudence; I almost cried to-night."

"So that is the story I find in your eyes. But you haven't asked me the news."

"You haven't seen mother, or Linnet, or Morris,—they keep my news for me." But she flushed as she spoke, reproaching herself for not being quite sincere.

Prue stood on the hearth rug, looking up at the portrait of the lady over the mantel.

"Don't pretend that you don't want to hear that Nannie Rheid has put herself through," began Miss Prudence in a lively voice, "crammed to the last degree, and has been graduated a year in advance of time that she may be married this month. Her father was inexorable, she must be graduated first, and she has done it at seventeen, so he has had to redeem his promise and allow her to be married. Her 'composition'—that is the old-fashioned name—was published in one of the literary weeklies, and they all congratulate themselves and each other over her success. But her eyes are big, and she looks as delicate as a wax lily; she is all nerves, and she laughs and talks as though she could not stop herself. What do you think of her as a school girl triumph?"

"It isn't tempting. I like myself better. I want to be *slow*. Miss Prudence, I don't want to hurry anything."

"I approve of you, Marjorie. Now what is this little girl thinking about?"

"Is that your mamma up there?"

"Yes."

"She looks like you."

"Yes, I am like her; but there is no white in her hair. It is all black, Prue."

"I like white in hair for old ladies."

Marjorie laughed and Miss Prudence smiled. She was glad that being called "an old lady" could strike somebody as comical.

"Was papa in this room a good many times?"

"Yes, many times."

Miss Prudence could speak to his child without any sigh in her voice.

"Do you remember the last time he was here?"

"Yes," very gently.

"He said I would like your house and I do."

"Nannie is to marry one of Helen's friends, Marjorie; her mother thought he used to care for Helen, but Nannie is like her."

"Yes," said Marjorie, "I remember. Hollis told me."

"And my best news is about Hollis. He united with the Church a week or two ago; Mrs. Rheid says he is the happiest Christian she ever saw. He says he has not been *safe* since Helen died—he has been thinking ever since."

Tears were so near to Marjorie's eyes that they brimmed over; could she ever thank God enough for this? others may have been praying for him, but she knew her years of prayers were being answered. She would never feel sorrowful or disappointed about any little thing again, for what had she so longed for as this? How rejoiced his mother must be! Oh, that she might write to him and tell him how glad she was! But she could not do that. She could tell God how glad she was, and if Hollis never knew it would not matter.

"In the spring he is to go to Europe for the firm."

"He will like that," said Marjorie, finding her voice.

"He is somebody to be depended on. But there is the tea-bell, and my little traveller is hungry, for she would not eat on the train and I tempted her with fruit and crackers."

"Aunt Prue, I *like* it here. May I see up stairs, too?"

"You must see the supper table first. And then Marjorie may show you everything while I write to Uncle John, to tell him that our little bird has found her nest."

Marjorie gave up her place that night in the wide, old-fashioned mahogany bedstead beside Miss Prudence and betook herself to the room that opened out of Miss Prudence's, a room with handsome furniture in ash, the prevailing tint of the pretty things being her favorite shade of light blue.

"That is a maiden's room," Miss Prudence had said; "and when Prue has a maiden's room it shall be in rose."

Marjorie was not jealous, as she had feared she might be, of the little creature who nestled close to Miss Prudence; she felt that Miss Prudence was being comforted in the child. She was too happy to sleep that night. In the years afterward she did not leave Hollis out of her prayers, but she never once thought to pray that he might be brought back again to be her friend. Her prayer for him had been answered and with that she was well content.

XVII.

MORRIS.

"What I aspired to be comforts me."—*Browning*.

It was late one evening in November; Prue had kissed them both good-night and ran laughing up the broad staircase to bed; Miss Prudence had finished her evening's work and evening's pleasure, and was now sitting opposite Marjorie, near the register in the back parlor. A round table had been rolled up between them upon which the shaded, bronze lamp was burning, gas not having yet been introduced into old-fashioned Maple Street. The table was somewhat littered and in confusion, Prue's stereoscope was there with the new views of the Yosemite at which she had been looking that evening and asking Aunt Prue numerous questions, among which was "Shall we go and see them some day? Shall we go everywhere some day?" Aunt Prue had satisfied her with "Perhaps so, darling," and then had fallen silently to wondering why she and Prue might not travel some day, a year in Europe had always been one of her postponed intentions, and, by and by, how her child would enjoy it. Marjorie's books and writing desk were on the table also, for she had studied mental philosophy and chemistry after she had copied her composition and written a long letter to her mother. Short letters were as truly an impossibility to Marjorie as short addresses are to some public speeches; still Marjorie always stopped when she found she had nothing to say. To her mother, school and Miss Prudence and Prue's sayings and doings were an endless theme of delight. Not only did she take Marjoire's letters to her old father and mother, but she more than a few times carried them in her pocket when she visited Mrs. Rheid, that she might read them aloud to her. Miss Prudence's work was also on the table, pretty sewing for Prue and her writing materials, for it was the night for her weekly letter to John Holmes. Mr. Holmes did not parade his letters before the neighbors, but none the less did he pore over them and ponder them. For whom had he in all the world to love save little Prue and Aunt Prue?

Marjorie had closed the chemistry with a sigh, reserving astronomy for the fresher hour of the morning. With the burden of the unlearned lesson on her mind she opened her Bible for her usual evening reading, shrinking from it with a distaste that she had felt several times of late and that she had fought against and prayed about. Last evening she had compelled herself to read an extra chapter to see if she might not read herself into a comfortable frame of mind, and then she had closed the book with a sigh of relief, feeling that this last task of the day was done. To-night she fixed her eyes upon the page awhile and then dropped the book into her lap with a weary gesture that was not unnoticed by the eyes that never lost anything where Marjorie was concerned. It was something new to see a fretful or fretted expression upon Marjorie's lips, but it was certainly there to-night and Miss Prudence saw it; it might be also in her eyes, but, if it were, the uneasy eyelids were at this moment concealing it. "The child is very weary to-night," Miss Prudence thought, and wondered if she were allowing her, in her ambition, to take too much upon herself. Music, with the two hours a day practicing that she resolutely never omitted, all the school lessons, reading and letters, and the conscientious preparation of her lesson for Bible class, was most assuredly sufficient to tax her mental and physical strength, and there was the daily walk of a mile to and from school, and other things numberless to push themselves in for her comfort and Prue's. But her step was elastic, her color as pretty as when she worked in the kitchen at home, and when she came in from school she was always ready for a romp with Prue before she sat down to practice.

When summer came the garden and trips to the islands would be good for both her children. Miss Prudence advocated the higher education for girls, but if Marjorie's color had faded or her spirits flagged she would have taken her out of school and set her to household tasks and to walks and drives. Had she not taken Linnet home after her three years course with the country color fresh in her cheeks and her step as light upon the stair as when she left home?

The weariness had crept into Marjorie's face since she closed her books; it was not when she opened the Bible. Was the child enduring any spiritual conflicts again? Linnet had never had spiritual conflicts; what should she do with this too introspective Marjorie? Would Prue grow up to ask questions and need just such comforting, too? Miss Prudence's own evening's work had begun with her Bible reading, she read and meditated all the hour and a quarter that Marjorie was writing her letter (they had supper so early that their evenings began at half-past six), she had read with eagerness and a sense of deep enjoyment and appreciation.

"It is so good," she had exclaimed as she laid the Bible aside, and Marjorie had raised her head at the exclamation and asked what was so good. "Peter's two letters to the Church and to me."

Without replying Marjorie had dipped her pen again and written: "Miss
Prudence is more and more of a saint every day."

"Marjorie, it's a snow storm."

"Yes," said Marjorie, not opening her eyes.

Miss Prudence looked at the bronze clock on the mantel; it was ten o'clock. Marjorie should have been asleep an hour ago.

Miss Prudence's fur-trimmed slippers touched the toe of Marjorie's buttoned boot, they were both resting on the register.

"Marjorie, I don't know what I am thinking of to let you sit up so late; I shall have to send you upstairs with Prue after this. Linnet's hour was nine o'clock when she was studying, and look at her and Nannie Rheid."

"But I'm not getting through to be married, as Linnet was."

"How do you know?" asked Miss Prudence.

"Not intentionally, then," smiled Marjorie, opening her eyes this time.

"I'm not the old maid that eschews matrimony; all I want is to choose for you and Prue."

"Not yet, please," said Marjorie, lifting her hands in protest.

"What is it that tires you so to-night? School?

"No," answered Marjorie, sitting upright; "school sits as lightly on my shoulders as that black lace scarf you gave me yesterday; it is because I grow more and more wicked every night. I am worse than I was last night. I tried to read in the Bible just now and I did not care for it one bit, or understand it one bit; I began to think I never should find anything to do me good in Malachi, or in any of the old prophets."

"Suppose you read to me awhile—not in the Bible, but in your Sunday-school book. You told Prue that it was fascinating. 'History of the Reformation,' isn't it?"

"To-night? O, Aunt Prue, I'm too tired."

"Well, then, a chapter of Walter Scott, that will rest you."

"No, it won't; I wouldn't understand a word."

"'The Minister's Wooing' then; you admire Mrs. Stowe so greatly."

"I don't admire her to-night, I'm afraid. Aunt Prue, even a startling ring at the door bell will not wake me up."

"Suppose I play for you," suggested Miss Prudence, gravely.

"I thought you wanted me to go to bed," said Marjorie, suppressing her annoyance as well as she could.

"Just see, child; you are too worn out for all and any of these things that you usually take pleasure in, and yet you take up the Bible and expect to feel devotional and be greatly edified, even to find that Malachi has a special message for you. And you berate yourself for hardheartedness and coldheartedness. When you are so weary, don't you see that your brain refuses to think?"

"Do you mean that I ought to read only one verse and think that enough?
Oh, if I might."

"Have you taken more time than that would require for other things to-day?"

"Why, yes," said Marjorie, looking surprised.

"Then why should you give God's book just half a minute, or not so long, and Wayland and Legendre and every body else just as much time as the length of your lesson claims? Could you make anything of your astronomy now?"

"No, I knew I could not, and that is why I am leaving it till morning."

"Suppose you do not study it at all and tell Mr. McCosh that you were too tired to-night."

"He would not accept such an excuse. He would ask why I deferred it so long. He would think I was making fun of him to give him such an excuse. I wouldn't dare."

"But you go to God and offer him your evening sacrifice with eyes so blind that they cannot see his words, and brain so tired that it can find no meaning in them. Will he accept an excuse that you are ashamed to give your teacher?"

"No," said Marjorie, looking startled. "I will read, and perhaps I can think now."

But Miss Prudence was bending towards her and taking the Bible from her lap.

"Let me find something for you in Malachi."

"And help me understand," said Marjorie.

After a moment Miss Prudence read aloud:

"'And if ye offer the blind for sacrifice, is it not evil? And if ye offer the lame and sick, is it not evil? Offer it now unto thy governor; will he be pleased with thee, or accept thy person? saith the Lord of hosts.'"

Closing the book she returned it to Marjorie's lap.

"You mean that God will not accept my excuse for not feeling like reading to-night?"

"You said that Mr. McCosh would not accept such an excuse for your astronomy."

"Miss Prudence!" Marjorie was wide awake now. "You mean that I should read early in the evening as you do! Is *that* why you always read before you do anything else in the evening?"

"It certainly is. I tried to give my blind, tired hours to God and found that he did not accept—for I had no blessing in reading; I excused myself on your plea, I was too weary, and then I learned to give him my best and freshest time."

There was no weariness or frettedness in Marjorie's face now; the heart rest was giving her physical rest. "I will begin to-morrow night—I can't begin to-night—and read the first thing as you do. I am almost through the Old Testament; how I shall enjoy beginning the New! Miss Prudence, is it so about praying, too?"

"What do you think?"

"I know it is. And that is why my prayers do not comfort me, sometimes. I mean, the short prayers do; but I do want to pray about so many things, and I am really too tired when I go to bed, sometimes I fall asleep when I am not half through. Mother used to tell Linnet and me that we oughtn't to talk after we said our prayers, so we used to talk first and put our prayers off until the last thing, and sometimes we were so sleepy we hardly knew what we were saying."

"This plan of early reading and praying does not interfere with prayer at bedtime, you know; as soon as my head touches the pillow I begin to pray, I think I always fall asleep praying, and my first thought in the morning is prayer. My dear, our best and freshest, not our lame and blind, belong to God."

"Yes," assented Marjorie in a full tone. "Aunt Prue, O, Aunt Prue what would I do without you to help me."

"God would find you somebody else; but I'm very glad he found me for you."

"I'm more than glad," said Marjorie, enthusiastically.

"It's a real snow storm," Miss Prudence went to the window, pushed the curtain aside, and looked out.

"It isn't as bad as the night that Morris came to me when I was alone. Mr. Holmes did not come for two days and it was longer than that before father and mother could come. What a grand time we had housekeeping! It is time for the *Linnet* to be in. I know Morris will come to see us as soon as he can get leave. Linnet will be glad to go to her pretty little home; the boy on the farm is to be there nights, mother said, and Linnet will not mind through the day. Mother Rheid, as Linnet says, will run over every day, and Father Rheid, too, I suspect. They *love* Linnet."

"Marjorie, if I hadn't had you I believe I should have been content with Linnet, she is so loving."

"And if you hadn't Prue you would be content with me!" laughed Marjorie, and just then a strong pull at the bell sent it ringing through the house, Marjorie sprang to her feet and Miss Prudence moved towards the door.

"I feel in my bones that it's somebody," cried Marjorie, following her into the hall.

"I don't believe a ghost could give a pull like that," answered Miss Prudence, turning the big key.

And a ghost certainly never had such laughing blue eyes or such light curls sprinkled with snow and surmounted by a jaunty navy-blue sailor cap, and a ghost never could give such a spring and catch Marjorie in its arms and rub its cold cheeks against her warm ones.

"O, Morris," Marjorie cried, "it's like that other night when you came in the snow! Only I'm not frightened and alone now. This is such a surprise! Such a splendid surprise."

Marjorie was never shy with Morris, her "twin-brother" as she used to call him.

But the next instant she was escaping out of his arms and fleeing back to the fire. Miss Prudence and Morris followed more decorously.

"Now tell us all about it," Marjorie cried, stepping about upon the rug and on the carpet. "And where is Linnet? And when did you get in? And where's Will? And why didn't Linnet come with you?"

"Because I didn't want to be overshadowed; I wanted a welcome all my own. And Linnet is at home under her mother's sheltering wing—as I ought to be under my mother's, instead of being here under yours. Will is on board the *Linnet*, another place where I ought to be this minute; and we arrived day before yesterday in New York, where we expect to load for Liverpool, I took the captain's wife home, and then got away from Mother West on the plea that I must see my own mother as soon as time and tide permitted; but to my consternation I found every train stopped at the foot of Maple Street, so I had to stop, instead of going through as I wanted to."

"That is a pity," said Marjorie; "but we'll send you off to your mother to-morrow. Now begin at the beginning and tell me everything that you and Linnet didn't write about."

"But, first—a moment, Marjorie. Has our traveller had his supper?" interposed Miss Prudence.

"Yes, thank you, I had supper, a very early one, with Linnet and Mother West; Father West had gone to mill, and didn't we turn the house upside down when he came into the kitchen and found us. Mother West kept wiping her eyes and Linnet put her arms around her father's neck and really cried! She said she knew she wasn't behaving 'marriedly,' but she was so glad she couldn't help it."

"Dear old Linnet," ejaculated Marjorie. "When is she coming to see us?"

"As soon as Mother West and Mother Rheid let her! I imagine the scene at Captain Rheid's tomorrow! Linnet is 'wild,' as you girls say, to see her house, and I don't know as she can tear herself away from that kitchen and new tinware, and she's fairly longing for washday to come that she may hang her new clothes on her new clothes line."

"Oh, I wish I could go and help her!" cried Marjorie. "Miss Prudence, that little house does almost make me want to go to housekeeping! Just think of getting dinner with all her new things, and setting the table with those pretty white dishes."

"Now, Marjorie, I've caught you," laughed Morris. "That is a concession from the girl that cared only for school books."

"I do care for school books, but that house is the temptation."

"I suppose another one wouldn't be."

"There isn't another one like that—outside of a book."

"Oh, if you find such things, in books, I won't veto the books; but, Miss Prudence, I'm dreadfully afraid of our Marjorie losing herself in a Blue Stocking."

"She never will, don't fear!" reassured Miss Prudence. "She coaxes me to let her sew for Prue, and I found her in the kitchen making cake last Saturday afternoon."

Miss Prudence was moving around easily, giving a touch to something here and there, and after closing the piano slipped away; and, before they knew it, they were alone, standing on the hearth rug looking gravely and almost questioningly into each others' eyes. Marjorie smiled, remembering the quarrel of that last night; would he think now that she had become too much like Miss Prudence,—Miss Prudence, with her love of literature, her ready sympathy and neat, housewifely ways, Prue did not know which she liked better, Aunt Prue's puddings or her music.

The color rose in Morris' face, Marjorie's lip trembled slightly. She seated herself in the chair she had been occupying and asked Morris to make himself at home in Miss Prudence's chair directly opposite. He dropped into it, threw his head back and allowed his eyes to rove over everything in the room, excepting that flushed, half-averted face so near to him. She was becoming like Miss Prudence, he had decided the matter in the study of these few moments, that attitude when standing was Miss Prudence's, and her position at this moment, the head a little drooping, the hands laid together in her lap, was exactly Miss Prudence's; Miss Prudence's when she was meditating as Marjorie was meditating now. There was a poise of the head like the elder lady's, and now and then a stateliness and dignity that were not Marjorie's own when she was his little friend and companion in work and study at home. In these first moments he could discern changes better than to-morrow; to-morrow he would be accustomed to her again; to-morrow he would find the unchanged little Marjorie that hunted eggs and went after the cows. He could not explain to himself why he liked that Marjorie better; he could not explain to himself that he feared Miss Prudence's Marjorie would hold herself above the second mate of the barque *Linnet*; a second mate whose highest ambition to become master. Linnet had not held her self above Captain Will, but Linnet had never loved books as Marjorie did. Morris was provoked at himself. Did not he love books, and why then should he quarrel with Marjorie? It was not for loving books, but for loving books better than—anything! Had Mrs. Browning loved books better than anything, or Mary Somerville, or Fredrika Bremer?—yes, Fredrika Bremer had refused to be married, but there was Marjorie's favorite—

"Tell me all about Linnet," said Marjorie, breaking the uncomfortable silence.

"I have—and she has written."

"But you never can write all. Did she bring me the branch of mulberry from Mt. Vesuvius?"

"Yes, and will bring it to you next week. She said she would come to you because she was sure you would not want to leave school; and she wants to see Miss Prudence. I told her she would wish herself a girl again, and it was dangerous for her to come, but she only laughed. I have brought you something, too, Marjorie," he said unsteadily.

But Marjorie ignored it and asked questions about Linnet and her home on shipboard.

"Have I changed, Marjorie?"

"No," she said. "You cannot change for the better, so why should you change at all?"

"I don't like that," he returned seriously; "it is rather hard to attain to perfection before one is twenty-one. I shall have nothing to strive for. Don't you know the artist who did kill himself, or wanted to, because he had done his best?"

"You are perfect as a boy—I mean, there is all manhood left to you," she answered very gravely.

He colored again and his blue eyes grew as cold as steel. Had he come to her to-night in the storm to have his youth thrown up at him?

"Marjorie, if that is all you have to say to me, I think I might better go."

"O, Morris, don't be angry, don't be angry!" she pleaded. "How can I look up to somebody who was born on my birthday," she added merrily.

"I don't want you to look up to me; but that is different from looking down. You want me to tarry at Jericho, I suppose," he said, rubbing his smooth chin.

"I want you not to be nonsensical," she replied energetically.

How that tiny box burned in his pocket! Should he toss it away, that circlet of gold with *Semper fidelis* engraved within it? How he used to write on his slate: "Morris Kemlo, *Semper fidelis*" and she had never once scorned it, but had written her own name with the same motto beneath it. But she had given it a higher significance than he had given it; she had never once thought of it in connection with any human love.

"How often do you write to Hollis?" he inquired at last.

"I do not write to him at all," she answered.

73

"Why not? Has something happened?" he said, eagerly.

"I suppose so."

"Don't you want to tell me? Does it trouble you?"

"Yes, I want to tell you, I do not think that it troubles me now. He has never—answered my last letter."

"Did you quarrel with him?"

"Oh, no. I may have displeased him, but I have no idea how I did it."

She spoke very easily, not flushing at all, meeting his eyes frankly; she was concealing nothing, there was nothing to be concealed. Marjorie was a little girl still. Was he glad or sorry? Would he find her grown up when he came back next time?

"Do you like school as well as you thought you would?" he asked, with a change of tone.

He would not be "nonsensical" any longer.

"Better! A great deal better," she said, enthusiastically.

"What are you getting ready for?"

"*Semper fiddelis*. Don't you remember our motto? I am getting ready to be always faithful. There's so much to be faithful in, Morris. I am learning new things every day."

He had no reply at hand. How that innocent ring burned in his pocket! And he had thought she would accept that motto from him.

"I am not the first fellow that has gone through this," he comforted himself grimly. "I will not throw it overboard; she will listen next time."

Next time? Ah, poor Morris, if you had known about next time, would you have spoken to-night?

"Marjorie, I have something for you, but I would rather not give it to you to-night," he said with some confusion.

"Well," she said, quietly, "I can wait."

"Do you *want* to wait."

"Yes. I think I do," she answered deliberately.

Miss Prudence's step was at the front parlor door.

"You young folks are not observing the clock, I see. Marjorie must study astronomy by starlight to-morrow morning, and I am going to send you upstairs, Morris. But first, shall we have family worship, together? I like to have a priest in my house when I can."

She laid Marjorie's Bible in his hand as she spoke. He read a short Psalm, and then they knelt together. He had grown; Marjorie felt it in every word of the simple heartfelt prayer. He prayed like one at home with God. One petition she long remembered: "Lord, when thou takest anything away from us, fill us the more with thyself."

XVIII.
ONE DAY.

"Education is the apprenticeship of life."—*Willmott*.

Marjorie did not study astronomy by starlight, but she awoke very early and tripped with bare feet over the carpet into Miss Prudence's chamber. Deborah kindled the wood fire early in Miss Prudence's chamber that Prue might have a warm room to dress in. It was rarely that Marjorie studied in the morning, the morning hours were reserved for practicing and for fun with Prue. She said if she had guessed how delightful it was to have a little sister she should have been all her life mourning for one. She almost envied Linnet because she had had Marjorie.

The fire was glowing in the airtight when she ran into the chamber, there was a faint light in the east, but the room was so dark that she just discerned Prue's curls close to the dark head on the pillow and the little hand that was touching Miss Prudence's cheek.

"This is the law of compensation," she thought as she busied herself in dressing; "one has found a mother and the other a little girl! It isn't quite like the old lady who said that when she had nothing to eat she had no appetite! I wonder if Miss Prudence has *all* her compensations!"

She stepped noiselessly over the stairs, opened the back parlor door, and by the dim light found a match and lighted the lamp on the centre table.

Last night had come again. The face of the clock was the only reminder she had left the room, the face of the clock and a certain alertness within herself. As she settled herself near the register and took the astronomy from the pile her eye fell on her Bible, it was on the table where Morris had laid it last night. Miss Prudence's words came to her, warningly. Must she also give the fresh hour of her morning to God? The tempting astronomy was open in her hand at the chapter *Via Lactea*. She glanced at it and read half a page, then dropped it suddenly and reached forward for the Bible. She was afraid her thoughts would wander to the unlearned lesson: in such a frame of mind, would it be an acceptable offering? But who was accountable for her frame of mind? She wavered no longer, with a little prayer that she might understand and enjoy she opened to Malachi, and, reverently and thoughtfully, with no feeling of being hurried, read the first and second chapters. She thought awhile about the "blind for sacrifice," and in the second chapter found words that meant something to her: "My covenant was with him of life and peace." Life and peace! Peace! Had she ever known anything that was not peace?

Before she had taken the astronomy into her hands again the door opened, as if under protest of some kind, and Morris stood on the threshold, looking at her with hesitation in his attitude.

"Come in," she invited, smiling at his attitude.

"But you don't want to talk."

"No; I have to study awhile. But you will not disturb; we have studied often enough together for you to know how I study."

"I know! Not a word in edgewise."

Nevertheless he came to the arm-chair he had occupied last night and sat down.

"Did you know the master gave me leave to take as many of his books as I wanted? He says a literary sailor is a novelty."

"All his books are in boxes in the trunk room on the second floor."

"I know it. I am going up to look at them. I wish you could read his letters. He urges me to live among men, not among books; to live out in the world and mix with men and women; to live a man's life, and not a hermit's!"

"Is he a hermit?"

"Rather. Will, Captain Will, is a man out among men; no hermit or student about him; but he has read 'Captain Cook's Voyages' with zest and asked me for something else, so I gave him 'Mutineers of the Bounty' and he did have a good time over that. Captain Will will miss me when I'm promoted to be captain."

"That will not be this voyage."

"Don't laugh at me. I have planned it all. Will is to have a big New York ship, an East Indiaman, and I'm to be content with the little *Linnet*."

"Does he like that?"

"Of course. He says he is to take Linnet around the world. Now study, please. *Via Lactea*" he exclaimed, bending forward and taking the book out of her hand. "What do you know about the Milky Way?"

"I never shall know anything unless you give me the book."

"As saucy as ever. You won't dare, some day."

Marjorie studied, Morris kept his eyes on a book that he did not read; neither spoke for fully three quarters of an hour. Marjorie studied with no pretence: Master McCosh had said that Miss West studied in fifteen minutes to more purpose than any other of her class did in an hour. She did not study, she was absorbed; she had no existence excepting in the lesson; just now there had been no other world for her than the wondrous Milky Way.

"I shall have Miss West for a teacher," he had told Miss Prudence.

Marjorie wondered if he ever would. Mrs. Browning has told us:

"Girls would fain know the end of everything."

And Marjorie would fain have known the end of herself. She would not be quite satisfied with Miss Prudence's lovely life, even with this "compensation" of Prue; there was a perfection of symmetry in Miss Prudence's character that she was aiming at, her character made her story, but what Marjorie would be satisfied to become she did not fully define even to Marjorie West.

"Now, I'm through," she exclaimed, closing the book as an exclamation point; "but I won't bother you with what I have learned. Master McCosh knows the face of the sky as well as I know the alphabet. You should have heard him and seen him one night, pointing here and there and everywhere: That's Orion, that's Job's coffin, that's Cassiopeia! As fast as he could speak. That's the Dipper, that's the North Star!"

"I know them all," said Morris.

"Why! when did you see them?"

"In my watches I've plenty of time to look at the stars! I've plenty of time for thinking!"

"Have you seen an iceberg?"

"Yes, one floated down pretty near us going out—the air was chillier and we found her glittering majesty was the cause of it."

"Have you seen a whale?"

"I've seen black fish; they spout like whales."

"And a nautilus."

"Yes."

"And Mother Carey's chickens?"

"Yes."

"Morris, I won't tease you with nonsense! What troubles you this morning?"

"My mother," he said concisely.

"Is she ill? Miss Prudence wrote to her last week"

"Does she ever reply?"

"I think so. Miss Prudence has not shown me her letters."

"Poor mother. I suppose so. I'm glad she writes at all. You don't know what it is to believe that God does not love you; to pray and have no answer; to be in despair."

"Oh, dear, no," exclaimed Marjorie, sympathetically.

"She is sure God has not forgiven her, she weeps and prays and takes no interest in anything."

"I should not think she would. I couldn't."

"She is with Delia now; the girls toss her back one to the other, and Clara wants to put her into the Old Lady's Home. She is a shadow on the house—they have no patience with her. They are not Christians, and their husbands are not—they do not understand; Delia's husband contends that she is crazy; but she is not, she is only in despair. They say she is no help, only a hindrance, and they want to get rid of her. She will not work about the house, she will not sew or help in anything, she says she cannot read the Bible—"

Miss Prudence

"How long since she has felt so?"

"Two years now. I would not tell you to worry you, but now I must tell some one, for something must be done. Delia has never been very kind to her since she was married. I have no home for her; what am I to do? I could not ask any happy home to take her in; I cannot bear to think of the Old Lady's Home for her, she will think her children have turned her off. And the girls have."

"Ask Miss Prudence what to do," said Marjorie brightly, "she always knows."

"I intend to. But she has been so kind to us all. Indeed, that was one of my motives in coming here. Between themselves the girls may send her somewhere while I am gone and I want to make that impossible. When I am captain I will take mother around the world. I will show her how good God is everywhere. Poor mother! She is one of those bubbling-over temperaments like Linnet's and when she is down she is all the way down. Who would have anything to live for if they did not believe in the love of God? Would I? Would you?"

"I could not live; I would *die*," said Marjorie vehemently.

"She does not live, she exists! She is emaciated; sometimes she fasts day after day until she is too weak to move around—she says she must fast while she prays. O, Marjorie, I'm sorry to let you know there is such sorrow in the world."

"Why should I not know about sorrow?" asked Marjorie, gravely. "Must I always be joyful?"

"I want you to be. There is no sorrow like this sorrow. I know something about it; before I could believe that God had forgiven me I could not sleep or eat."

"I always believed it, I think," said Marjorie simply.

"I want her to be with some one who loves her and understands her; the girls scold her and find fault with her, and she has been such a good mother to them; perhaps she let them have their own way too much, and this is one of the results of it. She has worked while they slept, and has taken the hardest of everything for them. And now in her sore extremity they want to send her among strangers. I wish I had a home of my own. If I can do no better, I will give up my position, and stay on land and make some kind of a home for her."

"Oh, not yet. Don't decide so hastily. Tell Miss Prudence. Telling her a thing is the next best thing to praying about it," said Marjorie, earnestly.

"What now?" Miss Prudence asked. "Morris, this girl is an enthusiast!"

She was standing behind Marjorie's chair and touched her hair as she spoke.

"Oh, have you heard it all?" cried Marjorie, springing up.

"No, I came in this instant; I only heard that Morris must not decide hastily, but tell me all about it, which is certainly good advice, and while we are at breakfast Morris shall tell me."

"I can't, before Prue," said Morris.

"Then we will have a conference immediately afterward. Deborah's muffins must not wait or she will be cross, and she has made muffins for me so many years that I can't allow her to be cross."

Morris made an attempt to be his usual entertaining self at the breakfast table, then broke down suddenly.

"Miss Prudence, I'm so full of something that I can't talk about anything else."

"I'm full of something too," announced Prue. "Aunt Prue, when am I going to Marjorie's school."

"I have not decided, dear."

"Won't you please decide now to let me go to-day?" she pleaded.

Miss Prudence was sure she had never "spoiled" anybody, but she began to fear that this irresistible little coaxer might prove a notable exception.

"I must think about it awhile, little one."

"Would I like it, Marjorie, at your school?"

"I am sure of it."

"I never went to school. The day I went with you it was ever so nice. I want a copy-book and a pile of books, and I want the girls to call me 'Miss Holmes.'"

"We can do that," said Miss Prudence, gravely. "Morris, perhaps Miss Holmes would like another bit of steak."

"That isn't it," said Prue, shaking her curls.

"Not genuine enough? How large is your primary class, Marjorie?"

"Twenty, I think. And they are all little ladies. It seems so comical to me to hear the girls call the little ones 'Miss.' Alice Dodd is younger than Prue, and Master McCosh says 'Miss Dodd' as respectfully as though she were in the senior class."

"Why shouldn't he?" demanded Prue. "Miss Dodd looked at me in church Sunday; perhaps I shall sit next to her. Do the little girls come in your room, Marjorie?"

"At the opening of school, always, and you could come in at intermissions. We have five minute intermissions every hour, and an hour at noon."

"O, Aunt Prue! When *shall* I go? I wish I could go to-day! You say I read almost well enough. Marjorie will not be ashamed of me now."

"I'd never be ashamed of you," said Marjorie, warmly.

"Papa said I must not say my name was 'Jeroma,' shall I write it *Prue Holmes*, Aunt Prue?"

"Prue J. Holmes! How would that do?"

But Miss Prudence spoke nervously and did not look at the child. Would she ever have to tell the child her father's story? Would going out among the children hasten that day?

"I like that," said Prue, contentedly; "because I keep papa's name tucked in somewhere. *May* I go to-day, Aunt Prue?"

"Not yet, dear. Master McCosh knows you are coming by and by. Marjorie may bring me a list of the books you will need and by the time the new quarter commences in February you may be able to overtake them if you study well. I think that will have to do, Prue."

"I would *rather* go to-day," sobbed the child, trying to choke the tears back. Rolling up her napkin hurriedly, she excused herself almost inaudibly and left the table.

"Aunt Prue! she'll cry," remonstrated Marjorie.

"Little girls have to cry sometimes," returned Miss Prudence, her own eyes suffused.

"She is not rebellious," remarked Morris.

"No, never rebellious—not in words; she told me within the first half hour of our meeting that she had promised papa she would be obedient. But for that promise we might have had a contest of wills. She will not speak of school again till February."

"How she creeps into one's heart," said Morris.

Miss Prudence's reply was a flash of sunshine through the mist of her eyes.

Marjorie excused herself to find Prue and comfort her a little, promising to ask Aunt Prue to let her go to school with her one day every week, as a visitor, until the new quarter commenced.

Miss Prudence was not usually so strict, she reasoned within herself; why must she wait for another quarter? Was she afraid of the cold for Prue? She must be waiting for something. Perhaps it was to hear from Mr. Holmes, Marjorie reasoned; she consulted him with regard to every new movement of Prue's. She knew that when she wrote to him she called her "our little girl."

While Miss Prudence and Morris lingered at the breakfast table they caught sounds of romping and laughter on the staircase and in the hall above.

"Those two are my sunshine," said Miss Prudence.

"I wish mother could have some of its shining," answered Morris. "My sisters do not give poor mother much beside the hard side of their own lives."

When Miss Prudence's two sunbeams rushed (if sunbeams do rush) into the back parlor they found her and Morris talking earnestly in low, rather suppressed tones, Morris seemed excited, there was an air of resolution about Miss Prudence's attitude that promised Marjorie there would be some new plan to be talked about that night. There was no stagnation, even in the monotony of Miss Prudence's little household. Hardly a day passed that Marjorie did not find her with some new thing to do for somebody somewhere outside in the ever-increasing circle of her friends. Miss Prudence's income as well as herself was kept in constant circulation. Marjorie enjoyed it; it was the ideal with which she had painted the bright days of her own future.

But then—Miss Prudence had money, and she would never have money. In a little old book of Miss Prudence's there was a list of names,—Miss Prudence had shown it to her,—against several names was written "Gone home;" against others, "Done;" and against as many as a dozen, "Something to do." The name of Morris' mother was included in the last. Marjorie hoped the opportunity to do that something had come at last; but what could it be? She could not influence Morris' hardhearted sisters to understand their mother and be tender towards her: even she could not do that. What would Miss Prudence think of? Marjorie was sure that his mother would be comforted and Morris satisfied. She hoped Morris would not have to settle on the "land," he loved the water with such abounding enthusiasm, he was so ready for his opportunities and so devoted to becoming a sailor missionary. What a noble boy he was! She had never loved him as she loved him at this moment, as he stood there in all his young strength and beauty, willing to give up his own planned life to serve the mother whom his sisters had cast off. He was like that hero she had read about—rather were not all true heroes like him? It was queer, she had not thought of it once since;—why did she think of it now?—but, that day Miss Prudence had come to see her so long ago, the day she found her asleep in her chair, she had been reading in her Sunday school library about some one like Morris, just as unselfish, just as ready to serve Christ anywhere, and—perhaps it was foolish and childish—she would be ashamed to tell any one beside God about it—she had asked him to let some one love her like him, and then she had fallen asleep. Oh, and—Morris had not given her that thing he had brought to her. Perhaps it was a book she wanted, she was always wanting a book—or it might be some curious thing from Italy. Had he forgotten it? She cared to have it now more than she cared last night; what was the matter with her last night that she cared so little? She did "look up" to him more than she knew herself, she valued his opinion, she was more to herself because she was so much to him. There was no one in the world that she opened her heart to as she opened it to him; not Miss Prudence, even, sympathetic as she was; she would not mind so very, very much if he knew about that foolish, childish prayer. But she could not ask him what he had brought her; she had almost, no, quite, refused it last night. How contradictory and uncomfortable she was! She must say good-bye, now, too.

During her reverie she had retreated to the front parlor and stood leaning over the closed piano, her wraps all on for school and shawl strap of books in her hand.

"O, Marjorie, ready for school! May I walk with you? I'll come back and see Miss Prudence afterward."

"Will you?" she asked, demurely; "but that will only prolong the agony of saying good-bye."

"As it is a sort of delicious agony we do not need to shorten it. Good-bye, Prue," he cried, catching one of Prue's curls in his fingers as he passed. "You will be a school-girl with a shawl strap of books, by and by, and you will put on airs and think young men are boys."

Prue stood in the doorway calling out "goodbye" as they went down the path to the gate, Miss Prudence's "old man" had been there early to sweep off the piazzas and shovel paths; he was one of her beneficiaries with a history. Marjorie said they all had histories: she believed he had lost some money in a bank years ago, some that he had hoarded by day labor around the wharves.

Miss Prudence

The pavements in this northern city were covered with snow hard packed, the light snow of last night had frozen and the sidewalks were slippery; in the city the children were as delighted to see the brick pavement in spring as the country children were glad to see the green grass.

"Whew"! ejaculated Morris, as the wind blew sharp in their faces, "this is a stiff north-wester and no mistake. I don't believe that small Californian would enjoy walking to school to-day."

"I think that must be why Aunt Prue keeps her at home; I suppose she wants to teach her to obey without a reason, and so she does not give her one."

"That isn't a bad thing for any of us," said Morris.

"She has bought her the prettiest winter suit! She is so warm and lovely in it—and a set of white furs; she is a bluebird with a golden crest. After she was dressed the first time Miss Prudence looked down at her and said, as if excusing the expense to herself: 'But I must keep the child warm—and it is my own money.' I think her father died poor."

"I'm glad of it," said Morris.

"Why?" asked Marjorie, wonderingly.

"Miss Prudence and Mr. Holmes will take care of her; she doesn't need money," he answered, evasively. "I wouldn't like Prue to be a rich woman in this city."

"Isn't it a good city to be a rich woman in?" questioned Marjorie with a laugh. "As good as any other."

"Not for everybody; do you know I wonder why Miss Prudence doesn't live in New York as she did when she sent Linnet to school."

"She wanted to be home, she said; she was tired of boarding, and she liked Master McCosh's school for me. I think she will like it for Prue. I'm so glad she will have Prue when I have to go back home. Mr. Holmes isn't rich, is he? You said he would take care of Prue."

"He has a very small income from his mother; his mother was not Prue's father's mother."

"Why, do you know all about them?"

"Yes."

"Who told you? Aunt Prue hasn't told me."

"Mother knows. She knew Prue's father. I suspect some of the girls' fathers in your school knew him, too."

"I don't know. He was rich once—here—I know that. Deborah told me where he used to live; it's a handsome house, with handsome grounds, a stable in the rear and an iron fence in front."

"I've seen it," said Morris, in his concisest tone. "Mr. Holmes and I walked past one day. Mayor Parks lives there now."

"Clarissa Parks' father!" cried Marjorie, in an enlightened tone. "She's in our first class, and if she studied she would learn something. She's bright, but she hasn't motive enough."

"Do you think Mr. Holmes, will ever come home?" he asked.

"Why not? Of course he will," she answered in astonishment.

"That depends. Prue might bring him. I want to see him finished; there's a fine finishment for him somewhere and I want to see it. For all that is worth anything in me I have to thank him. He made me—as God lets one man make another. I would like to live long enough to pass it on; to make some one as he made me."

It was too cold to walk slowly, their words were spoken in brief, brisk sentences.

There was nothing specially memorable in this walk, but Marjorie thought of it many times; she remembered it because she was longing to ask him what he had brought her and was ashamed to do it. It might be due to him after her refusal last night; but still she was ashamed. She would write about it, she decided; it was like her not to speak of it.

"I haven't told you about our harbor mission work at Genoa; the work is not so great in summer, but the chaplain told me that in October there were over sixty seamen in the Bethel and they were very attentive. One old captain told me that the average sailor had much improved since he began to go to sea, and I am sure the harbor mission work is one cause of it. I wish you could hear some of the old sailors talk and pray. The *Linnet* will be a praise meeting in itself some day; four sailors have become Christians since I first knew the *Linnet*."

"Linnet wrote that it was your work."

"I worked and prayed and God blessed. Oh, the blessing! oh, the blessing of good books! Marjorie, do you know what makes waves?"

"No," she laughed; "and I'm too cold to remember if I did. I think the wind must make them. Now we turn and on the next corner is our entrance."

The side entrance was not a gate, but a door in a high wall; girls were flocking up the street and down the street, blue veils, brown veils, gray veils, were streaming in all directions, the wind was blowing laughing voices all around them.

Marjorie pushed the door open:

"Good-bye, Morris," she said, as he caught her hand and held it last.

"Good-bye, Marjorie,—*dear*" he whispered as a tall girl in blue brushed past them and entered the door.

Little Miss Dodd ran up laughing, and Marjorie could say no more; what more could she say than "good-bye"? But she wanted to say more, she wanted to say—but Emma Downs was asking her if it were late and Morris had gone.

"What a handsome young fellow!" exclaimed Miss Parks to Marjorie, hanging up her cloak next to Marjorie's in the dressing room. "Is he your brother?"

"My twin-brother," replied Marjorie.

"He doesn't look like you. He is handsome and tall."

"And I am homely and stumpy," said Marjorie, good-humoredly. "No, he is not my real brother."

"I don't believe in that kind."

"I do," said Marjorie.

"Master McCosh will give you a mark for transgressing."

"Oh, I forgot!" exclaimed Marjorie; "but he is so much my brother that it is not against the rules."

"Is he a sailor?" asked Emma Downs.

"Yes," said Marjorie.

"A common sailor!"

"No, an uncommon one."

"Is he before the mast?" she persisted.

"Does he look so?" asked Marjorie, seriously.

"No, he looks like a captain; only that cap is not dignified enough."

"It's becoming," said Miss Parks, "and that's better than dignity."

The bell rang and the girls passed into the schoolroom in twos and threes. A table ran almost the length of the long, high apartment; it was covered with green baize and served as a desk for the second class girls; the first class girls occupied chairs around three sides of the room, during recitation the chairs were turned to face the teacher, at other times the girls sat before a leaf that served as a rest for their books while they studied, shelves being arranged above to hold the books. The walls of the room were tinted a pale gray. Mottoes in black and gold were painted in one straight line above the book shelves, around the three sides of the room. Marjorie's favorites were:

TO DESIRE TO KNOW—TO KNOW, IS CURIOSITY.

TO DESIRE TO KNOW—TO BE KNOWN, IS VANITY.

TO DESIRE TO KNOW—TO SELL YOUR KNOWLEDGE, IS COVETOUSNESS.

TO DESIRE TO KNOW—TO EDIFY ONE'S SELF, IS PRUDENCE.

TO DESIRE TO KNOW—TO EDIFY OTHERS, IS CHARITY.

TO DESIRE TO KNOW—TO GLORIFY GOD, IS RELIGION.

The words were very ancient, Master McCosh told Marjorie, the last having been written seven hundred years later than the others. The words "TO GLORIFY GOD" were over Marjorie's desk.

The first class numbered thirty. Clarissa Parks was the beauty of the class, Emma Downs the poet, Lizzie Harrowgate the mathematician, Maggie Peet the pet, Ella Truman wrote the finest hand, Maria Denyse was the elocutionist, Pauline Hayes the one most at home in universal history, Marjorie West did not know what she was: the remaining twenty-two were in no wise remarkable; one or two were undeniably dull, more were careless, and most came to school because it was the fashion and they must do something before they were fully grown up.

At each recitation the student who had reached the head of the class was marked "head" and took her place in the next recitation at the foot. During the first hour and a half there were four recitations—history, astronomy, chemistry, and English literature. That morning Marjorie, who did not know what she was in the class, went from the foot through the class, to the head three times; it would have been four times but she gave the preference to Pauline Hayes who had written the correct date half a second after her own was on the slate. "Miss Hayes writes more slowly than I," she told Master McCosh. "She was as sure of it as I was."

The replies in every recitation were written upon the slate; there was no cheating, every slate was before the eyes of its neighbor, every word must be exact.

"READING MAKES A FULL MAN, CONFERENCE A READY MAN, WRITING AN EXACT MAN," was one of the wall mottoes.

Marjorie had an amusing incident to relate to Miss Prudence about her first recitation in history. The question was: "What general reigned at this time?" The name of no general occurred. Marjorie was nonplussed. Pencils were rapidly in motion around her. "Confusion" read the head girl. Then to her chagrin Marjorie recalled the words in the lesson: "General confusion reigned at this time."

It was one of the master's "catches". She found that he had an abundant supply.

Another thing that morning reminded her of that mysterious "vibgyor" of the old times.

Master McCosh told them they could *clasp* Alexander's generals; then Pauline Hayes gave their names—Cassander, Lysimachus, Antiognus, Seleucus and Ptolemy. Marjorie had that to tell Miss Prudence. Miss Prudence lived through her own school days that winter with Marjorie; the girl's enthusiasm reminded her of her own. Master McCosh, who never avoided personalities, observed as he marked the last recitation:

"Miss West studies, young ladies; she has no more brains than one or two of the rest of you, but she has something that more than half of you woefully lack—application and conscience."

"Perhaps she expects to teach," returned Miss Parks, in her most courteous tone, as she turned the diamond upon her engagement finger.

"I hope she may teach—this class," retorted the master with equal courtesy.

Miss Parks smiled at Marjorie with her lovely eyes and acknowledged the point of the master's remark with a slight inclination of her pretty head.

At the noon intermission a knot of the girls gathered around Marjorie's chair; Emma Downs took the volume of "Bridgewater Treatises" out of her hand and marched across the room to the book case with it, the others clapped their hands and shouted.

Miss Prudence

"Now we'll make her talk," said Ella Truman. "She is a queen in the midst of her court."

"She isn't tall enough," declared Maria Denyse.

"Or stately enough," added Pauline Hayes.

"Or self-possessed enough," supplemented Lizzie Harrowgate.

"Or imperious enough," said Clarissa Parks.

"She would always be abdicating in favor of some one who had an equal right to it," laughed Pauline Hayes.

"Oh, Miss West, who was that lovely little creature with you in Sunday school Sunday?" asked Miss Denyse. "She carries herself like a little princess."

"She is just the one not to do it," replied Miss Parks.

"What do you mean?" inquired Miss Harrowgate before Marjorie could speak.

"I mean," she began, laying a bunch of white grapes in Marjorie's fingers, "that her name is *Holmes*."

"Doesn't that belong to the royal line?" asked Pauline, lightly.

"It belongs to the line of *thieves*."

Marjorie's fingers dropped the grapes.

"Her father spent years in state-prison when he should have spent a lifetime there at hard labor! Ask my father. Jerome Holmes! He is famous in this city! How dared he send his little girl here to hear all about it!"

"Perhaps he thought he sent her among Christians and among ladies," returned Miss Harrowgate. "I should think you would be ashamed to bring that old story up, Clarissa."

Marjorie was paralyzed; she could not move or utter a sound.

"Father has all the papers with the account in; father lost enough, he ought to know about it."

"That child can't help it," said Emma Downs. "She has a face as sweet and innocent as an apple blossom."

"I hope she will never come here to school to revive the old scandal," said Miss Denyse. "Mother told me all about it as soon as she knew who the child was."

"Somebody else had the hardest of it," said Miss Parks; "*that's* a story for us girls. Mother says she was one of the brightest and sweetest girls in all the city; she used to drive around with her father, and her wedding day was set, the cards were out, and then it came out that he had to go to state-prison instead. She gave up her diamonds and everything of value he had given her. She was to have lived in the house we live in now; but he went to prison and she went somewhere and has never been back for any length of time until this year, and now she has his little girl with her."

Miss Prudence! Was that Miss Prudence's story? Was she bearing it like this? Was that why she loved poor little Prue so?

"Bring some water, quick!" Marjorie heard some one say.

"No, take her to the door," suggested another voice.

"Oh, I'm so sorry, so sorry!" This was Miss Parks.

Marjorie arose to her feet, pushed some one away from her, and fled from them all—down the schoolroom, though the cloak-room out to the fresh air.

She needed the stiff worth-wester to bring her back to herself. Miss Prudence had lived through *that*! And Prue must grow up to know! Did Miss Prudence mean that she must decide about that before Prue could come to school? She remembered now that a look, as if she were in pain, had shot itself across her eyes. Oh, that she would take poor little Prue back to California where nobody knew. If some one should tell *her* a story like that about her own dear honest father it would kill her! She never could bear such shame and such disappointment in him. But Prue need never know if Miss Prudence took her away to-day, to-morrow. But Miss Prudence had had it to bear so long. Was that sorrow—and the blessing with it—the secret of her lovely life? And Mr. Holmes, the master! Marjorie was overwhelmed with this new remembrance of him. He was another one to bear it. Now she understood his solitary life. Now she knew why he shrank from anything like making himself known. The depth of the meaning of some of his favorite sayings flashed over her. She even remembered one of her own childish questions, and his brief, stern affirmative: "Mr. Holmes, were you ever in a prison?" How much they had borne together, these two! And now they had Prue to love and to live for. She would never allow even a shadow of jealousy of poor little Prue again. Poor little Prue, with such a heritage of shame. How vehemently and innocently she had declared that she would not be called Jeroma.

The wind blew sharply against her; she stepped back and closed the door; she was shivering while her cheeks were blazing. She would go home, she could not stay through the hour of the afternoon and be looked at and commented upon. Was not Miss Prudence's shame and sorrow her own? As she was reaching for her cloak she remembered that she must ask to be excused, taking it down and throwing it over her arm she re-entered the schoolroom.

Master McCosh was writing at the table, a group of girls were clustered around one of the registers.

"It was mean! It was real mean!" a voice was exclaiming.

"I don't see how you *could* tell her, Clarissa Parks! You know she adores Miss Pomeroy."

"You all seemed to listen well enough," retorted Miss Parks.

"We were spell-bound. We couldn't help it," excused Emma Downs.

"I knew it before," said Maria Denyse.

"I didn't know Miss Pomeroy was the lady," said Lizzie Harrowgate. "She is mother's best friend, so I suppose she wouldn't tell me. They both came here to school."

Master McCosh raised his head.

"What new gossip now, girls?" he inquired sternly.

"Oh, nothing," answered Miss Parks.

"You are making quite a hubbub about nothing. The next time that subject is mentioned the young lady who does it takes her books and goes home. Miss Holmes expects to come here among you, and the girl who does not treat her with consideration may better stay at home. Jerome Holmes was the friend of my boyhood and manhood; he sinned and he suffered for it; his story does not belong to your generation. It is not through any merit of yours that your fathers are honorable men. It becomes us all to be humble?"

A hush fell upon the group. Clarissa Parks colored with anger; why should *she* be rebuked, she was not a thief nor the daughter of a thief.

Marjorie went to the master and standing before him with her cheeks blazing and eyes downcast she asked:

"May I go home? I cannot recite this afternoon."

"If you prefer, yes," he replied in his usual tone; "but I hardly think you care to see Miss Pomeroy just now."

"Oh, no, I didn't think of that; I only thought of getting away from here."

"Getting away is not always the best plan," he replied, his pen still moving rapidly.

"Is it true? Is it *all* true?"

"It is all true. Jerome Holmes was president of a bank in this city. I want you in moral science this afternoon."

"Thank you," said Marjorie, after a moment. "I will stay."

She returned to the dressing-room, taking a volume of Dick from the book-case as she passed it; and sitting in a warm corner, half concealed by somebody's shawl and somebody's cloak, she read, or thought she read, until the bell for the short afternoon session sounded.

Moral science was especially interesting to her, but the subject this afternoon kept her trouble fresh in her mind; it was Property, the use of the institution of Property, the history of Property, and on what the right of Property is founded.

A whisper from Miss Parks reached her:

"Isn't it a poky subject? All I care to know is what is mine and what isn't, and to know what right people have to take what isn't theirs."

The hour was ended at last, and she was free. How could she ever enter that schoolroom again? She hurried along the streets, grown older since the morning. Home would be her sanctuary; but there was Miss Prudence! Her face would tell the tale and Miss Prudence's eyes would ask for it. Would it be better for Prue, for Aunt Prue, to know or not to know? Miss Prudence had written to her once that some time she would tell her a story about herself; but could she mean this story?

As she opened the gate she saw her blue bird with the golden crest perched on the arm of a chair at the window watching for her.

She was at the door before Marjorie reached it, ready to spring into her arms and to exclaim how glad she was that she had come.

"You begin to look too soon, Kitten."

"I didn't begin till one o'clock," she said convincingly.

"But I don't leave school till five minutes past two, childie."

"But I have something to tell you to-day. Something *de*-licious. Aunt Prue has gone away with Morris. It isn't that, because I didn't want her to go."

Marjorie followed her into the front parlor and began to unfasten her veil.

"Morris' mother is coming home with her to-morrow to stay all winter, but that isn't it. Do guess, Marjorie."

She was dancing all around her, clapping her hands.

"Linnet hasn't come! That isn't it!" cried Marjorie, throwing off her cloak.

"No; it's all about me. It is going to happen to *me*."

"I can't think. You have nice things every day."

"It's this. It's nicer than anything. I am going to school with you to-morrow! Not for all the time, but to make a visit and see how I like it."

The child stood still, waiting for an outburst of joy at her announcement; but Marjorie only caught her and shook her and tumbled her curls without saying one word.

"Aren't you *glad*, Marjorie?"

"I'm glad I'm home with you, and I'm glad you are to give me my dinner."

"It's a very nice dinner," answered Prue, gravely; "roast beef and potatoes and tomatoes and pickled peaches and apple pie, unless you want lemon pie instead. I took lemon pie. Which will you have?"

"Lemon," said Marjorie.

"But you don't look glad about anything. Didn't you know your lessons to-day?"

"Oh, yes."

"I'll put your things on the hat-rack and you can get warm while I tell Deborah to put your dinner on the table. I think you are cold and that is why you can't be glad. I don't like to be cold."

"I'm not cold now," laughed Marjorie.

"Now you feel better! And I'm to sit up until you go to bed, and you are to sleep with me; and *won't* it be splendid for me to go to school and take my lunch, too? And I can have jelly on my bread and an orange just as you do."

Marjorie was awake long before Deborah entered the chamber to kindle the fire, trying to form some excuse to keep Prue from going to school with her. How could she take her to-day of all days; for the girls to look at her, and whisper to each other, and ask her questions, and to study critically her dress, and to touch her hair, and pity her and kiss her! And she would be sure to open the round gold locket she wore upon a tiny gold chain about her neck and tell them it was "my papa who died in California."

She was very proud of showing "my papa."

What excuse could she make to the child? It was not storming, and she did not have a cold, and her heart did seem so set on it. The last thing after she came upstairs last night she had opened the inside blinds to look out to see if it were snowing. And she had charged Deborah to have the fire kindled early so that she would not be late at breakfast.

She must go herself. She could concoct no reason for remaining at home herself; her throat had been a trifle sore last night, but not even the memory of it could bring it back this morning.

Deborah had a cough, if she should be taken ill—but there was the fire crackling in the airtight in confirmation of Deborah's ability to be about the house; or if Prue—but the child was never ill. Her cheeks were burning last night, but that was with the excitement of the anticipation. If somebody should come! But who? She had not stayed at home for Morris, and Linnet would not come early enough to keep them at home, that is if she ought to remain at home for Linnet.

What could happen? She could not make anything happen? She could not tell the child the naked truth, the horrible truth. And she could not tell her a lie. And she could not break her heart by saying that she did not want her to go. Oh, if Miss Prudence were only at home to decide! But would she tell *her* the reason? If she did not take Prue she must tell Miss Prudence the whole story. She would rather go home and never go to school any more than to do that. Oh, why must things happen all together? Prue would soon be awake and asking if it were storming. She had let her take it for granted last night; she could not think of anything to say. Once she had said in aggrieved voice:

"I think you might be glad, Marjorie."

But was it not all selfishness, after all? She was arranging to give Prue a disappointment merely to spare herself. The child would not understand anything. But then, would Aunt Prue want her to go? She must do what Miss Prudence would like; that would decide it all.

Oh, dear! Marjorie was a big girl, too big for any nonsense, but there were unmistakable tears on her cheeks, and she turned away from sleeping Prue and covered her face with both hands. And then, beside this, Morris was gone and she had not been kind to him. "Good-bye, Marjorie—*dear*" the words smote her while they gave her a feeling of something to be very happy about. There did seem to be a good many things to cry about this morning.

"Marjorie, are you awake?" whispered a soft voice, while little fingers were in her hair and tickling her ear.

Marjorie did not want to be awake.

"*Marjorie*," with an appeal in the voice.

Then the tears had to be brushed away, and she turned and put both arms around the white soft bundle and rubbed her cheek against her hair.

"Oh, *do* you think it's storming?"

"No."

"You will have to curl my hair."

"Yes."

"And mustn't we get up? Shan't we be late?"

"Listen a minute; I want to tell you something."

"Is it something *dreadful?* Your voice sounds so."

"No not dreadful one bit. But it is a disappointment for a little girl I know."

"Oh, is it *me?*" clinging to her.

"Yes, it is you."

"Is it about going to school?" she asked with a quick little sob.

"Yes."

"*Can't* I go, Marjorie?"

"Not to-day, darling."

"Oh, dear!" she moaned. "I did want to so."

"I know it, and I'm so sorry. I am more sorry than you are. I was so sorry that I could not talk about it last night."

"Can't I know the reason?" she asked patiently.

"The reason is this: Aunt Prue would not let you go. She would not let you go if she knew about something that happened in school yesterday."

"Was it something so bad?"

"It was something very uncomfortable; something that made me very unhappy, and if you were old enough to understand you would not want to go. You wouldn't go for anything."

"Then what makes you go?" asked Prue quickly.

"Because I have to."

"Will it hurt you to-day?"

"Yes."

"Then I wouldn't go. Tell Aunt Prue; she won't make you go."

"I don't want to tell her; it would make her cry."

"Then don't tell her. I'll stay home then—if I have to. But I want to go. I can stand it if you can."

Marjorie laughed at her resignation and resolution and rolling her over pushed her gently out down to the carpet. Perhaps it would be better to stay home if there were something so dreadful at school, and Deborah might let her make molasses candy.

"Won't you please stay home with me and make molasses candy, or peppermint drops?"

"We'll do it after school! won't that do? And you can stay with Deborah in the kitchen, and she'll tell you stories."

"Her stories are sad," said Prue, mournfully.

"Ask her to tell you a funny one, then."

"I don't believe she knows any. She told me yesterday about her little boy who didn't want to go to school one day and she was washing and said he might stay home because he coaxed so hard. And she went to find him on the wharf and nobody could tell her where he was. And she went down close to the water and looked in and he was there with his face up and a stick in his hand and he was dead in the water and she saw him."

"Is that true?" asked Marjorie, in surprise.

"Yes, true every word. And then her husband died and she came to live with Aunt Prue's father and mother ever so long ago. And she cried and it was sad."

"But I know she knows some funny stories. She will tell you about Aunt Prue when she was little."

"She has told me. And about my papa. He used to like to have muffins for tea."

"Oh, I know! Now I know! I'll take you to Lizzie Harrowgate's to stay until I come from school. You will like that. There is a baby there and a little girl four years old. Do you want to go?"

"If I can't go to school, I do," in a resigned voice.

"And you must not speak of school; remember, Prue, do not say that you wanted to go, or that I wouldn't take you; do not speak of school at all."

"No, I will not," promised Prue; "and when that thing doesn't happen any more you will take me?"

XIX.

A STORY THAT WAS NOT VERY SAD.

"Children have neither past nor future; and, what scarcely ever happens to us, they enjoy the present."—*Bruyére.*

Prue was watching at the window with Minnie Harrowgate, and was joyfully ready to go home to see Aunt Prue when Marjorie and Lizzie Harrowgate appeared.

Standing a few moments near the parlor register, while Prue ran to put on her wraps, Marjorie's eye would wander to the Holland plate on the bracket. She walked home under a depression that was not all caused by the dread of meeting Miss Prudence. They found Miss Prudence on the stairs, coming down with a tray of dishes.

"O, Aunt Prue! Aunt Prue!" was Prue's exclamation. "I didn't go to school, I went to Mrs. Harrowgate's instead. Marjorie said I must, because something dreadful happened in school and I never could go until it never happened again. But I've had a splendid time, and I want to go again."

Miss Prudence bent over to kiss her, and gave her the tray to take into the kitchen.

"You may stay with Deborah, dear, till I call you."

Marjorie dropped her shawl-strap of books on the carpet of the hall and stood at the hat-stand hanging up her cloak and hat. Miss Prudence had kissed her, but they had not looked into each other's eyes.

Was it possible that Miss Prudence suspected? Marjorie asked herself as she took off her rubbers. She suffered her to pass into the front parlor, and waited alone in the hall until she could gather courage to follow her. But the courage did not come, she trembled and choked, and the slow tears rolled over her cheeks.

"Marjorie!"

Miss Prudence was at her side.

"O, Miss Prudence! O, dear Aunt Prue, I don't want to tell you," she burst out; "they said things about her father and about you, and I can't tell you."

Miss Prudence's arm was about her, and she was gently drawn into the parlor; not to sit down, for Miss Prudence began slowly to walk up and down the long length of the room, keeping Marjorie at her side. They paused an instant before the mirror, between the windows in the front parlor, and both glanced in: a slight figure in gray, for she had put off her mourning at last, with a pale, calm face, and a plump little creature in brown, with a flushed face and full eyes—the girl growing up, and the girl grown up.

For fully fifteen minutes they paced slowly and in silence up and down the soft carpet. Miss Prudence knew when they stood upon the very spot where Prue's father—not Prue's father then—had bidden her that lifetime long farewell. God had blessed her and forgiven him. Was it such a very sad story then?

Miss Prudence dropped into a chair as if her strength were spent, and Marjorie knelt beside her and laid her head on the arm of her chair.

"It is true, Marjorie."

"I know it. Master McCosh heard it and he said it was true."

"It will make a difference, a great difference. I shall take Prue away. I must write to John to-night."

"I'm so glad you have him, Aunt Prue. I'm so glad you and Prue have him."

Miss Prudence knew now, herself: never before had she known how glad she was to have him; how glad she had been to have him all her life. She would tell him that, to-night, also. She was not the woman to withhold a joy that belonged to another.

Marjorie did not raise her head, and therefore did not catch the first flash of the new life that John Holmes would see when he looked into them.

"He is so good, Aunt Prue," Marjorie went on. "*He* is a Christian when he speaks to a dog."

"Don't you want to go upstairs and see Morris' mother? She was excited a little, and I promised her that she should not come down-stairs to-night."

"But I don't know her," said Marjorie rising.

"I think you do. And she knows you. She has come here to learn how good God is, and I want you to help me show it to her."

"I don't know how."

"Be your sweet, bright self, and sing all over the house all the comforting hymns you know."

"Will she like that?"

"She likes nothing so well. I sung her to sleep last night."

"I wish mother could talk to her."

"Marjorie! you have said it. Your mother is the one. I will send her to your mother in the spring. Morris and I will pay her board, and she shall keep close to your happy mother as long as they are both willing."

"Will Morris let you help pay her board?"

"Morris cannot help himself. He never resists me. Now go upstairs and kiss her, and tell her you are her boy's twin-sister."

Before the light tap on her door Mrs. Kemlo heard, and her heart was stirred as she heard it, the pleading, hopeful, trusting strains of "Jesus, lover of my soul."

Moving about in her own chamber, with her door open, Marjorie sang it all before she crossed the hall and gave her light tap on Mrs. Kemlo's door.

When Marjorie saw the face—the sorrowful, delicate face, and listened to the refined accent and pretty choice of words, she knew that Morris Kemlo was a gentleman because his mother was a lady.

Prue wandered around the kitchen, looking at things and asking questions.
Deborah was never cross to Prue.

It was a sunny kitchen in the afternoon, the windows faced west and south and Deborah's plants throve. Miss Prudence had taken great pleasure in making Deborah's living room a room for body and spirit to keep strong in. Old Deborah said there was not another room in the house like the kitchen; "and to think that Miss Prudence should put a lounge there for my old bones to rest on."

Prue liked the kitchen because of the plants. It was very funny to see such tiny sweet alyssum, such dwarfs of geranium, such a little bit of heliotrope, and only one calla among those small leaves.

"Just wait till you go to California with us, Deborah," she remarked this afternoon. "I'll show you flowers."

"I'm too old to travel, Miss Prue."

"No, you are not. I shall take you when I go. I can wait on Morris' mother, can't I? Marjorie said she and I were to help you if she came."

"Miss Marjorie is good help."

"So am I," said Prue, hopping into the dining-room and amusing herself by stepping from one green pattern in the carpet to another green one, and then from one red to another red one, and then, as her summons did not come, from a green to a red and a red to a green, and still Aunt Prue did not call her. Then she went back to Deborah, who was making lemon jelly, at one of the kitchen tables, in a great yellow bowl. She told Prue that some of it was to go to a lady in consumption, and some to a little boy who had a hump on his back. Prue said that she would take it to the little boy, because she had never seen a hump on a boy's back; she had seen it on camels in a picture.

Still Aunt Prue did not come for her, and she counted thirty-five bells on the arbutilon, and four buds on the monthly rose, and pulled off three drooping daisies that Deborah had not attended to, and then listened, and "Prue! Prue!" did not come.

Aunt Prue and Marjorie must be talking "secrets."

"Deborah," standing beside her and looking seriously up into the kindly, wrinkled face, "I wish you knew some secrets."

"La! child, I know too many."

"Will you tell me one. Just one. I never heard a secret in my life. Marjorie knows one, and she's telling Aunt Prue now."

"Secrets are not for little girls."

"I would never, never tell," promised Prue, coaxingly.

"Not even me!" cried Marjorie behind her. "Now come upstairs with me and see Morris' mother. Aunt Prue is not ready for you yet awhile."

Mrs. Kemlo's chamber was the guest chamber; many among the poor and suffering whom Miss Prudence had delighted to honor had "warmed both hands before the fire of life" in that luxurious chamber.

Everything in the room had been among her father's wedding presents to herself—the rosewood furniture, the lace curtains, the rare engravings, the carpet that was at once perfect to the tread and to the eye, the ornaments everywhere: everything excepting the narrow gilt frame over the dressing bureau, enclosing on a gray ground, painted in black, crimson, and gold the words: "I HAVE SEEN THY TEARS." Miss Prudence had placed it there especially for Mrs. Kemlo.

Deborah had never been alone in the house in the years when her mistress was making a home for herself elsewhere.

Over the mantel hung an exquisite engraving of the thorn-crowned head of Christ. The eyes that had wept so many hopeless tears were fixed upon it as Marjorie and Prue entered the chamber.

"This is Miss Prudence's little girl Prue," was Marjorie's introduction.

Prue kissed her and stood at her side waiting for her to speak.

"That is the Lord," Prue said, at last, breaking the silence after Marjorie had left them; "our dear Lord."

Mrs. Kemlo kept her eyes upon it, but made no response.

"What makes him look so sorry, Morris' mother?"

"Because he is grieving for our sins."

"I thought the thorns hurt his head."

"Not so much as our sins pierced his heart."

"I'm sorry if I have hurt him. What made our sins hurt him so?"

"His great love to us."

"Nobody's sins ever hurt me so."

"You do not love anybody well enough."

The spirit of peace was brooding, at last, over the worn face. Morris had left her with his heart at rest, for the pain on lip and brow began to pass away in the first hour of Miss Prudence's presence.

Prue was summoned after what to her seemed endless waiting, and, nestling in Aunt Prue's lap, with her head on her shoulder and her hand in hers, she sat still in a content that would not stir itself by one word.

"Little Prue, I want to tell you a story."

"Oh, good!" cried Prue, nestling closer to express her appreciation.

"What kind of stories do you like best?"

"Not sad ones. Don't let anybody die."

"This story is about a boy. He was like other boys, he was bright and quick and eager to get on in the world. He loved his mother and his brother and sister, and he worked for them on the farm at home. And then he came to the city and did so well that all his friends were proud of him; everybody liked him and admired him. He was large and fine looking and a gentleman. People thought he was rich, for he soon had a handsome house and drove fine horses. He had a lovely wife, but she died and left him all alone. He always went to church and gave money to the church; but he never said that he was a Christian. I think he trusted in himself, people trusted him so much that he began to trust himself. They let him have their money to take care of; they were sure he would take good care of it and give it safe back, and he was sure, too. And he did take good care of it, and they were satisfied. He was generous and kind and loving. But he was so sure that he was strong that he did not ask God to keep him strong, and God let him become weaker and weaker, until temptation became too great for him and he took this money and spent it for himself; this money that belonged to other people. And some belonged to widows who had no husbands to take care of them, and to children who had no fathers, and to people who had worked hard to save money for their children and to take care of themselves in their old age; but he took it and spent it trying to make more money for himself, and instead of making more money always he lost their money that he took away from them. He meant to give their money back, he did not mean to steal from any one, but he took what was not his own and lost it and the people had to suffer, for he had no money to pay them with."

"That is sad," said Prue.

"Yes, it was very sad, for he had done a dreadful thing and sinned against God. Do you think he ought to be punished?"

"Yes, if he took poor people's money and little children's money and could not give it back."

"So people thought, and he was punished: he was sent to prison."

"To *prison*! Oh, that was dreadful."

"And he had to stay there for years and work hard, with other wicked men."

"Wasn't he sorry?"

"He was very sorry. It almost killed him. He would gladly have worked to give the money back but he could not earn so much. He saw how foolish and wicked he had been to think himself so strong and trustworthy and good when he was so weak. And when he saw how wicked he was he fell down before God and asked God to forgive him. His life was spoiled, he could not be happy in this world; but, as God forgave him, he could begin again and be honest and trustworthy, and be happy in Heaven because he was a great sinner and Christ had died for him."

"Did his sins *hurt* Christ?" Prue asked.

"Yes."

"I'm sorry he hurt Christ," said Prue sorrowfully.

"He was sorry, too."

"Is that all?"

"Yes, he died, and we hope he is in Heaven tonight, praising God for saving sinners."

"I don't think that is such a sad story. It would be sad if God never did forgive him. It was bad to be in prison, but he got out and wasn't wicked any more. Did you ever see him, Aunt Prue?"

"Yes, dear, many times."

"Did you love him?"

"I loved him better than I loved anybody, and Uncle John loved him."

"Was he ever in this room?"

"Yes. He has been many times in this chair in which you and I are sitting; he used to love to hear me play on that piano; and we used to walk in the garden together, and he called me 'Prue' and not Aunt Prue, as you do."

"Aunt Prue!" the child's voice was frightened. "I know who your story is about."

"Your dear papa!"

"Yes, my dear papa!"

"And aren't you glad he is safe through it all, and God his forgiven him?"

"Yes, I'm glad; but I'm sorry he was in that prison."

"He was happy with you, afterward, you know. He had your mamma and she loved him, and then he had you and you loved him."

"But I'm sorry."

"So am I, darling, and so is Uncle John; we are all sorry, but we are glad now because it is all over and he cannot sin any more or suffer any more. I wanted to tell you while you were little, so that somebody would not tell you when you grow up. When you think about him, thank God that he forgav him,—that is the happy part of it."

"Why didn't papa tell me?"

"He knew I would tell you some day, if you had to know. I would rather tell you than have any one else in the world tell you."

"I won't tell anybody, ever. I don't want people to know my papa was in a prison. I asked him once what a prison was like and he would not tell me much."

She kept her head on Miss Prudence's shoulder and rubbed her fingers over
Miss Prudence's hand.

There were no tears in her eyes, Miss Prudence's quiet, hopeful voice had kept the tears from coming. Some day she would understand it, but to-night it was a story that was not very sad, because he had got out of the prison and God had forgiven him. It would never come as a shock to her; Miss Prudence had saved her that.

XX.

"HEIRS TOGETHER."

"Oh, for a mind more clear to see,
A hand to work more earnestly,
For every good intent."—*Phebe Cary*.

"Aunt Prue," began Marjorie, "I can't help thinking about beauty."

"I don't see why you should, child, when there are so many beautiful things for you to think about."

It was the morning after Prue had heard the story of her father; it was Saturday morning and she was in the kitchen "helping Deborah bake." Mrs. Kemlo was resting in a steamer chair near the register in the back parlor, resting and listening; the listening was in itself a rest. It was a rest not to speak unless she pleased; it was a rest to listen to the low tones of cultured voices, to catch bits of bright talk about things that brought her out of herself; it was a rest, above all, to dwell in a home where God was in the midst; it was a rest to be free from the care of herself. Was Miss Prudence taking care of her? Was not God taking care of her through the love of Miss Prudence?

Marjorie was busy about her weekly mending, sitting at one of the front windows. It was pleasant to sit there and see the sleighs pass and hear the bells jingle; it was pleasant to look over towards the church and the parsonage; and pleasantest of all to bring her eyes into Miss Prudence's face and work basket and the work in her lap for Prue.

"But I mean—faces," acknowledged Marjorie. "I mean faces—too. I don't see why, of all the beautiful things God has made, faces should be ignored. The human face, with the love of God in it, is more glorious than any painting, more glorious than any view of mountain, lake, or river."

"I don't believe I know what beauty is."

"You know what you think it is."

"Yes; Prue is beautiful to me, and you are, and Linnet, and mother,—you see how confused I am. The girls think so much of it. One of them hurts her feet with three and a half shoes when she ought to wear larger. And another laces so tight! And another thinks so much of being slight and slender that she will not dress warmly enough in the street; she always looks cold and she has a cough, too. And another said she would rather have tubercles on her lungs than sores on her face! We had a talk about personal beauty yesterday and one girl said she would rather have it than anything else in the world. But *do* you think so much depends upon beauty?"

"How much?"

"Why, ever so much? Friends, and being loved, and marriage."

"Did you ever see a homely girl with plenty of friends? And are wives always beautiful?"

"Why, no."

"One of the greatest favorites I know is a middle-aged lady,—a maiden lady,—not only with a plain face, but with a defect in the upper lip. She is loved; her company is sought. She is not rich; she has only an ordinary position—she is a saleswoman down town. She is not educated. Some of your school girl friends are very fond of her. She is attractive, and you look at her and wonder why; but you hear her speak, and you wonder no longer. She always has something bright to say. I do not know of another attraction that she has, beside her willingness to help everybody."

"And she's neither young nor pretty."

"No; she is what you girls call an old maid."

Marjorie was mending the elbow of her brown school dress; she wore that dress in all weathers every day, and on rainy Sundays. Some of the girls said that she did not care enough about dress. She forgot that she wore the same dress every day until one of the dressy little things in the primary class reminded her of the fact. And then she laughed.

"In the Bible stories Sarah and Rebekah and Esther and Abigail are spoken of as being beautiful."

"Does their fortune depend upon their beautiful faces?"

"Didn't Esther's?"

"She was chosen by the king on account of her beauty, but I think it was God who brought her into favor and tender love, as he did Daniel; and rather more depended upon her praying and fasting than upon her beautiful face."

"Then you mean that beauty goes for a great deal with the world and not with God?"

"One of Jesse's sons was so tall and handsome that Samuel thought surely the Lord had chosen him to be king over his people. Do you remember what the Lord said about that?"

"Not quite."

"He said: 'Look not on his countenance or the height of his stature, because I have refused him; for the Lord seeth not as man seeth; for man looketh on the outward appearance, but the Lord looketh on the heart!'"

"Then it does make a difference to man."

"It seems as if it made a difference to Samuel; and the Lord declares that man is influenced by the outward appearance. Well, now, taking it for granted from the Lord's own words, what then?"

"Then it is rather hard not to be beautiful, isn't it?"

"Genius makes a difference; is it rather hard not to be a genius? Money makes a difference; is it rather hard not to be rich? Position makes a difference; is it rather hard not to be noble?"

"I never thought about those things. They give you advantage in the world; but beauty makes people love you."

"What kind of beauty?"

"Lovable beauty," confessed Marjorie, smiling, feeling that she was being cornered.

"What makes lovable beauty?"

"A lovable heart, I suppose."

"Then I shouldn't wonder if you might have it as well as another. Is Clarissa Parks more loved than any one in your class?"

"Oh, no. She is not a favorite at all."

"Then, child, I don't see that you are proving your assertion."

"I know I'm not," laughed Marjorie. "Clarissa Parks is engaged; but so is Fanny Hunting, and Fanny is the plainest little body. But I did begin by really believing that beautiful faces had the best of it in the world, and I was feeling rather aggrieved because somebody described me yesterday as 'that girl in the first class who is always getting up head; she is short and rather stout and wears her hair in a knot at the back of her head?' Now wasn't that humiliating? Not a word about my eyes or complexion or manner!"

Miss Prudence laughed at her comically aggrieved tone.

"It is hard to be nothing distinctive but short and stout and to wear your hair in a knot, as your grandmother does! But the getting up head is something."

"It doesn't add to my beauty. Miss Prudence, I'm afraid I'll be a homely blue stocking. And if I don't teach, how shall I use my knowledge? I cannot write a book, or even articles for the papers; and I must do something with the things I learn."

"Every educated lady does not teach or write."

"You do not," answered Marjorie, thoughtfully; "only you teach Prue. And I think it increases your influence, Miss Prudence. How much you have taught Linnet and me!"

"I'm thinking about two faces I saw the other night at Mrs. Harrowgate's tea table. Both were strangers to me. As the light fell over the face of one I thought I never saw anything so exquisite as to coloring: the hair was shining like threads of gold; the eyes were the azure you see in the sky; lips and cheeks were tinted; the complexion I never saw excelled for dazzling fairness,—we see it in a child's face, sometimes. At her side sat a lady: older, with a quiet, grave face; complexion dark and not noticeable; hair the brown we see every day; eyes brown and expressive, but not finer than we often see. Something about it attracted me from her bewitching neighbor, and I looked and compared. One face was quiet, listening; the other was sparkling as she talked. The grave dark face grew upon me; it was not a face, it was a soul, a human life with a history. The lovely face was lovely still, but I do not care to see it again; the other I shall not soon forget."

"But it was beauty you saw," persisted Marjorie.

"Not the kind you girls were talking about. A stranger passing through the room would not have noticed her beside the other. The lovely face has a history, I was told after supper, and she is a girl of character."

"Still—I wish—story books would not dwell so much on attitudes; and how the head sets on the shoulders; and the pretty hands and slender figures. It makes girls think of their hands and their figures. It makes this girl I know not wrap up carefully for fear of losing her 'slender' figure. And the eyelashes and the complexion! It makes us dissatisfied with ourselves."

"The Lord knew what kind of books would be written when he said that man looketh on the out ward appearance—"

"But don't Christian writers ever do it?"

"Christian writers fall into worldly ways. There are lovely girls and lovely women in the world; we meet them every day. But if we think of beauty, and write of it, and exalt it unduly, we are making a use of it that God does not approve; a use that he does not make of it himself. How beauty and money are scattered everywhere. God's saints are not the richest and most beautiful. He does not lavish beauty and money upon those he loves the best. I called last week on an Irish washerwoman and I was struck with the beauty of her girls—four of them, the eldest seventeen, the youngest six. The eldest had black eyes and black curls; the second soft brown eyes and soft brown curls to match; the third curls of gold, as pretty as Prue's, and black eyes; the youngest blue eyes and yellow curls. I never saw such a variety of beauty in one family. The mother was at the washtub, the oldest daughter was ironing, the second getting supper of potatoes and indian meal bread, the third beauty was brushing the youngest beauty's hair. As I stood and looked at them I thought, how many girls in this city would be vain if they owned their eyes and hair, and how God had thrown the beauty down among them who had no thought about it. He gives beauty to those who hate him and use it to dishonor him, just as he gives money to those who spend it in sinning. I almost think, that he holds cheaply those two things the world prizes so highly; money and beauty."

After a moment Marjorie said: "I do not mean to live for the world."

"And you do not sigh for beauty?" smiled Miss Prudence.

"No, not really. But I do want to be something beside short and stout, with my hair in a knot."

The fun in her eyes did not conceal the vexation.

"Miss Prudence, it's hard to care only for the things God cares about," she said, earnestly.

"Yes, very hard."

"I think *you* care only for such things. You are not worldly one single bit."

"I do not want to be—one single bit."

"I know you do give up things. But you have so much; you have the best things. I don't want things you have given up. I think God cares for the things you care for."

"I hope he does," said Miss Prudence, gently. "Marjorie, if he has given you a plain face give it back to him to glorify himself with; if a beautiful face, give that back to him to glorify himself with. You are not your own; your face is not yours; it is bought with a price."

Marjorie's face was radiant just then. The love, the surprise, the joy, made it beautiful.

Miss Prudence could not forbear, she drew the beautiful face down to kiss it.

"People will always call you plain, dear, but keep your soul in your face, and no matter."

"Can I help Deborah now? Or isn't there something for me to do upstairs?
I can study and practice this afternoon."

"I don't believe you will. Look out in the path."

Marjorie looked, then with a shout that was almost like Linnet's she dropped her work, and sprang towards the door.

For there stood Linnet herself, in the travelling dress Marjorie had seen her last in; not older or graver, but with her eyes shining like stars, ready to jump into Marjorie's arms.

How Miss Prudence enjoyed the girls' chatter. Marjorie wheeled a chair to the grate for Linnet, and then, having taken her wraps, kneeled down on the rug beside her and leaned both elbows on the arm of her chair.

How fast she asked questions, and how Linnet talked and laughed and brushed a tear away now and then! Was there ever so much to tell before? Miss Prudence had her questions to ask; and Morris' mother, who had been coaxed to come in to the grate, steamer chair and all, had many questions to ask about her boy.

Marjorie was searching her through and through to discover if marriage and travel had changed her; but, no, she was the same happy, laughing Linnet; full of bright talk and funny ways of putting things, with the same old attitudes and the same old way of rubbing Marjorie's fingers as she talked. Marriage had not spoiled her. But had it helped her? That could not be decided in one hour or two.

When she was quiet there was a sweeter look about her mouth than there had ever used to be; and there was an assurance, no, it was not so strong as that, there was an ease of manner, that she had brought home with her. Marjorie was more her little sister that ever.

Marjorie laughed to herself because everything began with Linnet's husband and ended in him: the stories about Genoa seemed to consist in what Will said and did; Will was the attraction of Naples and the summit of Mt. Vesuvius; the run down to Sicily and the glimpse of Vesuvius were somehow all mingled with Will's doings; the stories about the priest at Naples were all how he and Will spent hours and hours together comparing their two Bibles; and the tract the priest promised to translate into Italian was "The Amiable Louisa" that Will had chosen; and, when the priest said he would have to change the title to suit his readers, Will had suggested "A Moral Tale." This priest was confessor to a noble family in the suburbs; and once, when driving out to confess them, had taken Will with him, and both had stayed to lunch. The priest had given them his address, and Will had promised to write to him; he had brought her what he called his "paintings," from his "studio," and she had pinned them up in her little parlor; they were painted on paper and were not remarkable evidences of genius. Not quite the old masters, although painted in Italy by an Italian. His English was excellent; he was expecting to come to America some day. A sea captain in Brooklyn had a portrait of him in oil, and when Miss Prudence went to New York she must call and see it; Morris and he were great friends. That naughty Will had asked him one day if he never wished to marry, and he had colored so, poor fellow, and said,

'It is better to live for Christ.' And Will had said he hoped he lived for Christ, too. The priest had a smooth face and a little round spot shaven on top of his head. She used to wish Marjorie might see that little round spot.

And the pilot, they had such a funny pilot! When anything was passed him at the table, or you did him a favor, he said "thank you" in Italian and in English.

And how they used to walk the little deck! And the sunsets! She had to confess that she did not see one sunrise till they were off Sandy Hook coming home. But the moonlight on the water was most wonderful of all! That golden ladder rising and falling in the sea! They used to look at it and talk about home and plan what she would do in that little house.

She used to be sorry for Morris; but he did not seem lonesome: he was always buried in a book at leisure times; and he said he would be sailing over the seas with his wife some day.

"Morris is so *good*," she added. "Sometimes he has reminded me of the angels who came down to earth as young men."

"I think he was a Christian before he was seven years old," said his mother.

At night Marjorie said, when she conducted Linnet up to her chamber, that they would go back to the blessed old times, and build castles, and forget that Linnet was married and had crossed the ocean.

"I'm living in my castle now," returned Linnet. "I don't want to build any more. And this is lovelier than any we ever built."

Marjorie looked at her, but she did not speak her thought; she almost wished that she might "grow up," and be happy in Linnet's way.

With a serious face Linnet lay awake after Marjorie had fallen asleep, thinking over and over Miss Prudence's words when she bade her goodnight:—

"It is an experience to be married, Linnet; for God holds your two lives as one, and each must share his will for the other; if joyful, it is twice as joyful; if hard, twice as hard."

"Yes," she had replied, "Will says we are *heirs together* of the grace of life."

XXI.
MORRIS AGAIN.

"Overshadow me, O Lord,
With the comfort of thy wings."

Marjorie stood before the parlor grate; it was Saturday afternoon, and she was dressed for travelling—not for a long journey, for she was only going home to remain over Sunday and Monday, Monday being Washington's Birthday, and a holiday. She had seen Linnet those few days that she visited them on her return from her voyage, and her father and mother not once since she came to Maple Street in September. She was hungry for home; she said she was almost starving.

"I wish you a very happy time," said Miss Prudence as she opened
Marjorie's pocketbook to drop a five-dollar bill into its emptiness.

"I know it will be a happy time," Marjorie affirmed; "but I shall think of you and Prue, and want to be here, too."

"I wish I could go, too," said Prue, dancing around her with Marjorie's shawl strap in her hand.

There was a book for her father in the shawl strap, "The Old Bibie and the New Science"; a pretty white cap for her mother, that Miss Prudence had fashioned; a cherry-silk tie for Linnet; and a couple of white aprons for Annie Grey, her mother's handmaiden, these last being also Miss Prudence's handiwork.

"Wait till next summer, Prue. Aunt Prue wants to bring you for the sea bathing."

"Don't be too sure, Marjorie; if Uncle John comes home he may have other plans for her."

"Oh, *is* he coming home?" inquired Marjorie.

"He would be here to-day if I had not threatened to lock him out and keep him standing in a snowdrift until June. He expects to be here the first day of summer."

"And what will happen then?" queried Prue. "Is it a secret?"

"Yes, it's a secret," said Miss Prudence, stepping behind Marjorie to fasten her veil.

"Does Marjorie know?" asked Prue anxiously.

"I never can guess," said Marjorie. "Now, Kitten, good-bye; and sing to
Mrs. Kemlo while I am gone, and be good to Aunt Prue."

"Marjorie, dear, I shall miss you," said Miss Prudence.

"But you will be so glad that I am taking supper at home in that dear old kitchen. And Linnet will be there; and then I am to go home with her to stay all night. I don't see how I ever waited so long to see her keep house. Will calls the house Linnet's Nest. I'll come back and tell you stories about everything."

"Don't wait any longer, dear; I'm afraid you'll lose the train. I must give you a watch like Linnet's for a graduating present."

Marjorie stopped at the gate to toss back a kiss to Prue watching at the window. Miss Prudence remembered her face years afterward, flushed and radiant, round and dimpled; such an innocent, girlish face, without one trace of care or sorrow. Not a breath of real sorrow had touched her in all her eighteen years. Her laugh that day was as light hearted as Prue's.

"That girl lives in a happy world," Mrs. Kemlo had said to Miss Prudence that morning.

"She always will," Miss Prudence replied; "she has the gift of living in the sunshine."

Miss Prudence

Miss Prudence looked at the long mirror after Marjorie had gone down the street, and wished that it might always keep that last reflection of Marjorie. The very spirit of pure and lovely girlhood! But the same mirror had not kept her own self there, and the self reflected now was the woman grown out of the girlhood; would she keep Marjorie from womanhood?

Miss Prudence thought in these days that her own youth was being restored to her; but it had never been lost, for God cannot grow old, neither can any of himself grow old in the human heart which is his temple.

Marjorie's quick feet hurried along the street. She found herself at the depot with not one moment to lose. She had brought her "English Literature" that she might read Tuesday's lesson in the train. She opened it as the train started, and was soon so absorbed that she was startled at a voice inquiring, "Is this seat engaged?"

"No," she replied, without raising her eyes. But there was something familiar in the voice; or was she thinking of somebody? She moved slightly as a gentleman seated himself beside her. Her veil was shading her face; she pushed it back to give a quick glance at him. The voice had been familiar; there was still something more familiar in the hair, the contour of the cheek, and the blonde moustache.

"Hollis!" she exclaimed, as his eyes looked into hers. She caught her breath a little, hardly knowing whether she were glad or sorry.

"Why, Marjorie!" he returned, surprise and embarrassment mingled in his voice. He did not seem sure, either, whether to be glad or sorry.

For several moments neither spoke; both were too shy and too conscious of something uncomfortable.

"It isn't so very remarkable to find you here, I suppose," he remarked, after considering for some time an advertisement in a daily paper which he held in his hand.

"No, nor so strange to encounter you."

"You have not been home for some time."

"Not since I came in September."

"And I have not since Will's wedding day. There was a shower that night, and your mother tried to keep me; and I wished she had more than a few times on my dark way home."

"It is almost time to hear from Will." Marjorie had no taste for reminiscences.

"I expect to hear every day."

"So do we. Mrs. Kemlo watches up the street and down the street for the postman."

"Oh, yes. Morris. I forgot. Does he like the life?"

"He is enthusiastic."

She turned a leaf, and read a page of extracts from Donald Grant Mitchell; but she had not understood one word, so she began again and read slowly, trying to understand; then she found her ticket in her glove, and examined it with profound interest, the color burning in her cheeks; then she gazed long out of the window at the snow and the bare trees and the scattered farmhouses; then she turned to study the lady's bonnet in front of her, and to pity the mother with the child in front of *her*; she looked before and behind and out the windows; she looked everywhere but at the face beside her; she saw his overcoat, his black travelling bag, and wondered what he had brought his mother; she looked at his brown kid gloves, at his black rubber watch chain, from which a gold anchor was dangling; but it was dangerous to raise her eyes higher, so they sought his boots and the newspaper on his knee. Had he spoken last, or had she? What was the last remark? About Morris? It was certainly not about Donald Grant Mitchell. Yes, she had spoken last; she had said Morris was—

Would he speak of her long unanswered letter? Would he make an excuse for not noticing it? A sentence in rhetoric was before her eyes: "Any letter, not insulting, merits a reply." Perhaps he had never studied rhetoric. Her lips were curving into a smile; wouldn't it be fun to ask him?

"I am going to London next week. I came home to say good-bye to mother."

"Will you stay long?" was all that occurred to her to remark. Her voice was quite devoid of interest.

"Where? In London, or at home?"

"Both," she said smiling.

"I must return to New York on Monday; and I shall stay in London only long enough to attend to business. I shall go to Manchester and to Paris. My route is not all mapped out for me yet. Do you like school as well as you expected to?"

"Oh, yes, indeed."

"You expect to finish this year?"

"I suppose I shall leave school."

"And go home?"

"Oh, yes. What else should I do?"

"And learn housekeeping from Linnet."

"It is not new work to me."

"How is Miss Prudence?"

"As lovely as ever."

"And the little girl?"

"Sweet and good and bright."

"And Mrs. Kemlo?"

"She is—happier."

"Hasn't she always been happy?"

"No; she was like your mother; only hers has lasted so long. I am so sorry for such—unhappiness."

"So am I. I endured enough of it at one time."

"I cannot even think of it. She is going home with me in June. Morris will be glad to have her with mother."

"When is Mr. Holmes coming here?"

"In June."

"June is to be a month of happenings in your calendar."

"Every month is—in my calendar."

He was bending towards her that she might listen easily, as he did not wish to raise his voice.

"I haven't told you about my class in Sunday school."

"Oh, have you a class?"

"Yes, a class of girls—girls about fourteen. I thought I never could interest them. I don't know how to talk to little girls; but I am full of the lesson, and so are they, and the time is up before we know it."

"I'm very glad. It will be good for you," said Marjorie, quite in Miss Prudence's manner.

"It is, already," he said gravely and earnestly "I imagine it is better for me than for them."

"I don't believe that"

"Our lesson last Sunday was about the Lord's Supper; and one of them asked me if Christ partook of the Supper with his disciples. I had not thought of it. I do not know. Do you?"

"He ate the passover with them."

"But this was afterward. Why should he do it in remembrance of his own death? He gave them the bread and the cup."

Marjorie was interested. She said she would ask her father and Miss Prudence; and her mother must certainly have thought about it.

The conductor nudged Hollis twice before he noticed him and produced his ticket; then the candy boy came along, and Hollis laid a paper of chocolate creams in Marjorie's lap. It was almost like going back to the times when he brought apples to school for her. If he would only explain about the letter—

The next station would be Middlefield! What a short hour and a half! She buttoned her glove, took her shawl strap into her lap, loosening the strap so that she might slip her "English Literature" in, tightened it again, ate the last cream drop, tossed aside the paper, and was ready for Middlefield.

As the train stopped he took the shawl strap from her hand. She followed him through the car, gave him her hand to assist her to the platform, and then there was a welcome in her ears, and Linnet and her father seemed to be surrounding her. Captain Rheid had brought Linnet to the train, intending to take Hollis back. Linnet was jubilant over the news of Will's safe arrival; they had found the letter at the office.

"Father has letters too," she said to Hollis; "he will give you his news."

As the sleigh containing Linnet, her father, and Marjorie sped away before them, Captain Rheid said to Hollis:—

"How shall I ever break it to them? Morris is dead."

"Dead!" repeated Hollis.

"He died on the voyage out. Will gives a long account of it for his mother and Marjorie. It seems the poor fellow was engaged to her, and has given Will a parting present for her."

"How did it happen?"

Will has tried to give details; but he is rather confusing. He is in great trouble. He wanted to bring him home; but that was impossible. They came upon a ship in distress, and laid by her a day and a night in foul weather to take them off. Morris went to them with a part of the crew, and got them all safely aboard the *Linnet*; but he had received some injury, nobody seemed to know how. His head was hurt, for he was delirious after the first night. He sent his love to his mother, and gave Will something for Marjorie, and then did not know anything after that. Will is heartbroken. He wants me to break it to Linnet; but I didn't see how I can. Your mother will have to do it. The letter can go to his mother; Miss Prudence will see to that.

"But Marjorie," said Hollis slowly.

"Yes, poor little Marjorie!" said the old man compassionately. "It will go hard with her."

"Linnet or her mother can tell her."

The captain touched his horse, and they flew past the laughing sleighload. Linnet waved her handkerchief, Marjorie laughed, and their father took off his hat to them.

"Oh, *dear*," groaned the captain.

"Lord, help her; poor little thing," prayed Hollis, with motionless lips.

He remembered that last letter of hers that he had not answered. His mother had written to him that she surmised that Marjorie was engaged to Morris; and he had felt it wrong—"almost interfering," he had put it to himself—to push their boy and girl friendship any further. And, again—Hollis was cautious in the extreme—if she did not belong to Morris, she might infer that he was caring with a grown up feeling, which he was not at all sure was true—he was not sure about himself in anything just then; and, after he became a Christian, he saw all things in a new light, and felt that a "flirtation" was not becoming a disciple of Christ. He had become a whole-hearted disciple of

Christ. His Aunt Helen and his mother were very eager for him to study for the ministry; but he had told them decidedly that he was not "called."

"And I *am* called to serve Christ as a businessman. Commercial travellers, as a rule, are men of the world; but, as I go about, I want to go about my Father's business."

"But he would be so enthusiastic," lamented Aunt Helen.

"And he has such a nice voice," bewailed his mother; "and I did hope to see one of my five boys in the pulpit."

XXII.

TIDINGS.

"He giveth his beloved sleep."

Sunday in the twilight Linnet and Marjorie were alone in Linnet's little kitchen. Linnet was bending over the stove stirring the chocolate, and Marjorie was setting the table for two.

"Linnet!" she exclaimed, "it's like playing house."

"I feel very much in earnest."

"So do I. That chocolate makes me feel so. Have you had time to watch the light over the fields? Or is it too poor a sight after gazing at the sunset on the ocean?"

"Marjorie!" she said, turning around to face her, and leaving the spoon idle in the steaming pot, "do you know, I think there's something the matter?"

"Something the matter? Where?"

"I don't know where. I was wondering this afternoon if people always had a presentiment when trouble was coming."

"Did you ever have any trouble?" asked Marjorie seriously.

"Not real, dreadful trouble. But when I hear of things happening suddenly, I wonder if it is so sudden, really; or if they are not prepared in some way for the very thing, or for something."

"We always know that our friends may die—that is trouble. I feel as if it would kill me for any one I love to die."

"Will is safe and well," said Linnet, "and father and mother."

"And Morris—I shall find a letter for me at home, I expect. I suppose his mother had hers last night. How she lives in him! She loves him more than any of us. But what kind of a feeling have you?"

"I don't know."

"You are tired and want to go to sleep," said Marjorie, practically. "I'll sing you to sleep after supper. Or read to you! We have 'Stepping Heavenward' to read. That will make you forget all your nonsense."

"Hollis' face isn't nonsense."

"He hasn't talked to me since last night. I didn't see him in church."

"I did. And that is what I mean. I should think his trouble was about Will, if I hadn't the letter. And Father Rheid! Do you see how fidgety he is? He has been over here four times to-day."

"He is always stern."

"No; he isn't. Not like this. And Mother Rheid looked so—too."

"How?" laughed Marjorie. "O, you funny Linnet."

"I wish I could laugh at it. But I heard something, too. Mother Rheid was talking to mother after church this afternoon, and I heard her say, 'distressing.' Father Rheid hurried me into the sleigh, and mother put her veil down; and I was too frightened to ask questions."

"She meant that she had a distressing cold," said Marjorie lightly. "'Distressing' is one of her pet words. She is distressed over the coldness of the church, and she is distressed when all her eggs do not hatch. I wouldn't be distressed about that, Linnet. And mother put her veil down because the wind was blowing I put mine down, too."

Linnet stirred the chocolate; but her face was still anxious. Will had not spoken of Morris. Could it be Morris? It was not like Will not to speak of Morris.

"Will did not speak of Morris. Did you notice that?"

"Does he always? I suppose Morris has spoken for himself."

"If Hollis doesn't come over by the time we are through tea, I'll go over there. I can't wait any longer."

"Well, I'll go with you to ease your mind. But you must eat some supper."

As Linnet placed the chocolate pot on the table, Marjorie exclaimed, "There they are! Mother Rheid and Hollis. They are coming by the road; of course the field is blocked with snow. Now your anxious heart shall laugh at itself. I'll put on plates for two more. Is there chocolate enough? And it won't seem so much like playing house."

While Marjorie put on the extra plates and cut a few more slices of sponge cake, Linnet went to the front door, and stood waiting for them.

Through the open kitchen door Marjorie heard her ask, "Is anything the matter?"

"Hush! Where's Marjorie?" asked Hollis' voice.

Was it her trouble? Was it Miss Prudence? Or Prue—it could not be her father and mother; she had seen them at church. Morris! *Morris!* Had they not just heard from Will? He went away, and she was not kind to him.

Who was saying "dead"? Was somebody dead?

She was trembling so that she would have fallen had she not caught at the back of a chair for support. There was a buzzing in her ears; she was sinking down, sinking down. Linnet was clinging to her, or holding her up. Linnet must be comforted.

"Is somebody—dead?" she asked, her dry lips parting with an effort.

"Yes, dear; it's Morris," said Mrs. Rheid. "Lay her down flat, Linnet. It's the shock? Hollis, bring some water."

"Oh, no, no," shivered Marjorie, "don't touch me. What shall I say to his mother? His mother hasn't any one else to care for her. Where is he? Won't somebody tell me all about it?"

"Oh, dear; I can't," sobbed Mrs. Rheid.

Hollis drew her into a chair and seated himself beside her, keeping her cold hand in his.

"I will tell you, Marjorie."

But Marjorie did not hear; she only heard, "Good-bye, Marjorie—*dear*."

"Are you listening, Marjorie?"

"Oh, yes."

Linnet stood very white beside her. Mrs. Rheid was weeping softly.

"They were near a ship in distress; the wind was high, and they could not go to her for many hours; at last Morris went in a boat, with some of the crew, and helped them off the wreck; he saved them all, but he was hurt in some way,—Will does not know how; the men tried to tell him, but they contradicted themselves,—and after getting safe aboard his own ship—do you understand it all?"

"Yes. Morris got back safe to the *Linnet*, but he was injured—"

"And then taken very ill, so ill that he was delirious. Will did everything for his comfort that he could do; he was with him night and day; he lived nine days. But, before he became delirious, he sent his love to his mother, and he gave Will something to give to you."

"Yes, I know," said Marjorie. "I don't deserve it. I refused it when he wanted to give it to me. I wasn't kind to him."

"Yes, you were," said Linnet, "you don't know what you are saying. You were always kind to him, and he loved you."

"Yes; but I might have been kinder," she said. "Must I tell his mother?"

"No; Miss Prudence will do that," answered Hollis. "I have Will's letter for you to take to her."

"Where is he? Where *is* Morris?"

"Buried in England. Will could not bring him home," said Hollis.

"His mother! What will she do?" moaned Marjorie.

"Marjorie, you talk as if there was no one to comfort her," rebuked Mrs. Rheid.

"You have all your boys, Mrs. Rheid, and she had only Morris," said Marjorie.

"Yes; that is true; and I cannot spare one of them. Do cry, child. Don't sit there with your eyes so wide open and big."

Marjorie closed her eyes and leaned back against Linnet. Morris had gone to God.

It was hours before the tears came. She sobbed herself to sleep towards morning. She did not deserve it; but she would keep the thing he had sent to her. Another beautiful life was ended; who would do his work on the earth. Would Hollis? Could she do a part of it? She would love his mother. Oh, how thankful she was that he had known that rest had begun to come to his mother, that he had known that she was safe with Miss Prudence.

It was like Marjorie, even in her first great sorrow, to fall asleep thanking God.

XXIII.

GOD'S LOVE.

"As many as I love I rebuke and chasten."

Marjorie opened her "English Literature." She must recite to-morrow. She had forgotten whom she had studied about Saturday afternoon.

Again Hollis was beside her in the train. Her shawl strap was at her feet; her ticket was tucked into her glove; she opened at the same place in "English Literature." Now she remembered "Donald Grant Mitchell." His "Dream Life" was one of Morris' favorites. They had read it together one summer under the apple-tree. He had coaxed her to read aloud, saying that her voice suited it. She closed the book; she could not study; how strange it would be to go among the girls and hear them laugh and talk; would any of them ask her if she were in trouble? They would remember her sailor boy.

Was it Saturday afternoon? Hollis wore those brown kid gloves, and there was the anchor dangling from his black chain. She was not too shy to look higher, and meet the smile of his eyes to-day. Was she going home and expecting a letter from Morris? There was a letter in her pocket; but it was not from Morris. Hollis had said he expected to hear from Will; and they had heard from Will. He would be home before very long, and tell them all the rest. The train rushed on; a girl was eating peanuts behind her, and a boy was studying his Latin Grammar in front of her. She was going to Morris' mother; the rushing train was hurrying her on. How could she say to Miss Prudence, "Morris is dead."

"Marjorie."

"Well," she answered, rousing herself.

"Are you comfortable?"

The voice was sympathetic; tears started, she could only nod in reply.

There seemed to be nothing to talk about to-day.

She had replied in monosyllables so long that he was discouraged with his own efforts at conversation, and lapsed into silence. But it was a silence that she felt she might break at any moment.

The train stopped at last; it had seemed as if it would never stop, and then as if it would stop before she could catch her breath and be ready to speak. If she had not refused that something he had brought her this would not have been so hard. Had he cared so very much? Would she have cared very much if he had refused those handkerchiefs she had marked for him? But Hollis had taken her shawl strap, and was rising.

"You will not have time to get out."

"Did you think I would leave you anywhere but with your friends? Have you forgotten me so far as that?"

"I was thinking of your time."

"Never mind. One has always time for what he wants to do most."

"Is that an original proverb?"

"I do not know that it is a quotation."

She dropped her veil over her face, and walked along the platform at his side. There were no street cars in the small city, and she had protested against a carriage.

"I like the air against my face."

That last walk with Morris had been so full of talk; this was taken in absolute silence. The wind was keen and they walked rapidly. Prue was watching at the window, loving little Prue, as Marjorie knew she would be.

"There's a tall man with Marjorie, Aunt Prue."

Aunt Prue left the piano and followed her to the door. Mrs. Kemlo was knitting stockings for Morris in her steamer chair.

Marjorie was glad of Prue's encircling arms. She hid her face in the child's hair while Hollis passed her and spoke to Miss Prudence.

Miss Prudence would be strong. Marjorie did not fear anything for her. It might be cowardly, but she must run away from his mother. She laid Will's letter in Hollis' hand, and slipping past him hastened up the stairway. Prue followed her, laughing and pulling at her cloak.

She could tell Prue; it would relieve her to talk to Prue.

They were both weeping, Prue in Marjorie's arms, when Miss Prudence found them in her chamber an hour later. The only light in the room came through the open door of the airtight.

"Does she know?" asked Marjorie, springing up to greet Miss Prudence.

"Yes; she is very quiet, I have prayed with her twice; and we have talked about his life and his death. She says that it was unselfish to the end."

"He sent his love to her; did Hollis tell you?"

"I read the letter—I read it twice. She holds it in her hand now."

"Has the tall man gone?" asked Prue.

"Yes, he did not stay long. Marjorie, you did not bid him good-night."

"I know it; I did not think."

"Marjorie, dear;" Miss Prudence opened her arms, and Marjorie crept into them.

"Oh, Aunt Prue, I would not be so troubled, but he wanted to give me something—some little thing he had brought me—because he always did remember me, and I would not even look at it. I don't know what it was. I refused it; and I know he was so hurt. I was almost tempted to take it when I saw his eyes; and then I wanted to be true."

"Were you true?"

"I tried to be."

"Then there is nothing to be troubled about. He is comforted for it now. Don't you want to go down and see his mother?"

"I'm afraid to see her."

"She will comfort you. She is sure now that God loves her. I have been trying to teach her, and now God has taught her so that she can rejoice in his love. Whom the Lord loveth, she says, he chastens; and he knows how he has chastened her. If it were not for his love, Marjorie, what would keep our hearts from breaking?"

"Papa died, too," said Prue.

Marjorie went down to the parlor. Mrs. Kemlo was sitting at the grate, leaning back in her steamer chair. Marjorie kissed her without a word.

"Marjorie! The girls ought to know. I don't believe I can write."

"I can. I will write to-night."

"And copy this letter; then they will know it just as it is. He was with you so long they will not miss him as we do. They were older, and they loved each other, and left him to me. And, Marjorie—"

"Yes'm."

"Tell them I am going to your mother's as soon as warm weather comes, unless one of them would rather take me home; tell them Miss Prudence has become a daughter to me; I am not in need of anything. Give them my love, and say that when they love their little ones, they must think of how I loved them."

"I will," said Marjorie, "You and mother will enjoy each other so much."

Marjorie wrote the letters that evening, her eyes so blinded with tears that she wrote very crookedly. No one would ever know what she had lost in Morris. He had been a part of herself that even Linnet had never been. She was lost without him, and for months wandered in a new world. She suffered more keenly upon the anniversary of the day of the tidings of his death than she suffered that day. Then, she could appreciate more fully what God had taken from her. But the letters were written, and mailed on her way to school in the morning; her recitations were gone through with; and night came, when she could have the rest of sleep. The days went on outwardly as usual. Prue was daily becoming more and more a delight to them all. Mrs. Kemlo's sad face was sweet and chastened; and Miss Prudence's days were more full of busy doings, with a certain something of a new life about them that Marjorie did not understand. She could almost imagine what Miss Prudence had been twenty years ago. Despite her lightness of foot, her inspiring voice, and her *young* interest in every question that pertained to life and work and study, Miss Prudence seemed old to eighteen-years-old Marjorie. Not as old as her mother; but nearly forty-five was very old. When she was forty-five, she thought, her life would be almost ended; and here was Miss Prudence always *beginning again*.

Answers to her letters arrived duly. They were not long; but they were conventionally sympathetic.

One daughter wrote: "Morris took you away from us to place you with friends whom he thought would take good care of you; if you are satisfied to stay with them, I think you will be better off than with me. Business is dull, and Peter thinks he has enough on his hands."

The other wrote: "I am glad you are among such kind friends. If Miss Pomeroy thinks she owes you anything, now is her time to repay it. But she could pay your board with me as well as with strangers, and you could help me with the children. I am glad you can be submissive, and that you are in a pleasanter frame of mind. Henry sends love, and says you never shall want a home while he has a roof over his own head."

The mother sighed over both letters. They both left so much unsaid. They were wrapped up in their husbands and children.

"I hope their children will love them when they are old," was the only remark she made about the letters.

"I am your child, too," said Marjorie. "Won't you take me instead—no, not instead of Morris, but *with* him?"

In April Will came home. He spent a night in Maple Street, and almost satisfied the mother's hungry heart with the comfort he gave her. Marjorie listened with tears. She went away by herself to open the tiny box that Will placed in her hand. Kissing the ring with loving and reverent lips, she slipped it on the finger that Morris would have chosen, the finger on which Linnet wore her wedding ring. "*Semper fidelis.*" She could see the words now as he used to write them on the slate. If he might only know that she cared for the ring! If he might only know that she was waiting for him to come back to bring it to her. If he might only know—But he had God now; he was in the presence of Jesus Christ. There was no marrying or giving in marriage in the presence of Christ in Heaven. Giving in marriage and marrying had been in his presence on the earth; but where fullness of joy was, there was something better. Marriage belonged to the earth. She belonged to the earth; but he belonged to Heaven. The ring did not signify that she was married to him—I think it might have meant that to her, if she had read the shallow sentimentalism of some love stories; but Miss Prudence had kept her from false ideas, and given her the truth; the truth, that marriage was the symbol of the union of Christ and his people; a pure marriage was the type of this union. Linnet's marriage was holier and happier because of Miss Prudence's teaching. Miss Prudence was an old maid; but she had helped others beside Linnet and Marjorie towards the happiest marriage. Marjorie had not one selfish, or shallow, or false idea with regard to marriage. And why should girls have, who have good mothers and the Old and New Testaments?

With no shamefacedness, no foolish consciousness, she went down among them with Morris' ring upon her finger. She would as soon have been ashamed to say that an angel had spoken to her. Perhaps she was not a modern school-girl, perhaps she was as old-fashioned as Miss Prudence herself.

XXIV.
JUST AS IT OUGHT TO BE.

"I chose my wife, as she did her wedding gown, for qualities that would wear well."—*Goldsmith.*

"Prudence!"

"Well, John," she returned, as he seemed to hesitate.

"Have we arranged everything?"

"Everything! And you have been home three hours."

"Three and a half, if you please; it is now six o'clock."

"Then the tea-bell will ring."

"No; I told Deborah to ring at seven to-night."

"She will think you are putting on the airs of the master."

"Don't you think it is about time? Or, it will be at half past six."

"Why, in half an hour?"

"Half an hour may make all the difference in the world."

"In some instances, yes?"

Miss Prudence

They were walking up and down the walk they had named years ago "the shrubbery path." He had found her in the shrubbery path in the old days when she used to walk up and down and dream her girlish dreams. Like Linnet she liked her real life better than anything she had dreamed.

Mr. Holmes had returned with his shoulders thrown back, the lines of care softened into lines of thought, and the slouched hat replaced by a broad-brimmed panama; his step was quick, his voice had a ring in it, the stern, determined expression was altogether gone; there was a loveliness in his face that was not in Miss Prudence's own; when his sterner and stronger nature became sweet, it was very sweet. Life had been a long fight; in yielding, he had conquered. He bubbled over into nonsense now and then. Twenty years ago he had walked this path with Prudence Pomeroy, when there was hatred in his heart and an overwhelming sorrow in hers. There always comes a time when we are *through*. He believed that tonight. Prue was not lighter of heart than he.

"Twenty years is a large piece out of a man's lifetime; but I would have waited twice twenty for this hour, Prudence."

"I wish I deserved my happiness as much as you do yours, John."

"Perhaps you haven't as much to deserve."

"I'm glad I don't deserve it. I want it to be all God's gift and his goodness."

"It is, dear."

"I wish we might take Marjorie with us," she said, after a moment; "she would have such an unalloyed good time."

"Any one else?"

"Mrs. Kemlo."

"Is that all?"

"There's Deborah."

"Prudence, you ought to be satisfied with me. You don't know how to be married."

"Suppose I wait twenty years longer and learn."

"No, it is like learning to swim; the best way is to plunge at once. And at once will be in about twenty minutes, instead of twenty years."

"What do you mean?" she asked, standing still in unfeigned astonishment.

"I mean that your neighbor across the way has been invited to call at half past six this evening to marry me, and I supposed you were willing to be married at the same time."

"John Holmes!"

"Do you want to send me off again?"

"But I never thought of such a thing."

"It wasn't necessary; one brilliant mind is enough to plan. What did you ask me to come home for?"

"But not now—not immediately."

"Why not?" he asked, gravely.

"Because," she smiled at her woman's reason, "I'm not ready."

"Don't you know whether you are willing or not?"

"Yes, I know that."

"Aren't you well enough acquainted with me? Haven't you proved me long enough?"

"O, John," her eyes filling with tears.

"What else can you mean by 'ready'?"

She looked down at her dress; a gray flannel—an iron gray flannel—a gray flannel and linen collar and cuffs to be married in. But was it not befitting her gray locks?

"John, look at me!"

"I am looking at you."

"What do you see?"

"You were never so lovely in your life."

"You were never so obstinate in your life."

"I never had such a good right before. Now listen to reason. You say this house is to be sold; and the furniture, for future housekeeping, is to be packed and stored; that you and Prue are to sail for Havre the first steamer in July; and who beside your husband is to attend to this, and to get you on board the steamer in time?"

"But, John!" laying her hand in expostulation upon his arm.

"But, Prudence!" he laughed. "Is Deborah to go with us? Shall we need her in our Italian palace, or are we to dwell amid ruins?"

"Nothing else would make her old heart so glad."

"Marjorie and Mrs. Kemlo expect to go home to-morrow."

"Yes."

"Don't you want Marjorie to stay and help you?"

"With such a valiant husband at the front! I suspect you mean to create emergencies simply to help me out of them."

"I'm creating one now; and all I want you to do is to be helped out—or in."

"But, John, I must go in and fix my hair."

"Your hair looks as usual."

"But I don't want it to look as usual. Do you want the bride to forget her attire and her ornaments?"

A blue figure with curls flying and arms outstretched was flying down towards them from the upper end of the path.

"O, Aunt Prue! Mr. March has come over—without Mrs. March, and he asked for you. I told him Uncle John had come home, and he smiled, and said he could not get along without him."

"John, you should have asked Mrs. March, too."

"I forgot the etiquette of it. I forgot she was your pastor's wife. But it's too late now."

"Prue!" Miss Prudence laid her hand on Prue's head to keep her quiet. "Ask Marjorie and Mrs. Kemlo and Deborah to come into the parlor."

"We are to be married, Prue!" said John Holmes.

"*Who* is?" asked Prue.

"Aunt Prue and I. Don't you want papa and mamma instead of Uncle John and Aunt Prue?"

"Yes; I do! Wait for us to come. I'll run and tell them," she answered, fleeing away.

"John, this is a very irregular proceeding!"

"It quite befits the occasion, however," he answered gravely. Very slowly they walked toward the house.

All color had left Miss Prudence's cheeks and lips. Deborah was sure she would faint; but Mrs. Kemlo watched her lips, and knew by the firm lines that she would not.

No one thought about the bridegroom, because no one ever does. Prue kept close to Miss Prudence, and said afterward that she was mamma's bridesmaid. Marjorie thought that Morris would be glad if he could know it; he had loved Mr. Holmes.

The few words were solemnly spoken.

Prudence Pomeroy and John Holmes were husband and wife.

"What God hath joined—"

Oh, how God had joined them. She had belonged to him so long.

The bridegroom and bride went on their wedding tour by walking up and down the long parlor in the summer twilight. Not many words were spoken.

Deborah went out to the dining-room to change the table cloth for one of the best damasks, saying to herself, "It's just as it ought to be! Just as it ought to be! And things do happen so once in a while in this crooked world."

XXV.

THE WILL OF GOD.

"To see in all things good and fair,
Thy love attested is my prayer."—*Alice Cary.*

"Linnet is happy enough," said their mother; "but there's Marjorie!"

Yes; there was Marjorie! She was not happy enough. She was twenty-one this summer, and not many events had stirred her uneventful life since we left her the night of Miss Prudence's marriage. She came home the next day bringing Mrs. Kemlo with her, and the same day she began to take the old household steps. She had been away but a year, and had not fallen out of the old ways as Linnet had in her three years of study; and she had not come home to be married as Linnet had; she came home to do the next thing, and the next thing had even been something for her father and mother, or Morris' mother.

Annie Grey went immediately, upon the homecoming of the daughter of the house, to Middlefield to learn dressmaking, boarding with Linnet and "working her board." Linnet was lonely at night; she began to feel lonely as dusk came on; and the arrangement of board for one and pleasant companionship for the other, was satisfactory to both. Not that there was very much for Annie to do, beside staying at home Monday mornings to help with the washing, and ironing Monday evening or early Tuesday. Linnet loved her housekeeping too well to let any other fingers intermeddle. Will decided that she must stay, for company, especially through the winter nights, if he had to pay her board.

Therefore Marjorie took the place that she left vacant in the farmhouse, and more than filled it, but she did not love housekeeping for its own comfortable sake, as Linnet did; she did it as "by God's law."

Her father's health failed signally this first summer. He was weakened by several hemorrhages, and became nervous and unfitted even to superintend the work of the "hired man." That general superintendence fell to Mrs. West, and she took no little pride in the flourishing state of the few acres. Now she could farm as she wanted to; Graham had not always listened to her. The next summer he died. That was the summer Marjorie was twenty. The chief business of the nursing fell to Marjorie; her mother was rather too energetic for the comfort of the sickroom, and there was always so much to be attended to outside that quiet chamber.

"Marjorie knows her father's way," Mrs. West apologized to Mrs. Kemlo. "He never has to tell her what he wants; but I have to make him explain. There are born nurses, and I'm not one of them. I'll keep things running outside, and that's for his comfort. He is as satisfied as though he were about himself. If one of us must be down, he knows that he'd better be the one."

During their last talk—how many talks Marjorie and her father had!—he made one remark that she had not forgotten, and would never forget:—

"My life has been of little account, as the world goes; but I have sought to do God's will, and that is success to a man on his death-bed."

Would not her life be a success, then? For what else did she desire but the will of God.

The minister told Marjorie that there was no man in the church whose life had had such a resistless influence as her father's.

The same hired man was retained; the farm work was done to Mrs. West's satisfaction. The farm was her own as long as she lived; and then it was to belong equally to the daughters. There were no debts.

The gentle, patient life was missed with sore hearts; but there was no outward difference within doors or without. Marjorie took his seat at table; Mrs. Kemlo sat in his armchair at the fireside; his wife read his *Agriculturist*; and his daughter read his special devotional books. His wife admitted to herself that Graham lacked force of character. She herself was a *pusher*. She did not understand his favorite quotation: "He that believeth shall not make haste."

Marjorie had her piano—this piano was a graduating present from Miss Prudence; more books than she could read, from the libraries of Mr. and Mrs. Holmes; her busy work in the household; an occasional visit to the farmhouse on the sea shore, to read to the old people and sing to them, and even to cut and string apples and laugh over her childish abhorrence of the work. She never opened the door of the chamber they still called "Miss Prudence's," without feeling that it held a history. How different her life would have been but for Miss Prudence. And Linnet's. And Morris's! And how many other lives, who knew? There were, beside, her class in Sunday school; and her visits to Linnet, and exchanging visits with the school-girls,—not with the girls at Master McCosh's; she had made no intimate friendships among them. And then there were letters from Aunt Prue, and childish, affectionate notes from dear little Prue.

Marjorie's life was not meagre; still she was not "happy enough." She wrote to Aunt Prue that she was not "satisfied."

"That's a girl's old story," Mrs. Holmes said to her husband. "She must *evolve*, John. There's enough in her for something to come out of her."

"What do girls want to *do*?" he asked, looking up from his writing.

"Be satisfied," laughed his wife.

"Did you go through that delusive period?"

"Was I not a girl?"

"And here's Prue growing up, to say some day that she isn't satisfied."

"No; to say some day that she is."

"*When* were you satisfied?"

"At what age? You will not believe that I was thirty-five, before I was satisfied with my life. And then I was satisfied, because I was willing for God to have his way with me. If it were not for that willingness, I shouldn't be satisfied yet."

"Then you can tell Marjorie not to wait until she is half of three score and ten before she gives herself up."

"Her will is more yielding than mine; she doesn't seek great things for herself."

The letter from Switzerland about being "satisfied" Marjorie read again and again. There was only one way for childhood, girlhood, or womanhood to be satisfied; and that one way was to acknowledge God in every thing, and let him direct every step. Then if one were not satisfied, it was dissatisfaction with God's will; God's will was not enough.

Hollis had made short visits at home twice since she had left school. The first time, she had been at her grandfather's and saw him but half an hour; the second time, they met not at all, as she was attending to some business for Mrs. Holmes, and spending a day and night with Mrs. Harrowgate.

This twenty-first summer she was not happy; she had not been happy for months. It was a new experience, not to be happy. She had been born happy. I do not think any trial, excepting the one she was suffering, would have so utterly unsettled her. It was a strange thing—but, no, I do not know that it was a strange thing; but it may be that you are surprised that she could have this kind of trial; as she expressed it, she was not sure that she was a Christian! All her life she had thought about God; now, when she thought about herself, she began to fear and doubt and tremble.

No wonder that she slept fitfully, that she awoke in the night to weep, that she ate little and grew pale and thin. It was a strange thing to befall my happy Marjorie. Her mother could not understand it. She tempted her appetite in various ways, sent her to her grandfather's for a change, and to Linnet's; but she came home as pale and dispirited as she went.

"She works too hard," thought the anxious mother; and sent for a woman to wash and iron, that the child might be spared. Marjorie protested, saying that she was not ill; but as the summer days came, she did not grow stronger. Then a physician was called; who pronounced the malady nervous exhaustion, prescribed a tonic—cheerful society, sea bathing, horseback riding—and said he would be in again.

Marjorie smiled and knew it would do no good. If Aunt Prue were near her she would open her heart to her; she could have told her father all about it; but she shrank from making known to her mother that she was not ill, but grieving because she was not a Christian. Her mother would give her energetic advice, and bid her wrestle in prayer until peace came. Could her mother understand, when she had lived in the very sunshine of faith for thirty years?

She had prayed—she prayed for hours at a time; but peace came not. She had fasted and prayed, and still peace did not come.

Her mother was as blithe and cheery as the day was long. Linnet was as full of song as a bird, because Will was on the passage home. In Mrs. Kemlo's face and voice and words and manner, was perfect peace. Aunt Prue's letters were overflowing with joy in her husband and child, and joy in God. Only Marjorie was left outside. Mrs. Rheid had become zealous in good works. She read extracts from Hollis' letters to her, where he wrote of his enjoyment in church work, his Bible class, the Young Men's Christian Association, the prayer-meeting. But Marjorie had no heart for work. She had attempted to resign as teacher in Sunday school; but the superintendent and her class of bright little girls persuaded her to remain. She had sighed and yielded. How could she help them to be what she was not herself? No one understood and no one helped her. For the first time in her life she was tempted to be cross. She was weary at night with the effort all day to keep in good humor.

And she was a member of the church? Had she a right to go to the communion? Was she not living a lie? She stayed at home the Sabbath of the summer communion, and spent the morning in tears in her own chamber.

Her mother prayed for her, but she did not question her.

"Marjorie, dear," Morris' mother said, "can you not feel that God loves you?"

"I *know* he does," she replied, bursting into tears; "but I don't love him."

In August of this summer Captain Will was loading in Portland for Havana. She was ready for sea, but the wind was ahead. After two days of persistent head wind Saturday night came, and it was ahead still. Captain Will rushed ashore and hurried out to Linnet. He would have one Sunday more at home.

Annie was spending a week in Middlefield, and Linnet was alone. She had decided not to go home, but to send for Marjorie; and was standing at the gate watching for some one to pass, by whom she might send her message, when Will himself appeared, having walked from the train.

Linnet shouted; he caught her in his arms and ran around the house with her, depositing her at last in the middle of the grass plat in front of the house.

"One more Sunday with you, sweetheart! Have you been praying for a head wind?"

"Suppose I should pray for it to be ahead as long as we live!"

"Poor little girl! It's hard for you to be a sailor's wife, isn't it?"

"It isn't hard to be your wife. It would be hard not to be," said demonstrative Linnet.

"You are going with me next voyage, you have promised."

"Your father has not said I might."

"He won't grumble; the *Linnet* is making money for him."

"You haven't had any supper, Will! And I am forgetting it."

"Have you?"

"I didn't feel like eating, but I did eat a bowl of bread and milk."

"Do you intend to feed me on that?"

"No; come in and help, and I'll get you the nicest supper you ever had."

"I suppose I ought to go over and see father."

"Wait till afterward, and I'll go with you. O, Will! suppose it is fair to-morrow, will he make you sail on Sunday?"

"I never *have* sailed on Sunday."

"But he has! He says it is all nonsense not to take advantage of the wind."

"I have been in ships that did do it. But I prefer not to. The *Linnet* is ready as far as she can be, and not be in motion; there will not be as much to do as there is often in a storm at sea; but this is not an emergency, and I won't do it if I can help it."

"But your father is so determined."

"So am I," said Will in a determined voice.

"But you do not own a plank in her," said Linnet anxiously. "Oh, I hope it *won't* be fair to-morrow."

"It isn't fair to-night, at any rate. I believe you were to give a hungry traveller some supper."

Linnet ran in to kindle the fire and make a cup of tea; Will cut the cold boiled ham and the bread, while Linnet brought the cake and sugared the blueberries.

"Linnet, we have a precious little home."

"Thanks to your good father."

"Yes, thanks to my father. I ought not to displease him," Will returned seriously.

"You do please him; you satisfy him in everything. He told Hollis so."

"Why, I didn't tell you that Hollis came in the train with me. See how you make me forget everything. He is to stay here a day or so, and then go on a fishing excursion with some friends, and then come back here for another day or so. What a fine fellow he is. He is the gentleman among us boys."

"I would like to know what you are," said Linnet indignantly.

"A rough old tar," laughed Will, for the sake of the flash in his wife's eyes.

"Then I'm a rough old tar too," said Linnet decidedly.

How short the evening was! They went across the fields to see Hollis, and to talk over affairs with the largest owner of the *Linnet*. Linnet wondered when she knelt beside Will that night if it would be wrong to ask God to keep the wind ahead until Monday morning. Marjorie moaned in her sleep in real trouble. Linnet dreamed that she awoke Sunday morning and the wind had not changed.

But she did not awake until she heard a heavy rap on the window pane. It was scarcely light, and Will had sprung out of bed and had raised the window and was talking to his father.

"I'll be here in an hour or less time to drive you into Portland. Hollis won't drive you; but I'll be here on time."

"But, father," expostulated Will. He had never resisted his father's will as the others had done. He inherited his mother's peace-loving disposition; he could only expostulate and yield.

"The Linnet must sail, or I'll find another master," said his father in his harshest voice.

Linnet kept the tears back bravely for Will's sake; but she clung to him sobbing at the last, and he wept with her; he had never wept on leaving her before; but this time it was so hard, so hard.

"Will, how *can* I let you go?"

"Keep up, sweetheart. It isn't a long trip—I'll soon be home. Let us have a prayer together before I go."

It was a simple prayer, interrupted by Linnet's sobbing. He asked only that God would keep his wife safe, and bring him home safe to her, for Jesus' sake. And then his father's voice was shouting, and he was gone; and Linnet threw herself across the foot of the bed, sobbing like a little child, with quick short breaths, and hopeless tears.

"It isn't *right*" she cried vehemently; "and Will oughtn't to have gone; but he never will withstand his father."

All day she lived on the hope that something might happen to bring him back at night; but before sundown Captain Rheid drove triumphantly into his own yard, shouting out to his wife in the kitchen doorway that the *Linnet* was well on her way.

At dusk, Linnet's lonely time, Marjorie stepped softly through the entry and stood beside her.

"O, Marjorie! I'm *so* glad," she exclaimed, between laughing and crying.
"I've had a miserable day."

"Didn't you know I would come?"

"How bright you look!" said Linnet, looking up into the changed face; for Marjorie's trouble was all gone, there was a happy tremor about the lips, and peace was shining in her eyes.

"I *am* bright."

"What has happened to you?"

"I can tell you about it now. I have been troubled—more than troubled, almost in despair—because I could not feel that I was a Christian. I thought I was all the more wicked because I professed to be one. And to-day it is all gone—the trouble. And in such a simple way. As I was coming out of Sunday school I overheard somebody say to Mrs. Rich, 'I know I'm not a Christian.' 'Then,' said Mrs. Rich, 'I'd begin this very hour to be one, if I were you.' And it flashed over me why need I bemoan myself any longer; why not begin this very hour; *and I did.*"

"I'm very glad," said Linnet, in her simple, hearty way. "I never had anything like that on my mind, and I know it must be dreadful."

"Dreadful?" repeated Marjorie. "It is being lost away from Christ."

"Mrs. Rheid told Hollis that you were going into a decline, that mother said so, and Will and I were planning what we could do for you."

"Nobody need plan now," smiled Marjorie. "Shall we have some music? We'll sing Will's hymns."

"How your voice sounds!"

"That's why I want to sing. I want to pour it all out."

The next evening Hollis accompanied Linnet on her way to Marjorie's to spend the evening. Marjorie's pale face and mourning dress had touched him deeply. He had taught a class of boys near her class in Sunday school, and had been struck with the dull, mechanical tone in which she had questioned the attentive little girls who crowded around her.

It was not Marjorie; but it was the Marjorie who had lost Morris and her father. Was she so weak that she sank under grief? In his thought she was always strong. But it was another Marjorie who met him at the gate the next evening; the cheeks were still thin, but they were tinted and there was not a trace of yesterday's dullness in face or voice; it was a joyful face, and her voice was as light-hearted as a child's. Something had wrought a change since yesterday.

Such a quiet, unobtrusive little figure in a black and white gingham, with a knot of black ribbon at her throat and a cluster of white roses in her belt. Miss Prudence had done her best with the little country girl, and she was become only a sweet and girlish-looking woman; she had not marked out for herself a "career"; she had done nothing that no other girl might do. But she was the lady that some other girls had not become, he argued.

The three, Hollis, Linnet, and Marjorie, sat in the moon lighted parlor and talked over old times. Hollis had begun it by saying that his father had shown him "Flyaway" stowed away in the granary chamber.

He was sitting beside Linnet in a good position to study Marjorie's face unobserved. The girl's face bore the marks of having gone through something; there was a flutter about her lips, and her soft laugh and the joy about the lips was almost contradicted by the mistiness that now and then veiled the eyes. She had planned to go up to her chamber early, and have this evening alone by herself,—alone on her knees at the open window, with the stars above her and the rustle of the leaves and the breath of the sea about her. It had been a long sorrow; all she wanted was to rest, as Mary did, at the feet of the Lord; to look up into his face, and feel his eyes upon her face; to shed sweetest tears over the peace of forgiven sin.

She had written to Aunt Prue all about it that afternoon. She was tempted to show the letter to her mother, but was restrained by her usual shyness and timidity.

"Marjorie, why don't you talk?" questioned Linnet.

Marjorie was on the music stool, and had turned from them to play the air of one of the songs they used to sing in school.

"I thought I had been talking a great deal. I am thinking of so many things and I thought I had spoken of them all."

"I wish you would," said Hollis.

"I was thinking of Morris just then. But he was not in your school days, nor in Linnet's. He belongs to mine."

"What else? Go on please," said Hollis.

"And then I was thinking that his life was a success, as father's was. They both did the will of the Lord."

"I've been trying all day to submit to that will," said Linnet, in a thick voice.

"Is that all we have to do with it—submit to it?" asked Hollis with a grave smile. "Why do we always groan over 'Thy will be done,' as though there never was anything pleasant in it?"

"That's true," returned Linnet emphatically. "When Will came Saturday, I didn't rejoice and say 'It is the Lord's will,' but Sunday morning I thought it was, because it was so hard! All the lovely things that happen to us *are* his will of course."

"Suppose we study up every time where the Lord speaks of his father's will, and learn what that will is. Shall we, Marjorie?" proposed Hollis.

"Oh, yes; it will be delightful!" she assented.

"And when I come back from my fishing excursion we will compare notes, and give each other our thoughts. I must give that topic in our prayer-meeting and take it in my Bible class."

"We know the will of God is our sanctification," said Marjorie slowly. "I don't want to sigh, 'Thy will be done,' about that."

"Hollis, I mean to hold on to that—every happy thing is God's will as well as the hard ones," said Linnet.

"And here come the mothers for some music," exclaimed Marjorie. "They cannot go to sleep without it."

And Marjorie's mother did not go to sleep with it. Hollis had invited himself to remain all night, saying that he was responsible for Linnet and could not go home unless she went home.

XXVI.

MARJORIE'S MOTHER.

"Leave to Heaven the measure and the choice."—*Johnson*.

Marjorie fell asleep as happy as she wanted to be; but her mother did not close her eyes in sleep all that night. She closed them in prayer, however, and told Miss Prudence afterward that she "did not catch one wink of sleep." All night long she was asking the Lord if she might intermeddle between Marjorie and Hollis. As we look at them there was nothing to intermeddle with. Marjorie herself did not know of anything. Perhaps, more than anything, she laid before the Lord what she wanted him to do. She told him how Marjorie looked, and how depressed she had been, and her own fear that it was disappointment that was breaking her heart. The prayer was characteristic.

"Lord, thou knowest all things; thou knowest the hearts of both, and what is in thy will for both; but thou dost choose means, thou hast chosen means since the world began; and if thou hast chosen me, make me ready to speak. Soften the heart of the young man; show him how ill he has done; and knit their hearts to each other as thou didst the hearts of David and Jonathan. Make her willing as thou didst make Rebekah willing to go with the servant of Abraham. Give her favor in his eyes, as thou gavest favor to Abigail in the eyes of David. Bring her into favor and tender love, as thou broughtest Daniel. Let it not be beneath thy notice; the sparrows are not, and she is more than many sparrows to thee. Give me words to speak, and prepare his heart to listen. The king's heart is in thine hand, and so is his heart. If we acknowledge thee in all our ways, thou wilt direct our steps. I do acknowledge thee. Oh, direct my steps and my words."

With variety of phrasing, she poured out this prayer all through the hours of the night; she spread the matter before the Lord as Hezekiah did the letter that troubled him. Something must be *done*. She forgot all the commands to *wait*, to *sit still* and see the salvation of the Lord; she forgot, or put away from her, the description of one who believeth: "He that believeth shall not make haste." And she was making haste with all her might.

In the earliest dawn she arose, feeling assured that the Lord had heard her cry and had answered her; he had given her permission to speak to Hollis.

That he permitted her to speak to Hollis, I know; that it was his will, I do not know; but she was assured that she knew, and she never changed her mind. It may be that it was his will for her to make a mistake and bring sorrow upon Marjorie; the Lord does not shrink from mistakes; he knows what to do with them.

Before the house was astir, Hollis found her in the kitchen; she had kindled the fire, and was filling the tea-kettle at the pump in the sink.

"Good morning, Mrs. West. Excuse my early leave; but I must meet my friends to-day."

"Hollis!"

She set the tea-kettle on the stove, and turned and looked at him. The solemn weight of her eye rooted him to the spot.

"Hollis, I've known you ever since you were born."

"And now you are going to find fault with me!" he returned, with an easy laugh.

"No, not to find fault, but to speak with great plainness. Do you see how changed Marjorie is!"

"Yes. I could not fail to notice it. Has she been ill?"

"Yes, very ill. You see the effect of something."

"But she is better. She was so bright last night."

"Yes, last night," she returned impressively, setting the lid of the tea-kettle firmly in its place. "Did you ever think that you did wrong in writing to her so many years and then stopping short all of a sudden, giving her no reason at all?"

"Do you mean *that* has changed her, and hurt her?" he asked, in extreme surprise.

"I do. I mean that. I mean that you gained her affections and then left her," she returned with severity.

Hollis was now trembling in every limb, strong man as he was; he caught at the back of a chair, and leaned on his two hands as he stood behind it gazing into her face with mute lips.

"And now, what do you intend to do?"

"I never did that! It was not in my heart to do that! I would scorn to do it!" he declared with vehemence.

"Then what did you do?" she asked quietly.

"We were good friends. We liked to write to each other. I left off writing because I thought it not fair to interfere with Morris."

"Morris! What did he have to do with it?"

"She wears his ring," he said in a reasoning voice.

"She wears it as she would wear it if a brother had given it to her. They were brother and sister."

Hollis stood with his eyes upon the floor. Afterward Mrs. West told Miss Prudence that when it came to that, she pitied him with all her heart, "he shook all over and looked as if he would faint."

"Mrs. West!" he lifted his eyes and spoke in his usual clear, manly voice, "I have never thought of marrying any one beside Marjorie. I gave that up when mother wrote me that she cared for Morris. I have never sought any one since. I have been waiting—if she loved Morris, she could not love me. I have been giving her time to think of me if she wanted to—"

"I'd like to know how. You haven't given her the first sign."

"She does not know me; she is shy with me. I do not know her; we do not feel at home with each other."

"How are you going to get to feel at home with each other five hundred miles apart?" inquired the practical mother.

"It will take time."

"Time! I should think it would." Mrs. West pushed a stick of wood into the stove with some energy.

"But if you think it is because—"

"I do think so."

"Then she must know me better than I thought she did," he continued, thoughtfully.

"Didn't she go to school with you?"

"Not with me grown up."

"That's a distinction that doesn't mean anything."

"It means something to me. I am more at home with Linnet than I am with her. She has changed; she keeps within herself."

"Then you must bring her out."

"How can she care, if she thinks I have trifled with her?"

"I didn't say she thought so, I said *I* thought so!"

"You have hastened this very much. I wanted her to know me and trust me. I want my wife to love me, Mrs. West."

"No doubt of that, Master Hollis," with a sigh of congratulation to herself. "All you have to do is to tell her what you have told me. She will throw you off."

"Has she *said* so?" he inquired eagerly.

"Do you think she is the girl to say so?"

"I am sure not," he answered proudly.

"Hollis, this is a great relief," said Marjorie's mother.

"Well, good-bye," he said, after hesitating a moment with his eyes on the kitchen floor, and extending his hand. "I will speak to her when I come back."

"The Lord bless you," she answered fervently.

Just then Marjorie ran lightly down-stairs singing a morning hymn, entering the kitchen as he closed the door and went out.

"Hollis just went," said her mother.

"Why didn't he stay to breakfast?" she asked, without embarrassment.

"He had to meet his friends early," replied her mother, averting her face and busying herself at the sink.

"He will have to eat breakfast somewhere; but perhaps he expects to take a late breakfast on the fish he has caught. Mother, Linnet and I are to be little girls, and go berrying."

"Only be happy, children; that's all I want," returned Mrs. West, her voice breaking.

While Marjorie fried the fish for breakfast her mother went to her chamber to kneel down and give thanks.

XXVII.

ANOTHER WALK AND ANOTHER TALK.

"We are not to lead events but to follow them."—*Epictetus*.

Marjorie was so happy that she trembled with the joy of it. The relief from her burden, at times, was almost harder to bear than the burden itself. She sang all day hymns that were the outpouring of her soul in love to Christ.

"What a child you are, Marjorie," her mother said one day. "You were as doleful as you could be, and now you are as happy as a bird."

"Do you remember what Luther says?"

"Luther says several wise and good things."

"And this is one of them; it is one of Aunt Prue's favorite sayings: 'The Christian should be like a little bird, which sits on its twig and sings, and lets God think for it.'"

"That's all very well for a bird; but we have to *do*," replied her mother sharply.

"We have to *do* what God *thinks*, though," returned Marjorie quickly.

"Child, you are your father all over again; he always wanted to wait and see; but mine was the faith that acted."

"But now can we act, until we wait and see?" persisted Marjorie. "I want to be sure that God means for us to do things."

"Many a thing wouldn't have happened if I hadn't pushed through—why, your father would have been willing for Linnet to be engaged years and years."

"So would I," said Marjorie seriously.

A week later, one afternoon towards dusk, Marjorie was walking home from her grandfather's. Her happy face was shaded by a brown straw hat, her hands were sunburned, and her fingers were scratched with numerous berrying expeditions. There was a deepened color in the roundness of her cheeks; she was a country maiden this afternoon, swinging an empty basket in her hand. She was humming to herself as she walked along, hurrying her steps a little as she remembered that it was the mail for her long, foreign letter. This afternoon she was as happy as she wanted to be. Within half a mile of home she espied a tall figure coming towards her,—a figure in a long linen duster, wearing a gray, low-crowned, felt hat. After an instant she recognized Hollis and remembered that to-day he was expected home. She had not thought of it all day.

"Your mother sent me to meet you," he said, without formal greeting. Instantly she detected a change in his manner towards her; it was as easy as if he were speaking to Linnet.

"I've been off on one of my long walks."

"Do you remember our walk together from your grandfather's—how many years ago?"

"When I appealed to your sympathies and enlisted you in my behalf?"

"You were in trouble, weren't you? I believe it is just seven years ago."

"Physiologists tell us we are made over new every seven years, therefore you and I are another Hollis and another Marjorie."

"I hope I am another Hollis," he answered gravely.

"And I am *sure* I am another Marjorie," she said more lightly. "How you lectured me then!"

"I never lectured any one."

"You lectured me. I never forgot it. From that hour I wanted to be like your cousin Helen."

"You do not need to copy any one. I like you best as yourself."

"You do not know me."

"No; I do not know you; but I want to know you."

"That depends upon yourself as well as upon me."

"I do not forget that. I am not quick to read and you are written in many languages."

"Are you fond of the study—of languages? Did you succeed in French?"

"Fairly. And I can express my wants in German. Will you write to me again?"

There was a flush now that was not sunburn; but she did not speak; she seemed to be considering.

"Will you, Marjorie?" he urged, with gentle persistence.

"I—don't know."

"Why don't you know."

"I have not thought about it for so long. Let me see—what kind of letters did you write. Were they interesting?"

"*Yours* were interesting. Were you hurt because—"

It happened so long ago that she smiled as she looked up at him.

"I have never told you the reason. I thought Morris Kemlo had a prior claim."

"What right had you to think that?"

"From what I heard—and saw."

"I am ignorant of what you could hear or see. Morris was my twin-brother; he was my blessing; he *is* my blessing."

"Is not my reason sufficient?"

"Oh, yes; it doesn't matter. But see that sumach. I have not seen anything so pretty this summer; mother must have them. You wouldn't think it, but she is very fond of wild flowers."

She stepped aside to pluck the sumach and sprays of goldenrod; they were growing beside a stone wall, and she crossed the road to them. He stood watching her. She was as unconscious as the goldenrod herself.

What had her mother meant? Was it all a mistake? Had his wretched days and wakeful nights been for nothing? Was there nothing for him to be grieved about? He knew now how much he loved her—and she? He was not a part of her life, at all. Would he dare speak the words he had planned to speak?

"Then, Marjorie, you will not write to me," he began afresh, after admiring the sumach.

"Oh, yes, I will! If you want to! I love to write letters; and my life isn't half full enough yet. I want new people in it."

"And you would as readily take me as another," he said, in a tone that she did not understand.

"More readily than one whom I do not know. I want you to hear extracts from one of Mrs. Holmes' delicious letters to-night."

"You are as happy as a lark to-day.

"That is what mother told me, only she did not specify the bird. Morris, I *am* happier than I was Sunday morning."

He colored over the name. She smiled and said, "I've been thinking about him to-day, and wanting to tell him how changed I am."

"What has changed you?" he asked.

Her eyes filled before she could answer him. In a few brief sentences, sentences in which each word told, she gave him the story of her dark year.

"Poor little Mousie," he said tenderly. "And you bore the dark time all by yourself."

"That's the way I have my times. But I do not have my happy times by myself, you see."

"Did nothing else trouble you?"

"No; oh, no! Nothing like that. Father's death was not a trouble. I went with him as far as I could—I almost wanted to go all the way."

"And there was nothing else to hurt you?" he asked very earnestly.

"Oh, no; why should there be?" she answered, meeting his questioning eyes frankly. "Do you know of anything else that should have troubled me?"

"No, nothing else. But girls do have sometimes. Didn't your mother help you any? She helps other people."

"I could not tell her. I could not talk about it. She only thought I was ill, and sent for a physician. Perhaps I did worry myself into feeling ill."

"You take life easily," he said.

"Do I? I like to take it as God gives it to me; not before he gives it to me. This slowness—or faith—or whatever it is, is one of my inheritances from my blessed father. Who is it that says, 'I'd see to it pretty sharp that I didn't hurry Providence.' That has helped me."

"I wish it would some one else," he said grimly.

"I wish it would help *every one* else. Everything is helping me now; if I were writing to you I could tell you some of them."

"I like to hear you talk, Marjorie."

"Do you?" she asked wonderingly. "Linnet does, too, and Mrs. Kemlo. As I shall never write a book, I must learn to talk, and talk myself all out. Aunt Prue is living her book."

"Tell me something that has helped you," he urged.

She looked at the goldenrod in her hand, and raised it to her lips.

"It is coming to me that Christ made everything. He made those lilies of which he said, 'Consider the lilies.' Isn't it queer that we will not let him clothe us as he did the lilies? What girl ever had a white dress of the texture and whiteness and richness of the lily?"

"But the lily has but one dress; girls like a new dress for every occasion and a different one."

"'Shall he not much more clothe you?' But we do not let him clothe us. When one lily fades, he makes another in a fresh dress. I wish I could live as he wants me to. Not think about dress or what we eat or drink? Only do his beautiful work, and not have to worry and be anxious about things."

"Do you *have* to be?" he asked smiling.

"My life is a part of lives that are anxious about these things. But I don't think about dress as some girls do. I never like to talk about it. It is not a temptation to me. It would not trouble me to wear one dress all my life—one color, as the flowers do; it should be a soft gray—a cashmere, and when one was soiled or worn out I would have another like it—and never spend any more thought about it. Aunt Prue loves gray—she almost does that—she spends no thought on dress. If we didn't have to 'take thought,' how much time we would have—and how our minds would be at rest—to work for people and to study God's works and will."

Hollis smiled as he looked down at her.

"Girls don't usually talk like that," he said.

"Perhaps I don't—usually. What are you reading now?"

"History, chiefly—the history of the world and the history of the church."

They walked more and more slowly as they drifted into talk about books and then into his life in New York and the experiences he had had in his business tours and the people whom he had met.

"Do you like your life?" she asked.

"Yes, I like the movement and the life: I like to be 'on the go.' I expect to take my third trip across the ocean by and by. I like to mingle with men. I never could settle down into farming; not till I am old, at any rate."

They found Marjorie's mother standing in the front doorway, looking for them. She glanced at Hollis, but he was fastening the gate and would not be glanced at. Marjorie's face was no brighter than when she had set out for her walk. Linnet was setting the tea-table and singing, "A life on the ocean wave."

After tea the letter from Switzerland was read and discussed. Miss Prudence, as Mrs. West could not refrain from calling her, always gave them something to talk about. To give people something to think about that was worth thinking about, was something to live for, she had said once to Marjorie.

And then there was music and talk. Marjorie and Hollis seemed to find endless themes for conversation. And then Hollis and Linnet went home. Hollis bade them good-bye; he was to take an early train in the morning. Marjorie's mother scanned Marjorie's face, and stood with a lighted candle in her hand at bedtime, waiting for her confidence; but unconscious Marjorie closed the piano, piled away the sheets of music, arranged the chairs, and then went out to the milkroom for a glass of milk.

"Good-night, mother," she called back. "Are you waiting for anything?"

"Did you set the sponge for the bread?"

"Oh, yes," in a laughing voice.

And then the mother went slowly and wonderingly up the stairs, muttering
"Well! well! Of all things!"

Marjorie drew Aunt Prue's letter from her pocket to think it all over again by herself. Mr. Holmes was buried in manuscript. Prue was studying with her, beside studying French and German with the pastor's daughter in the village, and she herself was full of many things. They were coming home by and by to choose a home in America.

"When I was your age, Marjorie, and older, I used to fall asleep at night thinking over the doings of the day and finding my life in them; and in the morning when I awoke, my thought was, 'What shall I *do* to-day?' And now when I awake—now, when my life is at its happiest and as full of doings as I can wish, I think, instead, of Christ, and find my joy in nearness to him, in doing all with his eye upon me. You have not come to this yet; but it is waiting for you. Your first thought to-morrow morning may be of some plan to go somewhere, of some one you expect to see, of something you have promised to-day; but, by and by, when you love him as you are praying to love him, your first thought will be that you are with him. You can imagine the mother awaking with joy at finding her child asleep beside her, or the wife awaking to another day with her husband; but blessed more than all is it to awake and find the Lord himself near enough for you to speak to."

Marjorie went to sleep with the thought in her heart, and awoke with it; and then she remembered that Hollis must be on his way to the train, and then that she and Linnet were to drive to Portland that day on a small shopping excursion and to find something for the birthday present of Morris' mother.

Several days afterward when the mail was brought in Mrs. West beckoned
Marjorie aside in a mysterious manner and laid in her hand a letter from
Hollis.

"Yes," said Marjorie.

"Did you expect it?"

"Oh, yes."

Mrs. West waited until Marjorie opened it, and felt in her pocket for her glasses. In the other time she had always read his letters. But Marjorie moved away with it, and only said afterward that there was no "news" in it.

It was not like the letters of the other time. He had learned to write as she had learned to talk. Her reply was as full of herself as it would have been to Morris. Hollis could never be a stranger again.

XXVIII.

THE LINNET.

"He who sends the storm steers the vessel."—*Rev. T. Adams*

August passed and September was almost through and not one word had been heard of the *Linnet*. Linnet lived through the days and through the nights, but she thought she would choke to death every night. Days before she had consented, her mother had gone to her and urged her with every argument at her command to lock up her house and come home until they heard. At first, she resented the very thought of it; but Annie Grey was busy in Middlefield, Marjorie was needed at home, and the hours of the days seemed never to pass away; at last, worn out with her anguish, she allowed Captain Rheid to lift her into his carriage and take her to her mother.

As the days went on Will's father neither ate nor slept; he drove into Portland every day, and returned at night more stern and more pale than he went away in the morning.

Linnet lay on her mother's bed and wept, and then slept from exhaustion, to awake with the cry, "Oh, why didn't I die in my sleep?"

One evening Mrs. Rheid appeared at the kitchen door; her cap and sunbonnet had fallen off, her gray hair was roughened over her forehead, her eyes were wild, her lips apart. Her husband had brought her, and sat outside in his wagon too stupefied to remember that he was leaving his old wife to stagger into the house alone.

Mrs. West turned from the table, where she was reading her evening chapter by candle light, and rising caught her before she fell into her arms. The two old mothers clung to each other and wept together; it seemed such a little time since they had washed up Linnet's dishes and set her house in order on the wedding day. Mrs. Rheid thrust a newspaper into her hand as she heard her husband's step, and went out to meet him as Mrs. West called Marjorie. Linnet was asleep upon her mother's bed.

"My baby, my poor baby!" cried her mother, falling on her knees beside the bed, "must you wake up to this?"

She awoke at midnight; but her mother lay quiet beside her, and she did not arouse her. In the early light she discerned something in her mother's face, and begged to know what she had to tell.

Taking her into her arms she told her all she knew. It was in the newspaper. A homeward-bound ship had brought the news. The *Linnet* had been seen; wrecked, all her masts gone, deserted, not a soul on board—the captain supposed she went down that night; there was a storm, and he could not find her again in the morning. He had tried to keep near her, thinking it worth while to tow her in. Before she ended, the child was a dead weight in her arms. For an hour they all believed her dead. A long illness followed; it was Christmas before she crossed the chamber, and in April Captain Rheid brought her downstairs in his arms.

His wife said he loved Linnet as he would have loved an own daughter. His heart was more broken than hers.

"Poor father," she would say, stroking his grizzly beard with her thin fingers; "poor father."

"Cynthy," African John's wife, had a new suggestion every time she was allowed to see Linnet. Hadn't she waited, and didn't she know? Mightn't an East Indian have taken him off and carried him to Madras, or somewhere there, and wasn't he now working his passage home as she had once heard of a shipwrecked captain doing! Or, perhaps some ship was taking him around the Horn—it took time to go around that Horn, as everybody knew—or suppose a whaler had taken him off and carried him up north, could he expect to get back in a day, and did she want him to find her in such a plight?

So Linnet hoped and hoped. His mother put on mourning, and had a funeral sermon preached; and his father put up a grave-stone in the churchyard, with his name and age engraved on it, and underneath, "Lost at sea." There were, many such in that country churchyard.

It was two years before Linnet could be persuaded to put on her widow's mourning, and then she did it to please the two mothers. The color gradually came back to her cheeks and lips; she moved around with a grave step, but her hands were never idle. After two years she insisted upon going back to Will's home, where the shutters had been barred so long, and the only signs of life were the corn and rye growing in the fields about it.

Annie Grey was glad to be with her again. She worked at dressmaking; and spent every night at home with Linnet.

The next summer the travellers returned from abroad; Mr. Holmes, more perfectly his developed self; little Prue growing up and as charming a girl as ever papa and mamma had hoped for, prayed for, and worked for; and Mrs. Holmes, or "Miss Prudence" and "Aunt Prue," as she was called, a lady whose slight figure had become rounded and whose white hair shaded a fair face full of peace.

There was no resisting such persuasions as those of Mrs. Kemlo, the girls' mother, and the "girls" themselves; and almost before they had decided upon it they found themselves installed at Mrs. West's for the summer. Before the first snow, however, a house was rented in New York City, the old, homelike furniture removed to it, and they had but to believe it to feel themselves at home in the long parlor in Maple Street.

Linnet was taken from her lonely home by loving force, and kept all winter. She could be at rest with Miss Prudence; she could be at rest and enjoy and be busy. It was wonderful how many things she became busied about and deeply interested in. Her letters to Marjorie were as full of life as in her school days. She was Linnet, Mrs. Holmes wrote to her mother; but she was Linnet chastened and sanctified.

And all this time Hollis and Marjorie had written to each other, and had seen each other for two weeks every day each year.

During the winter Linnet spent in New York the firm for which he travelled became involved; the business was greatly decreased; changes were made: one of the partners left the firm; the remaining head had a nephew, whom he preferred to his partner's favorite, Hollis Rheid; and Hollis Rheid found himself with nothing to do but to look around for something to do.

"Come home," wrote his father. "I will build you a house, and give you fifty acres of good land."

With the letter in his pocket, he sought his friends, the Holmes'. He was not so averse to a farmer's life as he had been when he once spoke of it to Marjorie.

He found Prue practicing; papa was in the study, she said, and mamma and
Linnet had gone to the train to meet Marjorie.

"Marjorie did not tell me that she was coming."

"It was to be your surprise, and now I've spoiled it."

"Nothing can spoil the pleasure of it," he returned.

Prue stationed herself at the window, as when she was a little girl, to watch for Marjorie. She was still the blue bird with the golden crest.

XXIX.

ONE NIGHT.

"We are often prophets to others only because we are our own historians."—*Madame Swetchine*.

The evening before Marjorie started for New York she was sitting alone in her father's arm chair before the sitting-room fire. Her mother had left her to go up to Mrs. Kemlo's chamber for her usual evening chat. Mrs. Kemlo was not strong this winter, and on very cold days did not venture down-stairs to the sitting-room. Marjorie, her mother, and the young farmer who had charge of the farm, were often the only ones at the table, and the only occupants of the sitting-room during the long winter evenings. Marjorie sighed for Linnet, or she would have sighed for her, if she had been selfish; she remembered the evenings of studying with Morris, and the master's tread as he walked up and down and talked to her father.

Now she was alone in the dim light of two tallow candles. It was so cold that the small wood stove did not sufficiently heat the room, and she had wrapped the shawl about her that Linnet used to wear to school when Mr. Holmes taught. She hid herself in it, gathering her feet up under the skirt of her dress, in a position very comfortable and lazy, and very undignified for a maiden who would be twenty-five on her next birthday.

The last letter from Hollis had stated that he was seeking a position in the city. He thought he understood his business fairly, and the outlook was not discouraging. He had a little money well invested; his life was simple; and, beyond the having nothing to do, he was not anxious. He had thought of farming as a last resort; but there was rather a wide difference between tossing over laces and following the plow.

"Not that I dread hard work, but I do not love the *solitude* of country life. 'A wise man is never less alone than when he is alone,' Swift writes; but I am not a wise man, nor a wild beast. I love men and the homes of men, the business of men, the opportunities that I find among men."

She had not replied to this letter; what a talk they would have over it! She had learned Hollis; she knew him by heart; she could talk to him now almost as easily as she could write. These years of writing had been a great deal to both of them. They had educated each other.

The last time Mrs. West had seen Hollis she had wondered how she had ever dared speak to him as she had spoken that morning in the kitchen. Had she effected anything? She was not sure that they were engaged; she had "talked it over" with his mother, and that mother was equally in the dark.

"I know what his intentions are," confided Marjorie's mother "I know he means to have her, for he told me so."

"He has never told me so," said Hollis' mother.

"You haven't asked him," suggested Mrs. West comfortably.

"Have *you*?"

"I made an opportunity for it to be easy for him to tell me."

"I don't know how to make opportunities," returned Mrs. Rheid with some dignity.

"Everybody doesn't," was the complacent reply.

Marjorie had had a busy day arranging household matters for her mother while she should be gone, and was dozing with her head nestled in the soft folds of the shawl when her mother's step aroused her.

"Child, you are asleep and letting the fire go down."

"Am I?" she asked drowsily, "the room *is* cold."

She wrapped the shawl about her more closely and nestled into it again.

"Perhaps Hollis will come home with you," her mother began, drawing her own especial chair nearer the fire and settling down as if for a long conversation.

"Mother, you will be chilly;" and, with the instinct that her mother must be taken care of, she sprang up with her eyes still half asleep and attended to the fire.

The dry chips soon kindled a blaze, and she was wide awake with the flush of sleep in her cheeks.

"Why do you think he will?" she asked.

"It looks like it. Mrs. Rheid ran over to-day to tell me that the Captain had offered to give him fifty acres and build him a house, if he would come home for good."

"I wonder if he will like it."

"You ought to know," in a suggestive tone.

"I am not sure. He does not like farming."

"A farm of his own may make a difference. And a house of his own. I suppose the Captain thinks he is engaged to you."

Mrs. West was rubbing her thumb nail and not looking at Marjorie. Marjorie was playing with a chip, thrusting it into the fire and bringing it out lighted as she and Linnet used to like to do.

"Marjorie, *is* he?"

"No, ma'am," answered Marjorie, the corners of her lips twitching.

"I'd like to know why he isn't," with some asperity.

"Perhaps he knows," suggested Marjorie, looking at her lighted chip. It was childish; but she must be doing something, if her mother would insist upon talking about Hollis.

"Do *you* know?"

Marjorie dropped her chip into the stove and looked up at the broad figure in the wooden rocker—a figure in a black dress and gingham apron, with a neat white cap covering her gray hair, a round face, from which Marjorie had taken her roundness and dimples, a shrewd face with a determined mouth and the kindliest eyes that ever looked out upon the world. Marjorie looked at her and loved her.

"Mother, do you want to know? I haven't anything to tell you."

"Seems to me he's a long time about it."

Marjorie colored now, and, rising from her seat in front of the fire, wrapped the shawl again around her.

"Mother, dear, I'm not a child now; I am a woman grown."

"Too old to be advised," sighed her mother.

"I don't know what I need to be advised about."

"People never do. It is more than three years ago that he told me that he had never thought of any one but you."

"Why should he tell you that?" Marjorie's tone could be sharp as well as her mother's.

"I was talking about you. I said you were not well—I was afraid you were troubled—and he told me—that."

"Troubled about *what*?" Marjorie demanded.

"About his not answering your letter," in a wavering voice.

The words had to come; Mrs. West knew that Marjorie would have her answer.

"And—after that—he asked me—to write to him. Mother, mother, you do not know what you have done!"

Marjorie fled away in the dark up to her own little chamber, threw herself down on the bed without undressing, and lay all night, moaning and weeping.

She prayed beside; she could not be in trouble and not give the first breath of it to the Lord. Hollis had asked her to write because of what her mother had said to him. He believed—what did he believe?

"O, mother! mother!" she moaned, "you are so good and so lovely, and yet you have hurt me so. How could you? How could you?"

While the clock in Mrs. Kemlo's room was striking six, a light flashed across her eyes. Her mother stood at the bedside with a lighted candle in her hand.

"I was afraid you would oversleep. Why, child! Didn't you undress? Haven't you had anything but that quilt over you?"

"Mother, I am not going; I never want to see Hollis again," cried Marjorie weakly.

"Nonsense child," answered her mother energetically.

"It is not nonsense. I will not go to New York."

"What will they all think?"

"I will write that I cannot come. I could not travel to-day; I have not slept at all."

"You look so. But you are very foolish. Why should he not speak to me first?"

"It was your speaking to him first. What must he think of me! O, mother, mother, how could you?"

The hopeless cry went to her mother's heart.

"Marjorie, I believe the Lord allows us to be self-willed. I have not slept either; but I have sat up by the fire. Your father used to say that we would not make haste if we trusted, and I have learned that it is so. All I have done is to break your heart."

"Not quite that, poor mother. But I shall never write to Hollis again."

Mrs. West turned away and set the candle on the bureau. "But I can," she said to herself.

"Come down-stairs where it is warm, and I'll make you a cup of coffee. I'm afraid you have caught your death of cold."

"I *am* cold," confessed Marjorie, rising with a weak motion.

Her new gray travelling dress was thrown over a chair, her small trunk was packed, even her gloves were laid out on the bureau beside her pocket-book.

"Linnet has counted on it so," sighed her mother.

"Mother!" rising to her feet and standing by the bedside. "I will go. Linnet shall not be disappointed."

"That's a good child! Now hurry down, and I'll hurry you off," said her mother, in her usual brisk tone.

An hour and a half later Mrs. West kissed Marjorie's pale lips, and bade her stay a good while and have a good time. And before she washed up the breakfast dishes she put on a clean apron, burnished her glasses, and sat down to write to Hollis. The letter was as plain as her talk had been. He had understood then, he should understand now. But with Marjorie would be the difficulty; could he manage her?

XXX.

THE COSEY CORNER.

"God takes men's hearty desires and will instead of the deed where they have not the power to fulfill it; but he never took the bare deed instead of the will."—*Richard Baxter.*

Prue opened the door, and sprang into Marjorie's arms in her old, affectionate way; and Marjorie almost forgot that she was not in Maple Street, when she was led into the front parlor; there was as much of the Maple Street parlor in it as could be well arranged. Hollis was there on the hearth rug, waiting modestly in the background for his greeting; he had not been a part of Maple Street. The greeting he waited for was tardy in coming, and was shy and constrained, and it seemed impossible to have a word with her alone all the evening: she was at the piano, or chatting in the kitchen with old Deborah, or laughing with Prue, or asking questions of Linnet, and when, at last, Mr. Holmes took her upstairs to show her his study, he said good night abruptly and went away.

Marjorie chided herself for her naughty pride and passed another sleepless night; in the morning she looked so ill that the plans for the day were postponed, and she was taken into Mrs. Holmes own chamber to be petted and nursed to sleep. She awoke in the dusk to find Aunt Prue's dear face beside her.

"Aunt Prue," she said, stretching up her hands to encircle her neck, "I don't know what to do."

"I do. Tell me."

"Perhaps I oughtn't to. It's mother's secret."

"Suppose I know all about it."

"You can't! How can you?"

"Lie still," pushing her back gently among the pillows, "and let me tell you."

"I thought I was to tell you."

"A while ago the postman brought me a note from your mother. She told me that she had confessed to you something she told me last summer."

"Oh," exclaimed Marjorie, covering her face with both hands, "isn't it too dreadful!"

"I think your mother saw clearly that she had taken your life into her own hands without waiting to let God work for you and in you. I assured her that I knew all about that dark time of yours, and she wept some very sorrowful tears to think how heartbroken you would be if you knew. Perhaps she thought you ought to know it; she is not one to spare herself; she is even harder upon herself than upon other sinners."

"But, Aunt Prue, what ought I to do now? What can I do to make it right?"

"Do you want to meddle?"

"No, oh no; but it takes my breath away. I'm afraid he began to write to me again because he thought I wanted him to."

"Didn't you want him to?"

"Yes—but not—but not as mother thought I did. I never once asked God to give him back to me; and I should if I had wanted it very much, because I always ask him for everything."

"Your pride need not be wounded, poor little Marjorie! Do you remember telling Hollis about your dark time, that night he met you on your way from your grandfather's?"

"Yes; I think I do. Yes, I know I told him; for he called me 'Mousie,' and he had not said that since I was little; and with it he seemed to come back to me, and I was not afraid or timid with him after that."

"You wrote me about the talk, and he has told me about it since. To be frank, Marjorie, he told me about the conversation with your mother, and how startled he was. After that talk with you he was assured that she was mistaken—but, child, there was no harm, no sin—even if it had been true. The only sin I find was your mother's want of faith in making haste. And she sees it now and laments it. She says making haste has been the sin of her lifetime. Her unbelief has taken that form. You were very chilly to Hollis last night."

"I couldn't help it," said Marjorie. "I would not have come if I could have stayed at home."

"Is that proud heart satisfied now?"

"Perhaps it oughtn't to be—if it is proud."

"We will not argue about it now as there's somebody waiting for you down-stairs."

"I don't want to see him—now."

"Suppose he wants to see you."

"Aunt Prue! I wish I could be selfish just a few minutes."

"You may. A whole hour. You may be selfish up here all by yourself until the dinner bell rings."

Marjorie laughed and drew the lounge afghan up about her shoulders. She was so happy that she wanted to go to sleep;—to go to sleep and be thankful. But the dinner bell found her in the parlor talking to Linnet; Prue and Hollis were chattering together in French. Prue corrected his pronunciation and promised to lend him books.

The most inviting corner in the house to Marjorie was a cosey corner in the library; she found her way thither after dinner, and there Hollis found her, after searching parlors, dining-room, and halls for her. The cosey corner itself was an arm-chair near the revolving bookcase; Prue said that papa kept his "pets" in that bookcase.

Marjorie had taken a book into her hand and was gathering a thought here and there when Hollis entered; he pushed a chair to her side, and, seating himself, took the book from her fingers.

"Marjorie, I have come to ask you what to do?"

"About your father's offer?"

"Yes. I should have written to-day. I fancy how he watches the mail. But I am in a great state of indecision. My heart is not in his plan."

"Is your heart in buying and selling laces?"

"I don't see why you need put it that way," he returned, with some irritation. "Don't you like my business?"

"Do you?"

"I like what it gives me to do."

"I should not choose it if I were a man."

"What would you choose?"

"I have not considered sufficiently to choose, I suppose. I should want to be one of the mediums through which good passed to my neighbor."

"What would you choose for me to do?"

"The thing God bids you do."

"That may be to buy and sell laces."

"It may be. I hope it was while you were doing it."

"You mean that through this offer of father's God may be indicating his will."

"He is certainly giving you an opportunity to choose."

"I had not looked upon it in that light. Marjorie, I'm afraid the thought of his will is not always as present with me as with you."

"I used to think I needed money, like Aunt Prue, if I would bless my neighbor; but once it came to me that Christ through his *poverty* made us rich: the world's workers have not always been the men and the women with most money. You see I am taking it for granted that you do not intend to decide for yourself, or work for yourself."

"No; I am thinking of working for you."

"I am too small a field."

"But you must be included."

"I can be one little corner; there's all Middlefield beside. Isn't there work for you as a citizen and as a Christian in our little town? Suppose you go to Middlefield with the same motives that you would go on a mission to India, Africa, or the Isles of the Sea! You will not be sent by any Board of Commissioners for Foreign Missions, but by him who has sent you, his disciple, into the world. You have your experience, you have your strength, you have your love to Christ and your neighbor, to give them. They need everything in Middlefield. They need young men, Christian young men. The village needs you, the Church needs you. It seems too bad for all the young men to rush away from their native place to make a name, or to make money. Somebody must work for Middlefield. Our church needs a lecture room and a Sunday school room; the village needs a reading room—the village needs more than I know. It needs Christian *push*. Perhaps it needs Hollis Rheid."

"Marjorie, it will change all my life for me."

"So it would if you should go West, as you spoke last night of doing. If you should study law, as you said you had thought of doing, that would change the course of your life. You can't do a new thing and keep to the old ways."

"If I go I shall settle down for life."

"You mean you will settle down until you are unsettled again."

"What will unsettle me?"

"What unsettled you now?"

"Circumstances."

"Circumstances will keep on being in existence as long as we are in existence. I never forget a motto I chose for my birthday once on a time. 'The Lord shall fight for you, and ye shall hold your peace.'"

"He commands us to fight, sometimes."

"And then we must fight. You seem to be undergoing some struggles now.
Have you any opening here?"

"I answered an advertisement this morning, but we could not come to terms. Marjorie, what you say about Middlefield is worth thinking of."

"That is why I said it," she said archly.

"Would _you_ like that life better?"

"Better for you?"

"No, better for yourself."

"I am there already, you know," with rising color.

"I believe I will write to father and tell him I will take his kindness into serious consideration."

"There is no need of haste."

"He will want to begin to make plans. He is a great planner. Marjorie! I just thought of it. We will rent Linnet's house this summer—or board with her, and superintend the building of our own, Do you agree to that?"

"You haven't taken it into serious consideration yet."

"Will it make any difference to you—my decision? Will you share my life—any way?"

Prue ran in at that instant, Linnet following. Hollis arose and walked around among the books. Prue squeezed herself into Marjorie's broad chair; and Linnet dropped herself on the hassock at Marjorie's feet, and laid her head in Marjorie's lap.

There was no trouble in Linnet's face, only an accepted sorrow.

"Marjorie, will you read to us?" coaxed Prue. "Don't you know how you used to read in Maple Street?"

"What do you feel like listening to?"

"Your voice," said Prue, demurely.

XXXI.

AND WHAT ELSE?

"What is the highest secret of victory and peace?
To will what God wills."—*W.R. Alger*.

And now what further remains to be told?

Would you like to see Marjorie in her new home, with Linnet's chimneys across the fields? Would you like to know about Hollis' success as a Christian and a Christian citizen in his native town? Would you like to see the proud, indulgent grandmothers the day baby Will takes his first steps? For Aunt Linnet named him, and the grandfather declares "she loves him better than his mother, if anything!"

One day dear Grandma West came to see the baby, and bring him some scarlet stockings of her own knitting; she looked pale and did not feel well, and Marjorie persuaded her to remain all night.

In the morning Baby went into her chamber to awaken her with a kiss; but her lips were cold, and she would not open her eyes. She had gone home, as she always wanted to go, in her sleep.

That summer Mrs. Kemlo received a letter from her elder daughter; she was ill and helpless; she wanted her mother, and the children wanted her.

"They *need* me now," she said to Marjorie, with a quiver of the lip, "and nobody else seems to. When one door is shut another door is opened."

And then the question came up, what should Linnet and Marjorie do with their father's home? And then the Holmeses came to Middlefield for the summer in time to solve the problem. Mrs. Holmes would purchase it for their summer home; and, she whispered to

Marjorie, "When Prue marries the medical student that papa admires so much, we old folks will settle down here and be grandpa and grandma to you all."

In time Linnet gave up "waiting for Will," and began to think of him as waiting for her. And, in time, they all knew God's will concerning them; as you may know if you do the best you can before you see it clearly.

THE END.